ENCOUNTERS OF SHERLOCK HOLMES

Coming soon from George Mann and Titan Books

Sherlock Holmes: The Will of the Dead
The Casebook of Newbury & Hobbes
Further Encounters of Sherlock Holmes

ENCOUNTERS OF SHERLOCK HOLMES

BRAND-NEW TALES OF THE GREAT DETECTIVE

Edited by George Mann

TITAN BOOKS

Encounters of Sherlock Holmes
Print edition ISBN: 9781781160039
E-book edition ISBN: 9781781160107

Published by Titan Books
A division of Titan Publishing Group Ltd
144 Southwark Steet, London SE1 0UP

First edition: February 2013
1 3 5 7 9 10 8 6 4 2

What did you think of this book? We love to hear from our readers.
Please email us at: readerfeedback@titanemail.com,
or write to us at the above address.

To receive advance information, news, competitions, and exclusive offers online,
please sign up for the Titan newsletter on our website: www.titanbooks.com

CONTENTS

INTRODUCTION

What is it about the character of Sherlock Holmes that has made him such an enduring creation? When Sir Arthur Conan Doyle first sat down to set pen to paper, could he ever have imagined the great legacy his creation would inspire? I do not believe, even in his wildest dreams, that Doyle could have envisioned the manner in which this discourteous, drug-addicted, charismatic genius might develop into one of the world's best known and most loved fictional creations, let alone the fact his stories would go on to inspire an entire sub-genre of detective fiction.

When Doyle, tired of his character and looking for a reprieve, sent Holmes tumbling to his death over the Reichenbach Falls, the public outcry was so cacophonous that Doyle was forced to raise him from the dead. Yet the public appetite was such that, even after Doyle's own death in 1930, people continued to hunger for new Holmes adventures.

Consequently, there is a proud legacy of continuing Sherlock Holmes stories, sometimes referred to, perhaps unkindly, as "pastiches". Indeed, Holmes must, I suspect, be one of the most written-about characters in the English language, and probably in many other languages besides. Books, theatre, radio plays, television shows, films – all have played a part in continuing Doyle's legacy. Holmes has lived a thousand lifetimes, with twice as many adventures, but still he persists, the master of deduction, the template for most future detectives, a hero whose comforting presence can always be felt, lurking on the edges of popular culture.

Holmes, it seems, is more than just a character. He's an *idea*, a cipher; a metaphor for the articulate, intelligent hero that, just like Watson, we all want in our lives.

This volume, then, serves to fulfil that function, at least for a time: to provide the reader with fourteen brand-new tales of Sherlock Holmes. Here we see Holmes encounter strange patchwork men in the dark alleyways of London; meet a dying Sir Richard Francis Burton, who needs his help to locate a missing manuscript; go head to head with A.J. Raffles; unravel a bizarre mystery on the Necropolis Express; meet with H.G. Wells in the strangest of circumstances; unpick a murder in a locked railway carriage; explain the origins of his famous Persian slipper and more. We also see Watson and Mrs Hudson enjoying their own adventures, although Holmes forever looms large, even if he is working quietly to manipulate events from behind the scenes.

I hope you read on to enjoy these "encounters" of Sherlock Holmes. I've been privileged enough to be the first to read them as I've assembled this volume, and I already know what treats lay in store. So, without further ado, allow me to offer you one simple reassurance – the spirit of Sherlock Holmes lives on in every one of them.

Now go! The game's afoot!

George Mann
September 2012

THE LOSS OF
CHAPTER TWENTY-ONE

BY MARK HODDER

Throughout my long acquaintance with Sherlock Holmes I was frequently astonished by the insights I gained into his remarkable mind and the wholly unique manner in which it functioned. Over the years, as these revelations accumulated, I slowly came to understand how his great gift of observational and deductive intellect was also a terrible curse, for it robbed him of those warmer aspects of personality which we depend upon for the establishment and maintenance of friendships and emotional attachments. Indeed, Holmes often appeared to be little more than a machine built to gather and compare facts, calculating probabilities and interconnections until some final set of correspondences was revealed in which lay the solution to whatever problem had been set before him. I found this heartless efficiency disturbing, not only because it so separated him from society, but also because it caused me to often feel regarded as little more than a functional component of his existence. Admittedly, this might be regarded as insecurity on my part, but Holmes did little to assuage it, and I never felt it more deeply than during the case of *The Greek Interpreter*, when he finally revealed to me that he had a brother.

One night, shortly after the completion of that affair, Holmes and I were sitting up into the early hours, reading and smoking, when I found myself unable to hold my tongue any longer, and, out of the blue, blurted, "Really, Holmes! You are positively inhuman!"

My companion sighed, shifted in his armchair, put aside his book, and levelled his piercing eyes at me, saying nothing.

"Why did you never mention Mycroft before?" I continued. "All this time we've known one another, and you kept your brother a secret from me!"

Holmes glanced into his pipe bowl, leaned over and knocked it against the hearth, and set about refilling it. "I didn't mention him, Watson, simply because there was no reason to do so."

"No reason? Do you not see that the sharing of personal details about one's family, upbringing, past and associates establishes deeper bonds of friendship? Is that not reason enough?"

"Do you not consider us friends, then?"

"Of course we're friends! You purposely overlook my use of the word *deeper*. Friendship is not a static thing. It must be continually strengthened if it is to survive the naturally degenerative effects of time. You make no effort!"

Holmes waved a hand dismissively. "I have detected no lessening of my attachment to you, despite my apparent neglect."

"Ha!" I cried out. "*Detected*! Not *felt*, but *detected*! Even in your choice of words you reveal that you do not operate as a normal person. You are thoroughly cold and dispassionate!"

He struck a match and spent a few moments sucking at the stem of his pipe until the tobacco was burning and plumes of blue smoke were curling into the air, then murmured, "An advantage, it would seem. I am not dependent upon the fuel of emotive displays and reassurances."

I threw down my newspaper in exasperation, jumped to my feet, and paced over to the sideboard to pour myself a drink. "For all your criticism of his sedentary ways, I found Mycroft to be a warmer fellow than you are. Your only passion, Holmes, is the solving of puzzles!"

"Not passion," he responded. "Vocation. Look out of the window, would you? If I'm not mistaken, a carriage has just pulled up outside. The sound is somewhat muffled. I'll wager a fog has got up while we've been sitting here."

I frowned, annoyed that our conversation had been interrupted, and pulled aside the curtain. "A peasouper. I can't see a blessed thing. Great heavens!"

My exclamation came in response to a high-pitched screeching that penetrated both the pall and our windowpane, the words plainly audible. "Absurd! Absurd! It's a shilling, I tell you! I'll not be swindled! A shilling! A shilling and not a ha'penny more, confound you!"

I looked back at Holmes, who arched an eyebrow and said, "Down the stairs with you, there's a good fellow. If paying a cab fare engenders such hysteria, then our street door is about to suffer a dose of unrestrained hammering. Answer it before Mrs Hudson is roused, would you?"

Laying aside my untouched brandy, I left the consulting room, hurried down the staircase, and yanked open the front door just as the first knock impacted against it. A man of about fifty was on our doorstep. He was tiny, barely touching five feet in height, with a fragile-looking slope-shouldered body upon which was mounted a ridiculously outsized head, its bald cranium fringed with bright red hair that curled down around the jawline to form a small unkempt beard. Waving his bowler in the air, he hopped up and down and shrieked, "Help! Help! Sherlock Holmes!"

"Calm yourself!" said I. "Mr Holmes is just upstairs. Allow me to show you up to —"

Before I could finish, the visitor pounced through the door, ducked under my outstretched arm, and scampered up the staircase. "Holmes! Holmes! Murder! Theft! Murder! Help!"

"Hey there! I say!" I protested, setting off in pursuit.

The intruder reached the landing and pounded on the first door he came to, which happened to be that of the consulting room. Holmes called "Come!" and the little man plunged in.

I followed. Holmes hadn't moved from his armchair and was looking curiously at the apparition that stood twitching and gesticulating wildly in the middle of the room.

"Murder! Theft! Murder! Hurry! We can't delay the police for much longer!"

I opened my mouth to speak but Holmes stopped me with a small gesture, lay down his pipe, rested his chin on steepled fingers, and continued to watch the bizarre performance.

It occurred to me that our visitor's face was somewhat familiar, but he was so wildly animated I found it impossible to place him, so waited patiently – as did my colleague – for the histrionics to end.

Three or four minutes of almost incomprehensible jabbering passed before the man threw his hat onto the floor, spread his arms wide, and said, "Well?"

"Well," Holmes echoed. "Shall we begin with your name, sir?"

"What?" our guest squealed. "What? What? What? My name? Don't you realise the urgency of the situation? My name? Swinburne. Algernon Swinburne. It's murder, Holmes! Murder!"

I gasped, and Holmes looked at me enquiringly.

"Mr Swinburne is one of our most accomplished and admired poets," I said, knowing where that particular art was concerned, my friend's oddly compartmentalised knowledge didn't extend far beyond the Petrarch he habitually carried in his coat pocket. "His work is extraordinary."

"Poetry be damned!" Swinburne shouted. "By heavens, this could kill Burton! You have to help, Holmes! Get up! Out of that chair! We must leave at once! It's life or death!"

"Who is Burton?" Holmes asked.

Swinburne let loose a piercing scream of frustration, leaped into the air and landed with both feet on his hat, completely flattening it. "Burton! Burton! Sir Richard Francis Burton! Who else would I mean?" He bent, picked up the bowler, punched it back into shape, and suddenly became calm and earnest. "Mr Holmes, please, you must come with me to the St James Hotel right away. I will explain all *en route*. We cannot lose a further moment!"

Sherlock Holmes stood, cast off his threadbare dressing gown, and kicked the slippers from his feet. "Sir Richard Francis Burton, you say? Very well, Mr Swinburne, Watson and I will accompany you. I ask only that, on the way, you give a full and detailed account of the affair in the most rational manner you can muster. By that, I mean less of the dramatics, if you please."

"Rational?" Swinburne exclaimed, slapping the dented hat onto his bald cranium. "I assure you, I'm as rational as I've ever been!" He turned to me. "Dr Watson, do you have your medical kit?"

I nodded. "Is it required, Mr Swinburne?"

"It may be. Please bring it with you."

I left the room and entered my bedchamber, where I donned my shoes and jacket and took up my bag. When I returned to the consulting room, Holmes was ready to depart. Swinburne hustled us down the stairs and out into the swirling fog of Baker Street, where he emitted another of his shrill squeals. "Gone! The Brougham! Blast that driver! I knew he couldn't be trusted! He tried to charge me two and six!"

"That is the approximate fare from the St James Hotel," Holmes noted.

"Nonsense! A cab ride is a shilling!" Swinburne protested. "The distance is immaterial!"

Holmes and I exchanged a glance. I felt slightly disorientated by the poet's eccentricity. The detective, by contrast, appeared to be rather amused by it.

Despite the hour and the awful weather, we were able to hail a four-wheeler and were soon rattling southward towards Green Park.

"It is a short journey, Mr Swinburne," Holmes said. "Please start at the beginning and be concise. What has happened?"

"Murder! Theft!" The poet twitched and jerked spasmodically. It was plainly apparent to me that he suffered a congenital excess of electric vitality, but he managed to bring himself under control, took a deep breath, let it out slowly, and continued, "Sir Richard, his wife Isabel, and their personal physician, Dr Grenfell Baker, arrived in London three days ago, having travelled from their home in Trieste, where Burton is consul."

"Physician?" Holmes asked. "Are the Burtons unwell?"

"Yes. Sir Richard's heart is giving out. He suffered an attack a few weeks ago and remains frail. But he pushes himself so. He absolutely refuses to rest."

"And Lady Burton?"

"She's generally strong but suffers the minor and multiple ailments one must endure with old age." Swinburne shook his head and murmured:

"Time turns the old days to derision,
Our loves into corpses or wives;
And marriage and death and division
Make barren our lives."

Holmes clicked his tongue in irritation. "The facts, sir. Nothing more. No embellishments required."

The little man shuddered from head to foot, slapped his own cheek, tugged at his beard, then went on. "It so happens that our mutual friend, Thomas Bendyshe, was putting up at the St James, too, so the Burtons took a room next to his. Earlier tonight, Isabel went to meet with her sister —"

"Where?" Holmes cut in.

"At Bartolini's Restaurant in Leicester Square. Dr Baker, meanwhile, visited with his family in Islington, while Sir Richard, Tom Bendyshe and I dined together at the Athenaeum."

I asked, "For how long have you known the Burtons?"

"Nigh on thirty years," Swinburne replied.

Holmes muttered, "Immaterial. Do be quiet, Watson."

I glared at him, but my colleague's attention was wholly focused upon the poet, who said, "At about nine o'clock, Tom — whose heart is also weak — complained of slight palpitations and left us. Sir Richard and I stayed on at the club until half past eleven. I then accompanied him to the hotel, where he intended to show me a manuscript, of which I shall say more in a moment. When we arrived, the manager was waiting for us in the lobby. He rushed us up to the Burtons' suite. Apparently, Isabel had returned shortly before us and found Tom Bendyshe lying dead inside it. The aforementioned manuscript was missing. It appears a thief had entered through the window, which had been left open, was interrupted in his work by Tom, and murdered him before fleeing the scene."

"On which floor is the Burtons' room?" Holmes asked.

"The fourth. The window is accessible via an exterior metal staircase that runs up to the roof at the rear of the hotel."

"I see. Why is this not a police matter, Mr Swinburne? Why consult me?"

Swinburne threw his hands into the air. "No! No! Police? Impossible! The hotel manager insisted on calling them but we asked him to delay until I could fetch you. The problem, Mr Holmes, is that we cannot admit the existence of the manuscript to the police."

"Why not?"

Swinburne levelled his bright green eyes at the detective. "What do you know of Burton, sir?"

Holmes looked at me, said, "Watson?" then sat back and closed his eyes.

"I can speak now?" I asked in an indignant tone.

Holmes flicked his fingers.

"He is – or, rather, was, when in his prime – an explorer," I said. "He more or less single-handedly opened central Africa, leading to the discovery of the source of the River Nile. He also examined the cultures of West Africa, was one of the first Englishmen to enter forbidden Mecca, and, I believe, was a secret agent for Sir Charles Napier in India."

"Oh, he's much more than that," Swinburne interjected. "Sir Richard is fluent in at least thirty languages. He's counted as one of the best swordsmen in Europe. He's a scholar, a disguise artist, an author, a poet, a mesmerist, and an anthropologist."

Much to my discomfort, a tear rolled down the poet's cheek.

"But I fear these are his twilight years," he said. "My friend is not the man he used to be. He's sixty-seven years old, and the hardships of Africa have caught up with him. But, by God, he's determined not to go without making one last contribution to man's knowledge! Two years ago, Mr Holmes, he translated and published an Arabian manuscript entitled *The Perfumed Garden of the Cheikh Nefzaoui*. It is a treatise concerning the art of physical love between a man and a woman."

I cleared my throat. "Is it – is it – *decent*, Mr Swinburne?"

The poet snorted derisively. "Some idiots claim it to be naught but erotica." He leaned forward. "But do you not agree, Mr Holmes, that through the detailed study of every aspect of human behaviour – *every* aspect – we can gain a better understanding not only of individual motivations, but also of the racial and cultural proclivities that inform those motivations?"

Holmes opened his eyes and looked a little surprised. "That is a very astute observation, and I agree without reservation."

"Then you'll understand the dissatisfaction Sir Richard has felt concerning that volume, for it was published incomplete."

"In what respect?"

"He'd been unable to locate a version of the work in its original Arabic, and so was forced to translate from a French edition from which the notorious twenty-first chapter had been omitted. That chapter, by itself, is almost the same length as the entirety of the remaining material. It deals with what we English refer to as unnatural vices – that is to say, physical relations between men."

"Holmes," I murmured, "I'm not sure we should involve ourselves with –"

"Nonsense!" my friend snapped. "Continue, please, Mr Swinburne."

"Last year, Sir Richard discovered that an Algerian book dealer owned a copy of the work in its original language and with chapter twenty-one intact. He purchased it, and now intends to re-translate and annotate the entire volume, complete with the missing material. He regards it as his greatest project."

"And it is this manuscript that has been stolen?" Holmes asked.

"Not the complete thing; just chapter twenty-one. You can see why the police can't be informed. They couldn't possibly understand the anthropological value of the document. To them, it would be classed as filth of the worst kind. Sir Richard would be arrested."

Holmes grunted. "From where, exactly, was the chapter taken?"

"From a travelling trunk in his hotel bedroom." The poet suddenly slapped a fist into the palm of his hand and cried out, "A curse on Avery, damn him! May the hound rot!"

"You're getting ahead of yourself," Holmes said. "Avery?"

Swinburne shook his fist and snarled, "Edward Avery. A bookseller. The Burtons had hardly arrived in London before they learned that the swine has been illegally publishing and selling the earlier edition of *The Perfumed Garden*. Sir Richard confronted the rogue who, knowing that there could be no legal redress, brazenly offered to publish chapter twenty-one as a supplement. This was refused, of course, and Avery responded by declaring that, one way or another, he would see the chapter in print to his own benefit."

The little man angrily swept the tears from his cheek. "I lost my good friend Tom Bendyshe tonight, Mr Holmes. I want vengeance. Bring Edward Avery to justice, and restore that chapter to Burton before I lose him as well."

The carriage came to a jolting halt and the driver shouted down to us, "St James Hotel, gents!"

We disembarked.

"Two and six, please."

"Again?" Swinburne yelled. "It's a confounded conspiracy!"

Holmes took the poet by the elbow, dragged him away, and called, "Pay and follow, Watson!"

I fished in my pocket for change, passed the coins up to the cabbie, and chased after my companions.

The St James Hotel, off Piccadilly and at the northeast end of Green Park, was familiar to Holmes and me, as was its manager, Joseph McGarrigle. A concierge ushered us up to the fourth floor and to suite 106, which we found guarded by two constables, both of whom recognised Holmes. They opened the door and we stepped through into a sitting room where Inspector Lestrade of Scotland Yard greeted us somewhat grudgingly. The pallid, rat-faced police detective was standing beside a chair occupied by a large, elderly woman who appeared to be in considerable distress. She was attired in an old-fashioned jacket and voluminous skirt, with a frilly bonnet pinned to her long, tightly wound hair. A large crucifix dangled from the end of her beaded necklace.

I looked from her to the body of a slightly built man sprawled face down between the fireplace and the suite door. His head was turned to one side and a deep and bloody dent was visible between his eyebrows.

Mr McGarrigle was seated at a table by the window.

"Really, Holmes!" Lestrade exclaimed. "This is a very straightforward business. There's nothing for you here."

"I shall be the judge of that, if you please, Lestrade," Holmes replied. He bowed to the woman. "Lady Burton?"

"Yes," she responded huskily. "Thank you for coming, Mr Holmes.

My husband has often expressed a desire to meet you. I wish it could have been under different circumstances." Holding out a hand to Swinburne, who took it, she added, "Thank you, too, Algy."

"How is he?" the poet asked.

"Terribly upset." She sniffed and raised a handkerchief to her eyes.

"Interrupted burglary," Lestrade announced. "It's as plain as a pikestaff. Thief came up the stairs outside, climbed in through the window, and was interrupted by Mr Bendyshe. Panicked, killed him, made off. Nothing stolen."

Sherlock Holmes stepped over to the body and squatted beside it. "How did he get in?"

"I just said. Through the window."

"Not the burglar, Lestrade. Mr Bendyshe."

Lady Burton pointed across the chamber at a door opposite the fireplace. "Connecting rooms, Mr Holmes. Thomas was a dear friend. We had that door unlocked so he could come and go as he pleased."

Lestrade added, "He must have heard movement in here and came to investigate."

Holmes knelt and bent his head down close to the carpet. "I suppose you've been stamping around in your usual clumsy manner?"

"I arrived little more than five minutes ago."

"Time enough to destroy evidence. I want to turn the body over. Do you object?"

Lestrade hesitated then gave a curt nod of permission.

Holmes indicated that I should draw closer. "Watson, come and help, but watch where you tread. Take the feet."

I joined him. We carefully rolled the corpse onto its back. I pointed to the head wound and noted, "Not much blood." Holmes clicked his tongue and impatiently waved me away. He pulled a magnifying lens from inside his jacket and began a meticulous examination of the corpse, lingering over the watch that was hanging by its chain from Bendyshe's waistcoat pocket. Without looking up, he said, "Tell me what occurred, please, Lady Burton."

Sir Richard's wife gave her eyes a final dab with the handkerchief then folded it and pushed it into her sleeve. "I met Blanche – my sister – for dinner. When I came back, I found the room as you see it now, with poor Thomas on the floor. My husband and Algernon returned from their club almost immediately after I had alerted Mr McGarrigle. That is all."

The hotel manager interjected, "Mr Bendyshe arrived just a few minutes before Lady Burton. He asked if Dr Baker was here. I had been busy overseeing the change of staff to the night shift, and didn't know whether he was or not. I suppose Mr Bendyshe came looking for him."

Algernon Swinburne said to Lady Burton, "May I go to Richard?"

She nodded. "Take Dr Watson with you, Algy." She turned to me. "I'd like your opinion of my husband's condition, Doctor."

The poet gestured for me to follow, crossed to a door to the left of the chimneybreast, tapped on the portal, and entered.

I glanced back at Holmes. He was now on his hands and knees, with his nose less than an inch from the carpet, snuffling around like a bloodhound between the dead man and the fireplace.

I stepped into what proved to be the bedroom.

A lean-faced man was sitting in a chair beside the bed. He stood and came forward.

"Dr Watson? I'm Dr Grenfell Baker. I'm pleased to meet you."

"Um. The pleasure's mine," I responded, distractedly. My eyes were not on Baker but on his patient, who was sitting up in the bed.

Sir Richard Francis Burton was glowering at me like the Devil incarnate. Though elderly, white haired, and plainly ill, he was as impressive an individual as I'd ever seen. His deep-set eyes cut me through just as Holmes' always did, but they had none of the detective's aloof coldness about them; instead, there was an angry sullenness that both warned and challenged, a look I had often observed in dangerous criminals but which was here supported by a very obvious and ferocious intellect. Burton was a man, I instantly perceived, who'd been tested at every turn, who'd battled his way through one obstacle after another, who had been hurt and defeated and insulted, but who absolutely refused to lie down and take it. That he bore emotional scars was plainly evident – one could see it in that terrible gaze – but he was marked by physical ones, too. A long, savage furrow scored his left cheek; a smaller one, on the opposite side, puckered the skin at the angle of his jaw; and there were pockmarks and old wounds visible all over his face and hands.

Partly concealed by a moustache and short beard, his determined mouth was set hard, though it now twitched at the corners in what might have been an attempted smile.

"Watson, hey?" His voice was deep and gruff. "I have read your accounts with great interest, sir."

He stretched out his hand to clasp mine. I stepped forward to take it, and, in doing so, suddenly saw through the famous explorer's brutal appearance and recognised the frail old man beneath. Burton's eyes were bulging unnaturally, his breathing was too fast and too shallow, his skin felt cold and clammy, and there was a blue tinge to his lips. I had seen the symptoms many times before. His heart was giving out. He was dying.

"Sir Richard," I said. "It is truly an honour to meet you. As your wife observed, it's a shame it isn't under different circumstances. Sherlock Holmes is looking for evidence in the other room and will be with you presently."

"No," he growled. "I'll not receive him as a blasted invalid. I want to watch him work."

He swung his legs over the side of the bed and pushed himself up.

"For crying out loud!" Dr Baker exclaimed. "Why do you insist on disobeying my every order? Lie down at once!"

"Squawk, squawk!" Burton grumbled. He reached for a robe that hung from the bedpost and shrugged into it. "You're like a parakeet, Baker! Always making noise! Algy, offer me your shoulder, there's a good chap."

Swinburne scuttled forward and gave Burton support.

"Lead on, Dr Watson. You come too, Baker. Perhaps exposure to a scientific intellect will cure you of your quackery."

Baker and I fell in behind Burton and Swinburne as they slowly shuffled towards the door. Baker leaned close to me and whispered, "First I'm a parakeet, now I'm a duck. He is a perfectly impossible patient."

No sooner had we entered the lounge than Burton halted in front of us and uttered an oath in Arabic. "Bismillah!"

Looking past him, I saw that Lestrade and McGarrigle were holding Sherlock Holmes by the ankles and dangling him out of the window.

"What in blue blazes?" I cried out, rushing over. I leaned over the sill and saw that the detective was hanging upside down beside the metal staircase. He was holding a lighted match next to one of the points where the structure was bolted into the brickwork.

"Give them a hand hauling me in, Watson!" he called.

I reached down, dug my fingers into the top of his trousers, and helped Lestrade and McGarrigle drag him back to safety.

Burton, who was being fussed over by his wife, steered her back into the chair she'd risen from, then turned to Holmes and said, "I never imagined I might meet you feet first, Mr Holmes. What in heaven's name were you up to?"

Holmes smiled. "As I am frequently forced to remind Inspector Lestrade, one does not collect evidence by treading on it." He paced over to Burton and shook him by the hand. "I have read a great many of your accounts, Sir Richard. It is a rare pleasure to meet a man who knows not only how to look, but how to *see*."

I gritted my teeth at this. In the cab, Holmes had acted as if he knew little or nothing of the famous explorer when, in truth, he was almost certainly better informed than I. As he so often did, he'd encouraged me to display my knowledge not for information, but for its insufficiency, as if my inadequacies somehow aided him in the clarification of his own thoughts.

"And what I see," Burton said, "is that you have an unfortunate habit, Mr Holmes. Cocaine, is it? Forgive my bluntness, but you're a bloody fool. If the damnable stuff doesn't kill you, it will rob you −" to my utter astonishment, he lifted his hand and used his forefinger to tap Holmes sharply on the forehead "− of that exceptional mind of yours."

Sherlock Holmes appeared to be so taken aback by this that he was quite lost for words.

"Dick," Lady Burton objected. "Mr Holmes is here to help."

My friend recovered himself, bowed his head to her, and said, "It is perfectly all right, madam. Your husband is absolutely correct." He turned back to Burton. "My eyes?"

"Yes. Your pupils are slightly mismatched in size – the left being dilated – and your lower lids are too dark for your complexion. There are other indications. You are unnaturally gaunt. Your gums are slightly receded. No doubt, if you raised your sleeve, I would see needle marks. What is it, a ten per cent solution taken at regular intervals?"

"Seven," Holmes answered quietly. "And irregular."

"Ah! So Dr Watson is weaning you off it, then?"

"He is."

"Then you are blessed with a very good friend indeed." Burton was still using Swinburne as a physical support. He looked down at the little poet and said, "As am I. Thank you, Algy. I can stand unassisted, I think."

Dr Baker protested, "You shouldn't be standing at all."

"Indeed not!" Lady Burton added.

Burton turned to the hotel manager. "Mr McGarrigle, would you take my wife and Dr Baker downstairs and provide them with a pot of tea? Algy, go with them, please."

Swinburne flapped his arms. "What? What? What?"

"I would like to speak in private with Mr Holmes. Dr Watson is his trusted confidant, so must stay. Inspector Lestrade represents Scotland Yard and will refuse to go. The rest of you, let us give Mr Holmes some space to do his work. No doubt he is dismayed to have so many people milling around the scene of a crime." He clapped his hands together. "Out with you! Out! Out! We shall talk later!"

Burton walked unsteadily over to his wife, who had resumed her weeping, and tenderly brushed her cheek with his hand. He kissed her and said softly, "You are tired, darling. Go downstairs. Rest. Don't worry. I shall be fine, and I won't be long."

She clung to him for a moment then reluctantly followed the others. As they were passing through the door, Holmes called, "One moment! Mr McGarrigle, can you tell me how often the exterior staircase is used?"

"It's not used at all, Mr Holmes," the hotel manager responded, "and hasn't been for years. It is unsafe. As I'm sure you saw, the bolts that hold it against the wall are loose."

When the group had departed, Sir Richard Francis Burton gazed sadly at Bendyshe's body for a moment before then turning to face Lestrade. "My apologies, Inspector, I did not greet you. What is your opinion of this affair?"

Lestrade hooked his thumbs into his waistcoat. "As I told Holmes, Sir Richard, it is a simple matter. A burglar risked those outside stairs, climbed in through the open window, but was confronted by Mr Bendyshe before he could make off with anything."

Burton glanced at Holmes, sharing, with that quick look, the secret of the stolen chapter.

"The intruder attacked Bendyshe," Lestrade went on, "and struck him a fatal blow to the head before escaping back the way he had come."

"I see. Do you agree with that assessment, Holmes?"

"No, I do not."

"Good. Neither do I."

Lestrade emitted a groan, screwed up his eyes, massaged his temples, and whispered, "Oh, spare me! Now there are two of them!"

Burton said, "And you, Dr Watson. Do you see where Lestrade's theory stumbles and falls?"

I looked at Holmes. He was regarding me with arms folded and an amused twinkle in his eyes. He murmured, "You know my methods, Watson."

I sighed and cast my eyes over the room.

"The head wound," I said.

"Ah ha!" Burton responded.

"Bravo!" Holmes added.

"And the position of the body. If Bendyshe entered through the connecting door, why is he now closer to the suite's entrance? One might suppose that he grappled with the burglar, was forced back across the room, and was murdered where we now see him lying. But there are no signs of a struggle and the wound is on the front of his skull. If he was struck there with enough force to kill him, why did he not fall backwards, as you'd expect? Why is he stretched out face down?"

"Exactly!" Burton exclaimed. "So, Holmes, reveal all! What really happened in this room?"

Sherlock Holmes unfolded his arms and shrugged. "I haven't the faintest idea."

Burton, Lestrade and I gaped at him and choroused, "What?"

"I don't know. I'm baffled. The position of Bendyshe's body is certainly inconsistent with the picture Lestrade has painted, but I can find no explanation for it. Perhaps, when he was struck, he was clinging to his attacker, who backed away, dragging him forward as he fell, but I've found no evidence to support that supposition. I'm sorry, Sir Richard, but, on this occasion, I must give Lestrade his due. What he thinks happened is probably what happened."

Lestrade clapped his hands together and said, "Finally!"

I saw Burton stagger slightly and, in three rapid strides, rushed to his side and caught him by the elbow. "Enough!" I snapped. "You are in no condition for this, sir. Back to bed, at once. Come!"

The explorer was a big man – in his younger days, he must have been as strong as an ox – but as I guided him slowly back into the bedchamber, with my left hand still gripping his elbow and my right arm about his waist, he seemed to deflate and wither.

I kicked the door shut behind us and whispered, "I don't know what Holmes is playing at, but I don't believe a word of it. He's up to something, of that you can be sure!"

"Bismillah!" Burton croaked, as I helped him out of his gown. "Don't let him give up on me, Watson. If he can't recover the manuscript, I might as well die this very night. You have no idea what it means to me."

I helped him to lie back on the bed, and felt his pulse. It was fluttering wildly. He was struggling for air.

"I'll do what I can," I said. "Don't speak. Lie still and try to regulate your breathing. I'm going to give you a sedative."

His fingers closed around my wrist. "No! No drugs. The only thing that'll save me now is chapter twenty-one. My translation will be the crown of my life, Watson! The crown!"

I frowned. "But it's – it's *pornography*, Sir Richard!"

A hoarse chuckle escaped him. It turned into an outburst of coughing. I used my handkerchief to wipe the sweat from his brow and waited for the fit to pass.

"No one understands," he wheezed. "What is illegal and shocking in 1888 was once the very basis of Plato's philosophy. What we decry as unnatural and immoral today was considered the noblest form of affection yesterday. Time changes everything, Watson. Everything! And if we refuse to record that which we disapprove of now, then the future will be erected upon foundations so riddled with holes, omissions and misapprehensions that the entire edifice of civilisation might come tumbling down. Dispassionate knowledge! It is − it is − *essential!*"

A tremor shook him. He moaned and his eyes began to slip up into his head.

"Holmes!" I bellowed. "My bag! For the love of God, bring my bag!"

Seconds later, the door burst open and Sherlock Holmes raced in and handed me my medical kit. Working as rapidly as I could, I loaded a syringe with a solution of morphine and injected it into Burton's arm. Almost immediately, I observed his muscles relaxing, his breathing became less laboured, and, when I placed my stethoscope to his chest, I found that his heart was beating regularly, though with the slight "echo" I've often heard moments after a patient has experienced a heart attack.

"Unconscious," I said. "It was a close call but he'll live. For how long I can't say. What's your game, Holmes?"

"Later!" the detective replied in a brusque tone. "When you shouted, I sent Lestrade to fetch back Lady Burton. They'll be here momentarily. We must take this opportunity while we have it." He crossed to a large Saratoga trunk in the corner of the room, bent over it, and applied his magnifying lens to its lock. "Scratches!" he muttered. "Ha! It gives every appearance of having been picked." He lifted the lid to reveal books and papers within. "It was from here that chapter twenty-one was removed, but the marks around the lock are an attempted deception. It was opened in the normal manner, with a key."

"Deception by whom?" I asked.

He straightened. "Have you not seen through the duplicity yet, Watson?"

"Duplicity? No, I can't say I have. Why did you claim defeat?"

We heard the suite door open and feet crossing the carpet.

"Hush!" Holmes hissed.

Dr Baker, Algernon Swinburne and Lady Burton rushed in, the latter crying out "Dick!" and throwing herself down beside her husband.

"He suffered a mild heart attack," I told her. "I treated him with morphine. It has stabilised him but he must sleep and avoid any further distress."

Baker mumbled a thank you and set about examining his patient.

Sherlock Holmes moved over to stand beside Lady Burton and placed a hand gently upon her shoulder. "Madam," he said. "I must ask something of you."

She raised her face to him. Tears streamed down her plump cheeks. "What is it, Mr Holmes?"

"I wish you to call upon me at 221b Baker Street tomorrow at ten in the morning. It is of the utmost importance."

"I can't leave my husband."

Holmes looked at me. I said, "The crisis has passed, Lady Burton. I wouldn't allow you to leave Sir Richard's side were I not positive that you could afford to do so. The drug will keep him asleep and out of danger while you visit Baker Street."

Swinburne put in, "I shall remain with him while you are gone, Isabel."

"But —"

Holmes cut her off. "I must insist upon it."

She nodded. "Very well. Ten o'clock."

"Good. Then Watson and I will bid you farewell. Get some sleep, dear lady. You must be exhausted. Mr Swinburne, may I speak with you in the other room for a moment?"

The little man nodded and followed us out. Inspector Lestrade was standing at the suite entrance talking quietly with the two constables. Holmes led Swinburne to the corner farthest from the policemen and the bedroom. He whispered, "Watson and I will take our leave now. This entire matter will be resolved tomorrow and chapter twenty-one will be returned."

Swinburne gasped. "What? What? What? You've solved the case? Will Avery swing for it?"

"Can you call on me at three o'clock tomorrow afternoon?"

The poet nodded eagerly.

Holmes added, "Keep the appointment secret, please. Tell no one. Not even the Burtons."

We left suite 106 just as a police coroner arrived to remove the body of Thomas Bendyshe.

"You can't win 'em all, Holmes!" Lestrade called after us.

"Well done, Lestrade," Holmes responded cheerily. "It'll certainly raise your stock at the Yard if you find the murderer!" Under his breath, he added, "Not that you will, you insufferable dolt!"

"Explain!" I demanded. "I'm completely in the dark!"

"Tomorrow," he replied, and I could get nothing more from him.

Mr McGarrigle had one of the hotel's four-wheelers carry us home. By the time we arrived, it was half past three and I could barely keep my eyes open. I went straight to bed, fell asleep, and was shaken awake, it seemed, after just five minutes.

"Blast it, Holmes, can't it wait until morning?" I mumbled.

"It *is* morning," he said. "Lady Burton is due here in forty minutes."

I opened an eye and looked him up and down. "Those are the same clothes you wore last night. Have you not been to bed?"

"I'll sleep when the manuscript is back in Sir Richard's hands. Rouse yourself! Out of your nest!"

I heaved a sigh, opened my other eye, and sat up. "All right! All right! I'll be down presently."

I washed, shaved and dressed, and entered the consulting room just as the doorbell jangled. Holmes was standing before the fireplace with his hands behind his back.

We heard Mrs Hudson ascending the stairs. She knocked and poked her head around the door. "There's a Lady Isabel Burton to see you, Mr Holmes."

"Good show! Send her up, Mrs Hudson!"

Moments later, our visitor stepped in. She appeared tired but much recovered after last night's anxieties, and, in the light of day, I saw she'd once been a tall and handsome woman, though old age had now taken its toll.

Holmes greeted her and waved her to an armchair.

I asked, "How is your husband this morning, Lady Burton?"

"He has not awoken," she answered, "but Dr Baker assures me his slumber is natural and is the best thing for him."

"Quite so," I agreed.

Holmes indicated that I should settle into the other armchair, and, after I had done so, he strode into the middle of the room and turned to face us.

"I wonder, Lady Burton, if there is anything you wish to tell me."

"In regard to what, Mr Holmes?" she asked.

"Why, in regard to the events of yesterday evening, of course. What else?"

She started to pick nervously at the edge of her shawl. "I rather thought it would be you telling me something about it, sir."

"If you wish it, I can do so."

Puzzled, I began, "Holmes —"

He whipped up a hand with the palm facing me and snapped, "Not now, Watson!"

Lady Burton looked at him quizzically. "Well then?"

"Well then," Holmes said. "Since only chapter twenty-one of the Arabian manuscript was stolen, it's safe to proceed on the premise that it was removed by someone who knew exactly what they wanted and exactly where it could be found. To reach it, that person had only to do as Inspector Lestrade suggested: ascend the exterior staircase, climb in through the window, cross to the door on their left, enter the bedchamber, and open the trunk."

"Edward Avery," Lady Burton muttered. "We did not inform Inspector Lestrade of our suspicions, Mr Holmes, as we thought it better that you approach the bookseller."

Ignoring her statement, Holmes went on. "The assumption is that, just as the thief entered, Thomas Bendyshe came into the room through the connecting door, which would be to the intruder's right, immediately spotted him, attempted to apprehend him, and was struck a killing blow to the forehead. But why, then, Lady Burton, did Bendyshe not fall backwards? And why was he at the other end of the room?"

"I don't know, Mr Holmes."

"It is because there was no intruder, Edward Avery or otherwise."

"If there was no burglar," I protested, "how can the manuscript have gone missing, and who killed Bendyshe?"

"I shall answer the last question first, Watson. No one killed Thomas Bendyshe. He died of natural causes, almost certainly a heart attack. When he fell, he struck his head on the corner of the hearth. You yourself noted the lack of blood. He didn't bleed because his heart had stopped before he even hit the floor."

"But his body wasn't by the fireplace!"

"There were carpet fibres caught up in his watch chain. The only way they could have got there is if his body was dragged across the room. Also, the corner of the hearth was conspicuously cleaner than the rest. It had been wiped down."

"By whom?" I asked.

"That, Watson, is the question. The metal staircase provides the answer. Observe."

Holmes turned to his left and held his arms out, angled downward, with his fingers and thumbs curled as if gripping a rail. He marched up and down on the spot, and, while giving this peculiar performance, said, "When one descends a staircase of that sort, one's hands do not grip the rails to either side tightly, but simply slide along them, to aid balance." He turned to face the right, raised his arms higher, and mimicked the movements of a person ascending. "But when going up, the hands grip tightly, and one pulls hard in order to relieve some of the effort required by the legs."

He stopped his mimicry and looked at us. Lady Burton and I returned his gaze blankly. He sighed. "The bolts, Watson! As Mr McGarrigle noted, they were loose in the brickwork. If someone had climbed those metal stairs, the action of their hands would have put great pressure on the bolts and brick dust would have been dislodged around them, from the top section of the staircase in particular, due to the effect of leverage. If, on the other hand, a person had only descended, there would be a lesser amount of dust and it would be more evenly distributed from the topmost to the bottommost bolts. As, indeed, it was."

Holmes fixed his penetrating eyes upon Lady Burton.

"Furthermore, there was a thin film of soot on the stairs, deposited there, no doubt, by our London peasoupers. What say you, madam?"

She said nothing, but her face went white to the lips.

"It had been disturbed," Holmes went on. "And I noticed that the hem of the dress you were wearing last night was stained with the stuff. Had you gone up the staircase, the stain would have been at the front. It was at the back. Hence, you only went down."

Lady Burton burst into tears.

Holmes waited patiently. I looked from him to our guest and back again. Slowly, a fog of confusion cleared from my mind, and I realised what had happened.

"You were trying to protect your husband's reputation!" I exclaimed.

She nodded, and sobbed, "I was the first to return to the hotel that night. Mr McGarrigle was engaged with his staff and did not notice me enter." She pulled her handkerchief from her sleeve and wiped the tears from her face. "I'd been back less than ten minutes before there came a knock at the door. It was poor Thomas. He was suffering from chest pains and had come looking for Dr Baker."

I interjected, "But why did he go to the door of your suite rather than entering through the connecting door?"

"He's known Dick and me for many years," she replied, "but is not well acquainted with our physician. He wasn't aware that I was back, and did not want to burst in upon a man who was a virtual stranger to him."

"And he collapsed in front of you," Holmes said.

She sniffed and more tears fell. "He suddenly clutched his chest and dropped like a stone. As you say, his head impacted against the hearth, but I'm convinced he died instantly, even before his knees gave way. I rushed to him, found him to be dead, and was about to ring for the hotel manager when – when –"

Another fit of weeping interrupted her discourse. When I moved to comfort her, Holmes made a terse gesture to stop me. We waited, and after a couple of minutes, she started to speak again, though her voice rasped with emotion.

"You must understand," she said, "there has been a stain on my husband's character since he was a very young man. He spent his childhood on the continent, and has, in consequence, been regarded by many as somehow un-English. This prejudice increased when he worked for Sir Charles Napier in India and was sent to investigate certain establishments of bad repute. His report was rather too detailed, and when it fell into the wrong hands, it was employed by those jealous of his accomplishments to cast a shadow over him. He has been forced to work long and hard to prove the suspicions unfounded, and has taken risks and endured hardships that would have killed lesser men. And now, just as he's achieved widespread acclaim for his translation of *A Thousand Nights and a Night*, this – this – this *awful* chapter twenty-one! I cannot allow him to be remembered for such a monstrosity. It would eclipse everything good he has ever done!"

Holmes said, "So you saw your chance, dragged Bendyshe away from the fireplace – which you then wiped – took the manuscript, climbed out of the window, descended the metal stairs, and re-entered the hotel through the main doors, making sure to be seen by Mr McGarrigle."

"Yes. I am an old woman, but love for my husband gave me strength enough for all of that."

"Did it not occur to you that by staging the burglary you could have sent an innocent man to the scaffold?"

"Edward Avery? He is not an innocent man, Mr Holmes. He is pocketing money that should go to Richard. Besides, I knew there'd be nothing but circumstantial evidence to implicate him. His name might have been ruined – which he deserves – but it would have gone no further."

Sherlock Holmes paced over to the window and looked down at Baker Street. He took his pipe from his pocket and tapped its stem against his chin. "I understand your motives, Lady Burton, but I cannot agree with them. Sir Richard's achievements will be remembered not because he followed the mob, or did as he was told, or allowed others to make decisions for him, but because he acted independently and used his own judgement. If he believes that chapter twenty-one of *The Perfumed Garden* will contribute to mankind's knowledge and understanding, then I cannot doubt him, and neither should you."

"He regards it as his final project," I added. "He told me it is his most important work. Do you really intend to deprive him of it?"

She buried her face in her hands. "He will be vilified."

"Perhaps so," Holmes murmured. "But he knows the risk and he chooses it. Obviously, he's prepared to sacrifice his reputation in the short term in order to contribute certain insights to future generations, who might find them less shocking than we do."

The detective turned away from the window and faced Lady Burton. "I'm afraid I cannot permit your interference. You will tell me where chapter twenty-one is hidden and I will see to it that the material is returned to Sir Richard. Your part in its disappearance will not be mentioned. Not, that is, unless you refuse me."

Isabel Burton looked at me, as if expecting my support. There was such anguish in her expression, and she possessed such obvious devotion to her spouse, that, for a moment, I was tempted to throw my lot in with her, but then I remembered what Burton had said: *If he can't recover the manuscript, I might as well die this very night!*

"You acted with noble intentions," I said. "But I must agree with my friend. Sir Richard is infirm, but his mind is as sound as a bell, and if he – who has achieved so much – believes the chapter should be translated and published, then it probably should."

Holmes said, "Where is the manuscript, Lady Burton?"

She slumped in her seat. Her mouth worked silently for a moment. She whispered, "I wrapped it in a pillowcase and threw it into a coalbunker by the mews behind the hotel."

"Watson!" Holmes barked. "Leave immediately. Find it!"

I stood, put my hand on Lady Burton's arm, murmured, "He was, is, and shall always be regarded as a great man," and departed.

A fast hansom delivered me to the St James Hotel, and, within minutes, while the carriage waited, I'd located the coalbunker and discovered the package inside it. I returned to Baker Street. Holmes was alone, sitting in a haze of tobacco smoke.

"A truly remarkable woman, Watson!" he declared. "Such loyalty is commendable, don't you think?"

I left chapter twenty-one on the table, crossed to the sideboard, and drank the brandy I'd poured the night before. "Even if it leads to misjudged actions, Holmes?"

"Ha! She allowed her faith in her husband's intellect to be adversely influenced by emotion."

"Her love for him?"

"No. Her fear that she'd outlive him and have to endure alone the ruination of his good name."

I shook my head. "Poor woman. It must be exceedingly difficult to live in the shadow of such a giant."

My friend gave me a peculiar look. "Those who do, and who provide support and stability, are the very best of us all."

For the next few hours, I read and dozed while Holmes stared into space and filled the room with noxious tobacco fumes. Neither of us touched chapter twenty-one.

At three o'clock, Algernon Swinburne arrived and Holmes handed the manuscript to him.

The little poet leaped into the air and emitted a triumphant squeal. "How, Holmes? Who? Why? Avery?"

"No, Mr Swinburne, the bookseller was not involved. I can say nothing more. Take the chapter and return it to Sir Richard. Inform him that it was my pleasure to assist him, and there is no fee."

"Thank you, Holmes! Thank you!"

With that, Swinburne left us and, I would like to say, the affair of the missing chapter came to a satisfying conclusion. Except, it didn't.

One evening, nearly three years later, in July of 1891, I was dining alone in the Athenaeum. Sherlock Holmes was dead – or so I believed – having plunged with Professor Moriarty into the Reichenbach Falls, and I was still in the throes of a deep depression.

I had just finished my meal when a man, uninvited, pulled out a chair and sat at my table.

"My condolences, Dr Watson," he said.

"Mr Swinburne! It is good to see you!" I gripped the little poet's hand, and, remembering that Sir Richard Francis Burton had passed away in Trieste nine months previously, added, "We have both suffered a terrible loss."

He nodded, swallowed, then bunched his fingers into a fist and slammed it down on the table, causing the cutlery and crockery to rattle. "Did you hear what she did?"

"Yes."

It had been in all the newspapers. Burton had completed his translation, which he'd retitled *The Scented Garden*, but a heart attack had taken him before it could be published, and, in the wake of his death, Lady Burton had gathered together all his papers, correspondence, and journals, and made a bonfire of them. Into this, she threw her husband's *magnum opus*.

"It was his masterpiece," Swinburne said. "And she destroyed it. I will never forgive her. I will never speak to her again."

We ordered coffee, and for many minutes sat in silence, contemplating, remembering, and mourning.

Swinburne suddenly stated, "He was not an easy man to be with."

"Nor Sherlock Holmes," said I.

"He was bullish and provocative, argumentative and occasionally brutal in his choice of words. But here is the strange thing, Dr Watson: whenever I was in his company, no matter how awkward and frustrating a companion he may have been, I never felt so thoroughly *engaged* with the business of living."

I nodded. "Yes, Mr Swinburne. I know exactly what you mean."

ABOUT THE AUTHOR

Mark Hodder is the author of the Philip K. Dick Award-winning series of Burton and Swinburne adventures, beginning with *The Strange Affair of Spring Heeled Jack*, in which the famous explorer and poet play Holmes and Watson-like roles in slightly twisted versions of true history. Hodder has also written *A Red Sun Also Rises*, an homage to the nineteenth-century novel and the planetary romances of Edgar Rice Burroughs.

Born in Southampton, Hodder worked for many years in London, including a five-year stint at the BBC, but now lives in Valencia, Spain, where he writes on a full-time basis. He collects and preserves Sexton Blake stories, and is a fan of the old ITC TV shows, such as *The Persuaders*, *The Champions*, *Department S*, and *The Prisoner*.

SHERLOCK HOLMES AND THE INDELICATE WIDOW

BY MAGS L HALLIDAY

It was the winter of 1894, and a pearlescent light was flooding my friend Holmes' sitting room. The clouds that had cast their shadows over me for the three years Holmes had been presumed dead had lifted, and I was wont to finding myself, whenever an idle hour presented itself, sat in my old chair at Baker Street. On this morning, the rare clear air I had breathed walking from Paddington had swept away any lingering gloom, and I was feeling quite jovial.

Naturally, the case that then presented itself was one that would cast the shadow of mortality over us once again.

I was reading a surprisingly dull article about the medicinal use of kif when the front door bell rang and Mrs Hudson informed us there was a widow, a Mrs Stephen Perkins, to see us. The woman who was shown upstairs was indeed in secondary mourning of a dark grey dress trimmed black, a jet bead necklace − adorned with a jet rose rather than a crucifix or cross − and a grey hat. She was doughtily set, with a more weather-browned face than I would have expected of someone who must only have emerged from a mourning veil but recently.

"Ah, Mrs Perkins," Holmes greeted her, gesturing towards a chair, "and how was your journey from Woking? You must have been on the 08.23."

Like so many of our visitors before her, the woman was surprised by his insight. I, however, had noticed the traces of dried yellowish mud on her black fustian-trimmed skirts and congratulated myself on noting that she must have come from out of town.

"It was right enough," she said, "but I'm not 'ere to discuss the railway timetables. I'm 'ere because I'm concerned me Stephen is to lose his job when it ain't his fault."

"Stephen?" I asked. "Is he your son?"

"No, no. He's me husband."

I must have shown my surprise at this pronouncement, as Sherlock barked a laugh and even Mrs Perkins' mouth turned up in amusement.

"Watson, my friend, your delicacy is much to be admired, but you've read the situation wrong. Mrs Perkins has come up this morning from Brookwood, where Londoners are sent to be buried, and where Mr Stephen Perkins works. I think perhaps Mrs Perkins also works there, hence having suitably sombre attire but the sun-dappled skin of someone who is often outside."

Our guest nodded, and folded her ungloved hands over her reticule. "You'll be right, Mr Holmes. My husband is the stationmaster at the north station, where we take care of the non-conformists. I help by offering much-needed sustenance to both the bereaved and the workers."

Holmes smiled again. "You run the bar, do you not, Mrs Perkins? The calluses on your hands are suggestive of those generated from the regular pulling on bar taps."

She laughed this time, which I could not but help find shocking in someone dressed as she was. Her behaviour was at great odds with her appearance and with what one would expect of a widow.

"I do, 'cept when we have some Quakers or other temperance-minded souls to lay to rest. They have lemonade and sandwiches."

"So what brings you to me?" Holmes asked. "How is your Stephen in trouble?"

"That's the rub of it, Mr Holmes, I don't right know. We've been there for a couple of year now, with the Company most happy with the way we runs things. Never a complaint, not like that Mr Kitching at the south station. He's been fined for refusing to serve someone who was more'n half cut, but we don't get any trouble like that. But three times in the last two months, we've had unexpected visits from the Company. Going through our papers, inspecting our rooms. And I keep 'em spotless. No one, not even some of the heathen types we have come through, likes to say their final farewells in a room that ain't been swept."

I could not see how this case would interest Holmes. It sounded like a petty tangle of jealousy or pilfering. After all, we had only Mrs Perkins' word that her husband was honest and she herself was falsely dressed in mourning. She had fallen silent and was looking earnestly at my friend.

"There's more to your story, though, is there not?" Holmes asked her. She nodded, and her face, which till then had been serene, grew agitated.

"It's the noises at night, Mr Holmes, that really bother me."

"That seems quite natural," I remarked, "Given you live by a graveyard."

"It's not a graveyard, Mr Watson, it's a cemetery. Built within these last forty years to hold the dead of London. That don't bother me, as I used to live by Russell Court graveyard. And it ain't the sounds of the countryside at night neither, though the quiet did bother me at first. No, it's a creaking, and voices, and the sound of people trying to be silent."

That afternoon, we walked over to the offices of the London Necropolis Railway. Their premises were purpose built hard by the London and South Western Railway's viaduct at Waterloo, onto which their trains ran. When I had more time for my practice, I had a good proportion of patients who, once I could relieve their suffering no more, had chosen to be transported from the city in which they lived to the green fields of Surrey. Their families had assured me, as I signed the death certificate needed to book a journey upon that sorrowful train, that the service provided was excellently run and the resting places most charming. This was, however, my first visit to their premises and I looked around with not a little curiosity.

An archway of handsome red brick and Portland stone provided access for hearses and mourners from Westminster Bridge Road with a dog-legged tunnel leading out under the viaduct ensuring the vehicles could be unloaded and moved on without any unseemly manoeuvring back out. At ground level were the Company's offices and waiting rooms reserved for the lowest class of funeral. For there were three classes, mirroring the distinctions of the regular railway. Along the passageway, the windows were brightly furnished with winter-blossoming flowers and it was lit through a glass roof several storeys above us, at track level.

We were greeted by a clerk, who was calm, quiet and respectful. He led us up a wide stone staircase onto the second-class floor, where there was a room set aside for displaying the Company's range of coffins, and began providing us with the advantages of each design.

"This is one of our most popular designs for the second-class funeral, in simple elm coffin and shell. Many customers wish to have something refined to demonstrate the level of respect due to their beloved relative. We are also able to provide the 'earth-to-earth' papier-mâché design, for people who wish to eschew the gaudy displays of life in favour of a natural burial. Unless, sirs, you are looking on behalf of a parish, perhaps? We have a simple box wood design, not available for viewing here, which enables us to offer most reasonable terms…"

"Alas, sir," said Holmes, "You have mistaken us for possible customers, perhaps misled by my friend's profession. I need to see one of your directors." He held up a thin finger before the startled man could speak. "One of the Company directors, not a funereal one."

As the clerk rushed off, I remonstrated with Holmes. "You should not have allowed him to continue in his misunderstanding."

"On the contrary, Watson, he has given us a great deal of information about the company and its practices without any awareness that he was doing so. I am also desirous of seeing these designs."

I looked around the room. Each coffin was held on a trestle and presented as it would be in a chapel of rest, although no religious symbols were visible. I tried to suppress a shudder looking at these promises of the future. Mortality is part of my job, and I have seen a great many deaths on the battlefield besides. Yet undertakers, and their work, made me uncomfortable in a way that those moments of death did not. I think perhaps it is the idea that they make their money by disposing of the dead with distraught relatives as customers. I tried to express this disquiet to Holmes.

"Really, Watson, is it so different to you charging a fee for seeing someone in pain? Your own customers, your patients as you call them, are themselves not always in the most rational of states."

"Nor yet are yours," I retorted.

One of the Company directors entered the room before we could continue, and Holmes turned his focus on him. He was approaching his middle years gracefully, without the ruddy complexion of so many of my more well-heeled patients. His greying hair was neat, and his salt-and-pepper beard trimmed. He gave every appearance of a man in full control of his world.

"Mr Holmes? I am Mr James Arrowsmith, one of the three directors of the London Necropolis Company. I cannot pretend not to know your name, nor your occupation. I can assure you we will be happy to assist you in an investigation, within the limits of both the law and discretion. I presume that you are investigating the death of someone whose mortal remains we have laid to rest?"

Holmes raised an eyebrow. "That's possible, of course, but not the prime reason we are here. Would you be willing to accept my presence if my investigations turn out not to be in the best interests of the company?"

There was a long, uncomfortable pause. Arrowsmith paced the room twice, with his hands clasped behind his back and his head bowed. When he reached the mantelpiece, he looked upwards at the discreet clock before turning back to face us.

"It is possible," he said so quietly I strained to hear, "that our thoughts bend to the same subject. I, too, have been investigating something that concerns me greatly."

"Something that concerns what is happening in Surrey?" Holmes asked.

"Quite, quite. There are… irregularities. I've had a clerk looking at what is happening here in London, and have myself travelled to

Brookwood three times to go over the books at both stations. There are too many people, Mr Holmes."

"I don't quite follow, Mr Arrowsmith."

"Perhaps I am explaining it ill. One of the clerks, an excellent lad with a head for numbers, noticed that the number of people travelling on the returning train on Tuesdays was greater than the number of tickets out."

"Local people are using the trains to get to London?" I asked.

"That's what I suspect, and it would be most unfortunate if it is true. Our lease of the line from the London and South Western Railway depends upon us only serving funeral parties and mourners visiting their beloveds' resting places. The Railway could terminate our contract if we were found in breach of it."

"And your relationship with the Railway has always been a little… strained, I believe?" asked Holmes.

"Quite. Even if they did not choose to tear up our lease, they could make it more difficult for us to run the professional and calm service we take pride in. We've had to ask them to ensure the train crews who run our engines can be discreet, after one driver was drunk and nearly overran the buffers at the cemetery. The relationship between the two companies cannot take additional strains."

"On which of the station masters does your suspicion fall?"

"On both. Kitching in the south station has already been reprimanded for his behaviour towards a customer, but the north station is closer to the village. I have not, as yet, been able to find any clear evidence on either of them. Neither has access to ticket rolls, but both take monies over the bar. Their books are all accurate."

"Is there a pattern to the additional passengers?"

"There is not, though it is always on a day when we are running pauper funerals, so on a Tuesday or a Thursday."

Holmes brought his hands together and tapped his lips with his fingers, a sure sign that he was thinking through the possible reasons for both the numerical disparity and the vague fears of Mrs Perkins.

"Very well, Mr Arrowsmith, I would be happy to take up the investigation on your behalf. I, like your Company, pride myself on a discrete service that will not draw unwelcome attention on the people involved. If I can, I shall report my findings to yourself to take action. Unless, that is, laws are being broken when I may have no option but to call in the authorities."

Mr Arrowsmith looked alarmed at the idea of the police, and the possibility of his Company appearing in the press. Given the nature of their work, any such story would likely be taken up with prurient enthusiasm by the gutter press eager to tell sensational stories. I was not alone, after all, in my disquiet about undertakers. The one before us, however, nodded slowly.

"Tell me what else you need," he said.

Thus it was that the following Tuesday, Holmes and I found ourselves dressed in our mourning attire watching a coffin being loaded onto a train in Waterloo.

Mr Arrowsmith had fixed for us to travel upon the train by recording us as the mourners of one Mrs Langhurst, a widow of some six-and-fifty years who had no family or friends to accompany her. Her solicitor had arranged for her to have a second-class funeral and we had duly been shown to a private room on the middle floor of the Railway's building, where Mrs Langhurst was already in situ, arrayed in an elm coffin with simple details. I found I could not look upon this poor widow, whose laying to rest we were using for our own ends. Holmes, for his part, glanced at her dismissively and began inspecting the room.

His air of distraction, which I soon realised was being assumed, increased when we were invited up to the platform to watch the coffin, now securely closed, be loaded into a compartment of a hearse van. A small card carrying the name of the occupant was on the outside of the hearse van. Matching cards was also inserted into the compartment doors of the passenger coach, so that each funeral party travelled in seclusion.

Further down the platform from us, several clusters of mourners stood about. Most were in some form of mourning, though some of the dresses looked freshly dyed. There were but two of these impoverished grievers per coffin, and I realised that these would be the pauper burials and the bereaved were reliant on parish travel warrants to follow their beloved to their rest. Unlike our own class, these disparate parties were offered no privacy and were all on the platform together.

Our second-class carriages were rather busier, with mourning parties ranging from half a dozen to a score embarking on the journey. All were dressed in fresh attire from Jay's outfitters, with only the children exempted from the donning of full black. In some parties, the widow stood out most with her thick veil obscuring her face and her long weeds announcing her status. In one party, there was instead a widower and I saw the undertakers loading both an adult and a child coffin into their section. I was reminded briefly of my own loss, and that sorry procession through Kensal Green.

The journey itself was uneventful. I watched as the scene beyond our half-lowered blind changed from the squalid, soot-blackened backs of slum housing to neatly trimmed suburban villa gardens and then fields and woodland. Outside the city, a frost still glistened in the shadows and the air was sharper. This was a very different journey even from that up Swains Lane in Highgate or along the Harrow Road in Kensal Rise. Certainly, this world was Elysian when compared to the horrors of the old enclosed churchyards in the centre of the city, where bodies had piled so deep that the very height of the ground was raised up to the windowsills of the houses that overlooked them.

The train jolted as we went over the points onto the spur line into the cemetery, lifting me out of my reverie. We went slowly along this section, allowing any passengers able to raise their eyes a first view of this modern Necropolis. A laurel hedge ran alongside the train, so that it did not intrude too egregiously on the landscape. Beyond that were gently sloping lawns and curved paths, interspersed not only with recent planting but also with copses of the ancient woodland the cemetery had been built in.

The station buildings formed three sides of a square, with the platform as the fourth. The train drew up alongside so that the funereal wagons came to a halt alongside the two spurs of the buildings, where the platform had been slightly raised. As we passengers disembarked and were guided towards the appropriate wing of the premises, based on the class of funeral we were attending, the stationmaster and his porters unloaded the grim cargo and took the coffins into the waiting rooms.

Throughout, Holmes was looking around himself and playing the role of a man half-parted with his senses through grief. It was a very convincing guise that enabled him to show curiosity in the surroundings without raising suspicions. My discomfort at his dissembling, for its part, must have looked like a friend uneasy at such a public display.

Our coffin was soon taken from the waiting area in the station up a slope to a plot in the conformist section. My unease continued as the appointed curate ran through the shortest ceremony we could have chosen, and laid to rest someone we had never known in life into the frosty ground. To date I had seen nothing untoward or unusual, save our own fraudulent loss.

We returned to the south station, where the stationmaster was at work in the yard against the building, chopping wood to feed the fires that burned in every grate. His wife, a thin, quiet woman lacking the vitality of her counterpart to the north, was offering a warm luncheon of soup, bread and beer in the bar. The train crew stood at one end, nursing their small beer and eating large hunks of bread. There was just one other occupant, a widow already seated by the fire, when we walked in. Her face was veiled, but her hands trembled as she raised a small glass of sherry from the table. More mourners arrived hard behind us, and the room soon became hot and musky.

"Excuse me," Holmes asked the stationmaster's wife, "what time does the train return to London?"

"In perhaps another three-quarters of an hour," she replied.

"Would we be able to walk to the other station in that time?"

"Why, yes, if you wish it. Sometimes people need some air, don't they, afore they go back to the city? The train don't wait, though. If you miss it, you'll need to walk on to the LSWR's station by the village and pay for another ticket."

Holmes thanked her and we set off down the road.

Holmes walked in silence, and I knew he would not want my

questions at this stage. He was gathering evidence, or working through the details he had already seen. Instead I admired the sylvan scene around us.

"Watson, as a doctor you must sign a deal of death certificates?" he suddenly asked.

"Of course, it is part of our duty to ascertain the person is indeed dead, and what the causes of that death are."

"And no funeral can take place without a certificate?"

"Certainly not. Only a medical professional can be certain all life has indeed left a body. Without our confirmation, it might be possible for someone who has fallen into a deep coma to be mistakenly buried."

"Ah, the fear of being buried still alive. Tell me, have you ever heard of such a thing? From a reliable witness?"

"Never from a reliable person. It is always possible that death could be mistakenly identified, but our custom of laying out the body and waiting for a few days before the funeral prevents any such horrific confusion."

We were approaching the north station, for dissenters and non-conformists, and Holmes reassumed his faux-distraught air.

"Watson, I telegraphed Mrs Perkins last night and told her we would be here today. Pray do not show any signs of recognition, as I have asked her to do likewise."

We entered the bar, and looked around. Unlike the other station, this one contained a range of different attitudes to death. A Roman Catholic family took up two settles, arrayed in mourning, wearing crucifixes and holding breviaries. A smaller group of three Quakers stood nearby, in plain garb, wide-awake hats still on their heads. As at the south station, there were a handful of pauper mourners who sat in a separate section. Unlike the other station, there were no employees of the Railway.

Mr Perkins was a broad-shouldered man with dark whiskers and rolled-up sleeves. As with his wife's false mourning colours, he wore a mourning band around his upper arm and maintained an air of courteous respect. He accepted my friend's claim to have walked from the other station but quietly requested sight of our mourners' tickets before serving us.

The return train was due imminently, so Mrs Perkins began to speak quietly to each group, asking them to move onto the platform. She did her best not to react when she reached us.

As the train pulled in, its locomotive pushing it in reverse back towards the mainline, Holmes' air of distraction increased. As I moved towards the part of the second-class carriage with the Langhurst name on it, I realised he was not beside me. Instead he was opening the doors of each compartment of the carriage, apologising profusely and continuing to the next.

"What are you doing?" I asked, taking him by his arm, for he was receiving startled responses from the occupants of each compartment whose private grief he was so abruptly interrupting. Having disturbed each compartment, he allowed me to guide him to our own, and sank back into the corner seat with a smile on his face. He pulled our door to and lowered the blinds entirely.

"Watson, I think I have it. When we get back to the city, I will need you to apply some of your forensic skills to the books of the Necropolis Company."

"But, Holmes, Mr Arrowsmith has already assured us the paperwork is in order."

"I'm counting on that very fact, my dear fellow. I need you to look at the names on the death certificates."

"And what will you be doing?" For I had guessed at once that he would not be joining me in going through the papers, but was in one of his adrenaline-inspired enthusiasms.

"I, Watson, will be following the spare body."

At the London terminus, I set to work with the ledgers for the last six months of funerals. The Company had performed some five hundred and sixty-two funerals in that time, to a wide range of clientele. Holmes had tasked me to first look at the records for that very day, to see if any funerals had not been accompanied by mourners. There were two such ceremonies besides Mrs Langhurst: a slum-dwelling elderly pauper of the rookery at St Giles-in-the-Fields, and an office manager of some seven-and-twenty years from the parish of St

Saviours, Southwark. Both had been conformists, and neither had been accompanied by any living soul down to the gardens of rest.

As Holmes had requested, I noted the names of the doctors who had signed the death certificates. Without sight of such a certificate, the Company would not perform a funeral, and they were meticulous in recording that they had followed due process. I then began to look back through the ledgers to find other funerals without mourners, and to note any where the doctor matched those from today. It soon became apparent to me that Dr P– of Lambeth frequently appeared in my annotations, and had a greater proportion of such funerals than any other doctor whose patients chose the Brookwood Necropolis for their final resting place.

Before I could speculate on what this pattern might indicate, Holmes reappeared. He had some colour high in his cheeks, suggesting he had run part of the way back from wherever the trail had taken him. A messenger boy straggled behind him.

"Where is Mr Arrowsmith?" he asked.

"In his office, I believe. What have you found out?"

"In a moment. Tell me, did your search uncover a single name?"

"Yes, Dr P– of Lambeth."

Holmes added the name to the piece of paper in his hand, and bade the boy to race across to Scotland Yard, just across the bridge from us, and deliver it to one Inspector Bradstreet. He then hastened me from the ledger room towards Arrowsmith's office. Arrowsmith was sat at his desk, looking over some papers when Holmes brushed past his clerk and shut the door.

"Well, I had found out why your clerk counted more people coming back than leaving. I'm afraid I have had to involve the police to prevent the criminals fleeing. Moreover, I will need to ask the police to interview some of the Company, so I must ask you to remain silent for another hour. I hope we can minimise the interest of the press, or at least ensure no censure attaches itself to your Company. Have I your word you will tell no one for another hour?"

The man looked shaken, as well he might. This had been the very scenario he had hoped to avoid. "Can I at least warn my fellow directors?" he asked.

"Absolutely not! I fear complicity in these crimes includes one of them. I recommend you spend the next hour preparing a statement to offer any journalists who ask for your view. Come on, Watson, we need to reach Victoria before the hour is out!"

Out on Waterloo Bridge Road, Holmes had a hansom cab waiting, and hurried me into it, calling the driver to make haste to Victoria station on the other side of the Thames. As we jolted across the bridge and turned into Westminster, Holmes explained what he had uncovered.

"My theory formed when a study of the line indicated that people could only board the Necropolis train at the cemetery. There are no other stops along the route. It would also make no sense to travel to London from a home in Surrey with no option for returning. What purpose would the minimal saving on fare serve?

"So I began to think the real fraud must lie in the number of bodies going out. I made a careful inventory of the number of coffins and mourners who travelled this morning. I also noted that the coffins are transported on biers rather than carried by pall bearers."

"So there are fake bodies going out? But why? And how can that result in extra passengers back?"

"Think, Watson! Consider what I asked you to look into…"

The cab turned the corner by the Houses of Parliament and onto the long straight road to the station.

"There had to be a doctor falsifying the death certificates," I reasoned aloud. "So that's how Dr P– was involved! But to what end?"

"To receive a percentage on a fraud, of course. Did you note the widow at the south station? Did you perceive that her face was entirely obscured by her veil? That is, of course, not uncommon when a woman is in full mourning. I also perceived that she had not been on the train out. As I was checking the compartments when we reboarded the train, I surprised her sitting in rather a masculine pose."

"I'm afraid I don't follow. This false widow was… what?"

"She was one Albert Richards, late of Falcon Court, Southwark. I followed him from the Necropolis station and observed him return to his home. A talkative neighbour informed me both that Mr Richards had died, despite the best efforts of that lovely Dr P–, and that his widow had received a goodly payout on the life insurance this very day and was packing up the family to move to her cousin's house at Whitstable in Kent."

We had reached the giant terminus of the London Chatham and Dover Railway, and the cab had slowed in the melee of other vehicles attempting to draw up under its canopy. Holmes spotted some of Inspector Bradstreet's men and leapt out to race after them.

I flung some money at the cabbie and ran after Holmes as he weaved through the crowds. The boat trains to Dover were due to depart in another fifteen minutes, so there were many passengers looking for their platforms, and porters with trolleys stacked high with luggage. A half-score of uniformed policemen were closing in on a family all attired in mourning, save the father. He was looking around with a wild cast in his eyes, searching for a way to evade Bradstreet's men. He made a break for it, his wife calling for him not to, and was brought down quickly.

My conversation with Holmes had been interrupted when we reached Victoria, so I took it up again with him that evening.

"I am still unclear on why they went to the effort of travelling out to the cemetery, and what the strange noises were that Mrs Perkins recounted to us."

"You said it yourself, when we were at Brookwood. We have the custom in this country of leaving the coffin unsealed until it takes its final journey. Generally, the undertakers will screw the coffin lid on themselves. So there had to be a body. The other Company director could not draw too many of his employees into the scheme, since that would diminish his percentage of the payout. So instead Dr P– supplied a drug to induce the appearance of death. From the description, I suspect it was a combination of laudanum and a barbiturate which would slow the breathing sufficiently for it not to be visible, and reduce any involuntary eye movement.

"What the director did do was introduce the use of the papier-mâché 'earth-to-earth' design, which you'll have noticed each of the suspicious funerals had as their box of choice. By their very design, these coffins could easily be pierced to create airholes, ensuring the false corpses could breathe during their final journey, and were built to quickly decay.

"At the station, Kitching would ensure the coffin was placed in one of the private waiting rooms, enabling the erstwhile corpse to slip out and be disguised prior to returning to London. The simplest disguise, and one that would not draw attention on a train from a cemetery, is, of course, a widow in full weeds whose face is obscured. Such was our false widow. It was then a simple matter to replace the man's weight with wood and to go through the pretence of a funeral."

"And the noises?"

"Most of the men taking advantage of this scheme had to return to London, either to collect their money and their families or to start a new life in a different part of the city. I suspect a handful, however, were no mere insurance fraudsters but criminals of a more serious bent who had a need to escape the city entirely without notice. Rather than taking the railway back, they will have walked the same road we did in order to reach the nearest mainline station, and thus make their way further afield without returning to a city whose constabulary were watching for them."

I contemplated what it must have been like to take those journeys, even drugged half insensate. Perhaps the drugs themselves had made the journey yet more disorientating? How desperate must these men have been to put their trust in Dr P– and his escape route? How often must they have hoped or prayed that the stationmaster would unseal their coffin and free them from its claustrophobic embrace? And how much had they dwelled on the fear that they would not be freed, would not step back onto the train but would instead feel the heavy thump of soil on the lid above them?

"Holmes," I said. "Do you think all the men who undertook this plan were safely delivered from the grave?"

Holmes steepled his fingers and looked at the ceiling. "We must surely hope so."

ABOUT THE AUTHOR

Mags L Halliday writes historical science fiction and fantasy, including the steampunk novel, *Warring States*, set during the 1901 Boxer War in China. Her most recent work includes an essay in *Chicks Unravel Time* (Mad Norwegian Press), and a daughter (still a work in progress). More details are available from www.magslhalliday.co.uk.

THE DEMON SLASHER
OF SEVEN SISTERS

BY CAVAN SCOTT

Henrietta Stead was many things to many people. To her father she was a disappointment. To her sister she was an embarrassment. To Bramwell Applegarth, distinguished editor of *The London Examiner*, she was an irritant and to me, well, a man is allowed his secrets, isn't he?

To Sherlock Holmes, however, she was always *the* woman; the woman who nearly bludgeoned him to death, that is.

Never in my wildest dreams did I imagine I'd meet the celebrated consulting detective, let alone almost find myself an accomplice to his murder.

I'd read about the great man. Who hadn't? The papers were always full of his exploits and I never missed any of Dr Watson's little melodramas in *The Strand*. Violence, jeopardy and derring-do, just the thing to get a chap's pulse racing.

Of course, violence, jeopardy and derring-do were the last things I wanted when I became a journalist. Yes, there were newspapermen who thrived on such experiences, I just wasn't one of them.

I became a journalist for the money.

There, I've admitted it and even today I am not ashamed. Not everyone read the news for grisly murders, blazing conflagrations or political wrangling. Many of our readers headed straight for the gossip columns. They wanted to wallow in the scandal and intrigue of high society; to be titillated by the hypocrisy, illicit liaisons and outright debauchery of those who ought to know better.

No matter what my colleagues at *The Examiner* thought of our more sensational, and sometimes downright steamy, content, my column helped keep our circulation figures healthy and Mr Applegarth off our backs. It may not have been one of the most honourable ways to earn a living, but as long as there were loose-lipped servants or unscrupulous socialites in the city, my position at *The Examiner* was secure. I'd spent long enough waiting on the great and good of London. Now they would serve me.

The chain of events that led to the near demise of Sherlock Holmes began on 21 October 1902. It was late afternoon and I was putting the finishing touches to my next column. I have to admit I was struggling to concentrate. My head was pounding thanks to the flagons of mild I'd been forced to consume the night before. I'd known that if Albert Wilkes became merry enough, the most indiscreet butler in Belgravia would soon start spilling his mistress's secrets. I'd just not prepared myself for the man's tolerance to alcohol: he had the constitution of a particularly resilient ox. Thankfully, by the time I helped the old soak home − a task all the more difficult as I was seeing double myself − I had my story. Lady Mary Crawford would wake red-faced in the morning and her lover would probably be looking for a new position. All I had to do was make sense of my increasingly erratic notes.

I was reaching the end of my report when something slapped down on my desk, causing me to start.

"Have you read this?" Henrietta stood in front of me, cheeks flushed with excitement and hazel eyes dancing. I recognised that look. I should, it had got me into enough scrapes in the last few months.

I picked up the periodical she had tossed before me. "*The Adventure Weekly?*" I remembered the infamous little rag from my Chester Place days, one of the other boys had positively devoured each number, but I had no idea it was still being published. A quick flick through its badly printed pages told me that nothing had changed. Tales of murder most horrid and terror to curl your toenails. All pretty lurid stuff. "What's a well-to-do young lady like you reading a penny blood like this, Hettie? Need a little more excitement in your life?"

"If I were that well-to-do I doubt I'd spend so much time in your company, George Rayne," she shot back, a familiar smile tugging at the corner of those devastating lips. "Look at the cover."

I obliged and flipped back to a garish illustration of a maiden in distress – pretty standard fare for the *Weekly*. A monstrous figure was looming out of the shadows, arms raised, ready to bring bloody death raining down on its terrified victim.

"'The Demon Slasher Strikes Again,'" I read, putting on my best music-hall voice, "'The Terror of Tottenham'. Yes, very good. Worthy of Dickens himself."

Hettie snatched the magazine out of my hands, her pretty face creased in a frustrated frown.

"You must have read the reports," she snapped, "of the Demon Slasher?"

"Of course I have. Applegarth's been running them every day for a fortnight. 'Mysterious Stranger Stalks Seven Sisters', 'Plucky Hero Slashed by Hideous Phantom'. I'm not surprised *The Weekly* has picked up on it. It's Springheeled Jack all over again."

The first attack had hit the headlines two weeks previously, on a cold Thursday evening. Hilda Gledhill, a twenty-four-year-old washerwoman, had been returning home from work when she'd heard a noise behind her. She'd turned to see a man towering over her, obscenely long arms raised above his head. She screamed, barely noticing the flash of a blade before it was too late. The razor had sliced across her front, cutting through her clothes and opening her chest. Hilda had fallen back in fear, convinced she was about to meet her maker, but the stranger had leapt over her cringing body and fled into the night, leaving nothing but maniacal laughter hanging in the air.

The following night another woman, Mary Waddington, was assaulted in the adjoining street, again by a razor-wielding rogue wearing a long, heavy greatcoat. For the next week not a night passed without a fresh appearance of the fiend the papers were soon calling the "Demon Slasher". I glanced down at the illustration of the brute on the front of *The Adventure Weekly*. The artist had perfectly captured the grisly description given by the phantom's many victims. A tall, gaunt fellow with ghastly features: a thin cruel mouth, a nose worthy of Mr Punch and wide owl-like eyes that seemed to burn with infernal fire.

But that wasn't the worst of it. Where you and I have index fingers, the monster was said to have long, curved blades. No wonder the poor people of Seven Sisters had begun to live in terror of nightfall, although none of this explained why Hettie was so agitated.

"Don't you see, George?" Hettie said, a worrying glimpse of eagerness flashing across her eyes. "This is my chance."

"Your chance for what, exactly?"

"To prove my worth to Applegarth once and for all."

She paused for effect, placing her hands on her hips and thrusting out her chest theatrically.

"I'm going to catch the Slasher!"

This was worse than I feared.

"You are?" I queried, knowing full well I wouldn't like the answer to my next question. "And how exactly are you going to do that?"

Hettie perched herself on my desk and gave me her most winning smile.

"That's where you come in…"

My headache suddenly felt a lot worse.

I knew from the moment I met Hettie Stead that she would be the death of me. Up to that point my life had been proceeding according to plan. I'd used my contacts to sell my first story, secured my desk at *The Examiner* and greased enough palms to keep the gossip columns full. I was happy, filed my stories mostly on time and looked forward to frittering away my pay packet at the weekend. An easy life, that's all I wanted.

Chasing violent men twice my size through moonlit backstreets had never been part of the deal.

So why did I find myself doing just that? Oh, yes. Hettie.

My quarry tore down the lane, heavy boots pounding against the pavement. The face that glanced over his broad shoulder was not a handsome one. Piggy eyes stared out from beneath a thick brow, ragged whiskers erupting from a nose that had been broken one too many times.

Usually, trying to apprehend such a rogue would be the last thing on my mind. I mean, what exactly was I going to do with him if I succeeded? This was a man I'd just seen kicking another poor soul to death. I was sure it was only the element of surprise that had prompted him to flee in the first place. If he had taken the time to evaluate his pursuer, he'd soon have realised that I was no threat.

And yet Hettie had used that tone I never seemed able to ignore, a tone developed from years of expecting people to do what they were told.

"Get after him, George."

So I did.

My legs were burning as Broken Nose darted left, barrelling down the alley that ran along the back of Birstall Road. Even if I weren't still suffering from the excesses of the previous evening, my body wasn't built for this kind of punishment.

The only thing that kept me going was the thought of telling Hettie I'd let him escape, a prospect considerably more terrifying than the thought of wrestling this chap to the floor.

Thankfully, for once the universe seemed to smile down upon me. As Broken Nose reached the end of the road my salvation strode into view. A policeman, on his beat, crossing the junction ahead. God bless London's bluebottles.

Broken Nose spotted the newcomer and scrambled to a halt, not knowing where to run. Unfortunately, his indecision was so sudden that I didn't have time to react. Still running full pelt, I barged into my prey, knocking him flying and tumbling to the pavement myself. A boot smashed into my shoulder as Broken Nose tried to get away, my second stroke of luck as I'm pretty sure he had been aiming at my face. The sudden burst of pain stunned me for a second, but my part in his arrest had been played. Broken Nose had been well and truly nabbed by the long arm of the law.

"Calm down lad," the burly policeman was shouting even as he slammed Broken Nose into a brick wall. "What's all this about?"

"I've done nothing wrong, guv," the villain growled, struggling against the officer's grip. I knew differently.

"He's lying, constable," I wheezed, dragging myself back to my feet. "We saw him beating a man back on Greenfield Road. There were three of them, all laying into the chap."

"We?"

"Me and my friend, Hettie."

"And where is this Hettie, sir?"

"Back with the victim. He's badly –"

A scream cut me off mid-sentence. A girl's voice. Hettie's voice.

No! I should never have left her alone.

"Hettie!"

The plan had been predictably foolhardy. The Slasher had so far attacked eight women and two men, always between dusk and midnight. The police had failed to apprehend any suspects and tensions were running high along the terraced streets of the area. No one had been killed, but folk were understandably nervous about being on the streets at night.

Not so Henrietta Stead. She had decided to trap the Slasher by offering herself as bait. A young woman alone and vulnerable, waiting beneath the lamppost on the corner of Roselyn Road, a treat no self-respecting, razor-blade-fingered maniac could resist.

My job was to lie in wait, ready to pounce on the criminal as he struck. Simple, if reckless, traits shared by most of Hettie's schemes.

What we hadn't expected was happening across a bunch of rogues kicking the living daylights out of a chap beneath the self-same lamppost. I'd been all for turning about and returning to the safety of the offices of *The Examiner*, but Hettie wasn't having any of it. Her defiant yell had scattered the mob and I had taken off after Broken Nose, leaving my friend alone with a badly beaten man.

Alone and vulnerable.

If anything had happened to her…

Accompanied by the sound of police whistles I tore back down Birstall Road, turning into Greenfield, already fearing the worst.

Then I saw Hettie, standing where I'd left her, the bodies still at her feet.

Wait a minute. Bodies? Plural?

"Hettie," I wheezed as I ran to her side, "what happened? I thought I heard you…"

The second body – the new body – let out a groan.

"George," she gasped, turning to me, a lock of her usually immaculate russet-brown hair hanging loose against her pale face, "he grabbed me as I was examining this unfortunate fellow." I glanced from the moaning figure to the man I'd hoped we had saved from the beating. It was obvious that we had been too late.

"What did you do?" I asked, pulling her into the gaslight to check for any razor-marks. Thankfully, while she looked a little dishevelled, my impetuous friend seemed unhurt.

"Why, hit him with this of course." Hettie raised the velvet chatelaine bag that usually hung from her waist. I took it from her and, surprised by its weight, flicked open the clasp.

"Since when have you taken to carrying around half a brick in your purse?" I asked, not really wanting to know the answer.

"Since I've been offering myself up as a lamb for the slaughter," came the reply. "Do you think I'd put myself in peril without a means to defend myself?"

"I thought *I* was your means to defend yourself?"

The look I received for that comment told me everything I needed to know.

"What's going on here?" said a gruff voice behind me. I turned to see my fortuitous policeman from Seven Sisters Road, accompanied by a further two officers.

"My friend was attacked," I explained.

"By the Demon Slasher no less," Hettie cut in, her nose held high in victory, "who I have single-handedly managed to apprehend."

I couldn't help but think that the word "single-handedly" was aimed squarely in my direction.

"I hate to disappoint you, young lady," came a voice somewhere near our feet, "but I am no demon. I was merely attempting to stop you destroying vital evidence by moving the body."

The befuddled policeman pushed past me to help Hettie's victim to his feet. The stranger took the officer's arm gratefully, rising shakily to his feet, a trickle of blood running down from an angry-looking graze on his high forehead.

"Then who are you?" I asked, putting myself between Hettie and the fellow.

"I, sir, am Sherlock Holmes."

An hour later, Hettie was still apologising. Once the police had taken our statements, she had insisted that we take Holmes to the hospital to be checked over, but the detective refused. He had, however, been persuaded into accepting an early supper in a nearby hotel.

Hettie had taken this as evidence of her powers of persuasion, but I couldn't help but notice that Holmes had only agreed when she revealed she had already interviewed one of the Slasher's victims. I must admit it had come as news to me. Hettie had obviously been planning tonight's activities for days.

"Beatrice Kelly was the fourth woman to be attacked," Holmes was recalling, staring intently at my colleague, "on the Chiltern Works."

"That's right," Hettie replied, buzzing with excitement. "On Sunday the fifth. Her story matched the others exactly. The Slasher appeared out of nowhere when she was walking home."

"She was injured?"

"Not seriously. Apparently, she threw up her hand to protect herself and the blade passed through her thick sleeve, only scratching her arm beneath."

"A lucky escape," Holmes mused. "And you believe her account?"

Hettie frowned. "Well, she showed me the clothes she was wearing at the time. They were cut to ribbons."

"And the scratch upon her arm?"

"Healed, but still visible."

"Why wouldn't Hettie believe her?" I asked, only to be ignored. I was beginning to feel like the proverbial gooseberry.

"So you are investigating the Slasher, Mr Holmes?" Hettie asked, unable to keep the obvious hero worship from her voice.

"It's true I have accepted the case," Holmes replied, taking a sip from his glass of medicinal brandy. "Usually I wouldn't give much credence to such sensationalism, although I have been following the story in the morning papers, including your own."

"Wait a minute," I interjected, "how did you know we are journalists?"

Holmes finally looked at me, although his expression was of complete bemusement.

"Mr Rayne, while I have received a blow to the head, I am not deaf," Holmes replied coldly, leaving me none the wiser.

"You told Constable Terry who we were," prompted Hettie, her look warning me not to embarrass her. "And who we worked for. Remember?"

"Oh, yes." I nodded as if it had been obvious all along. "I just assumed it was part of your turn."

Holmes' face darkened.

"My... turn?"

"You know, your act." My head knew I should stop talking, but my mouth had yet to take the hint. "Impressing us with your observations and deductions." I leant in, feigning an air of brotherly conspiracy, hoping Holmes would see in me a kindred spirit rather than a young fool woefully out of his depth. I'm ashamed to say I even added a wink. "I've read Dr Watson's stories. I know how this works."

"Do you indeed?" If Holmes' tone had been frosty before, it was positively Antarctic now. "What a relief not to have to impress anyone, especially you."

I laughed and leant back in my chair, stubbornly refusing to acknowledge the baleful glare that Hettie was no doubt casting over me. I willed myself to shut up, realising I'd gone too far, knowing that no good would come of continuing the conversation. At this point in the proceedings Georgie-boy needed to be seen and not heard.

"Besides, I doubt there's little you could deduce from me anyway."

Georgie-boy was an imbecile.

Holmes smiled, although the expression didn't reach his eyes.

"You're right. Nothing whatsoever. You, Mr Rayne, are a closed book. Save for the fact that you overslept this morning and were no doubt late for work. If I was performing my turn I would probably enquire if you enjoyed your lunch of beetroot sandwiches and advise you to purchase a new pen."

Yes, yes, I thought, forcing myself to grin like idiot, very good. You've put me in my place. Shall we return to the mystery in hand now? Unfortunately it appeared that while Sherlock Holmes was a man of rare talents, his abilities didn't include mind reading.

"Then there is the question of what led a footman such as yourself to leave service and move to Fleet Street in the first place? Or why you have never made your feelings known to the woman you love?"

I have no idea how long I sat there, feeling my cheeks colour and my heart sink. It felt as if the entire world had paused, waiting for a witty retort worthy of a man in my profession. I wouldn't say I hated Holmes at that moment, but I'd be lying if the thought of wiping that smug sneer off his grey face didn't cross my mind.

The detective held my gaze for a second longer than was tolerable and turned his attention back to Hettie, who, to her credit, was looking distinctly uncomfortable.

"Where was I? Ah yes," Holmes continued, barely pausing for breath, "I have been hired by a guild representing the local businesses of the area. It appears the nocturnal activities of the so-called Slasher are having rather a negative effect on trade. The streets of South Tottenham are considered too dangerous to walk alone."

"As we witnessed tonight…" Hettie commented, her expression grave. "That poor man…"

"The mania caused by the attacks has reached fever pitch. When an innocent fellow is kicked to death by a mob of blood-thirsty vigilantes just because his face isn't known in the area…"

Holmes let his words hang, the memory of the man's bloody corpse on the corner of Roselyn Road still painfully fresh in our minds. Terrance Rudge had been a passing tradesman, whose only crime had been to cross the path of a drunken group of locals who had taken to patrolling the streets to protect their women folk from the Slasher. He'd paid with his life. Suddenly the events in Seven Sisters had taken a somewhat more sinister turn. Someone had died, not at the hands of a razor-wielding phantom, but a band of scared, paranoid locals.

"What about the police?" Hettie asked. "Have they any leads?"

"Unfortunately not. I have conferred with a colleague at Scotland Yard and they simply do not have the manpower to investigate further."

"But that's dreadful," Hettie exclaimed, appalled at what she was hearing. "People around here are terrified."

"Indeed they are, but no lives have been lost – until tonight that is. Trust me Miss Stead, our law enforcers have enough problems without chasing after ghosts and goblins."

"So you think that the Slasher is of supernatural origin, then?" I asked, only to be rewarded by another of Holmes' icy glares.

"You claim to have read my friend's accounts, Mr Rayne?"

"I have, sir."

"Then you will be aware that preternatural phenomena has no place in my world."

"Of course, 'The world is big enough for us. No ghosts need apply.'" I stammered, remembering a line from one of the recent editions of *The Strand*. "Where is Dr Watson, by the way?"

"Sadly, the good doctor had business of his own to attend to."

If Holmes had been kinder to me, then I would have tried to hide my disappointment.

"That's a shame. I would have loved to meet the man behind the stories."

"You already have," Holmes retorted, before turning his attention to my friend. "Miss Stead, after you introduced my head to the contents of your handbag you said you would do anything to make amends."

I didn't like the sound of that.

"Of course, anything," Hettie replied.

"Excellent," said Holmes, smiling with genuine affection this time. "I would like to make the acquaintance of Mrs Beatrice Kelly."

At first Beatrice hadn't been pleased to see us.

"Our Henry's paid what he owed," she'd screamed after finding us standing on her doorstep. "Why can't you people leave us be?" Then she'd spotted Hettie and her demeanour had instantly changed. The woman beckoned us in to her distinctly murky kitchen and immediately busied herself in boiling the kettle. However, when Hettie revealed the identity of our companion, Mrs Kelly all but dropped the grimy crockery she was gathering from a battered sideboard.

"Sherlock Holmes," she shrieked. "In me 'ouse. God 'elp us, what has Henry done now? He's a good man, Mr Holmes, a good man. He just gets in with the wrong sort, always 'as. Very easily led, my Henry."

Holmes amazed me by displaying more charm and diplomacy than I had thought possible during our short acquaintance. He calmed the flustered woman, insisting that he just wanted to ask a few questions about the Slasher. At the very name of the fiend, Beatrice's lined face became positively electrified. This was a subject that she was more than happy to talk about. After all, as she explained, it had made her "a right royal celebrity around these parts", although it had been "a terrible ordeal" of course.

"'Orrible it was, Mr Holmes. 'orrible. Jumped me he did, with no warning. I thought my time had come, so I did."

Holmes turned over Beatrice's dirty woollen jacket in his hands. "And this is where his blade struck home?"

"Yes, sir. Cut clean through the sleeve, it did." Beatrice indicated where the fabric had been sliced. "Ruined my best blouse too. 'Ere, I'll show you." She produced a garment that could be only generously referred to as "off-white". If this was Beatrice's Sunday best, I'd hate to see the rest of her wardrobe.

"So I see," Holmes said, taking the blouse from her. "But you escaped being cut yourself."

"Oh I felt the blade against my skin sure enough. Cold as ice it was. Left a nasty scratch although it didn't break the skin, thank God. Me guardian angel must have been watching over me that night, Mr Holmes," she added with a toothless grin.

"May I see?"

"Of course." Beatrice was already rolling up an equally grubby sleeve. We all peered closer, but could see nothing of note on the woman's arm. "As I said, it was nothing more than a scratch really. Healed up nicely, it has. I'm one of the lucky ones."

"Compared to the Slasher's other victims, you mean?"

"I've been too scared to leave the house, but Henry's been bringing the papers 'ome. I can barely bring myself to look at them. Brings it all flooding back it does, especially that 'orrible picture. Gave me a right funny turn that did."

"The police sketch, you mean?" asked Hettie.

Beatrice pushed herself up from the table.

"No, dear, the one on the front of that dreadful magazine. Where did Henry put it? That man can never leave things where they were."

She began shuffling through the detritus of the cramped worktops, huffing and puffing to herself.

"You mean *The Adventure Weekly*?" I offered, "The story paper?"

"That's the one, love," Beatrice replied, finally finding the paper under a pile of cloths. "'Ere it is. Yeah, that's the geezer who tried to do me in, large as life and twice as ugly."

She passed the periodical to Holmes, who regarded it with interest.

"I had no idea the Slasher's exploits had found their way into the penny dreadfuls," he commented, flicking through the pages. "A five-part story by Mr Marcus Riggs. Fascinating."

"Does Mr Kelly regularly buy *The Weekly*, Beatrice?" asked Hettie, drawing a cackle from our hostess.

"Mercy me, dear, no. I didn't even know he could read."

"Where is your husband employed, Mrs Kelly?" Holmes enquired.

"Works at the glue factory, up Wilcox Street," came the reply. "Ever since he was a boy."

"But he had built up debts in the past." It was not a question, more a statement of fact. Beatrice visibly stiffened.

"What makes you ask that?"

Holmes raised a placating palm.

"My apologies, madam. I meant no offence. It was just the manner in which you greeted us…"

"He used to gamble," Beatrice replied, the warmth instantly extinguished from her voice. "Got 'imself in trouble."

"But he's paid his debts now."

"That he has," she snapped. "Came into some money, although what that's got to do with the Slasher, I don't know."

"Nothing at all," Holmes replied, rising to his feet. Apparently he'd decided we were leaving. "Thank you for your hospitality."

* * *

"What was all that about," I asked as we were all but bundled out of the Kelly household.

"Not here, Mr Rayne," Holmes warned, striding down the street. "Walls have ears, especially around this neighbourhood."

"But you saw something in her story?" interjected Hettie, pulling gloves from her bag. "Something I missed?"

Holmes didn't get a chance to answer. As we turned the corner, we found our path blocked by a portly figure – a portly figure I recognised.

"Terry Anders," I exclaimed. "What are you doing here?"

"I could ask you the same question, Rayne," Anders replied, a sly smile spreading across his greasy, corpulent face. "There's no high-class muck to be raked up around these parts, unless you've decided to become a proper journalist." He turned his unwanted attention on Hettie. "Like the delectable Miss Stead. Many of my colleagues at the *Echo* still have their doubts about lady reporters such as yourself, but this will show them. Your big scoop."

"What scoop are you talking about, Anders?" Hettie all but hissed.

Anders beamed, finally turning his attention to our companion.

"The fact that the great Sherlock Holmes is on the trail of the Demon Slasher. Of course, it would have been a scoop if a little bird hadn't told me what was occurring tonight. Have you time for a quick interview, Mr Holmes?"

For once, I was glad of Holmes' brusqueness. He stepped forward, almost barging Alders' considerable bulk out of the way.

"No comment," he shouted over his shoulder, leaving Anders spluttering as we sidestepped the well-padded hack and scurried after the detective.

"The man has no shame," I said, shoving the next edition of the *Echo* under Hettie's nose. "'Sherlock Holmes Stumped by Seven Sisters Slasher.' Only Terry Anders could translate 'No comment' as, and I quote, 'the world-renowned detective admitted last night that the case of the Demon Slasher has him beaten. After an evening investigating the strange Tottenham-based attacks, Mr Holmes is as much in the dark as His Majesty's Police Force.' It's rubbish like this that gives journalists a bad name."

"While your own work does nothing but reinforce our good reputation."

"Yes, very droll." I folded the copy of the *Echo* and deposited it into the wastepaper basket where it belonged. "Been taking lessons from Holmes on how to be completely objectionable, have we?"

The name of the detective brought a dazzling smile to her face.

"Funny you should mention your friend and mine."

She handed me a telegram, the contents of which made my eyebrows raise and my heart sink.

Miss Stead, it read, *I have a story for you. STOP. Please be at 120 Chancery Lane at noon. STOP. Mr Rayne may attend, if he must.*

"If he must?" I repeated, trying to sound as outraged as possible. "Who does he think he is?"

"Oh, no one in particular," replied Hettie, kicking away from her seat. "Just your common-or-garden genius, I expect." She grabbed her notebook and, when she noticed the look on my face, stuck out her bottom lip.

"Oh, don't worry Georgie, I'll never leave you for him. I've never been one for the older man." With that she turned on her heel and marched to the coat stand. I glanced at my watch and sighed. It was half past already. Best to get this over with.

"But this is the offices of the –"

"*Adventure Weekly,*" Holmes announced as he appeared beside our cab door to help Hettie to the pavement, a smart leather portfolio folder held under his arm. "We have an appointment with Mr Roger Pearson, the publisher." The detective bowed in greeting. "It is a pleasure to see you again, Miss Stead. I trust that your chatelaine is a great deal lighter this afternoon?"

I tried not to notice the blush that rose to Hettie's cheeks as I paid for the cab. This was another detail Watson had failed to publicise.

Holmes may have been knocking on fifty, but whatever Hettie said, the old rogue obviously had a way with the ladies.

You didn't have to be a consulting detective to see that *The Adventure Weekly* had obviously seen better days. The office's spartan furnishings were tired to say the least and the framed front covers that lined the walls had faded with age. Roger Pearson, on the other hand, was younger than I expected, perhaps no more than twenty-five years old, with an eager face, strong jaw and slicked-back hair.

"Mr Sherlock Holmes," he enthused, pumping our associate's hand with vigour. "What an unexpected honour. I have long been an admirer of Dr Watson's stories."

An expression suspiciously like frustration passed across Holmes' face for a split second. "Yes, so many people are these days. May I introduce Miss Stead and Mr Rayne of *The London Examiner*?"

"*The Examiner*?" Pearson's smile didn't falter, although his eyes betrayed a sudden flash of concern. "I don't understand."

"They are writing a story on your paper, Mr Pearson, and I am hoping you will be able to supply them with a few facts."

Now it was my turn to look confused. We were?

"Of course," Pearson said nervously, indicating for us to take a seat. "We never refuse a spot of publicity." I found myself standing as Holmes pulled out a chair for Hettie and took the remaining seat himself.

"Even when it is bad?" Holmes questioned, drawing a frown from the publisher.

"Again, I'm afraid I don't follow."

You and me both, I thought to myself.

"If I am correct," Holmes continued, "your father left the business to you in his will earlier this year."

Pearson nodded gravely. "Indeed, Mr Holmes. I am still reeling from the loss."

"Not to mention the circulation figures, I'd wager. Is it fair to say that the glory days are behind your once-*great* publication?"

If Pearson noticed the sarcasm Holmes ladled onto the question, he didn't react.

"I admit that our figures had been dropping, but I wouldn't write off *Adventure Weekly* just yet, Mr Holmes. In our heyday we sold a great deal more than Dr Watson's beloved *Strand* and I firmly believe –"

"That you will once again? That's the spirit."

I had a sudden vision of a cat playing with its prey. The glance that I swapped with Hettie told me she was thinking the same. The tension of the room had intensified.

"Especially with the success of last week's number," Holmes said.

"I had no idea we had such a celebrated devotee," Pearson said, the skin around his collar starting to flush. "Of course, I would be happy to arrange a complimentary subscription."

"Most kind –" Holmes raised a hand from the portfolio in his lap "– but I'm afraid that your run is about to be cut short." He unzipped the folder and drew out a copy of the story paper. "Sadly, you are never going to print the conclusion of Marcus Riggs's thrilling series."

He threw the paper across Pearson's desk so it landed in front of the publisher. Pearson's face now matched his neck.

"I'm not sure what you are suggesting, Mr Holmes," the publisher barked, "but if this is some kind of threat..."

"I paid Mr Riggs a visit earlier today," Holmes interjected, ignoring Pearson's rant. "Or at least I tried to. It appears your star writer is currently visiting his sister in Edinburgh. He left for Scotland three weeks ago. According to his landlady he had just delivered his account of the Slasher to you, based on the news reports, obviously. Almost as if he wanted to be out of the way when the first instalment was published."

"What of it?" Pearson asked. "A man's allowed to visit his relatives."

"Three weeks ago?" interrupted Hettie, her brow creasing in confusion. "But that's –"

"Exceptionally interesting," Holmes interposed. "Indeed it is, Miss Stead. As is the story Mrs Kelly spun last evening. Her description of the Slasher perfectly matched that found in Mr Riggs's story. Almost word for word."

"As you said," Pearson replied, "Riggs based his tale on the news reports."

"Reports which didn't appear until a week after he delivered his manuscript," pointed out Hettie. My eyes widened, even as the colour drained from Pearson's face.

"I believe," Holmes began, his voice rising to a crescendo, "that the reason the police haven't been able to find the Slasher –"

"Is that he doesn't exist," Hettie concluded, her pen frozen above her pad. "It was all a publicity stunt for the *Weekly*."

"Hang on," I said, tired of being a spectator. "Are you really suggesting Pearson hired someone to dress up as the Slasher and attack those people?"

"I did no such thing!" exploded Pearson, beads of sweat forming on his brow.

"There was no need," agreed Holmes, "not when you could merely pay people to say they'd been attacked."

"It was all a hoax?" I asked, confounded. Hettie at least had recovered her composure and was scribbling away on her pad.

"Seven Sisters is not an affluent neighbourhood. It must have been simplicity itself to find a number of people willing to claim they had been attacked. Much like Mr Kelly. Paying off the man's gambling debts was a small price to pay for the continued propagation of the Slasher stories. And you have to admire dear Mrs Kelly. Cutting through her own clothes with knife to simulate the attack. Of course, a close examination soon revealed that the damage wasn't caused by a razor-sharp blade. The fibres of her best jacket were virtually hacked apart. A razor's cut would be clean and straight. Then there was her blouse. It's hard to believe a blade could work its way through such a thick woollen sleeve, shredding a blouse in the process, and not break the skin. There was no sign of blood, despite the fact the garment obviously hadn't been laundered for quite some time."

"This is preposterous," Pearson spluttered, eyes flashing with a combination of fury and unmistakable alarm. "People have been injured, Mr Holmes. The attacks were real."

"The injuries were real. When folk are living in abject poverty it is staggering what they will do to earn a few bob."

"Even drag a razor over their own chest?" I asked, not wanting it to be true. "Or kick a man to death in the streets?"

"I had nothing to do with that," Pearson blurted out, getting to his feet, chair legs squealing across the floor. "I never even met those men."

"And I suspect there were other 'victims' you have never met. The poor souls so hungry for attention that they would turn a knife on themselves to grab their moment in the spotlight. The drunken louts who thought they were protecting their neighbourhood when they turned on an innocent stranger.

"The story – *your* story – grew with every new day. Fear, panic, mania. All to sell a few more copies of a squalid little magazine."

Holmes let his words hang in the stuffy air of the office. Broken, Pearson stumbled back, letting himself fall into his chair, lost for words.

"Fortunately, thanks to the story Miss Stead is about to write, everyone will soon know the true horror of the Demon Slasher."

A crowd had gathered around the offices of *The Adventure Weekly*, Pearson's dream made flesh. They gawped and gaped as the disgraced publisher was bundled into the back of a police wagon.

Holmes himself paid no attention to the man he had just ruined. Instead, he was giving Hettie one last quote. What did he care? As far as he concerned his work was done. The case was now in the hands of the authorities and a young journalist from *The London Examiner.*

I still didn't really know what I was doing here. It wasn't as if I had contributed anything to the great reveal. Perhaps Holmes just liked an audience. Was that why he kept Watson near, to have someone on hand to be amazed by his brilliance? A sickening thought occurred to me – was that the real reason Hettie endured my company?

"Mr Rayne, I must take my leave of you." Holmes' voice made me jump. The detective was standing beside me, his hand outstretched. I took it happily. The thought of being shot of him was cheering me no end.

"My pleasure, Mr Holmes."

"I doubt that very much." He paused for a moment, as if suddenly in uncharted territory. "I owe you an apology."

I hadn't been expecting that.

"What for?"

"For the way I embarrassed you in the hotel. There was no need to make such a show. Sometimes, when Watson is not around…"

For a second, those grey eyes shifted, the familiar proud mask slipping away to reveal a weary soul, beset by secret concerns. He looked so old, so alone.

I coughed, embarrassed for the man, and in an instant he had snapped back to his usual self-assured demeanour.

"Of course, for the record, my observations were mere trifles. I knew you had been late for work as there was a spot of blood on your collar. That, and the general slovenly nature of your chin told me that you had rushed your morning shave."

"Very good, Mr Holmes. Now let me guess, the stains on my finger betrayed my fondness for beetroot sandwiches and the stain on the inside of my jacket –"

"Is evidence that you carry a pen that is in the habit of leaking in your breast pocket." Holmes let out a genuine laugh. "You were obviously paying attention when you read Watson's little stories."

"And the other points?" I asked. "About my past –"

"And the woman you love?" A smile played on Holmes' thin lips. "Your shoes are perfectly polished, Mr Rayne, the kind of workmanship only practised by soldiers or servants. I can tell from your hairstyle that you have never been a military man, so a servant it must be. No doubt how you persuade all those cooks and butlers to reveal all. As for the love of your life…"

He paused, raising one eyebrow as he considered his next comment.

"Let's just say that you don't have to be a detective to see the obvious."

I felt my face flush as he unzipped his portfolio and produced the latest edition of the *The Strand*. "Before I forget, I have something for you. A gift from a friend. I suggest you turn to page seventeen."

And with that Holmes was gone, leaving me holding the magazine. I flicked through the pages to find an inscription above this week's tale of Sherlock Holmes.

Dear Mr Rayne,
You have my deepest sympathies. He can be utterly intolerable at times.
                                                    Yours,
                                          John H. Watson.

ABOUT THE AUTHOR

Cavan Scott has written novels, comics, audiobooks and dramas for series such as *Doctor Who*, *The Sarah Jane Adventures*, *Judge Dredd*, *Highlander* and *Blake's 7*, as well as numerous books for children. His latest novel, *Blake's 7: The Forgotten*, written with Mark Wright, was published by Big Finish in 2012.

Cavan lives near Bristol with his wife and two daughters and is currently working on a new fantasy trilogy.

THE POST-MODERN PROMETHEUS

BY NICK KYME

A t the corner of Brick Lane my colleague stoops, his nose within close proximity to a corpse. It takes little deduction, especially for one of his superlative talents, to realise how this unfortunate wretch met his end.

Head sits separate to body, the neck cavity a ragged and bloody mess that sees one of Lestrade's junior officers relinquish his hasty breakfast and me reaching for the menthol. Neither is a pleasant aroma – putrefying corpse or actinic, mildly acerbic reek – but the latter is most certainly preferable to the former.

It is a dingy place, a dark little alcove where light does not penetrate or is too afraid to venture. A killer's alleyway in many respects, of rough cobblestone, rotted shutters and dirty awnings that funnel the rain down into grimy gutters that carry off this patina of filth to the rest of London.

There are five of us present, myself included, two of whom are wearing the uniform of the Queen's Constabulary. A third is not in uniform, but his manner betrays his profession as the self-same as the officers. The fourth wears a long, tan coat, suit and waistcoat underneath.

"What do you estimate as the cause of death?" asks my colleague, his attempt at gallows humour lost on the vomiting constable.

"Very droll, Holmes," I rejoinder, pitying the poor constable as one of his fellows slaps his back. The bile of his stomach lining jolts out to join his expelled breakfast in a merry union.

It's raining, and I pull up the collar on my greatcoat and pull down the brim of my hat, over which a cataract is falling.

"I would suggest death by decapitation," I posit, as my mind wanders to a warm fire back at Baker Street and some of Mrs Hudson's homemade scones.

Holmes looks sharply over his shoulder at me, one knee sodden where it supports him next to the corpse, his deerstalker similarly overflowing with the deluge from the grey clouds above.

"Is that your professional opinion, Doctor?"

Despite having been his acquaintance – I hesitate to say "friend" – for several years, and although it was doubtful anyone could ever say they actually "knew" Sherlock Holmes, I do, for the most part, believe I can decipher his mores and whimsies better than most. Yet I could rarely tell with any certainty when he was being serious and when he favoured sarcasm.

I considered it a test, of character, of my intelligence – which, by the barometer of most scholars, is well above average but pales to the remarkable ingenuity and mental faculty of my colleague – but most pointedly, I believed, of my capacity for forbearance, for Holmes was not an easy companion.

"Yes, death by beheading, Holmes," I concede, eager to be away from this squalor and to environs entirely more salubrious. Brick Lane has ever been the refuge of the poor and the deprived, and, while not blind to their plight, I had no wish to associate with it any longer than I had to.

"Wrong!" he snaps, standing straight and sweeping across the narrow alley to a pool of viscera, thinning with every passing second as the pouring rain diluted it. "Watson, you are as blind as you are drenched. A layman's assessment," he went on, revelling, I suspect, in the theatre of it, "little better than the observations of Inspector Lestrade." He turns to the inspector to whom he refers, who looks hawkish and miserable in a long black coat and hat. "Wouldn't you say, Inspector?"

"Get on with it, Holmes," he gripes, not bothering to hide the scowl or his obvious displeasure at the inclement weather.

"Just so," says Holmes, smiling with unfettered delight at a truth to which only he, with his prodigious deductive abilities, can see. "And here," he adds, crouching down again to wet his other knee and more ostensibly to lift the victim's right hand, "is the proof of it." Dropping the hand, he skips over to the head next. "And here, also. See it?"

He puts this last question to me.

I frown, asking, "What am I supposed to be —"

"No, of course you don't," he interrupts, "none of you do, having already demonstrated the abject mediocrity of your observational skills."

"So illuminate us, Mr Holmes," says Lestrade. He pronounces the words, "illoomanate" and "ohms", but I can see his patience is wearing thin.

Holmes sees it too and starts to bring down the curtain on his performance.

"Doctor, consult your notebook, if you will, and tell me the approximate time of death based on this unfortunate individual's liver temperature, as noted when we first entered Brick Lane and beheld this grisly scene now before us."

Slightly wrong-footed but quick to react, I leaf through my notebook and find the requested answer.

"Approximately two hours, Holmes."

He clicks his fingers, a tutor happy with his slightly dimwitted student. "Precisely!"

"Meaning?" asks Lestrade, still not following.

"Have you seen this man's hands, Inspector?" says Holmes. "Have you seen his face? Have you examined, observed or noticed his other extremities at all? In short, have you perceived or inspected anything in this alley to make the warranting of your profession and rank a just one?"

"Watch it," he warns, but stoops alongside Holmes anyway.

So do I, eager to witness the conclusion of my colleague's antics, despite my distaste for them.

"What do you see?" Holmes asks of us both, looking either side as we flank him.

Up close, and with the time of death in mind, I see.

"Looks like rigor mortis in the hand," I say, and cannot help a self-indulgent flush of pride at Holmes' guarded smile, "which should be impossible after only two hours, yet this man's hands are curled into claws. Of course," I continue, moving down the body to the feet, removing the boots and socks myself, "there is a margin for error with such diagnoses…"

Barring a rather ugly carbuncle, the toes are perfectly fine.

"No apparent rigor on the other extremities," I say, continuing my examination. I move to the head, bringing my menthol handkerchief closer to my mouth and nose.

Between inhalations, I add, "The face is similarly contorted, an almost rictus *grin*," I sneer the word, "upon it. Eyes are wide, pupils dilated. No purpling or swelling of the tongue…"

"And what is your analysis, my dear Watson?"

Holmes has followed me and I can practically smell the tobacco on his breath.

"Well, I would say this man was dead before his head was removed and furthermore, that… it sounds ridiculous… but…"

"He was scared to death!" declares Holmes. "Something so terrible, some apparition resolving from the London fog, his nightmares coalesced into solid form, prompted such a reaction from this man that he died from sheer fright."

"If he was already dead, then why remove his head?" Lestrade chips in.

Holmes turns to him, face aglow with excitement. "That, my cognitively challenged inspector," he says, "is the question before us."

"Not to mention what that God-awful, bloody mess is," I say, pointing to the pool of viscera slowly sluicing into Brick Lane's streets for stray dogs to lap at.

"Indeed," says Holmes, equally ebullient as he turns his razor-like attention on me. "Do you know, my dear Watson," he adds, his expression almost paternal, his tone most certainly patronizing, "I do believe there is hope for you yet."

He stands and stalks from the alley, having seen all he needs to of the evidence.

"Holmes, where are you going now?" I hope it's back to Baker Street to dry out.

"Mrs Hudson's home cooking will have to wait, Watson," he replies, edging out of sight as he leaves the crime scene, as if reading my mind.

"And, I suppose, a hot bath and a warm fire will too, then?" I ask, following him and cursing the weather.

"You really are on good form today, old man," Holmes gibes.

We take a winding path through London's gloomy districts, Holmes unwilling or unable to tell me our destination. I content myself with following him, knowing that often the only possible recourse when he is in one of his moods is to simply accept it and let it run its course.

He moves swiftly, taking obscure turns, doubling back, about to take one street before favouring another and taking that instead. By the time we reach Trafalgar Square, I am utterly out of breath and at a loss as to what he is trying to achieve.

"Holmes!" I gripe, having to shout to be heard, my earlier attempts at getting my colleague's attention falling on deaf ears.

"Yes," says Holmes, to himself and not to me, I realise, "I believe we've been standing out in the rain for long enough."

Holmes is flat against a brick wall, breathing hard and utterly soaked. We both are.

"Long enough for what?" I ask.

He smiles superciliously, and it takes some effort for me not to throw a right hook. "Time for tea, Watson?"

"Tea?" I ask, my incredulity yet to wane in the face of such bizarre behaviour. "Tea!" I repeat, turning to anger. "Yes, I'd like a bloody cup of tea. An hour ago might have been nice."

Holmes smiles again. "Tea it is then." He proceeds to slap me on the arm as he sets off at a brisk pace in the direction of our by-now-distant lodgings. "Come now, Doctor, you'll catch a death out here in this rain."

He is fortunate I am tired and a few paces behind, or I may well have thrown that punch after all.

But as we walked back to Baker Street like two drowned rats, I wonder what has set him off; what has arrested Sherlock Holmes' senses to make him wander off and take such a circuitous route back to our abode? If I didn't know any better I would say he is trying to discern if someone is following us. I look back on several occasions but see nothing out of the ordinary. In a city like London, with its black, beating heart, there is no shortage of ne'er-do-wells, ruffians and assorted vermin that would do well-heeled, law-abiding folk harm. I see plenty of these but none whom I believed Holmes would regard as a threat.

It is with grateful eyes, then, that I finally behold 221b Baker Street and imagine the warm welcome we will receive within.

Still, the chill that something or someone has alarmed my colleague persists even after the fire is lit and a hot towel is curled around my shoulders. It is to be as nothing to what we will encounter later.

"What are you looking at, Holmes?" I ask, mildly exasperated. I have a small glass of whisky in my left hand, a cigar in my right and am warming my bare feet on the fire. I have changed my clothes, dispensing with my sodden garments for Mrs Hudson's expert attention. The towel around my shoulders is warming my neck and I sit in a plush armchair, glad to be out of the storm lashing the streets outside.

Holmes is transfixed on the gloom below our window, staring seemingly without blinking at some unknown and unseen terror only he can perceive.

He doesn't answer.

"Holmes, you are soaked and will catch a death of cold if you do not change. At once, old boy, doctor's orders. I insist."

"Watson," he replies, "you are as badgering and ineffectual as our old nanny. Mrs Hudson has tried, and failed, to dislodge me. I shall not be moved."

"At least take a towel, Holmes, or remove your jacket. I have no wish to be ministering to a dose of influenza because of your recalcitrant attitude."

"On the contrary, Watson," he corrects me, unflinching in his dedication, "it is essential."

I decide to drop the matter. In a battle of wills, I am wise and humble enough to accept that Sherlock Holmes would always be the victor. Instead, I cast my mind back to the alley and that scene of utter horror and bodily devastation.

"What manner of man could do something like that?" I wonder out loud. "How," I say, turning away quickly from the fire to regard my colleague again, "could a man possess the strength to remove another man's head, and why?'

"I feel it is connected," says Holmes.

"Is that a joke?" The seriousness of my colleague's expression suggests it is not. "Connected?' I continue, glad that we are at least engaging in conversation. "To what, old boy?"

"To whatever else that was layering Brick Lane. Certainly not the victim's neck though, dear Doctor."

"The blood and viscera? Outside of a slaughterhouse, I have never seen such a mess."

"Vile indeed," Holmes agrees. "Are you so sure though, Watson?"

"Sure? Of what?"

He turns quickly, bolting from the window like he's been bitten by an adder.

"Holmes?" I ask. "What the devil —"

"Come, Watson!" he shouts, throwing open the door. "And bring your gun, if you please."

"What?"

I am pulling on my socks and shoes, still damp from the rain, as I hear him call from the corridor.

"Are you so sure it is a man at all?" Holmes' voice echoes.

Feeling that now familiar chill up my spine, I take my gun from the drawer in my office, grab my coat and give chase.

I race into the street outside our lodgings, very nearly colliding with a clutch of lingering street urchins. Bullying them with harsh words, even though I know I am at fault, I find Holmes standing by the corner of Baker Street looking out into the void.

Night is encroaching, brought on faster by the rain, and my colleague is a tall and gaunt silhouette.

He seizes an urchin as they scurry past, teasing the wretch's ear and having a quiet word. By the time I catch up to them, Holmes has released the boy and is proffering a pocket watch I recognise.

"Yours, I believe, Watson," he says, without looking at me.

I take it, staring vengefully after the little hellion that's just disappeared into the darkness, and am about to thank my colleague when he exclaims, "There!" and hares off into the night.

"Holmes?"

I follow, keeping a hand near the pocket where I've put my gun.

"This way, Watson," I hear him cry, his form becoming ever more spectral and seemingly incorporeal the farther ahead he gets.

"Slow down, Holmes," I urge, but he is a hound with the scent of the fox and has no intention of losing the hunt. It is all I can do to keep him vaguely in my line of sight.

We are racing through the London streets and despite my best efforts I lose track of exactly where, my bearings foiled by the night's darkness.

After a long and enervating sprint, Holmes takes a sharp turn and I lose him, just for a few moments. I barrel around the end of a street corner and find it empty.

"Holmes!" I call, worried that I might have lost his trail or my colleague had fallen foul to some urban predator. The area is industrial, as is much of London beyond the tenement squalor, and I hear the action of distant machineries going through their circadian motions.

"Shhh…" I hear from behind me, and turn to see Holmes crouched down in the lee of a doorway. More precisely, I realise, we are in a warehouse district and enclosed on either side by buildings devoted to public works. In the sudden stillness, above the frenzied beating of my own heart, I discern the mechanical grind of the pumping works that services all of London's sewers and drains. The stink of that dank place is strong here too and I wonder suddenly what we have unwittingly walked into.

Holmes is pointing. "At the end of the alley," he says.

I follow his extended finger and see only darkness at first.

My breathing is rapid, my heart rate elevated, and not from the impromptu burst of exercise.

"From Brick Lane," Holmes adds in a rasp, "we were followed."

I can still see only darkness, and then, with all the slow resolution of an eclipse, a shadow detaches itself from another and, at the back of the alley, I see what appears to be a man.

Certainly it is human in shape, two arms, two legs, a head, but the silhouette it creates is massive. I gauge it then as over seven feet tall, but my estimate is later proven false.

"Reveal yourself!" I declare with greater courage than I feel.

He has an odour, this giant, one of ammonia and embalming fluid, of naphtha and menthol. There is something else too, a hint only. Decomposition.

Holmes hisses in my ear, and it takes all of my resolve not to cry out in panic, "Did you bring your gun, Doctor?"

Silence has fallen upon the narrow cordon in which we have found ourselves, the actions of the pistons and the wheels of the waterworks unable to lift the strange quietude that has descended. I am not ashamed to admit my hand is trembling as I reach for the gun.

The giant man advances a step, and I am suddenly, disquietingly reminded of how empty the streets now are, of how isolated we must be in a city teeming with souls. None have ventured here, braving the shadows and the rain-soaked night. Save us.

A word manifests in my brain as I look upon this hulking brute and brandish my pistol.

Monster.

"Halt," I warn the man. "Do not come any closer or I will shoot. I am a trained military marksman, I warn you. I shall not miss."

Holmes steps out from the alcove. I see he too has brought a gun.

The giant comes closer and a baleful moan passes his lips, like air escaping a leather balloon through its stitches. I hear something else too, the scrape of metal against stone, and I realise that the giant walks with a limp.

"Halt, I say!" shouting to convey my vehemence and commitment. "Step no closer."

Then I fire, a single shot aimed at the heart.

Holmes fires a fraction before me, targeting the head.

There is a brief flash of light from the muzzles of our guns, in which I see the suggestion of something grotesque and misshapen, pallid flesh and a snarl of blackened teeth. The after-flare blinds me, but I hear Holmes reloading for a second shot. I do too, but by the time I have the bullet primed the giant figure has gone.

"Where is he?" I ask, searching the shadows, half-expecting one of them to move.

"John…" says Holmes, pistol held forward in his outstretched hand, advancing into the darkness.

He rarely uses my Christian name. It is usually something he holds in reserve for when he wants to express sentiment but finds he does not possess the emotional faculty to do so. I think now he means to convey the seriousness of the danger we are in and his own exasperation at being confounded by what we had just witnessed.

"I have you covered, old boy," I reply. "Proceed with caution, Sherlock."

He does, the veneer of the reckless showman he often adopts dissolving like all the light of the gas lamps behind us. We are surrounded, he and I, by the shadows and everything they might harbour.

Lowering the pistol, he quickens his pace, just as I settle into a two-handed firing stance. My hands are steady as I am suddenly cast back to Afghanistan and the ranges where I learned my craft as a soldier before being deployed more usefully as a medic. At this moment, I would prefer those war-torn fields to this endless and unknown dark.

Holmes ducks down and I lose him to the shadows.

"Sherlock?" I call.

A few seconds lapse without answer. They stretch into minutes.

"I'm all right, John," he says at last, before adding, "Join me, if you please. I believe I have found how our ugly duckling flew the coop."

I venture into the alley, following my colleague's footsteps, and note as I get closer that there is a dead end, a blank wall to which the grotesque giant could not simply have dematerialised.

Holmes is crouching by a barred vent through which the noisome gases of the sewer emanate. As I join him, I try not to gag.

"Holmes, how can you not retch at the smell of it?"

He doesn't say, but instead directs my attention to a faint scraping next to the sewer grate.

"Light?" he asks.

"I beg your pardon, Holmes?"

"Light, illumination, a match, Watson," he expounds with some exasperation. "Do you have a match upon your person, Doctor?"

I do, and produce the book from my pocket, which Holmes snatches in short order. Striking one before I can protest, the scratches next to the grate are revealed in greater detail, as is the size and heft of the iron barrier blocking our own ingress in the dank darkness of London's effluent underworld.

"It would take three men to lift that," I observe, not bothering to hide my shock that our giant seemingly managed the feat alone.

"A pity then," says Holmes, "that we are only two."

After a tense pause as we stare into the mouth of the grate, I say, "I hit him, Holmes. A heart shot, I have no doubt."

Holmes looks at me sidelong. "No doubt, Doctor? In this gloom, your body fighting to overwhelm its very natural urge to flee? Can you be that precise?"

I nod. "In the heart, Holmes. I am sure."

He regards me for a moment then nods himself. "Very well then."

"And you?" I ask.

"The head. Left temple. Certain to kill or severely debilitate in the unlikely probability the bullet ricocheted off the skull and away from the brain."

"Then why –" I begin, before Holmes interrupts.

"Is our grotesque not dead? That is an excellent question."

His gaze has returned to the grate, and I see the yearning in his eyes to know the solution to this puzzle before us. Then the match fades and we are enveloped by shadow again.

"Would you venture down there?" I ask.

There is a moment of silence from Holmes when I assume he is contemplating that very course, before he stands up straight and dusts off his hands.

"No, I think that would be unwise. Our grotesque is not far away,

I believe. He is waiting for us," he says louder, presumably for the benefit of the giant.

We leave the alleyway and the sounds of the waterworks behind us. It is a long way back to Baker Street, made longer by my imaginings. I am not ashamed to admit the experience shook me to my core. Not since the moors and our encounter with the beast that preyed there have I been so afraid.

Upon our return, a fugue-like state settles on my companion as the deep contemplation needed to unwrap this ghastly conundrum begins. We exchange few words before Holmes retreats into himself and indulges in habits I would rather not be privy to.

I retire to my quarters and, despite my fear, try to bring to mind every detail of that night. The sheer strength of this misshapen man, his obvious and terrible injuries, his seemingly impervious nature, or un-nature – I am at a loss to explain it, especially the latter. At the time I wonder if I am in fact mistaken, that my shot went wide of the mark; my colleague's too. Certainly, there is a great deal I bring into question about my understanding of science and nature on account of this night. Holmes is not only a champion of the law, he is a champion of enlightenment, of science and reason. I am his able batman, I am not too proud to admit, as well as a subscriber to the same beliefs. But what we witnessed defied our logical creed and threatened to bring it burning down around us.

Sleep, when it comes that night, is fitful and fraught with images of a giant patchwork man, glowering from the shadows, resurrected from the grave.

The next morning I cannot rouse Holmes from whatever drug-induced torpor he has inflicted upon himself. Perforce, I keep an appointment I had made with the physician conducting the autopsy on the poor, unfortunate wretch we discovered in Brick Lane.

A walk in the fog-laden day does little to banish the demons plaguing my nocturnal hours, but I feel a measure of calm return.

London's warts are ugly to behold in the naked light of the sun, as is its dirt and squalor – but they are at least entirely corporeal, rational things and I find the solidity of that reassures me.

The visit to the attending physician is of little import, so I will not recount the details of it here. Most saliently, I discover the victim's name is Bartholomew Shelley. Upon inspection of his internal organs, the viscera and other matter also found on Brick Lane are determined not to belong to the man, thus suggesting a second victim.

According to Lestrade's investigations, Shelley is a chemist and owns property in the vicinity of where his headless body was discovered. Several chemicals are noted in the autopsy, the evidence of which is found on his clothes, fingertips, even his hair. I catalogue mercury, antimony and arsenical salts; charcoal, clay and ethanol, all of which are or could be used in the process of embalming.

Despite all of this additional information, I am no closer to understanding the grotesque man, although his candidacy for the role of murderer has been greatly enhanced. My intention is to take all of this to Holmes, but by the time I return to our lodgings he is no longer there and a note remains in his stead with instructions to meet him at an address in London.

I take a carriage and do just that.

Late into the afternoon, I arrive in Southwark and the somewhat forbiddingly named Ossory Road. According to Holmes' directions I am in the right place, standing in front of a dishevelled building which looks as if it hasn't been occupied for some time. A notice for public demolition is pinned to the door.

I am about to knock when a shuttered window on the second floor opens and my colleague leans out, a distinct cloud of dust billowing free behind him.

"It's neither locked nor barred, Watson," he says, and promptly disappears again.

With little other recourse, I wrench open the door and am conveyed up to the second floor by a flight of worn and rickety stairs. Through a second door, I emerge into a room that has every appearance of a study. It is a closeted space, festooned with nook and cranny, antechambers and shadow-swathed corridors. There is one desk, fully laden, and a great many bookcases and glass cabinets.

"Holmes?" I enquire, not seeing my colleague amongst the raft of books, papers and academic materials. He surfaces from behind a stack of volumes dedicated to anatomy, chemistry and thanatology amongst other more esoteric subject matter.

"Glad you could join me, Watson," he says, a fat bell jar held aloft in one hand as he examines it in what little light penetrates the grimy window.

Coughing up some of the dust from my lungs, I say, "Join you in what, Holmes? What is this place? And why are we here?"

"August Wilhelm von Hofmann," he replies, failing to elucidate me.

My frown evidently spurs a more detailed response as Holmes brandishes the bell jar, a briny-looking liquid sloshing within.

"Formaldehyde," he adds. "A solution used in the process of embalming. Von Hofmann's invention." Holmes smiles as if indulging an indolent child. "A better question, Doctor, would be to whom does this domicile belong?"

Outside, the sun is dipping below the London horizon and with the coming of the dark I feel the slightest resonance of the previous night's anxiety.

Distracted, I answer, "I have no idea."

"Look around, John," he says, setting down the bell jar so he can encompass the room with the spreading of his arms, "and tell me what you see."

My brow wrinkling further, I do as he requests.

"Books, papers, beakers, jars, vials… dust," I add, ruefully.

"No, no, no," Holmes impatiently snaps. "Those are all objects in this room as any fool with eyes can perceive. Tell me what you *see*."

I look again, and at first notice nothing further, but then a pattern begins to form in the madness. At first, I merely thought the place to be untidy, forgotten and left to decay, but that wasn't true.

"It has been ransacked," I say, touring the small study.

"More…" Holmes cajoles, patiently following in my stead.

I see a recent paper, some damage to one of the many bookcases that looks fresh and a smashed beaker, the glass crunching underfoot.

"Someone has been living here, but not the owner. He left long ago," I say, pausing by a stack of scientific journals unobscured by the dust which is ubiquitous throughout the rest of this abode. "These are a much more recent addition." I see a treatise by von Hofmann; a paper written by Frederik Ruysch; another in Russian, which I cannot read but am able to discern its author as a Ilya Mechnikov.

A quiet moment of contemplation settles in, so, belatedly, I recall my conversation with the physician and reach for my notebook.

"I met with the physician conducting the autopsy and discovered that the victim's name was –"

"Bartholomew Shelley," says Holmes. "A backstreet chemist and former associate of one J.G. Utterson." He produces a yellowed piece of paper from his breast pocket and brandishes it with aplomb. "A receipt for services rendered, I believe. One that the unfortunate Mr Shelley had concealed about his person and which I liberated during my examination of the body."

"And you felt that was unworthy of Lestrade's attention?"

Holmes returns the paper to his pocket. "The good inspector has enough to deal with without adding this to his already challenged and overworked mind."

By now, the light outside the window has all but disappeared and Holmes ignites the oil lamps in the room to provide some meagre illumination.

"Very well," I say, not entirely in agreement, adding, "But that is not all I learned. There were chemicals found on the victim's body common with the process of –"

"Embalming," Holmes interrupts again, prompting me to fold my arms in exasperated consternation.

"If you already knew all of this then what was the point of my visit to the autopsy physician?"

"What indeed, good Doctor, but no matter; we are here now, if a little behind speed."

I am about to protest again but see no point in it, opting for a different tack.

"Who, then, is this J.G. Utterson? The owner of this hovel?"

"No. He is, in fact, a lawyer who uncovered the deeds to this 'hovel', including the identity of its previous owner, and then granted access to our now-headless Bartholomew Shelley."

I am still, at this point, nonplussed. "So who was the previous owner and how is this relevant to our murder?"

Night having now fallen, the shadows have deepened in the room, the paltry light from the oil lamps doing little to lift the gloom.

"One Victor Frankenstein," Holmes declares, and in that moment of revelation I feel a creeping dread up my spine as a solemn voice issues from the back of the room.

"He was my father…"

It was a grave rasp, a deep and forbidding cadence best left to the darkest corners of the mind.

Surprised, I turn to face the speaker and am confronted with the same diabolic image as we saw in the alleyway next to the waterworks.

The grotesque, the giant man is here!

"Holmes, get behind me!" I shout, pulling out my gun, though more to bolster my courage than in the hope it could actually protect us from this monster.

Holmes raises his hand, his eyes on the lumpen silhouette at the back of the room.

"A secret passage," he says, and I am unsure if he is making a statement or asking the grotesque. To me, he adds, "Put down your gun, Watson. It will not avail us here."

I hesitate, gauging the distance to the door and Holmes' distance from the man.

"Down, if you please?" Holmes requests calmly a second time, while beckoning the man forward.

I raise my gun anyway, unconvinced of our safety at this point.

"Holmes, what are you doing?"

"If he meant us harm he would have done so already," Holmes replies. "And I do not think that is why you were following us," he addresses the man.

To call it such would be a gross dereliction of the term, for as it steps forward into the wan lamplight, we see it fully revealed for the first time.

It is… a monster, in the truest sense of the word. Large and lumpen, grotesquely muscled, it has stitches running across its face, bisecting its ugly visage. Now I look closer, I see the pale and wasted texture of its flesh, the mismatched nature of its limbs. A crude metal brace attached to its left leg reveals the source of the scrape I heard and the limp I saw the previous night. It is rank, this "man", a thing not created by natural means but fashioned through some devilish artifice; hubris given form.

I recall the terrible plight and malformation of Joseph Carey Merrick when I visited London Hospital as part of a delegation of medical professionals invited to comment and theorise on the poor man's condition. His affliction was horrifying and evinced an equal sense of dread and pity, but this creature before me is far worse and I can find no empathy for it.

But as it stands before us in the half-light, its head bowed, eyes unblinking, I do wonder if there is a mote of humanity contained within its patchwork frame.

"Remarkable," says Holmes, absorbing the full horror of the creature. "Victor Frankenstein was a doctor who hailed from Geneva, one of dubious reputation. Are you asking us to believe you are his offspring?"

The creature nods, slowly and forlornly like a dog that has taken one too many beatings.

"He was my father," it says again, "my creator."

Holmes draws closer and I am about to warn him off again, but the creature makes no move, no threat.

I lower the gun.

"A simulacrum of a man, fashioned from the concomitant parts of other men," says Holmes, walking around the grotesque creature in our midst.

"I am a man!" declares the monster, a sudden apoplexy filling it as it snarls through rotten teeth and clenches its club-like fists.

Holmes takes a backward step; I, a forward one with pistol extended once more.

"The gun, Watson!" says my colleague. "Down, if you please."

Reluctantly, I obey, but keep it close at hand just in case.

The creature calms down, but I cannot calm the thunderous refrain of my heart. I feel Holmes must be similarly afflicted but masks it expertly.

"Tell us then," I demand, "what are you doing here and why are you following us?"

As it shifts its dead gaze to me, I fight every instinct not to flinch before it. As if I am facing off against a feral dog, I give no quarter and try to establish my dominance.

"These are my father's lodgings, his study," the creature explains, "but they have been defiled, as have his works."

"You," I say, "are his works."

"They are much more than that," it retorts, and I am surprised by its obvious intellect and capacity for cognisance; surprised and, at the same time, disturbed. "I am not the scientist my father was, I cannot create life, though I dearly wish I could. I came here seeking to learn how, after all of my father's work at home was destroyed. But someone discovered this place and took it for themselves."

"And you were driven to the sewers, the only safe place for a man as unique as you," says Holmes.

The creature nods again. "Yes. I will not stand by and let my father's works be perverted by those who would see them turned towards ill."

"Was this why you killed Bartholomew Shelley?" I ask, my tone accusing. "Is perverting your father's works excuse enough for murder?"

It roars and, despite its intelligent veneer, Holmes and I are reminded of the monster this thing truly is. "No! I do not kill. I will not. I have seen enough of that to last several lifetimes. But the man you speak of is involved in this." It turns to Holmes then, a doleful look in its eyes. "Please, help me put a stop to this."

"A stop to what?" I cry. "Holmes, what is the meaning of all of this?"

Holmes does not answer me. Instead, he regards the creature as if measuring the veracity of its words and declaration.

"For certain there is perfidy of a most unique and horrifying stripe afoot here," he says. "You wish us to help you track down the man responsible for perverting your father's works? I believe I know where he is to be found, and furthermore," he adds, looking askance at me, "I believe we will discover the identity of Bartholomew Shelley's murderer at the same time. We have already met him, Watson," he states, now looking directly and only at me.

"We have?"

"Indeed. Not far from here is Greenland Dock, one of several yards in close proximity, but with one pertinent difference."

"I'm afraid I don't follow, Holmes."

"You will, Watson. You will."

I turn sharply, noting a sudden change in the room. The monster has gone, evaporated into the shadows like so much London fog.

"How is that even possible?" I ask, and make for the back of the room, where the creature must have retreated, until Holmes puts out a hand to stop me.

"You won't find him, John, and I think pursuit at this point would be most unwise." He is staring straight ahead, but pats my shoulder and concludes, "Our destination is Greenland Dock and the resolution of this most disturbing case, I think. Come!"

We leave the study of the departed Dr Victor Frankenstein as we found it. Bartholomew Shelley or his employers are not coming back, and neither is the creature. As we emerge onto the streets again, I imagine it travelling the sewers beneath and wonder where its path will end up leading us. I am not to wait long for my answer.

Holmes is checking his pistol as I catch up to him at the edge of Greenland Dock and, more specifically, the block of warehouses appended to it. One in particular has my colleague's undivided attention.

"A tannery?" I ask.

"Even a cursory examination of the sadly deceased Bartholomew Shelley would have revealed his background in chemistry, specifically his recent predilection for embalming. However, a much more detailed analysis, such as that which I was able to conduct while inspecting the dead man's apparent rigor mortis, would reveal an additional chemical concealed by the compound of the others." Now he turns to me, a satisfied and beaming smile broadening his face, and says, "Tannin, my dear doctor."

"Tannin?"

"Yes, derived from the German oak and fir, a chemical most commonly used in the process of tannery. I'd also wager that the viscera we discovered alongside the body had similar traces of the substance. And, here, dear doctor, we are."

Not bothering to try and fathom the inner-workings of my colleague's exceptional mind, I return my attention to the tannery. Much like the offices down Ossory Road, it is a broken-down and ramshackle building.

"And what, old boy, do you expect to find in there?"

Holmes' smile loses its warmth. "Monsters, my dear Watson."

We enter through a side door, noting that its lock has been forced and eventually broken. Within, the tannery is gloomy and we proceed slowly and with care down a narrow channel, flanked either side by large copper vats that have long since fallen to disuse. Overhead I make out the ragged silhouettes of rawhide and other partially cured flesh hanging from stout metal hooks suspended from thick beams set into the ceiling. The effect is both grisly and disconcerting. Ahead is a set of black iron steps leading to an upper level, where I assume the offices of this establishment are located.

Just as I am wondering what has happened to our monstrous companion, we hear voices coming from the upper level.

Holmes turns to me with a finger on his lips and, pistols drawn, we advance quietly up the steps.

Upon reaching the summit, my suspicions about the upper level are confirmed as we are presented with an office area. There is a desk and a similar array of papers and scientific paraphernalia as we saw in Victor Frankenstein's study. I realise then that this is no office, but in fact a crude laboratory.

Three men are present: one a burly-looking thug, the other two well attired and evidently gentlemen, if in name and not manner. The first is wiry, his suit jacket buttoned and pressed, hair slicked back. The second is rangier still, but without jacket, shirtsleeves rolled up over his elbows, top button loose. Dark rings around his eyes suggest fatigue; the sweat upon his brow, stress. He is talking animatedly to the other gentleman – I take this to be the lawyer, J.G. Utterson – who listens as the other man frantically leafs through the myriad papers on the desk.

I am about to remark my findings to Holmes, but in the short time it has taken me to compile this observational analysis, my colleague has mounted the upper level and is proceeding to advance boldly on the three men.

Cursing Holmes', at times, suicidal craving for drama, I follow.

The thuggish brute sees my colleague first and grunts to the others. There's a nervous tic affecting the man's right eye and what appears to be delirium tremens shaking his thick fingers. Still, he appears to have no weapon or I believe he would have already drawn it.

Both gentlemen look up but it is the lawyer who speaks first. "This is private property," he says, reaching for his inside pocket until I glare and slowly shake my head. "What are you doing here?"

Holmes answers, "I should like to put the same question to you, my good man."

The lawyer's eyes narrow. "Who are you?"

The other, as yet unknown gentleman now joins in, "Why, John," he says, referring to his friend, "don't you recognise them?" Leaving the papers to the chaos he has made of them, he steps around the desk and stands alongside John Utterson. The brute is still in the background, but looms large over the other two. "This is the inestimable Sherlock Holmes and his redoubtable servant, Dr John Watson."

Utterson stiffens at the revelation, just as my colleague deigns the unknown man with a short bow.

"And you are Dr Henry Jekyll, are you not?" says Holmes, and my eyes widen at the name.

The man before us is a wraith, a mass murderer several years dead, or so I had believed. I am unable to recall the full details but remember a strange case involving Henry Jekyll and another man, Edward Hyde. What he is doing here is, as yet, a mystery.

"How long have you been hiding in the shadows, good Doctor?"

Holmes asks. "Was Bartholomew Shelley your apprentice? Was he to walk in the light where you could not for fear of being recognised? Did he baulk at what you were doing here and refuse to assist you further? Is that why you had one of your thugs separate his head from his shoulders?"

Jekyll merely smiles, running a hand through the feverish sweat in his hair.

"How did you find me?" he asks, a subtle change in his tone and diction that I thought I imagined at first.

Holmes returns the smile. "It was elementary."

Utterson then turns to Jekyll. "Henry, I cannot be implicated in this…"

'Nor I," Jekyll replies, "the formula isn't perfected yet." And at this point I note the many vials and philtres set out on a shorter bench behind the two men. I know not what they are concocting but I recognise an experiment when I see it.

Without further conversation, Jekyll steps to one side.

"Zeus. Kill them both."

The brute lurches into motion, swift as a charging ape, arms swinging low by his sides to cement the image. Holmes and I fire as one, but the brute's sudden speed puts off our aim and he grunts in pain as our shots strike him in the arm and torso respectively.

It is barely enough to slow him.

We run.

Taking two stairs at a time, I feel sure we are outpacing the brute until it leaps down in front of us to block our exit.

"Please tell me you discussed this with Lestrade before we came here," I say, backing off in lockstep with my colleague.

"Afraid not, Watson," replies Holmes, as our simian aggressor advances on us.

"Can't let you live, Holmes," Jekyll calls from above us, "nor you, Dr Watson. I am truly sorry, but even with Victor Frankenstein's research my work is incomplete, and I fear your untimely intervention would delay it indefinitely."

"Quite understandable, Dr Jekyll, but I am afraid we shall have to disappoint," Holmes replies.

We are almost with our backs to the steps again, and out of room to manoeuvre.

"Oh?" asks Jekyll.

He sounds amused and I don't appreciate the humour of the situation until I notice the shadow looming behind Zeus. The thug sniffs the air, realising his error a fraction too late, as Victor Frankenstein's monstrous creation enfolds him in its arms and starts to squeeze.

I hear a shout from above us, but can't discern if it's Jekyll or Utterson. Most of my attention is focused on getting Holmes and myself out of harm's way as the monster and the brute wrestle. We duck off to the side, hurrying around them until we're at a safe distance, and watch the brawl from behind one of the tanning vats.

Honestly, I am expecting Frankenstein's monster to tear the other man apart, but I have not considered the sheer depths of turpitude to which Dr Jekyll has sunk in his nefarious endeavours.

Face reddening by the second, Zeus breaks the hold of the creature, and is seemingly… grown. His entire body, his musculature, his hands but not his head, have enlarged. Veins stand out on his neck, rope-like and thick. His small eyes bulge. Like a silverback gorilla, he strikes out at the monster, a palpable blow that sends it to its knees.

Shaking, growing further, this new abomination looms over the monster and prepares to hit it again. Interlacing both hands, it will smash the creature while its head is down.

"If he kills it…" I mutter.

"Then our exit is behind us, John," Holmes answers, "and Godspeed that we reach it in time." He glances up from the fight between the two titans. "Come on," he says, deciding, "we cannot allow Jekyll or Utterson to escape."

Only half paying attention, I watch as the monster seizes the brute's wrists before his fists can fall.

"Go!" it snarls at us. "For my father."

"For the law of everything that is right and decent," says Holmes, but nods to the creature nonetheless.

We run, back up the steps this time, passing the two massive brawlers.

By the time we reach the upper level again, Utterson has fled but

Jekyll remains. He is hunched over the small bench, a steel syringe in his right hand that he drops to the floor where it clatters.

"Henry Jekyll," I shout, my pistol held out before me, "turn and raise your hands."

As he does, I see the dark rings around the doctor's eyes have deepened and there is a transformation occurring within them. And not only his eyes – his entire body is reshaping.

"I doubt he's coming quietly, old boy," says Holmes, and I cannot argue.

We exchange the briefest look before discharging our weapons in unison.

Unlike the monsters grappling below us, Jekyll is shaken by the impact of both bullets. He staggers back, two crimson stains blossoming from around the holes in his shirt, before merging and overlapping in the middle.

He falls off the edge of the upper level and into one of the tanning vats below.

Holmes and I rush after him, stopping short at the edge of the wooden platform and looking down as we try to discover the doctor's fate.

At first there is nothing, then the viscous contents of the vat start to bubble and froth.

"How many more bullets do you have, Watson?" Holmes asks, rising from a crouching position and backing away from the edge. He doesn't have to tell me to do the same.

I check. "Just one. You?"

"The very same."

We get as far as halfway back to the steps when something large and formidable springs from the vat where we saw Henry Jekyll fall to his certain death not a moment ago. It is massive and hulking, the equal of the brute but with a feral intelligence in its eye that the other abomination does not possess. Clothes torn, dripping with acidic tannin, it looks raw and bestial despite the cognition in its eyes.

"Jekyll," I gasp.

The thing wearing the doctor's shredded attire slowly shakes its head and corrects me in a deep voice, "Hyde."

In my gut, I feel that the thing Jekyll has turned into is about to pounce, and there is nothing Holmes or I can do to prevent it.

Or so I believe.

Holmes tilts his aim wide and fires off his last shot. It clips the lamp Jekyll had been using to see in the dingy confines of the tannery, and Hyde laughs at my colleague's apparent ineptitude until the spark from the shot ignites the spilled oil and sets him aflame.

With a roar, Hyde goes up in conflagration. Drenched in tannin, the flames burn eagerly. He leaps again, straight up, and catches hold of one of the rafters in the ceiling. Brachiating from beam to beam, he seeks to swing his way free and douse the fire ravaging his flesh.

"After him, Watson!" Holmes cries, and I marvel at the sheer courage of the man as he throws himself across the wooden platform and down the iron steps.

Blindly pursuing my colleague, I come to an abrupt and sudden halt, almost barrelling into Holmes' back.

The brute is larger still and has the monster in a vice-like grip around the neck, but just as he is about to dispatch it, he changes again. Mutation is rapid this time and, far from apotheosis, signals the brute's demise. Like a bellows filled with too much air, the brute expands, skin stretching to accommodate.

"Behind me...." rasps the monster, shielding us, and through the gaps in its massive frame I witness an explosion of flesh, blood and matter as the brute combusts before our very eyes. Nothing is left following this violent reaction, nothing but a pool of sticky red viscera.

There is little time to appreciate the connection. I had misinterpreted Hyde's intentions – he wasn't trying to escape, he was tying up his loose ends, including the tannery and us.

Fire is spreading quickly across the roof, virulent like a plague, colonising every foot and yard, dissolving it in a black and orange sea.

Smoke thickens the air, so much that I raise my handkerchief to my mouth.

"Holmes," I shout above the din of burning timber and the crackle of flames, "we have to get out of here."

"Agreed," Holmes replies, looking up.

I follow his gaze but can find no sign of Hyde.

"You too," Holmes says to the creature, which nods once.

The monster leads us. Parts of the wooden roof are collapsing around us now, and our way back is far from straightforward. A huge burning beam crashes down in our path and we are almost immolated. Our grotesque companion shoves it aside, despite the obvious pain it causes, and I find myself wondering if I have misjudged this poor creature.

"Nearly there," I hear Holmes say, though I can scarcely see him through the grey pall of smoke that is billowing around us.

Mere paces from the door, we are stopped again by the hulking form of Hyde. The fire has wreaked havoc on his body. His hair is burned off, his skin scorched and blistered. Vengeance and anger fill his eyes, his next actions telegraphed by his posture and obvious demeanour.

The monster intercedes again, catching hold of Hyde and throwing him from our path.

"Now," it urges us, "flee!'

I have a bullet left in my pistol, and for a fleeting moment consider if it will be any use to the monster in its fight. In the end, the choice is made for me when Holmes grabs my jacket and hauls me, bodily, through the tannery door. My last sight before I turn towards the night and the cold air is of the monster hurling itself towards Hyde, its ragged coat alight.

Smoke funnels upwards in the night sky, blighting the moon and casting a murky, grey shadow. In it, the tannery burns. Fire engulfs it and the vats cook off in a series of sporadic, slightly muffled explosions.

Sitting on the edge of Greenland Dock, Holmes and I watch the blaze, grateful to be alive.

"Hyde and Jekyll," I say, coughing up a wad of charcoal-coloured phlegm.

"Jekyll and Hyde," Holmes ripostes.

"They were one and the same."

Holmes nods. His face is black from the smoke and soot, and I have never seen him looking quite so dishevelled. I expect I look no better.

"Jekyll possessed the intelligence, Hyde the brawn."

"So where does Victor Frankenstein fit into all of this?"

Part of the tannery collapses as the flames reach new heights into the London sky.

"We may never find out," Holmes admits, "but I suspect Jekyll wanted the best of both worlds, Watson. He wanted Hyde, he wanted to capture that brute strength, that power and fortitude, and marry it to his own intellect. Frankenstein's research was key to that. You saw his earlier attempts at perfecting the formula."

I am grimly reminded of the bloody remains in Brick Lane, and again in the tannery when Jekyll's bodyguard and test subject exploded.

"Victor Frankenstein created life from death, Watson," Holmes went on, "who knows what else he discovered before he died."

"Now we will never know."

"Perhaps," says Holmes, producing his pipe from his inside pocket and lighting up.

"How can you smoke at a time like this?" I ask.

"Can't think of a better time, Doctor."

I hear shouts in the distance: Lestrade and his constables come to find out the source of all the commotion.

He arrives shortly afterwards in person, a veritable battalion of officers in his charge.

"When I heard about a fire at Greenland Docs, I had an inkling I'd find you two at the scene," he says. Behind him, a forlorn John Utterson is being ushered away in handcuffs.

"Well, congratulations, Inspector," Holmes replies.

Lestrade scowls curiously.

"You've had your first inkling," Holmes tells him, beaming.

Muttering expletives to himself, Inspector Lestrade turns his back on us to direct his men.

"Back to Baker Street then, Watson?" Holmes asks brightly, ineffectually dusting off his soot-smeared jacket and getting to his feet. "We can both have a smoke and warm ourselves by the fire, eh?"

It takes all of my resolve not to show what I think of that suggestion.

Instead, I follow and hope we don't have far to walk before we can hail a cab.

* * *

In the aftermath of the fire only one body is found, that of Henry Jekyll, returned to his natural form. It is difficult to identify but I insist on performing the autopsy myself. I had hoped we would find them both; to have survived such devastation, surely the monster would be grievously injured.

Despite all of its efforts – it saved mine and Holmes' lives more than once – I cannot bring myself to think of it as anything but an abomination. As a doctor, I am a man of science and reason. The evidence of my eyes tells me that although it clearly exists, this monstrous creation of Victor Frankenstein is neither scientific nor reasonable.

As I pack my medical bag, the autopsy and my written findings complete, I make haste back to Baker Street. When a rational man is challenged by the irrational, his view of the world is thrown into jeopardy. I think my colleague feels this way too, for so much of his existence is predicated on logic and reason.

Climbing into the back of a black cab, far from comforted by the illusory safety of its walls, I fear one thing is for certain – Sherlock Holmes and I have not seen the last of this creature. Our paths will cross again. I hope to dear God that we are ready when they do.

ABOUT THE AUTHOR

Nick Kyme is an author and editor from Nottingham. He has written several novels and short stories set in the science fiction and fantasy worlds of Warhammer and Warhammer 40,000 for the Black Library, one of which, *The Primarchs* for the Horus Heresy series, was a *New York Times* bestseller. His most notable works include the popular Tome of Fire trilogy, and *The Fall of Damnos*. Most recently, he released the epic fantasy novel *The Great Betrayal*.

Find him at his website: www.nickkyme.com or follow him on Twitter @NickKyme.

MRS HUDSON AT THE
CHRISTMAS HOTEL

~~~

BY PAUL MAGRS

From the Journal of Dr John Watson.
November, 1925.

T his morning I received a rather large envelope postmarked
Sussex. Of course I knew at once that it came from my old
friend and, sure enough, amongst various yellowing papers
and envelopes there was a jar of his finest home-engineered honey,
wrapped in a protective bundle of muslin. Holmes' bees' honey is
a rare treat and a welcome addition to our breakfast table, though
my beloved does object to the occasional dead Hymenopteran found
suspended in the sticky stuff. Digging deeper in the brown paper
parcel proved there to be a further bundle and this was a padded
box, such as might contain an item of jewellery. Indeed, inside the
box there were two splendid multi-hued crystals. They looked rather
like a pair of eyes. I passed them to my beloved wife across the table
and she gasped. "Whatever is he doing, entrusting such things to the
Royal Mail?"

I couldn't answer her satisfactorily without first absorbing the import
of his note, which was folded neatly underneath these packages. I do
enjoy my former colleague-in-adventure's sporadic missives, touching
as they often do upon events in our shared past of which even I am
not fully cognisant. It seems that adventures and investigations were

going on continuously all around us, and I wasn't aware of even half of them. His letter of this morning – in rather shakier handwriting than ever, I am afraid – consisted of the following:

Watson – please find enclosed the latest production of my recalcitrant livestock. Cajole them as I might, they are very slow and perfectionist and what is contained in this jar represents almost a full year of squeezing and cudgeling of their small selves. I trust you will find it delicious. I also enclose the Eyes of Miimon, which belong to the people of Finland. They were smuggled here in the early 1890s by extraordinary means and the manner of their theft is still, I am afraid, a closed book. However, they have recently come to light again and were sent to me by the nieces of one Maude Sturgeon, a deceased spinster from the North Yorkshire coastal town of Whitby. They are a superstitious folk in that part of the islands, and will believe any silly piece of nonsense when it comes to matters of black magic and necromancy and so on. The nieces of this elderly, formidable lady – known as the local wise woman, apparently – believe that their ninety-four-year-old aunt was whisked away before her time at the behest of dark forces. (Before her time, I ask you! At the age of ninety-four…!) As you know, I will have no truck with such things as magic and dreadful sentimental drivel about demons and so on, especially at my time of life.

Nevertheless we must respect the beliefs of others – at least, in terms of how those beliefs might lead their owners to behave. Maude Sturgeon, I am informed, fully believed that these jewels are capable of exerting an influence of great evil. They had been in her possession ever since they were smuggled into this country, in 1895 – some thirty years ago. Her nieces found them amongst her precious belongings after her demise and they have decided to be rid of them. And so – in their great good wisdom – they have sent them to me. I was appalled to find that Maude Sturgeon never presented the jewels to the authorities three decades ago as she was plainly instructed to, but as you know, I have no faith in the doings of womankind. Especially not the kind of women who instruct their surviving relatives to sprinkle their ashes illegally and unhygenically around a national monument such as the ruined Abbey at Whitby.

Anyhow, I am too old and decrepit to run about the place with supposedly magical crystals. Would you, Watson, please see that they are disposed of correctly? My initial thought was that you should present them to my brother Mycroft, for official restoration to the Finns, who would no doubt be delighted. But then I thought... why not give the things to Professor Challenger, that old charlatan? If they are indeed magical stones – and I know you will guffaw at my entertaining the very idea, old friend – well, at the very least Professor Challenger might squeeze a little entertainment and amusement out of them. As might his new housekeeper, Mrs Hudson. She might even recognise the Eyes of Miimon, and be reminded of an escapade of her own from 1895.

An escapade which the also-enclosed packet of letters and postcards rather chaotically details. They are all addressed to you, my dear Watson, though somehow they have ended up amongst my many jumbled papers and effects.

Do you remember these rather strange communications which we received from Mrs Hudson during her holiday in the early summer of 1895? We both thought – as we read each one during our breakfasts at 221b – that our absent housekeeper was losing her mind.

Well, perhaps not. There is certainly something very odd about these twin jewels from Finland. Do you not find they give off a rather odd vibration? Don't they make you feel that there might actually be something in the superstitions of the wild north-easterners?

With great affection,
Holmes

June 15th, 1895
Whitby; The Royal Crescent, The West Cliff

Dear Dr Watson,
Now I hope you two sillies are seeing to yourselves properly. I put some nice jam on the kitchen counter, did you see? For breakfast.

Damson. Home-made. I won't be away for more than a week. My sister Nellie could never put up with me for longer than that. Today we have had a trip out to Scarborough, where folk go to take the waters. I much prefer the quieter seafront here in Whitby, though. Far more civilised than all that hullaballoo further down the coast. Here, life is much more sedate and genteel. As you yourself told me, Doctor, my nerves need soothing, rather than exciting further. Frazzled and malcontent, I think were the words you used to describe my recent moods. How your epithets rang in my ears when you left me on the station platform on Monday morning.

Anyhow, relax I must, the good Doctor tells me. To that end Nellie and I have been enjoying rather lazy days strolling about the intricate streets of this town, on both sides of the harbour. During yesterday's rather gusty afternoon we even took a bracing walk up the 199 steps to the old, broken-down Abbey. I am sure you approve of a little light exertion, though I must admit my legs were trembling this morning. Not that either of you wish to hear of my sundry complaints, of course. As far as the pair of you are concerned, all I *ever* do is run up and down staircases.

This evening we attend a special musical evening at one of the grander hotels on the West Cliff. Nellie has promised an evening of wonderment and enchantment. Nellie often exaggerates, though I must say, Whitby thus far is everything she has been promising me. Do you know this neck of the woods, Doctor?

I do hope all is peaceful at home. The two of you are, I imagine, embroiled in one of your dreadful investigations. I am sure ruffians of all kinds will be tracking muck up and down my stair carpets. I would not dream of asking a man of your elevation to run around with the ewbank, Dr Watson, but you would lighten my load considerably if you could manage it.

Now, please give Himself my warmest good wishes, and do save some for yourself.

Oh – the picture on the reverse shows the ruined Abbey and St Mary's Church, at the summit of the winding upward slope of 199 steps which Nellie and I doughtily tackled yesterday. You will be amused to note that, from this elevation, the stairs describe a reversed question mark upon the face of the steep, grassy cliff. Mysteries everywhere, you see.

Yours,
Mrs Hudson

Dear Dr Watson,

As you know I practise moderation in all things and I hardly ever touch a drop of alcohol, and so I don't know quite what came over me last night at the Christmas Hotel. There was, I think, a feverish and hysterical atmosphere about the place, and a sense that things were running ever so slightly amok.

Nellie and I arrived for dinner at the grand, imposing edifice of the one-hundred-year-old hotel and I admit to marvelling at its palatial splendour. It was painted pink and its windows were lit up charmingly with golden light. Inside, however, it was clear that all the guests were awash with the party spirit. There was dancing and hectic activity in every direction one cared to look. We found a foyer trimmed with every kind of gaudy Christmas decoration and barely room between flushed and overdressed guests to manouevre ourselves. As you know, my sister is lame and rather short, and so we had something of a trial, scuffling past the vast Scots fir and making for the ballroom at the far end of the first floor.

Nellie had already explained that the owner of the Christmas Hotel went in for these festive excesses all the year round. This was how she and her customers liked it. I found it all a bit much for a warm night in June. I did think it possibly irreligious, too.

Things are different in the north, as we both well know, Doctor, and though I should have turned on my heel and quit the Christmas Hotel at once, I felt I ought to linger a little for poor Nellie's sake. I don't believe she gets out much on her own, being as disfigured and generally malformed as she is.

Having said that, I was astonished that Nellie didn't seem perturbed by the abandonment and revelry all about us. It was a kind of cross between a rough Parisian dance hall and scenes from Bedlam. In fact, as she led the way into the ballroom, I realised that she seemed quite eager to take part in the dancing and the various hijinks in evidence.

Here there was a band, all the members of which were attired in green and scarlet outfits befitting of some species of pixie or elf. The music they were playing seemed unearthly and vulgar to my affronted ears.

Nellie must have noticed the expression on my face, for she turned to me, laughing. How strange, I thought, to see her so unselfconscious. Laughing, like this, in public. She must indeed feel at home here in this insalubrious place. Under the glittering lights of the ballroom her makeup seemed horribly garish and there were points of light dancing nastily in her single eye.

"The mistress wants to meet you," she told me.

I was duly introduced to the proprietress of this extraordinary establishment. It was a vast, blousy female form that came shunting towards us, her bloated body surmounting a kind of mechanised bath chair. Her revolting gown revealed a surplus of powdered bosom, and broken veins crisscrossed her face like contour lines on the Ordnance Survey Map for this part of North Yorkshire.

She cackled at me, "I am Mrs Claus," and the force of her breath was vile. She reeked like a pudding hot with flaming sauce and I took against her at once. "I feel honoured to meet poor Nellie's infamous sister."

"Infamous?" snapped I. As you know, Doctor, I do try not to be short with folk. But the fatuous remarks of others sometimes make it impossible for me not to snap at them.

"Oh, certainly. We all know who you work for, dear, and we're all very impressed. We keep up to date with his exploits through the scribblings of the good Dr Watson. We aren't so remote from the metropolis that we aren't bang up to the minute on unspeakable crimes in the south."

What a coarse way of referring to your various literary productions, Dr Watson! Suddenly, I felt exposed before this heinous female in this parochial pleasure parlour. I felt as if our entire lives had been laid bare. In that moment I knew that no matter that her hotel was geared to continuous celebration of the birth of our Saviour, there was an unholy stink of corruption about it and also about the occupant of that steam-driven bath chair.

Such was the extent of our discourse last evening, for Nellie swiftly dragged me away to sample the Christmas punch, which was being dispensed from a crystal bowl by another pair of waiters decked out as elves. We drank, and then we danced. Gentlemen gallantly offered themselves. We whirled about under lights to music I had never heard before. We made several return visits to the bottomless tureen of that delicious brew. We slaked our thirsts after our exertions and I marvelled again at Nellie's fleet-footedness on the floor. Never had I seen her less ungainly, with her clubfoot banging the sprung floor in perfect time. I think we both imbibed a little more of the heavenly beverage than we ought to have done.

Luckily, Nellie's compact cottage isn't far from the Christmas Hotel. We tottered easily down a few back alleys when it was time to drag ourselves away.

It had been a far more enjoyable evening that I had expected and really, Doctor, I am only telling you about it now in order to prove that I am taking seriously your exhortations that I should relax during my northern sojourn and do my level best to let down my hair.

This morning we are in disarray. My head and that of my sister are both pounding with the echoes of queer music. Nellie has made several large pots of tea to help us stir ourselves. Uppermost in my mind is the needling impression left upon me by that grotesque hostess, Mrs Claus. During our unexpectedly energetic dancing, I caught her watching us once or twice, through the crowd. She even had the nerve to waggle her fat fingers at me.

Also – and I haven't breathed a word of this to Nellie, of course – I happened to glimpse a poster advertising the very thing that you and Himself have asked me to watch out for.

In the ladies' lavatory there was a garish notice for An Extravaganza of Exorcism to be held at the Christmas Hotel. It's on every Tuesday night, apparently.

Yours,
Mrs Hudson

* * *

Dear Dr Watson,

It was evening before Nellie and I ventured out again and, in nostalgic vein, Nellie wanted to reminisce about our distant shared childhood in the Borders. I have no interest in looking back at a time when I was small, helpless and at the mercy of neglectful parents, and I can't see why she would care to dwell on such times when folk would call out names and throw rocks at her in the street. But my sister seems depressed and sunk into herself. Her flesh appears to hang off her distorted skeleton and her spirit is out of sorts, and so I indulged her for a portion of the evening, roving stiffly over old times. I also made half a dozen discreet enquiries about her health and state of mind, but about both my sister has not been forthcoming, poor mite.

Gabbling about a childhood expunged of all distressing details, she led me through the harbour and there we found a crowd gathered around a certain whaling vessel at the jetty. There was a flurry of excitement and kerfuffle going on as the ship docked and naturally we paused to see what was occurring. Nellie pointed to the cause of all the over-stimulation and it turned out to be a dark, dripping, unidentifiable carcass that was being roped into a harness on the deck of the ship. The sailors had brought something horrid out of the freezing sea. Some multi-limbed monstrosity that sent shivers through each of the observers, none of whom had seen anything like it.

We wandered to the swing bridge over the harbour and, standing downwind of its evil, brackish stench, we watched as the nasty thing was hauled aloft. I stared straight into its monstrous and sightless eyes.

And how do I explain this without sounding like a raging loon? Ach, Dr Watson. You will think that no more than two days away from Baker Street has turned me into a silly woman. For: I looked into the eyes of that beast. Eyes as large as side plates they were, and I felt I could see whole galaxies expand in their swirling depths. I saw stars blooming and worlds colliding and time telescoping into nothingness. I felt the whole of the future and past were laid out before me as I stood there on the bridge in the middle of that town, with the turbid North Sea all chilly around me. I experienced a small thrill of excitement, I have to say.

All of that I saw in the queer cephalopod's eyes.

Anyhow, then we had a very pleasant fish supper. Much, much better than the rubbish we get in London. I hope you and Himself are having a pleasant week, Doctor, and that there have been no untoward investigations thrust upon the two of you. You know how I fret. Tomorrow is Tuesday, as you know, and I shall be attending the Extravaganza of Exorcisms, just to see what it is like. I will report forthwith.

Yours,
Mrs Hudson

Dear Dr Watson,
Oh by jingo.

Why on earth did you ask me to go there? Why not leave a poor woman alone to potter about at the seaside and enjoy old ladyish things? Why make me undertake a mission of this nature?

I wish I had never gone.

Nellie is upstairs in her bed. It's past one in the morning. She's whimpering in her sleep, I can hear it through the floorboards. I'm just praying that she won't be permanently damaged by what she has been through tonight.

I'll tell you what it was. It was cruel, is what it was. It was shameful cruelty on the part of that woman and I blame myself. More than you and Himself, I blame myself, for letting my poor sister come along to the Christmas Hotel with me this evening.

But how was I to know?

I mean, with things of this sort, you expect them to be a den of charlatans, don't you? There's nothing in it, is there? All that table-rapping. Spirit-world mumbo jumbo. Why, I recall several occasions when you yourself and Himself have been called out on cases complicated by the carryings-on of fakers of psychic phenomena. I had assumed that much the same would be going on at the jamboree held at the Christmas Hotel and, indeed, when we first went in, it did seem like a fairly innocuous affair: a kind of bazaar for the feeble-minded. There were gypsies everywhere, reading palms in tents and at tables; there were Arabs and Jews and Chinese flogging their exotic wares; there were foreign folk consulting crystals and scrying mirrors and all types of occult artefacts. The very air was singing with the mystical mumblings of the fey folk crowded into the hotel's public rooms.

It was for the demonstrations of exorcisms that we were there, however, as you well know, Dr Watson. I guided my lumpen and somewhat sullen sister in the direction of the ballroom and there we were witness to a most peculiar performance. He was rather like a magician on that stage, with his assistant in a glamorous, beruffled frock. Denise and Wheatley, they were billed as, and, when they got going with a volunteer from the audience, I saw that it was the female Denise who took the lead. She was the one shouting and exhorting the devil to hie himself out of the volunteer elf. Mr Wheatley simply stood to one side, mumbling verses from a black-bound Old Testament and casting worried sideways glances at the supposedly possessed young man who then started vomiting on the stage.

It was a revolting spectacle, but my sister was enthralled. When I turned to tell her that I thought we had seen enough, I was startled to see that Nellie had an avid expression on her face. Her whole, twisted body was rigid and on the very point of surging forward through that crowd. "N– Nellie…?" I asked.

She looked at me and I saw a light in her eyes that I had never seen before. A wicked light, I thought.

We were interrupted then by the next act. Denise and Wheatley had apparently been successful in de-demonising the vomiting elf, and were replaced by a formidably ancient Romany woman with jet-black hair and dressed in hooped satin skirts. She was hard-faced and sinister and she appeared to be slipping into a trance.

"There are devils amongst us," she intoned, in a curious accent. "Beelzebub walks amongst us."

I turned to my sister to make a dry and jocular remark and was startled to find that Nellie had gone. She had slipped neatly through the press of bodies and was hauling herself onto the stage area. There was a roar of approval from the crowd.

"He is in me!" Nellie declared. She held out her arms and faced us, with a beatific smile upon her usually rather miserable-looking and crumpled face. "The devil is inside me! He has always been inside me! I have always been his plaything!"

The applause grew wilder, as if my unfortunate sister had won the approval of her fellow townsfolk; as if she were confirming the truth of something they had always suspected about her.

There was a string of words stuck in my throat. I tried repeatedly to shout them out at the stage, but they wouldn't come. I was suspended in horror, jostled in the crowd and helpless.

Now the Romany woman was laying her coarse, dirty hands on my sister and chanting some very strange verses indeed. I watched as Nellie went stiff as a board and started to froth at the mouth. That made me sick to the pit of my stomach. I could feel the Seafood Surprise from our early dinner start to rise in my gorge.

The gypsy woman's chanting was reaching a crescendo. I could have sworn I saw Nellie's eyes roll back and turn red.

Then there was a round of applause and it was over. Nellie was helped down from the stage and she was smiling shyly and nodding, acknowledging the applause. She wandered back through the crowd towards me.

On the stage the Romany exorcist flung up her arms and said, "The demon is powerfully strong! He will not leave this woman so easily. Nor will he leave any of you. All of you must buy…" And here she produced a pink jar of some kind of snake oil that she insisted we must all queue up and buy for four guineas a pop. Well, I was having none of it, and practically dragged my still-shaking and frothy-mouthed sister home.

So – thank you, indeed, Dr Watson. As if you even needed Nellie and I to investigate those charlatans at the Christmas Hotel. Naturally they are fakers. We knew that even before attending this macabre charade. But Nellie needn't have been frightened out of her wits in aid of your pursuit of knowledge. I wish you had never read those accounts in the first place, of the miraculous and mysterious events reported here in Whitby. I don't know why a sensible man such as yourself would have been at all bothered in the first place.

Yours,
Mrs Hudson

* * *

Dear Dr Watson,

This morning my poor sister was no better. She has gone a very odd colour indeed. Her usual hue isn't all that healthy looking, but this is downright alarming. I asked her if there was anything I could do for her.

"Maude will know," she said, tremulously. "Fetch Maude."

Well, it turns out her friend Maude Sturgeon lives down by the docks and she is what used to be called a local wise woman. Actually, there is a whole family of wise women, as it turns out, and these sisters occupy a tall house not far from the harbour. Downstairs it is a kind of herbalist shop – reeking of spices and curious unguents. I cast my eye around with some interest at the things they had on display. But I was there on a mission. "Maude will be able to help me," Nellie had insisted.

Now I was confronting the formidable Maude Sturgeon herself, in her witchy emporium. She listened disapprovingly as I described the previous evening's events. She seemed to take a very dim view of anything that went on at the Christmas Hotel.

"There's always someone dabbling with dark forces and things they should know better about," said Maude gruffly. She was more like a schoolmarm than a witch, I thought, in her plain grey suit and her steel-grey hair pinned up like so. It was reassuring to be in the presence of her stolid good sense. She asked me to come and sit in their parlour, where I found three of her rather more fey sisters engaged in a very odd task indeed.

Maude was fetching her shawl off the hat stand. "Oh, don't mind them," she told me. "They're stuffing it for the Whitby museum."

I looked harder and realised that the slippery dark thing they were all sewing wasn't some svelte garment after all. It was the gutted remains of the monstrous sea beast that had been landed yesterday. Those witchy sisters appraised me as they went on stitching, and I was very careful not to look into the behemoth's eyes again.

Then Maude was ready and I was glad to get out of the fishy smell of that back parlour. The wise woman led the way through the narrow streets towards Nellie's house, pausing on the way to buy her a fancy cake from a favoured bakery.

"How long have you been friends with my sister?" I asked conversationally.

"Ever since she's been here," said Maude, beaming brightly and brandishing her walking stick as we passed familiar faces. "Your sister has proved quite a reliable helper on a number of my more terrifying investigations and adventures here in Whitby."

Well, of course, you could have knocked me down with a feather. Our Nellie? Having adventures? Involved in investigations? Helping out a personage such as this Maude? For a second I experienced a slight dizziness. Did everyone I know get themselves involved in curious adventures behind my very back?

"Do you mean… crimes?" I asked, lowering my voice as we came within sight of Nellie's cottage.

"Crimes, indeed —" Maude nodded "— also supernatural and unexplained phenomena of all kinds. Whitby seems to be a kind of magnet for occult and devilish practices, schemes and unholy beings, y'know."

"Really?"

"Oh, yes —" Maude sniffed, giving me a very dark look indeed as I fumbled for my keys to Nellie's house "— it's to do with the presence of an interstitial dimensional gateway known as the Bitch's Maw in the grounds of the old Abbey, you see. A kind of gateway into hell. Very nasty indeed."

I'm afraid my mouth dropped open at her words and I busied myself with letting us into the cottage, which smelled reassuringly of newly brewed coffee and fresh wood smoke. Convinced I was bringing a raging lunatic to the rescue, I was delighted to see that my sister had risen from her bed. She was shuffling about in the kitchen in her nightie and pouring coffee for us all.

"I'm so sorry to call you out, Maude," she said, as her visitor produced the Victoria sponge from her shopping bag. "Ooh, lovely. I'll fetch plates. No, I thought I'd better call you over, because of this funny do that we had last night at the Exorcism Extravaganza."

"You were fools to go to such a thing," Maude growled, slicing the cake and dolloping wedges of it messily onto dainty china.

"I know, I couldn't help myself," said Nellie. "And we all know these things are about charlatans fleecing the public. But the thing is… I went there because Raphael was worried. He had felt a vibration. There was a genuinely powerful psychic up there at the hotel last night. He could feel them at work. They were malevolent. Harmful. Hiding their wicked selves away amongst the usual fakers. That's why we were there last night. So I could flush this person out."

I sat there with my wedge of cake halfway up to my mouth, staring at my sister. My malformed and shy younger sister, Nellie. Nellie with one eye, a crooked back and a clubfoot. Nellie who would never say boo to a goose. My poor Nellie was sitting there in her nightgown, eating cake for breakfast, and coming out with all of this gobbledegook, easy as you like. And that bullish Maude woman was simply nodding at her. Nodding as if they had little chats like this all the time. Nodding as if they were discussing something entirely reasonable.

Before they could carry on saying more to uproot my sense of the stability of all things, I broke in, "Erm, who is Raphael?"

My dear sister Nellie looked at me and I was astonished to see a hint of pity in her single eye. She was pitying me! "Oh dear," she said. "Well. I suppose needs must. After all these years, I must come clean. I must tell you the truth. After a lifetime of concealment."

"I think you're right," said Maude. "It's about time your sister knew the truth."

Nellie took a deep breath and looked at me dead in the eye. Both my eyes. With her single one. Which was wincing with pity. She said – in a very calm voice indeed – "You see, Raphael is my inner demon. And my spirit guide. He's been inside me all my life and he's been my little secret. And when that dreadful woman tried to exorcise him last night, it gave Raphael quite a turn, I can tell you."

I stared at her. I really didn't know what to say. What does one say, Dr Waston, in circumstances like these?

Yours,
Mrs Hudson

* * *

Dear Dr Watson,

I hope both your good self and our mutual friend, Himself, are faring rather better than I am this week. I have been in a whirl of perturbation for several days. Never have I been so steeped in strangeness and such eerie goings-on. Well, it turns out that my malformed sister and her bluff and hearty best friend are very well accustomed to all manner of supernatural things. Things I assumed simply should not be. Being, like our good friend Himself, a creature of rationality and good, plain commonsense, I am having problems. Here in the north I am finding more things in my philosophy – as the Danish prince would say – than I could shake a stick at.

Today is Thursday – honestly, I don't know where the time is going; I'm passively being led around by my sister, who seems to have a renewed vigour about her, now that she is embroiled in an investigation. I was compelled to attend an unveiling ceremony at the museum in the rather elegant park across the other side of town. This was for the stuffed squid that Maude's sisters had spent day and night stitching back into some semblance of life. When we arrived for the sherry cocktail reception this evening in that rather musty, dusty municipal establishment, the squid was suspended in a delicate cat's cradle of silver threads, which gave it the appearance of swimming through the cavernous room. All of the guests – Whitby's great and good in their finery – stood milling underneath, gazing up at the frozen tentacles and the shiny carapace of its purple skin.

I nodded politely and smiled as my sister gabbled away at Maude's sisters, who were attired in suitably witchy – and rather scandalous – gowns for the evening. They smiled demurely and seemed to be the toast of the town. I wandered about the other display cabinets, finding a bewildering selection of mouldering dolls' houses and ragged bears. There were Valentine's cards from the previous century; tiny gloves and shoes; stuffed woodland beasts and seabirds. It was a shabby miscellany, I thought, with hardly any rhyme or reason.

Anyhow, there was a proper ballyhoo when the Mayor of Whitby got up in all his robes and chains and made his speech. He stood on a podium – this oleaginous Mr Danby, as they called him – and chuntered on about their town and its glorious heritage. I was staring into the eyes of the monstrous beast, but its celestial orbs had been replaced, naturally enough, with something less potent. They looked rather like green glass plates and, indeed, Maude leaned in to me and hissed that they were two expensive serving platters she had brought back from a holiday on the island of Murano, near Venice. Oh, my heart leapt up at the mention of Venice, dear Dr Watson. And then I shivered as I recalled some of the deadlier details of our adventure there, last autumn.

It was just as the Mayor was coming to the end of his windy speech that I noticed something rather odd happening to the suspended squid. One of its attenuated limbs seemed to flex and lash, of its own accord. There was a sharp cry as someone else noticed the same thing. Then, all of a sudden, its other limbs were moving and screams rang out inside the stuffy museum. It was at this point that I noticed it was all due to the wires which suspended the beast: they were snapping, one by one, and the thick, heavy body of the squid was swaying and then galloping about in mid-air. There was such a pandemonium at this, and I felt Nellie grab me by both arms and drag me backwards into the alcove where the ships-in-bottles were tidily arrayed.

With a tremendous crash of breaking cabinets and glass displays, the giant squid came toppling down. Some innocent bystanders had been transfixed with horror – including the Mayor – and they were soon pinned and wriggling under that giant, piscine form.

After a few moments there was silence, and billowing clouds of dust.

I heard Maude Sturgeon cry out, "Sabotage…!"

And soon we were checking around to see who was hurt. Maude's witchy sisters were shaken, but not injured. The squid itself had barely a scratch on it. The Mayor's ancient, wizened mother was hyperventilating and had to be taken home.

Nellie and I went straight to the nearest hotel, where we sat in the bar and took a fortifyingly stiff nip of brandy. "Who would want to sabotage the unveiling of a squid?" I asked her.

She gave me a very dark look. "Perhaps it's not the squid itself. Perhaps it is all about what was inside the squid."

I raised my eyebrow at her as she downed her drink. "What could be inside a squid?" I laughed.

"Whatever it was, it isn't there now," she said cryptically. "The squid was, as we know, rammed full of stuffing."

She was mumbling rather drunkenly, and I thought I could detect a touch of Raphael, her supposed spirit guide, in her eyes. "Are you saying something was removed from the squid? By those who did the stuffing?"

She tapped her nose. "I am, indeed."

"Maude's sisters gutted the thing; what did they take out?"

"I don't know," she said primly. "I'm only surmising." Then she was peering across the elegant lounge bar of the Miramar Hotel at someone who had just stepped in, alone. "Isn't that Denise?" she said. "From Denise and Wheatley?"

And it was, Dr Watson. Away from the stage and out of her finery, Denise was a rather shabby genteel figure, all bundled up in worsted and tweed.

"She's entering the bar on her own," I observed.

"Oh, no one cares about that kind of propriety," said Nellie. "Not at the Miramar Hotel, anyway. Look, I'm going to call her over."

I wasn't sure I even wanted to be sociable with an exorcist, but voice my concerns about this I could not, for Nellie was on her feet and beckoning Denise by waving her skinny arms and winking at her with her one good eye.

"My life is in tatters." Denise wept copiously once my sister had started her talking.

"Why is that?" asked Nellie, agog at the spectacle of the blue-haired lady sobbing into her libation.

"He can be terrible, terrible –" her voice trembled "– when he's in a fury." Fear made her shiver and the brandy glass tinkled against her rotten stumps of teeth.

"Who, my dear?" Nellie pressed.

"Why, him. My husband. My terrible husband." Then Denise clapped a hand over her mouth, as if she had said too much.

Nellie was intrigued and kept badgering the old dear, and I felt myself growing uneasy. What was Nellie doing, getting so close? Hadn't Denise been one of the reasons Nellie had been up all night on Tuesday? All gut-churning and collywobbly as she was?

"There, there," Nellie kept saying, and the elderly exorcist burst into more violent tears. She put her head on Nellie's hump and gave full vent to her feelings as Nellie patted her wispy blue hair. I didn't know where to look.

"He makes me do heinous things," she said, through heaving breath and muffled by Nellie's hump.

"Where is he now?" asked Nellie.

"In our room, upstairs," said Denise. "He has gone to bed in fury and disgust. All because of that fracas at the museum."

"The museum?" I asked. "You mean, the cephalopod's unfortunate collapse?"

She sniffed. "Yes, I saw you both there. But you left with the crowd, shortly afterwards. You never saw him, berating those sisters. Getting me to cut open the thing. Feeling around inside those slippery limbs... Looking for... looking for..."

Nellie was looking excited now. She had a fervid expression. Rather like Himself gets. You know, when "the game's afoot". "Looking for what, Denise?"

"Those blasted jewels," cried the exorcist. "The Eyes of Miimon. Smuggled here in the body of that behemoth. The rarest of jewels. Possessed of untold occult powers."

Now, this was a surprise to Nellie. "Jewels?" she said. "Where from?"

"From the islands of Finland, far away," said the old lady. "And he has lost them forever, he fears."

"But −" I broke in, trying to grasp the situation "− the giant squid was stuffed, wasn't it? We saw Maude Sturgeon's sisters sewing it themselves in their backroom. Rather like a shroud. Surely, if there were jewels inside the beast's body, then..."

Denise Wheatley was staring at me and her eyes were hard and glittering with excitement. "Yes! Yes, you're right!"

I looked at Nellie and she was shaking her head at me fiercely. "But, I just thought −" I began.

"We must go at once," said Denise, slinging back the last of her brandy. "Where do they live, these Sisters Sturgeon? Where are they hiding the Eyes of Miimon?"

And then, rather like your own dear self, Dr Watson, I was left to straggle in the wake of the others as they dashed from the bar area, and out of the Miramar Hotel, into something of a balmy evening.

Yours,

Mrs Hudson

Dear Dr Watson,

I am writing this on the back of a laundry list I have found in my coat pocket and using a nub of pencil that has worn almost to nothing. This is possibly the most futile and hopeless message demanding help that you will never receive. Still, it seems preferable to write it all down, rather than sit here in the dark, doing nothing. At least my hands aren't tied, I suppose. That is something. I can twiddle my fingers at least.

Nellie is with me, absolutely furious at our predicament, for which she blames me. At this present time my malformed sister is refusing to speak to me.

"You had to blunder in, didn't you?" was one of the last things she said. "Everything was proceeding just as it ought, and you had to go and open your big fat trap."

Never have I heard such coarseness from my sister's rather blubbery and unattractive lips. For a few moments I was convinced that the vile spook she claims to harbour in her soul was speaking through her, but alas, no: it was Nellie herself who was livid with me. It turns out that I had burst out with quite the wrong thing, and shouldn't have told Denise the exorcist about the Sturgeon sisters and their skills in the art of taxidermy. Everything, it seems, was already in hand, and Nellie was on the point of ensnaring the blue-haired woman in a trap. My sister and Maude Sturgeon had had everything worked out, and the idea was, apparently, to lure Denise Wheatley up to the ruined Abbey to meet and greet her ultimate fate, as befitting a being as magically powerful as herself. She was to be lured there by the promise of having these magical Finnish crystals handed over to her by Maude, as the senior Sturgeon sister. Such had been the idea, anyhow.

But because of me, everything has gone to the bad. I never could hold my tongue, could I?

This house is silent now. The pair of us have been imprisoned in one of the attic rooms. We've tried to break out, smashing the few bits of old furniture against the solid door. We have shouted for help, but there is no one here. The Sturgeon house is quite empty. The lower rooms lie in messy chaos, following that terrible fight between the three Sturgeon sisters and Denise Wheatley. Shelves, jars, furniture and fittings – everything was smashed into smithereens by those… what would you call them? Lightning bolts? That they were all shooting out of their hands and eyes at each other. It was a terrible to-do. And all over a few bits of old jewellery that came out of a gutted fish.

LATER

Maude Sturgeon eventually arrived to let us out. By then I was exhausted and in no mood for a long disquisition or inquisition about what had been going on. She was filling in her partner-in-crime, my sister Nellie, about the latest developments. How it turned out that Denise Wheatley was, in fact, a powerful sorceress, and the supernatural powers of all four Sturgeon sisters combined hadn't been enough to hold her back. She had stormed into their home and stolen away the jewels she was after.

Both Nellie and Maude gave me a hard stare at this point, for giving away their location. I merely tutted and set off down the stairs of the Sturgeon residence, eager to be out of that dusty deathtrap, filled with antiques and black-magic paraphernalia.

I can tell you, Doctor, I wasn't at all impressed by this talk of sorceresses and so on, for all I had seen of them shooting bolts every which way.

Maude told us that the Finnish jewels had been discovered by her sisters during the stuffing process. They had been hidden inside the dead eyes of the giant squid. Maude had cleaned them up and popped them into the safe in her bedroom, which Denise Wheatley had no compunction about breaking into, blasting it apart with those queer bolts of lightning she manifested out of her limbs.

This was all rather too much for me. I didn't care who got hold of the jewels, and said so. What did Finland matter to me?

Maude glared at me angrily. By now we were in the smashed-up herbalist shop downstairs. "With the Eyes of Miimon, a powerful sorceress like Denise could do untold damage to the world."

Nellie was biting her lip. "We were going to shove her in the Bitch's Maw, up at the Abbey. The idea was to dispatch her to hell."

"But now she's on the alert," said Maude. "There's no way she'd let us lead her there. She knows full well now that we are set against her."

I was seeing the extent to which I had scuppered their plans. "Oh well, never mind. I'm very sorry and all that. I think my sister and I ought to be going, actually. It's terribly late and we've been through a great deal. Ah… where are your sisters now, Maude?"

It turns out they were out hunting Denise, who had gone to ground. They didn't come back until the early hours of the morning, apparently absolutely furious. By then, however, I was safely asleep in Nellie's spare bedroom. I was trying not to feel guilty for messing up their plans, and listening to the muffled voices of Nellie talking with her demon spirit guide, Raphael, in her bedroom. Really, it sounded just like Nellie talking to herself in a deeper, gruffer voice. I wasn't at all sure I believed in any of this occult stuff they were all talking about.

I went to sleep at last, and dreamed of those mesmerising squid eyes I had seen the other day.

Yours,
Mrs Hudson

Dear Dr Watson,

Tonight we return to the Christmas Hotel for another night of exorcisms. I'm really not sure it's a good idea at all.

Nellie demands (she's become rather forceful of late, and I'm not sure it's all down to her purported spirit demon) that we both don our finest gowns for the evening. I have told her that I prefer something I can run in easily, given the danger element inherent in these evenings out in Whitby. Nellie replied that it is possible to be mobile and ready for action, as well as maintaining an attractive and glamorous appearance. I did think this a bit rich coming from a hunchback with a clubfoot, one eye and permanently greasy hair, but I didn't say anything.

I did, in fact, wear my nicest gown – the emerald green silk – for our second Tuesday with the exorcists and I think we made rather a splendid entrance into that festive foyer. Again the elves were serving their punch and taking coats, and again there was yuletide music and frivolity in abundance as we moved graciously through the crowd.

We saw the raddled Mrs Claus again, dolled up even more extravagantly and cackling madly. She drew Nellie closer and whispered something about the missing jewels and the stuffed squid. She seemed to find the whole thing hilarious. She is remarkably well informed about goings-on in this town, it seemed.

Through the crowd we caught glimpses of folk we have met in recent weeks. I spied the Mayor and his tiny mother, both looking none the worse for being crushed beneath the collapsing sea monster. I noticed the witchy Sturgeon sisters moodily browsing the occult bazaar in the ballroom, but they took no heed of us. Clearly they were most vexed by my involvement in the Eyes of Miimon affair.

All of this fuss over some foreign jewels! It is ludicrous, is it not?

Then a crowd formed for the exorcism part of the evening, and my sister and I stood near the back to observe the same species of shenanigans as we were forced to witness last Tuesday night. It was clear, upon second viewing, that it was all a piece of well-rehearsed melodrama. We watched volunteers expelling quantities of ectoplasmic Scotch broth. Even the spinning heads and the forked tongues didn't impress me much, now that I was becoming a regular at these soirees at the Christmas Hotel. I knew it was all fakery and quackery.

Then, however, there was a hush of expectation, and the lights were lowered, as if for a special act. Mrs Claus trundled onto the stage, helped by two of her heftiest elves, and she made a rambling introduction for the winners of the Christmas Hotel's "Exorcist of the Year" competition. This was the first, actually, I'd heard of a competitive element to the proceedings. There was even a small trophy – in the shape of a disembodied and demonic soul – which the proprietress presented to the winner.

Which turned out to be Denise and Wheatley. He – sweating and red-faced in his evening dress – shuffled onto the podium first in order to accept the award. He seemed especially pleased by the engraved plaque on the front of the thing. Denise was beatific in a lacy black gown, holding up her hands for applause. Her blue hair was teased out very glamorously, and she seemed so very different from the shambolic and distraught creature in the bar of the Miramar Hotel, when she had hoodwinked information out of me.

I think you'll agree, Dr Watson, that I am far too soft-hearted and ingenuous for these kinds of adventures and investigations.

The winning exorcists were persuaded to put on a little demonstration. A kind of jubilant, celebratory rite. The lights were lowered once again, and the husband fetched out his bible while Denise turned to the audience and considered who could do with her attention.

And thus it was that my sister was called, once more, ineluctably, onto the stage at the Christmas Hotel.

There was something very odd about Denise's eyes as she called my sister forth, and a gap opened up in the audience. Nellie started walking through that channel to the stage and I grabbed hold of her stick-like arm. "Nellie, no!" I cried. "Can't you see? Her eyes... *her eyes are the Eyes of Miimon!*"

And it was true, though no one else seemed disturbed by the fact. Her human eyes were seemingly gone and Denise had glittering jewels in her cavities instead.

Maude Sturgeon appeared as if from nowhere at my side and held me back. "There is nothing you can do. Poor Nellie is under the spell of the sorceress now."

I stood helplessly by as my sister galumphed her way onto the stage. She was fighting the influence with every iota of her strength, I knew – but it was to no avail. Denise Wheatley had the upper hand.

"Raphael... Raphael..." cooed Denise, once she had Nellie where she wanted her. "Come out of this broken body. Leave this pathetic form and manifest yourself for me. Raphael... come to me..."

Denise's crystal orbs lit up in her head and seemed to shoot beams of blue light that bathed my sister in a spectral glow. The audience cheered at this. They obviously felt they were getting their money's worth this week.

Maude grunted and said, "That's what she's after. She wants Raphael for herself, the scheming besom."

My sister cried out, and writhed painfully as the demon struggled within her. She cried out, "No! Raphael, beloved! Do not leave me…!"

But it was very plain that something drastic was going on inside of her. Under the baleful influence of the purloined Eyes of Miimon, my sister was being exorcised, even though – it turned out – that was the last thing she wanted.

But what could I do? Tell me, Dr Watson, what would you have done? What *could* you have done? What could any ordinary, mortal being do in such circumstances?

Well, just then, something very unexpected happened.

Remember the gypsy? The woman we had seen on the previous Tuesday? The one who had seemed possessed of the true magical powers, who had first called my sister's demon hence?

All of a sudden, she was back on the stage. She darted forward, with her hooped skirts and her long black hair fanning out around her. The Romany exorcist looked absolutely livid.

"What's this?" shouted out the jocular Mr Wheatley, as his wife continued her arcane ritual. "The stage has been invaded! Hie thee hence, gypsy, and leave the exorcisms to your betters! Avaunt! I cast thee out, Romany witch!"

The gypsy woman snarled at this. She was well nigh feral, I thought. Maude and I exchanged a glance at this sudden turn in events. Denise's concentration had lapsed, and my poor sister sagged back onto the stage floor.

"You are dabbling in things you do not understand," said the gypsy, in rather screeching tones. She thrust a finger in the face of Denise Wheatley, who was out of breath and venomously cross.

"Get off the stage, Romany whore!" the prize-winning Denise thundered, and took a swing at her.

The gypsy dodged the blow and swung back with a rather swift uppercut to the jaw. Denise staggered backwards and put her hands up to her face. She shrieked and called the gypsy something I will not write down nor send through the Royal Mail. Soon, both female exorcists were engaged in a hand-to-hand catfight while the audience roared their approval.

"Someone should stop them," I said nervously to Maude.

She tossed her head. "Nothing wrong with a good grapple to sort things out. I just hope Nellie doesn't get hurt in the crossfire…"

Mr Wheatley was hovering anxiously as he watched his wife fighting the gypsy. He clutched his Old Testament to his chest and looked worriedly at Mrs Claus. "Fight! Fight! Fight!" cried the owner of the Christmas Hotel.

It seemed that all her magical powers couldn't help Denise Wheatley in a fair fight. Soon the gypsy had her pinned to the floor and was clawing at her face.

"Oh my god!" Mr Wheatley bleated. "She's pulling out her eyes…!"

But that wasn't happening at all. The gypsy was, in fact, removing the Eyes of Miimon, which Denise had affixed into her sockets in front of her already rather deep-set eyes using rather a lot of eyelash glue. We all cheered as the gypsy held up the two glittering jewels. We watched her clamber to her feet and keep the so-called champion exorcist on the ground by standing on her blue hair. Behind them, Mr Wheatley noticed that his prized trophy had been smashed in the kerfuffle.

"The Eyes of Miimon!" cried the gypsy, in a rather grand voice. Then she tossed them into the crowd, which I thought was a rather cavalier gesture. But the gypsy's aim was good and true. Maude Sturgeon plucked them out of the air and stowed them swiftly in her handbag. "Take good care of them," warned the gypsy.

And then she basked in a warm round of applause from the crowd.

Mrs Claus took the stage again, and declared the evening's bizarre entertainments over. She told us all to fetch ourselves another drink and to have fun. The dancing would recommence, just as soon as the band could set up.

We saw her in earnest conversation with the gypsy, and I hurried over to help Nellie, who seemed rather woozy after her ordeal.

"Are you all right, my dear?"

"I am… fine." Nellie struggled to her feet. "Raphael is still inside of me, which is the main thing."

"Oh good," I said, though I still felt very dismayed by the thought of my sister actually wanting to be possessed by this being, whatever he was.

Maude slapped her shiny leather handbag triumphantly. "And thanks to the gypsy, I've got the Eyes of Miimon! Safe, where no one can make mischief with them!"

Nellie looked rather pleased by that.

But we all had one remaining question, and it was to do with the gypsy woman. Why had that beaky-nosed creature helped us like that, in our moment of direst need?

It was some time later, in a quiet corner of the public rooms, near the roaring fire in the lounge, when we caught up with her.

"Look here, gypsy woman," said Maude Sturgeon, with her usual bluff heartiness. "I suppose we owe you our thanks for your intercession tonight. If that dreadful woman Denise had been allowed to keep these jewels, who knows what terrible sorceries she might have unleashed."

"Where is she now?" asked the gypsy sharply, glaring at the three of us in turn.

"That's a good point," said Nellie. "She vanished into the crowd, once you let her go. And so has her husband."

"They live to fight another day," shrugged the gypsy. "Ah well."

She was pulling a shawl around her, clearly ready for the off.

"Look here," I said, stepping forward. "You still haven't explained anything…"

The gypsy laughed. "I trust Maude Sturgeon to do the correct thing with the crystals. They were stolen from the Finnish people and they must be returned. Miss Sturgeon will act in accordance with the law."

I looked at Maude and she seemed determined – on the contrary – to dispatch the things straight into the Bitch's Maw, as planned.

"Well, yes," Maude said. "Quite right. I will contact the authorities tomorrow."

"Excellent," the gypsy nodded. "Then my work here is finished."

Nellie was frowning and her single eye was blazing. "Hang on a moment!" she cried. She had to yell over the noise of the band playing Christmas tunes. They were getting louder by the minute.

"Contact the authorities? Return the Eyes of Miimon to the Finnish people?" She sounded scornful. "What kind of gypsy exorcist are you, woman?"

The gypsy started laughing at us then. It was a harsh, gasping, somewhat sarcastic laughter that came bubbling out from under the shawl and her dark ringlets.

It was a laughter I took only a second or two to recognise.

The Romany woman reached up and dragged off her shawl and her wig and gave us one of those quicksilver grins I was so used to seeing.

A grin I was in no way expecting to see in a hotel on a cliff above the dark North Sea.

"Good Goddess!" cried Maude Sturgeon.

"I don't believe it," Nellie gasped. "Hettie –" she turned to me "– did you know about this?"

I stared at her and then back at Mr Sherlock Holmes. I couldn't help but laugh out loud. "I most certainly did not!"

And then, still half-garbed as a gypsy, our mutual friend Himself gave a theatrical bow and turned on his heel. Would you believe it, Dr Watson? He flew out of that Christmas Hotel without a single further word.

And I suppose he will be back with you now, Doctor. You will be reading this over breakfast. Perhaps reading this final missive aloud to him, as you scratch together your bachelors' breakfast and use the last of the damson jam I left out for you. Never fear, I will be back in Baker Street by tomorrow evening, to clear up the mess you have both undoubtedly made of the place.

Tell Mr Holmes that my sister and her partner in supernatural investigations both thank him profusely for his help in the case of the Eyes of Miimon and the Giant Finnish Squid and the Exorcists at the Christmas Hotel. Tell him from me that I will resist, in future, the temptation of ever again taking a relaxing fortnight by the sea.

Yours,
Mrs Hudson

* * *

From the Journal of Dr John Watson.
November, 1925.

That is the end of those letters which, now that I am reminded of them, strike as queer a chord in me as they did back then, some thirty years ago.

We were all so young in those days! Mrs Hudson included. Now she lives at the home of Professor Challenger in Norfolk, where she acts as his housekeeper and occasional companion on his bizarre adventures. All of a sudden I find myself keen to take a train journey to a reunion with Mrs H and the formidable Professor. Perhaps there really will be something in this business of the Finnish stones, found hidden in the eyes of a giant squid all those years ago.

Won't Mrs Hudson be surprised!

Yes, in fact, since I've nothing planned for the rest of the week – why ever not? My beloved wife surely won't mind if I go gallivanting in search of new adventures.

I shall make the journey at once and report back fully, later on.

NOTE, LATER ON

What followed is, of course, a tale for another day.

A ghastly tale for which I don't feel the world is yet ready.

ABOUT THE AUTHOR

Paul Magrs lives and writes in Manchester. He has published a number of novels over the years, his most recent being *Brenda and Effie Forever!* (Snowbooks), which is the sixth in his series about the Bride of Frankenstein running a B&B in Whitby and solving supernatural mysteries with her mardy best friend, Effie.

THE CASE OF THE NIGHT CRAWLER

BY GEORGE MANN

From the notebooks of John H. Watson, M.D.

During the many years in which I served as both a friend and chronicler of Sherlock Holmes, there were but a rarefied handful of occasions upon which I witnessed that cold logician rendered speechless or flustered by the unexpected outcome of a case. Irene Adler evoked one such response, and the events that I have come to consider as "The Case of the Night Crawler" elicited yet another. It is due in part to the sensitivities of my friend that I have never published my notes regarding this most singular of adventures, but I record them here for the sake of posterity and completeness. I am, if nothing else, a thorough man, and it would not do to allow such a startling series of incidents to go entirely unrecorded.

So, here, in this worn leather journal, where perhaps my words will go forever unread, I shall set it down. I am old now, and I have little better to do with my time but to reflect upon the more adventurous days of my past.

The biggest irony of all, of course, is that Holmes himself had very little to do with the unravelling of the case. Indeed, he resoundingly turned his nose up at the opportunity to involve himself in such "coarse, ridiculous matters," as I remember so well that he put it, plucking violently at his violin strings as if to underline the significance of his words. His dismissive attitude was, in this rare instance, a cause for his later embarrassment, as it would transpire that the matter in question was quite as far from ridiculous as one might ever imagine. Not that Holmes was ever one to learn from such mistakes.

The aforementioned events marked also my first encounter with that remarkable individual Sir Maurice Newbury and his most astonishing associate, Miss Veronica Hobbes. It was not, much to my regret, the beginning of a long-lasting friendship, but Newbury and I nevertheless identified a mutual respect, and there would follow a number of other occasions upon which we would throw our hats in the same ring – most notable amongst them that dreadful matter of the Kaiser's unhinged spiritualist during the early days of the war.

Holmes, of course, had quite a different opinion of Newbury, but I suppose that was only to be expected; although without equal in his field, Holmes was not above a modicum of professional rivalry if he felt his reputation – or more truthfully, his pride – was at risk. His attitude towards Newbury would change over time, and I believe by the end, following the resolution of that matter in 1915 and the destruction of the spectrograph generator, he might even have granted Newbury the respect he deserved. War does that to a man, I've found. It teaches him to work alongside those he might otherwise have considered, if not enemies, perhaps the unlikeliest of allies.

It was during that bitterly cold autumn of 1902, early in the season, when the leaves were first beginning to turn and the days were growing noticeably shorter, that the seeds of the affair were sown. My friend and fellow medical practitioner, Peter Brownlow, had called on me unexpectedly at my club. It was late in the evening and I'd been enjoying a solitary brandy by the fire when the poor chap practically collapsed into the chair opposite me, his face ashen. He generally suffered from a pale complexion and maintained a rake-thin physique, a condition he claimed was a result of a stomach disorder but which I attributed more to vanity than any inability to digest his food. Nevertheless, he had a good heart and was a fine doctor, but on that blustery September afternoon he had about him the look of a man who'd seen a ghost.

"Whatever is the matter with you, dear chap?" I said, leaning forward in concern and passing him my brandy. "Here, drink this."

Brownlow nodded, grabbed gratefully at the glass and choked it down in one long gulp. I could see his hand was trembling as he placed the glass on the side table beside his chair.

"Now, tell me what has perturbed you so."

Brownlow took a deep breath. "I barely know how to give voice to it, John. I'm sure you'll think me quite insane."

"Oh, I shouldn't worry about that," I said, chuckling. "I've grown quite used to seeing the impossible rendered mundane, and to madmen proved sane. Speak what's on your mind."

Brownlow smiled, but there was no humour in it. "I have seen the most terrible thing, John. A creature… a beast…" He held his hand to his mouth for a moment, unsure how to go on.

I frowned. "A beast?"

"Yes. Yes, that's the only word for it. A beast of the most diabolical appearance, as if it had dragged itself from the very depths of Hades itself." He turned, staring into the grate at the glowing embers of the fire, but I could tell that he was seeing something else.

"Go on," I prompted.

He closed his eyes, as if trying to blink away the after-image of whatever it was he was attempting to describe. "It had a fat, bulbous body, about the size of a hackney cab, and it pulled itself along on eight thick, tentacle-like limbs that wriggled beneath it like those of an octopus. The sound of its passing was like the screeching of a thousand tormented souls. It was devilish, John. The most horrendous thing I have ever seen."

"And where was this, man? Where did you see this beast?" I watched Brownlow shudder at the very thought of this terrible sight to which he claimed to have borne witness. My first thought was that he must have been drunk or otherwise inebriated, but Brownlow had never been much of a drinker, and he was clearly terrified. Whatever the truth of the matter – and I was sure it could not be that he had genuinely encountered such a bizarre specimen – Brownlow believed what he was saying.

"Cheyne Walk," he said, "about an hour ago. The darn thing

pulled itself out of the Thames right before me and slithered off down the street."

Well, I admit at this point I was close to rolling my eyes in disbelief, but Brownlow had such a desperate air about him, and I was sure there must have been more to his story.

"I came directly here. It was the closest place to hand. I couldn't think what else to do. And then I saw you sitting here and knew you'd know what to do."

In truth, I had no real notion of what to do with such a remarkable tale. Surely the police would have only sniggered at Brownlow's story and sent him on his way, putting it down to nothing but an hallucination or the fabrication of an unhinged mind. But Holmes aside, Brownlow was one of the most rational men I knew, and there was no reason he should lie.

"Well, first of all, I think you need another stiff drink for your nerves. I'll fetch you another brandy." He nodded enthusiastically at this. "Beyond that, I want you to set it out for me again, this time recalling as much of the detail as you can muster." I'd seen Holmes extract information from enough of his potential clients to know that this was the best way to begin unpicking Brownlow's story. Perhaps he might give something away, some little detail he had missed the first time around that might help to shed light on what had truly occurred. I admit, my interest had been piqued, and I felt pity for the chap, who had clearly had the wits scared out of him.

So it was that Brownlow downed another large brandy and set about relating his tale once again, this time in exquisite detail. I must admit the credibility of his words grew somewhat in the retelling, but there was nothing in it that could help me to discern what might truly have occurred. I had seen some things in my time, particularly since returning from Afghanistan and falling in with Holmes, but this tall tale seemed to test the bounds of even my well-trod credulity.

It was with a heavy heart that I sent Brownlow home to his bachelor's apartment that night, unable to offer him any real comfort, other than a prescription for a mild sedative should he find it necessary in order to sleep. I promised the man I would consider his story, and that I would contact him directly should I happen upon any possible hint of an explanation. There was little else to be done, and so I made haste to my bed, my mind restless with concern.

The next morning I approached breakfast with a mind to refer Brownlow to a nerve specialist I'd worked with on occasion. Having slept on the matter I was now convinced that his ungodly vision could have only been the result of an hallucination, and decided that, if it hadn't been brought about by drink or other mind-altering substances, it was most likely an expression of nervous exhaustion. Brownlow had always had a tendency to throw himself into his work, body and soul. Aside from his private, paying customers, I'd known him to spend hours in aid of the poor, administering free treatment to those wretches who lined the alleyways of the slums, or huddled in their masses beneath the bridges that crisscrossed the banks of the Thames. Perhaps he'd been overdoing it, and he simply needed some rest. Or perhaps he'd succumbed to a mild fever.

My theories were soon dispelled, however, as I set about hungrily tucking into my bacon and eggs. It is my habit to take the morning papers with my breakfast, and upon folding back the covers of *The Times*, I fixed upon a small report on the bottom of the second page. The headline read: EYEWITNESSES REPORT SIGHTINGS OF STRANGE BEAST.

My first thought was that Brownlow had gone to the papers with his story, but I quickly dismissed the notion. The previous night he'd been in no fit state to talk to anyone, and I'd seen him into the back of a cab myself.

I scanned the article quickly, and was surprised to see that there were, in fact, a number of reports that seemed not only to corroborate Brownlow's story, but also to expand somewhat upon it. It appeared the previous evening had been the third in a row during which sightings of this bizarre creature had been reported. Furthermore, one of the reports stated that the woman in question – a Mrs Coulthard of Brixton – had seen the beast give chase to a group of young vagabonds who had been generally up to no good, throwing rocks at nearby boats and jeering at passers-by. Many of the reports claimed, just as Brownlow had, that the creature had dragged itself out of the Thames, and what's more, that it had been seen returning to the water upon completion of its nightly sojourn.

I leaned back in my chair, sipping at my coffee and staring at the remnants of my breakfast in astonishment. So Brownlow had been telling the truth. He had seen something down by the river. And if the veracity of his story was no longer in question, then the beast was something truly diabolical. Could it have been some sort of throwback to the prehistoric past? Or some previously undocumented variety of gargantuan squid?

I resolved to visit Holmes directly. There was a mystery here, and people were potentially in grave danger. If only I could persuade him to apply his attention to the matter, there was hope that we could uncover precisely what was going on.

The drive to Baker Street passed in a blur. All the while, as the cab bounced and rattled over the cobbled roads, I couldn't help imagining the scene that must have confronted Brownlow and those others, the sight of that hulking beast dragging itself out of the inky black water. It would surely have been terrifying to behold.

I resolved then and there that I would find a way to look upon this creature with my own eyes. Only then could I be utterly sure of its existence and the nature of any threat it represented.

Upon my arrival at Baker Street I found Holmes in one of his peculiar, erratic moods. He was pacing back and forth before the fireplace, somewhat manically, pulling at his violin strings as if trying to wring some meaning out of the random, screeching sounds the instrument was making. It was icy cold in there, yet the fireplace remained untended to, heaped with ash and charred logs. If Holmes felt the chill he did not show it.

He had his back to me. I coughed politely from the doorway, noting with alarm that my breath actually fogged in the air before my face.

"Yes, yes, Watson. Do come in and stop loitering in the hallway. And since you're here, see about building up this fire, will you? It's perishing in here."

Shaking my head in dismay, but deciding it would do neither of us any good to take umbrage, I set about clearing the grate.

"I expect you're here about those wild reports in the newspapers this morning," he said, strolling over to the window and peering out at the busy street below. He gave a sharp twang on another violin string, and I winced at the sound.

"I won't bother to ask how you managed to discern that, Holmes," I said, sighing as a plume of soot settled on my shirt cuff and then smeared as I attempted to brush it away. "Can't Mrs Hudson do this?" I said, grumpily.

"Mrs Hudson has gone out to the market," he replied, turning back from the window to look at me.

"She was here a moment ago," I said, triumphantly. "She opened the door and let me in."

Holmes held up a single index finger to indicate the need for silence. I watched him for a moment, counting beneath my breath as I begged the gods to grant me patience. Downstairs, I heard the exterior door slam shut with a bang. "There!" he exclaimed with a beaming smile. "Off to the market."

I sighed and continued piling logs onto the fire. "Well, of course you're right."

"About Mrs Hudson?"

"About the reason I'm here. This supposed beast. I had the unhappy task of comforting a friend last night who claimed to have seen it. The poor man was terrified."

"Hmmm," said Holmes, resuming his pacing.

I waited for his response until it was evident that I'd already had the entirety of it. "Well?"

"Can't you see I'm in the middle of something, Watson?" he said, a little unkindly.

I glowered at him. "Really, Holmes! I thought you would be glad of the case. I mean, you've been holed up in here for weeks with nothing to occupy your mind. And poor Brownlow —"

"There's nothing in it, Watson. Some idle hoaxer looking to sell his story. Nothing more. I have no interest in such coarse, ridiculous matters." He plucked violently at three strings in succession.

"Besides," he continued, his tone softening, "I find myself in the midst of a rather sensitive affair. Mycroft has gone and lost his favourite spy, a government scientist by the name of Mr Xavier Gray. He's quite frantic about the whole matter, and he's prevailing on me to assist him in the search for the missing man."

"Well, what are you doing *here*?" I asked. Sometimes I found it very difficult to fathom the motives of my dear friend.

"Thinking," he replied, as if that explained everything. He reached for the bow that he'd balanced precariously on the arm of a chair and began chopping furiously at the violin, emitting a long, cacophonous screech. I rose from where I'd been crouching by the fire and dusted off my hands. Clearly, I was unlikely to gain anything further from Holmes. As I crossed the room, heading towards the door, the violin stopped abruptly behind me and I turned to see Holmes regarding me, a curious expression on his face. "Send your friend to see a man named Maurice Newbury, of 10 Cleveland Avenue, Chelsea. I understand he's an 'expert' in matters such as these." He spoke the man's name with such disdain that he clearly thought him to be no such thing.

"Very well," I said, curtly. "I hope you find your missing spy." But Holmes had already started up again with his violin.

As I clambered into a hansom outside number 221b, frustrated by Holmes' dismissive attitude, I made the sudden, snap decision to pay a visit to this Newbury character myself. I am not typically given to such rash acts, but I remained intent on discovering the truth about the infernal beast that had so terrified my friend. Brownlow, meek as he was, would never call on Newbury of his own account, no matter how I pressed him. I was sure that even now he would be reconciling himself to what had occurred, finding a way to accommodate the bizarre encounter into his own, conservative view of the world. He would rationalise it and carry on, returning to the distractions of his patients and his busy life. My interest, however, had been piqued and I was not prepared to allow the matter to rest without explanation.

I must admit that I was also keen to prove Holmes wrong. I realise now how ridiculous that sounds, how petty, but his attitude had galled me and I was anxious to prove to my friend that the matter was not beneath his attention. As things were to transpire, I would be more successful on that count than I could have possibly imagined.

The drive to Chelsea was brisk, and I passed it by staring out of the window, watching the streets flicker by in rapid, stuttering succession. Almost before I knew it we had arrived at Cleveland Avenue. I paid the driver and watched as the cab clattered away down the street, the horse's breaths leaving steaming clouds in the frigid air.

Number 10 was an unassuming terraced house, fronted by a small rose garden that in turn was flanked by a black iron railing. A short path terminated in three large stone steps and a door painted in a bright, pillar-box red. I approached with some hesitation, feeling a little awkward now after my somewhat hasty retreat from Baker Street. What would I say to this Newbury fellow? I was there on behalf of a friend who claimed to have seen a monster? Perhaps Holmes had been right. Perhaps it was ridiculous. But there I was, on the doorstep, and I'd never been a man to shy away from a challenge. I rapped firmly with the doorknocker.

A few moments later I heard footsteps rapping on floorboards from within, and then the door swung open and a pale, handsome face peered out at me. The man was dressed in a smart black suit and had an expectant look on his face. "May I help you?" he said, in warm, velvet tones.

"Mr Maurice Newbury?" I replied. "I was told I might find him at this address?"

The man gave a disapproving frown. "*Sir* Maurice is not receiving visitors at present, I'm afraid."

Holmes! He might have saved me that embarrassment if he'd wanted to. "Indeed," I replied, as graciously as I could muster. "I wonder if I might leave a card. My name is John Watson and I'm here on a rather urgent matter. I would speak with him as soon as convenient. He comes very highly recommended."

The man – whom I now realised was most likely Newbury's valet – raised his eyebrows in what appeared to be genuine surprise. "Dr John Watson? The writer?"

I smiled at this unexpected recognition. "Quite so."

The valet grinned. I had to admit, I was warming to the fellow. "Well, Dr Watson, I think you'd better come in. I'm sure Sir Maurice will be anxious to meet you when he discovers the nature of his caller." He coughed nervously as he closed the door behind me and took my hat and coat. "If you'd like to follow me?"

He led me along the hallway until we reached a panelled door. I could hear voices from inside, two of them, belonging to a man and a woman and talking in the most animated of tones. The valet rapped loudly on the door and stepped inside. I waited in the hallway until I knew I would be welcome.

"You have a visitor, Sir."

When it came the man's reply was firm, but not unkind. "I thought I'd explained, Scarbright, that I wished to receive no callers today? I have an urgent matter I must attend to with Miss Hobbes."

"Yes, Sir," replied the valet, a little sheepishly. "Only, it's Dr John Watson, Sir."

"Dr Watson?" said Newbury, as if attempting to recall the significance of my name. "Ah, yes, the writer chap. You're a follower of his work, aren't you, Scarbright?"

"Indeed, Sir," said the valet, and I couldn't suppress a little smile as I heard the crack of embarrassment in his voice. "He claims to have a rather urgent matter to discuss with you, Sir."

Newbury gave a sigh of resignation. "Very well, Scarbright. You'd better send him in."

The valet stepped back and held the door open to allow me to pass. I offered him a brief smile of gratitude as I passed over the threshold into what I took to be the drawing room. In fact, it was much like the room in Baker Street from which I'd recently departed, only decorated with a more esoteric flair. Where Holmes might have had a stack of letters on the mantelpiece, speared by a knife, Newbury had the bleached skull of a cat. Listing stacks of leather-bound books formed irregular sentries around the edges of the room, and two high-backed Chesterfields had been placed before a raging fire. Both were occupied, the one on the left by the man I took to be Sir Maurice Newbury, and the other by a beautiful young woman who smiled warmly at me as I met her gaze.

Newbury was up and out of his seat before I'd crossed the threshold, welcoming me with a firm handshake and beckoning me to take a seat on the low-backed sofa that filled much of the centre of the room. He was a wiry-looking fellow of about forty, and was dressed in an ill-fitting black suit that appeared to have been tailored for a slightly larger man. Either that, or he had recently lost weight. He was ruggedly handsome, with fierce, olive-green eyes and raven-black hair swept back from his forehead. He had dark rings around his eyes and a sallow complexion, and I saw in him immediately the hallmarks of an opium eater: perhaps not the most auspicious of beginnings for our acquaintance. Nevertheless, I'd made it that far and I was determined to see it out.

"You are very welcome, Dr Watson," said Newbury, genially. "I, as you might have gathered, am Sir Maurice Newbury, and this is my associate Miss Veronica Hobbes."

I took the young woman's hand and kissed it briefly, before accepting Newbury's offer of a seat. Miss Hobbes was stunningly beautiful, with dark brown hair tied up in a neat chignon. She was wearing dark grey culottes and a matching jacket – the picture of modern womanhood.

"Would you care for a drink, Doctor?" said Newbury, indicating the well-stocked sideboard with a wave of his hand. "A brandy, perhaps?"

I shook my head. "No, thank you. Most kind, but I'll abstain."

Newbury returned to his seat by the fire, angling his body towards me. "So, how may I be of assistance, Dr Watson? I presume it's not related to one of your journalistic endeavours?"

"Indeed not," I replied, gravely, "I'm here on behalf of an associate of mine, a man named Brownlow. It's connected with that business about the supposed beast that's been seen crawling out of the river. Last night Brownlow had an encounter with the thing, and it rather left him terrified out of his wits. It was… suggested to me that you might be able to help shed some light?"

The corner of Newbury's mouth twitched with the stirrings of a wry smile. "And this was not a matter that Mr Holmes was able to assist you with?"

"Holmes is busy," I said, a little defensively. "And besides, it was Holmes who recommended I call. He said you were considered rather an expert in matters such as these."

"I'm sure he did," said Newbury, knowingly.

"Tell us, Dr Watson –" Miss Hobbes interjected, offering Newbury a mildly disapproving look "– did Mr Brownlow give you any indication as to when and where this sighting occurred?" In truth, I couldn't blame the man for enjoying the moment. It was fair to imagine that Holmes himself would have done precisely the same. In fact, knowing him as I did, I'm convinced he would have taken the time to truly relish the irony of the situation.

I smiled at Miss Hobbes in gratitude for the timeliness of her interruption. "Cheyne Walk," I replied. "Close to eleven o'clock yesterday evening. Following the incident he came directly to my club, where he is also a member, and sought me out for my assistance."

Newbury looked thoughtful. "And did he offer a description of the beast?"

I hesitated for a moment as I considered the sheer ludicrousness of what I was about to relate. I felt ridiculous now for coming here and adding weight and validity to this story. How could it be real? Had I simply overreacted to Holmes' rebuttal?

Well, whatever the case, it was too late to back out. "Brownlow described it as having a large, bulbous body about the size of a hansom cab, and eight thick limbs like tentacles upon which it slithered in the manner of an octopus. Now, I'm a little unsure as to the veracity of my friend's description, but given the accounts in the newspapers this morning… well, you understand, I had to come. The poor man thinks he's going insane. He might yet be right."

Newbury glanced at Miss Hobbes. "Oh, I assure you, Dr Watson, that your friend is quite sane. His report is the same in every respect as the others. This 'beast', whatever it is, is quite real."

"Sir Maurice's clerk, Mrs Coulthard, was another of the witnesses," continued Miss Hobbes, smiling reassuringly. "You find us in the midst of a discussion over how best to approach the situation."

"Have you any thought yet as to what it might be? Some sort of primordial beast, woken after years of hibernation? The result of an experiment? A previously undiscovered species brought back from the colonies?" I sighed. "The mind boggles…"

I realise now that these suggestions may appear somewhat ignorant to a reader aware of the facts, but at the time I could think of no other reasonable explanation for what this beast might have been. As Holmes was fond of saying, "Once you've eliminated the impossible, whatever remains, however improbable, must be the truth." If that axiom was indeed correct – and Newbury, also, was right in his assertion that the beast was real – then I could see no other credible explanation.

"I think it would be wrong for us to jump to any conclusions at this stage, Doctor. At least before we've had chance to lay eyes upon the beast ourselves." Newbury glanced at his companion before continuing. "Miss Hobbes and I had only just resolved to take a stroll along Cheyne Walk this very evening. I'm of a mind to catch a glimpse of this creature myself. You'd be more than welcome to accompany us, if you so wished?"

"Well, it certainly makes sense to pool our resources," I said. "And I also tend to favour the evidence of my own eyes. I'd be delighted to join you, Sir Maurice." I admit to feeling a certain sense of relief at this rather unexpected development. I couldn't help but wonder what Holmes would make of it all.

"In that case, Doctor, I shall encourage you to make haste to your home and prepare for a cold evening by the river. Warm clothes, stout boots and a firearm would be advisable. We can meet here for an early dinner at, say, six o'clock, and then be on our way." Newbury smiled, and stood to accompany me to the door.

"Thank you, Sir Maurice," I said, taking him by the hand. "And good afternoon, Miss Hobbes."

"Until this evening, Dr Watson," she replied brightly.

It wasn't until I'd already left the house on Cleveland Avenue that it occurred to me that baiting monsters by the river might have been a rather unsuitable pursuit for a lady. Nevertheless, as I was soon to discover, Miss Veronica Hobbes was most definitely a woman who knew how to look after herself.

* * *

So it was that, a few hours later, my belly full of the most excellent beef Wellington, I found myself on the banks of the Thames, shivering beneath my heavy woollen overcoat as Newbury, Miss Hobbes and I took up our positions along Cheyne Walk.

I'd found myself warming to Newbury as we'd talked over dinner, discussing the nature of his work – or rather, as much of it as he was able to discuss, given the secrecy of his role. It transpired he worked in some obscure capacity for the Crown, on one hand aiding Scotland Yard in their ever-constant battle against the criminal elements of the capital, and on the other taking direction from Buckingham Palace itself, performing the role of a state spy and expert in the occult.

That was about as much as I could glean about the man himself, but he talked openly about his catalogue of bizarre experiences, including his encounters with plague-ridden Revenants in the slums; his investigation into the wreckage of *The Lady Armitage* – a terrible airship crash from the previous summer that I remembered well; his run-in with the Chinese crime lord Meng Li and other, increasingly surprising stories. He was a master at weaving a good yarn, and he held my attention throughout the three delicious courses of our meal. Miss Hobbes, herself a player in many of these exceptional tales, watched Newbury as he related these accounts of their adventures with no small measure of affection.

I came away from that dinner sure that, should Holmes ever decide to hang up his hat, I should readily have another subject upon which to focus my literary endeavours. Moreover, I decided that, despite Holmes' obvious disdain for the man's reputation, if the two of them were to actually meet they would surely find each other's company most invigorating.

I reflected on this as I stood in the shadow of Thomas Carlyle – or rather his memorial statue – at one end of the street, looking out over the Chelsea Embankment. We'd spread out along this stretch of the river, about a hundred yards apart. Miss Hobbes – wrapped in a dark, grey overcoat and wearing a wide-brimmed hat – was between Newbury and I, who, from this distance, I could just make out in the misty evening as a dark silhouette.

This, I understood from Newbury, was the location cited in the majority of the reports, including those of Brownlow and Newbury's clerk, Mrs Coulthard. Most claimed to have seen the creature scale the wall of the embankment and drag itself over the stone lip, pulling itself onto land and slithering off into the alleyways between the serried rows of terraced houses. One report, however, was of the creature also returning to the river by the same means, in or about the same spot. It seemed logical then that we should make our observation from this point, and we'd come prepared for a long wait.

Even so, my limbs were beginning to grow weary with the cold. It was a damp, miserable night, and the thick autumnal mist dulled even the glow of the street lamps. It seemed to wreath everything in its embrace, clinging to the trees and the buildings, curling its tendrils across the choppy surface of the Thames. There were but a few people abroad that night, passing along the embankment with their heads stooped low against the inclement weather. They appeared to me like ghostly shapes emerging from the mist, passing from one realm into another as they drifted along beside the river.

We must have waited there for hours without passing a word between us. I checked my timepiece at around eleven o'clock, stamping my feet in an attempt to warm my weary, frozen limbs. I was just about to hail Newbury in order to call it a night when I received my first indication that something was afoot.

I became aware of a low, mechanical sound coming from the river, not unlike the clanking of heavy iron chains being dragged through a winching mechanism. At first I imagined it to be a ship drawing anchor, but I could see no masts on the water. I glanced at Newbury and Miss Hobbes, who had evidentially both heard the same noise and had abandoned their posts to approach the embankment. I started after them, wondering if at last we were about to reap some reward from our long vigil.

My hopes were confirmed a moment later when I saw Miss Hobbes start and fall back to the cover of the trees. I ran to her side in time to see two thick probosces, each about the girth of a man's torso and covered in scores of tiny suckers like those of an octopus, come probing over the stone lip of the embankment. They squirmed and shifted as if feeling for the best possible hold, and then appeared to latch on to the uneven surface, providing purchase for the beast to haul itself out of the water.

It was difficult to ascertain much in the way of detail, due to the gloom and the pervasive mist, but I had already seen enough to set a cold lump of dread in the pit of my stomach. The sheer size of the thing to which such tentacles belonged... I could only stand there beside Miss Hobbes, looking on in abject fear as the beast slowly dragged itself onto land before us.

Newbury had continued to approach the water's edge but was now keeping himself at a safe distance, obviously keen not to find himself caught by one of the thrashing tendrils as the creature heaved itself further and further out of the Thames. The screeching noise continued, and I now realised that what I'd at first considered to be a mechanical noise must in fact have been the sound of the creature itself. I shuddered at the thought of such an infernal beast.

Another tentacle whipped over the side of the embankment, followed closely by a fourth. I had a sense, then, of the immensity of the thing, and as its body finally hove into view I had to fight the urge to run. Brownlow had been correct in his description of the creature and at that point I understood what had so disturbed him about his encounter with the creature the previous night. It was a thing to inspire madness. Simply to look upon it was to question one's own sanity.

As I watched, the monster slipped its bulk over the top of the embankment wall and raised itself up to its full height – at least twenty feet tall – twisting and turning as if trying to decide which direction it should now take. I could see very little of it, other than the silhouette of its mass and the gleam of its wet carapace, catching and reflecting what thin shafts of moonlight fell on it from above.

It appeared to settle on a course a moment later, shuffling off in the direction of the nearest side street. It had a curious ambulatory technique, part way between a crawl and a slither, and I couldn't help thinking, despite everything, that the beast was far more suited to water than to land. Nevertheless, it moved with a not inconsiderable momentum, dragging itself along with all the noise of Hades, screeching and grinding as its multiple limbs struck again and again upon the flagstones.

"After it!" bellowed Newbury, his words rousing me from my temporary stupor. I did as he said, charging after it as fast as my numb, tired legs would carry me.

The beast had dragged itself into a narrow opening between two rows of houses, leading to a dark, cobbled alleyway beyond. Now its limbs were splayed around it, grasping at the sides of the buildings, pulling chunks out of the brickwork as it swiftly propelled itself along.

"Stand aside!" called Newbury, coming up behind me at a run. I dived quickly to one side as Miss Hobbes ducked to the other, and Newbury lurched to a stop, hurling something high into the air in the direction of the creature.

There was a sudden explosion of bright, white light as the flare – for that was what Newbury had thrown – hissed to life, rendering the entire scene in a series of brilliant, stuttering flashes as it spun wildly through the air.

I fell back, awestruck, as I caught my first proper glimpse of the creature, and realised with shock that it wasn't in fact a creature at all. What had at first appeared as some kind of gargantuan, primitive animal was, in the harsh brilliance of the flare, shown to be nothing more than a huge mechanical construct. Its metallic limbs, now clearly a series of cleverly segmented iron coils, glinted with reflected light as they writhed and twisted, scrabbling at the walls. Its carapace was dull and black, still dripping with river water, and to my surprise I saw the startled face of a man inside, peering out through the thick glass of a riveted porthole. I realised it was some sort of amphibious vehicle, and that the man inside was most likely the pilot. Judging by the appearance of it, I guessed it was a submersible – but a remarkable submersible of the like I had never seen, with the ability to clamber out of the water and scale sheer walls. I wondered at who might have even conceived of such a thing.

The flare struck the back of the machine's carapace and rebounded, tumbling over and over until it struck the cobbles a few feet away and continued to fizz and sputter in the gutter.

I was still standing in awe of the machine when one of the tentacles whipped out and struck Newbury full in the chest, lifting him clean off his feet and sending him sprawling to the ground with a dull thud. It occurred to me later that the pilot had probably assumed he was under attack, and that the flare had been some sort of weapon or explosive device. At the time, however, I was quite unprepared for what happened next.

Miss Hobbes emitted a shrill cry of alarm, but rather than rush to Newbury's aid, she grabbed for a large stone from a nearby rockery and pitched it straight at the strange vehicle. It boomed as it struck the metal hull, causing the pilot's pod to rock back and forth upon the writhing cradle of its legs. In response, the machine reared up, twisting around and releasing its hold on the two buildings. One of its tentacles flicked out and caught Miss Hobbes around the waist, snaking around her and hoisting her high into the air. She looked like a fragile doll in its grip as it swung her around and thrust her, hard, against the nearest wall. She howled pain and frustration, clutching furiously at the iron tentacle in an attempt to prise herself free.

Incensed, I reached for my service revolver, which I'd secreted in the pocket of my overcoat before setting out from home. It felt cold but reassuring in my fist as I raised my arms, searching for a clear shot in the mist-ridden gloom.

Miss Hobbes gave a sharp cry of pain as she was slammed once more against the wall, lolling in the machine's terrible iron grip. Behind me, Newbury was silent and still where he lay on the pavement, unconscious or dead.

I cocked the hammer and took my aim, hoping beyond hope that my bullet would not ricochet and further injure Miss Hobbes. I could think of no other course of action, however; to get entangled in the machine's writhing limbs would mean certain death for us all. I was doubtful my bullets would puncture the vehicle's thick armour plating, but if I could create a distraction I thought I might be able to lure it away from Miss Hobbes.

By this time I was convinced that the people in the neighbouring houses must have raised the alarm, and I expected the police to appear on the scene at any moment. I hoped for it, concerned that what little I might be able to do would still not be enough.

I squeezed the trigger and braced myself as the weapon discharged. The report was like a thunderclap that echoed off the nearby buildings.

I heard the bullet ping as it struck the belly of the mechanical beast, and I ducked involuntarily in case it rebounded in my direction.

Just as I'd hoped, the shot seemed to startle the pilot enough to draw his attention. I squeezed off another bullet, then a third in quick succession. I was pleased to hear the satisfying splinter of glass, suggesting I'd managed to unwittingly strike one of the portholes.

The machine twisted around, releasing its stranglehold on Miss Hobbes and allowing her to slump heavily to the ground. With a terrible scraping of metal against stone, the vehicle lurched out of the mouth of the alleyway towards me. I stumbled back, trying desperately to keep myself out of reach of the probing limbs that thrashed across the cobbles before it. I stumbled then, catching my heel on a loose paving stone and tumbling backwards, jarring my elbow and sending my revolver skittering across the street.

Panicked, I tried to roll out of the way of the oncoming machine, but in my heart I knew it was over. The mechanical beast would crush me utterly beneath its massive bulk.

I closed my eyes, took a deep breath and felt a moment of strange, lucid calm as I waited for it to strike. At least I'd managed to save Miss Hobbes.

But the blow never came. To my amazement the vehicle veered away at the last moment, lurching back the way it had come, towards the river. I leapt to my feet, reclaiming my revolver and staggering after it, but within moments it had slithered over the edge of the embankment, dropping into the water with an almighty splash. I ran to the edge but could see nothing but a frothy ring of bubbles upon the surface.

I rushed back to where Miss Hobbes was struggling to pull herself upright in the mouth of the alley. "Are you hurt?" I asked, skipping the pleasantries.

She shook her head, gasping for breath. "No, not seriously. Please... Maurice." She pointed to the prone form of Newbury. He hadn't moved since he'd been thrown across the street by the beast. I went to his side.

He was still breathing. I checked him hurriedly for broken limbs. Miraculously, he appeared to be mostly unhurt. He'd have a few aches and bruises when he came round, perhaps even a mild concussion, but he'd sustained no serious injuries.

I realised Miss Hobbes was standing beside me and stood back to allow her room. She knelt on the ground beside him and cupped his face in her hands. "Maurice?" And then more firmly, "Maurice?"

Newbury stirred, groaning. His eyes flickered open, and he looked up at us, confused. "Has it gone?"

"Yes, it's gone," I said, with a heavy sigh. "Although we're lucky to be alive. I fear it was a rather abortive encounter."

Newbury grinned as he pulled himself up into a sitting position, dusting himself down. "On the contrary, Dr Watson. Now we know what it is. Tomorrow we'll be able to catch it."

I frowned. "Forgive me, Sir Maurice, but how exactly do you propose to capture a mechanical beast of that size?"

Newbury laughed and took Miss Hobbes's proffered hand in order to pull himself to his feet. "With an equally big net," he replied, clapping me boldly on the shoulder. He glanced at Miss Hobbes. "You look shaken, Miss Hobbes. Are you all right?"

"Yes," she replied, dabbing with a handkerchief at a minor cut on her temple. Her hair had shaken loose and she was flushed. I recall thinking at the time, however, that it was not so much the encounter with the submersible that had shaken her, but her fear for Newbury. "Yes, I'm quite well."

Newbury nodded, but it was clear he was not entirely satisfied with her answer. "Now, I'm sure we could all do with a stiff brandy. Let's repair to Cleveland Avenue where we can rest, tend our wounds, and discuss our strategy for tomorrow."

I found myself nodding and falling into step. I was keen to put some distance between our little band and the scene of the disturbance, and to find somewhere warm to rest my weary bones. I also must admit that, despite the danger, I had found myself quite swept up in the adventure and mystery of it all. There were questions to be answered. Who had that man been inside the strange submersible, staring out at me with such a pale, haunted expression? What was the purpose of the vehicle, and why had the pilot spared my life at the last moment?

I knew I'd be unable to rest until I had the answers to those questions. And besides, I was anxious to know more of these remarkable people with whom I had found myself working. Both Newbury and Miss Hobbes had shown remarkable courage in the face of terrible danger. Not only that, but they had remained entirely unperturbed by the appearance of the bizarre machine, as if they'd seen its like a hundred times before. I was intrigued to know how they planned to tackle the machine the following day, and I knew that whatever scheme was outlined to me that night, I would be unable to resist playing a role.

The following day I woke to a spasming muscle in my left calf. I felt tired and drained, and my body ached as it hadn't done for years. Nevertheless, I also felt somewhat invigorated by the recollection of my adventure the prior evening. It seemed to me as if I'd stumbled upon something momentous, and I was anxious to get to the bottom of the matter.

I washed and dressed and worked the muscle in my leg until the cramping eased. I was badly bruised from where I'd fallen, and my elbow was painful to move. I knew it wouldn't stop me, however. I might have been an old soldier, but I was a soldier still, and I knew how to pick myself up and carry on.

I took a stout breakfast of porridge and fruit, and then set out to call on Brownlow. A short trip on the Underground took me across town, and the brisk walk at the other end did much to clear my head. It was a cold, damp day, and the sky above was an oppressive canopy of grey, brooding and pregnant.

Upon my arrival, Brownlow's wife – a willowy woman in her late thirties, who wore a permanently startled expression – informed me that her husband was out, and so I trudged the quarter mile to his surgery, where I found him enjoying a momentary respite from his patients. He ushered me into his office and asked the clerk to organise a pot of tea.

It was clear almost immediately that I'd been correct in my assumption that Brownlow would have thrown himself into his work in an effort to dispel his anxiety over the events of two nights previous. He acted as if the encounter had never even occurred, and when I raised the subject he waved me down with a severe frown, indicating that he no longer wished to discuss it. Still, I persisted, and when I began to relate the story of my own encounter with the mechanical beast, he listened quietly, absorbing every detail.

"So I am not, after all, bound for Bedlam," he said when I'd finished. He did so with a jovial smile, but the relief was plain to see on his face. "Thank you, John."

"You were never bound for Bedlam, Peter. But I do believe you are guilty of overworking yourself. You should consider allowing yourself a holiday with that pretty wife of yours."

He smiled at this and poured the tea. "I think, my dear friend, that I should find such a holiday even more stress-inducing than a late-night encounter with a mechanical beast. I cannot abandon my patients."

I sighed and reached for my teacup.

It was approaching midday when I left Brownlow to his patients, feeling as if, for once, I'd been able to lift a weight from his shoulders. Newbury had said he'd need time to prepare for the evening's activities – that he needed to speak with a man named Aldous Renwick – and so, left to my own devices, I decided to head to Baker Street in order to take luncheon with Holmes. I was still rankled with him for his dismissive attitude the previous day, but felt it would not do to let things fester between us. He had, after all, no other friends upon which to prevail if he found himself in need. He was not a man that responded well to prolonged solitude; despite his protestations to the opposite, Holmes needed an audience.

I found him hunched over a leather-bound tome, poring over page after page of arcane diagrams, each of which appeared to depict complex chemical formulas. He was still wearing his ratty old dressing gown and his unlit pipe was clenched between his teeth. Dark rings had developed beneath his hooded eyes, and he appeared gaunt. I guessed he had not been to bed since I had last seen him, let alone the thought that he might have taken a bath or gone for a stroll.

He didn't look up when Mrs Hudson showed me into the room, but waved for me to take a seat. I shifted a heap of newspapers to the floor in order to do so.

"Well, Holmes!" I said, clutching the arms of the chair and leaning forward, hoping to draw his attention from the manual upon his lap. "Last night's activities by the river were quite invigorating."

"Hmmm," issued Holmes dismissively, still steadfastly refusing to look up from his book.

"I saw it for myself," I continued, determined that he'd hear me out. "The beast, that is. Turns out it's a ruddy great machine of some sort, a submersible with legs, containing a pilot. Things looked a bit hairy for a while, on account of the aforementioned pilot attacking Sir Maurice, his associate Miss Hobbes, and me. Had to chase him off with my revolver in the end. You should have seen it, Holmes. Quite remarkable."

At this, Holmes suddenly slammed his book shut and looked up, turning his familiar hawk-like gaze upon me. "What was that, Watson? I fear I didn't quite catch what you said."

I issued a long, familiar sigh. "Nothing, Holmes," I said, deflated. "It wasn't important."

Holmes raised a single eyebrow, and then tossed the book he'd been reading onto the floor. It landed with a dull thud on the carpet by my feet. He turned, stretching out upon the divan like a luxuriating cat, resting his slippered feet upon the arm.

I shook my head in resigned dismay. "How is your investigation going?" I asked. "It looks as if you've barely left the drawing room these past two days. Your search for Mr Xavier Gray is not, I presume, proving easy."

Holmes glanced at me, a thin smile forming upon his lips. "Oh, I'd say the investigation is proceeding quite as planned, Watson. The matter has my full attention."

I shrugged my shoulders in disbelief. Despite living with Holmes for many long years and chronicling all of his most notable investigations, his methods could still seem opaque to me.

"What time is lunch?" I asked, leaning back in my chair. "I'm famished and in need of one of Mrs Hudson's hearty broths." I knew it was a liberty, but I felt I'd earned it after the events of the following evening, and besides, it looked as if Holmes could do with a square meal. Perhaps if I stayed to accompany him, he might actually eat.

"You shall not be disappointed, Watson, if you have it in you to bide your time in that chair for another twenty-six minutes. Beef stew, I believe, with dumplings."

"Ah, my favourite! Let me guess," I said, grinning. "You heard Mrs Hudson place the pot upon the stove, and, over recent months – if not years – you've worked to memorised her routine from the very sounds she makes as she toils. Now, you're able to fathom her every movement from the noises issuing from the basement, and predict the dish and the exact moment upon which she will serve luncheon?"

Holmes gave a cheerful guffaw. "Close, Watson. Very close. She came to inform me just a few moments before you arrived – four minutes, in fact – that she would be serving beef stew, with dumplings, in half an hour's time."

I could not suppress a chuckle. "Well, I'd better pop down and ask if she wouldn't mind setting another place," I said, moving to rise from my chair.

"No need," said Holmes, waving his pipe, "I attended to that yesterday."

"Yesterday?" I asked, incredulous. "Whatever do you mean?"

"I mean that I asked Mrs Hudson to make a special effort to prepare a hearty lunch – your favourite stew, in fact – given that you'd be stopping by after what undoubtedly would have proved to have been a harrowing night on Cheyne Walk, grappling with monsters and such like." He struck a match with a flourish and lit his pipe.

"You astound me, Holmes," was about as much as I could muster.

He was still laughing when Mrs Hudson called us to the dining room for lunch.

Following my visit to Baker Street, still a little baffled by Holmes' unflappable mood and his apparent lack of progress in his case, I dropped in at my club to pass a few hours of quiet reflection. Duly restored, I called home to collect my revolver – carefully cleaned that morning – before setting out to meet Newbury and the others at Cheyne Walk. It was dark by then and the streets already had an abandoned, desolate air; a thick, syrupy fog had descended along with the darkness to smother everything in its damp embrace, sending the pedestrian population scuttling to the warmth of their homes.

We'd agreed to meet at the very same spot at which we'd encountered the strange machine the previous evening. Logic dictated that this was the most likely place for us to lay our trap. We had, while sat around the fire drinking brandy in Newbury's drawing room, discussed the possibility that the pilot might select a different stretch of the embankment to make his ascent that night, following his surprise confrontation with our little band. Miss Hobbes had argued, however, that there must have been some reason why he should so far have chosen to scale the walls at that particular point. All of the witness reports confirmed such was his habit. We'd decided between us that it would therefore make sense for us to stage our trap in the vicinity.

I was, as yet, unaware of the nature of this trap, and it wasn't until I rounded the corner of Cheyne Walk and saw the spectacle of it laid out before me that I began to get some sense of what Newbury had planned.

A large, box-shaped construct, about the height of a man and twice as wide again, sat squat at the far end of the street. Black smoke curled from the top of it, forming a dark, oily smudge, and even from ten feet away I could feel the heat of its furnace and smell the acrid stench of burning coal. The noise, too, was horrendous: a whirring, clacking cacophony, the sound of spinning turbines, powered by steam. Thick bunches of copper cable coiled from the belly of the portable generator, and a man with tufts of wild white hair was stretching them out upon the pavement, hands sheathed in thick rubber gloves. The cables sparked and popped with the violent electricity that coursed through them. Newbury stood over his shoulder, overseeing proceedings, and Miss Hobbes stood off to one side, watching the river for any signs of movement.

I coughed politely to announce my presence.

"Dr Watson!" Newbury called cheerfully, looking up for a moment from what the other man was doing. I was startled to see his expression alter suddenly from apparent pleasure to immediate concern. "Now, don't move an inch!"

I glanced down to see that, in my haste to join the others, I had strayed dangerously close to one of the live cables. My left boot was only a fraction of an inch from brushing against it, and the slightest adjustment in my posture would have seen thousands of volts hungrily discharge into my body.

Cautiously, I edged away from the live wire until I was comfortable enough to breathe a sigh of relief. I moved over to join Newbury and the man I took to be Aldous Renwick. "So you're planning to electrocute it?" I asked, impressed by the machinery they'd been able to erect in just a few hours.

"Quite so, Dr Watson. When that mechanical beast finds itself entangled in these electrified cables, the resulting surge of power should render it temporarily immovable," replied Newbury.

"Yes, and temporarily deadly to the touch, too," said the other man, gruffly. He straightened his back, laying the last of the cables into position and turning to face me. "When that happens, the last thing you should do is consider touching the machine itself. If you do, you'll be blown clear into the river by the resulting shock. They'll be fishing you out with a net."

Newbury laughed. "Dr Watson, meet my good friend, Aldous Renwick."

"A pleasure," I said, taking his hand.

In truth, I find it difficult to select words with which to adequately describe the appearance of such a unique and eccentric individual. Aldous Renwick defied easy interpretation. As I have already described, his hair was a wild, wispy mess upon his head, and he was unshaven, his lower face covered in wiry grey bristles. His teeth were yellowed from tobacco smoke and his complexion was that of a fifty-year-old, although I placed him closer to forty. He was dressed in an ill-fitting shirt, open at the collar, over which he wore a thick leather smock, such as one a butcher might don while carving meat. Most disturbing of all, however, was the appearance of his left eye, or rather the object embedded in the socket where his left eye should have been.

At first I had assumed that Renwick was wearing a jeweller's magnifying glass, using it to examine the electrical cables with which he had been busying himself, but upon closer inspection I saw that the lens was, in fact, an integral part of the man's face. The device had been inserted into the vacant socket where his eyeball had once been: an artificial replacement, much like a glass eye, but significantly more practical. I soon realised that, although it might have appeared a little ungainly to some, the false eye actually enabled Renwick to see.

I studied the device for a moment as it whirred and clicked, turning as if by its own volition. Deep inside, behind the curved glass lens, a tiny pinprick of fierce red light burned inside his skull. I wondered who had constructed and installed such a thing. It was at once remarkable and utterly disconcerting.

Renwick grinned, his face creasing with a thousand lines. "It's impressive, isn't it, Doctor?"

"It most certainly is, Mr Renwick. Quite remarkable. Tell me, does it offer the same clarity of vision as the original eye?"

Renwick shrugged. "It suits my needs," he said, glancing over at Newbury. "We're as ready as we'll ever be."

Newbury grinned. "Now to wait for the beast."

We fell back from the edge of the embankment, Miss Hobbes and I posted at opposite ends of the street to ensure that no innocent civilians inadvertently strayed into our trap, just as I had almost done a few moments earlier. The temperature had dropped dramatically, but I'd come prepared for a long wait, and had even thought to bring along a hip flask filled with brandy. I was careful to take only the shortest of warming nips, however, as I did not wish to face the infernal machine again while inebriated.

Hours passed. I began to grow weary. I could see the others growing impatient, also, stamping their feet and pacing up and down, anxious for something to occur. At one point Newbury abandoned his post to join me for a moment. I offered him my hip flask, which he received gratefully, taking a long draw. "Perhaps we scared him off," he said, studying the oily river, which stretched away into the night like a black ribbon. "Perhaps he isn't coming back tonight?"

"Perhaps," I replied, noncommittally.

"Another hour," he said, quietly. "We'll give it another hour." He trudged off to join Aldous Renwick beneath the cover of the trees.

In the event, it was closer to two before we heard the approach of the bestial machine. Just as the previous night, the first warning was a sound like chains being ratcheted through metal eyelets. I watched, wide-eyed, as the first of the tentacular limbs snaked over the top of the embankment wall. This was swiftly followed by another, and then another, and then finally the hulking body of the submersible, water streaming down its sides as it hauled itself from the river.

"Stay back!" called Newbury, and I admit that I had no desire to disobey his order. I could feel the trepidation like a dead weight in my belly. What if the trap didn't work? What if the machine proved impervious to the electrical storm, or the pilot chose to take an alternative route entirely? It would all have been for nothing. Worse, we might all have found ourselves once more in terrible danger.

Newbury, of course, was not leaving anything to chance. I watched, surprised, as he suddenly produced a hurricane lantern from somewhere beside him, raising the shutters so that bright, yellow light spilled out, encapsulating him in a glowing orb.

He marched forward, towards the electrical cables, waving the lantern above his head as if he were a matador taunting a bull.

"Maurice, be careful," I heard Miss Hobbes call out in the gloom, and I noted the edge of warning in her tone.

The machine started forward, and then stopped, as if the pilot was uneasy about this unexpected development.

"Over here!" shouted Newbury, waving the lantern back and forth. "Over here!"

The pilot seemed to make up his mind then and the submersible swept forward, its tentacles grinding across the pavement as it charged at Newbury.

With a triumphant cry, Newbury skipped backwards, leading the mechanical beast on.

The sound when the first of the tentacles struck the copper cables was like a thunderclap, a deafening blow that left me reeling with shock. The accompanying flash of sudden, sparking light was almost too much to bear, and I squeezed my eyes shut as it seared my retinas. For a moment everything seemed to take on a dream-like quality as, struck suddenly deaf and blind, I tried to regain my senses.

When I opened my eyes again a few moments later, the sight was utterly breathtaking.

Unable to halt its momentum, the submersible had slid fully onto the copper cables and was now caught in the full brunt of the electrical discharge. Blue lightning flickered over every surface, crawling like snakes across the carapace. The tentacles leapt and danced, thrashing about uncontrollably at the mercy of the current. The entirety of Cheyne Walk was lit up by the deadly – but irrefutably beautiful – storm.

"Halt the current!" I heard Newbury bellow, and Renwick rushed to the generator, forcing the lever into the "off" position. A few moments later, the submersible stuttered, gave a last, violent shudder, and then collapsed in a heap upon the ground.

I withdrew my revolver from my pocket and rushed over to where the others were gathering around the downed machine. Miss Hobbes was first to the site, and seemed about to clamber up onto the body of the machine itself in search of the hatch.

"Stand back, Miss Hobbes," called Renwick, running over in order to keep her from getting too close to the machine. "There may be some residual charge. Here, allow me." Renwick approached it gingerly, testing the surface with his gloved hands. He circled the vehicle once before turning to Newbury, a gleam in his single remaining eye. "It's quite something, isn't it? Just as you said."

"Indeed it is," said Newbury, although it was clear there was something else on his mind. "Aldous, the pilot…?"

Renwick frowned, as if he didn't understand the question.

"Will he be dead?" I asked, quietly.

Renwick shrugged. "It depends what protection he had inside." He glanced at each of us in turn. "Only one way to find out," he said. He reached up and took hold of a small metal wheel that jutted from the lower side of the hull and began twisting it, releasing the seal of the pilot's hatch. It loosened off a few seconds later with a pneumatic hiss, and the hatch hinged open with a metallic clang. We all waited with bated breath.

There was a low groan from inside the machine, followed by the sound of a man spluttering and coughing. I glanced at Newbury, who raised an eyebrow in surprise. "I suppose we'd better get him out of there, then?"

Together we worked to turn the hull of the vehicle until Newbury was able to reach inside and drag the pilot out onto the street. He was a sorry mess, shaking and spluttering as he propped himself up on one arm, staring up at us with a blank, pale expression. He was wearing a set of dark blue overalls that were covered in a week's worth of oil and grime, and blood was running freely from one nostril. He wiped at it ineffectually with his sleeve.

I stood over him with my revolver, although in truth it was an unnecessary gesture; there was no fight left in the man, and if he'd tried anything we should easily have been able to restrain him.

"Who are you?" asked Miss Hobbes, her voice more commanding than I'd come to expect from her. She was, if nothing else, a woman of many surprises.

The man gazed up at her, a haunted look in his eyes. "My name is Xavier Gray," he said.

I almost choked in surprise as I tried to assimilate this unexpected information. "Xavier Gray!" I exclaimed loudly.

"You know this man?" said Newbury.

I shook my head. "Indeed not. But I know a man who wants very much to find him. Mr Gray here is the quarry of none other than Sherlock Holmes."

Newbury emitted a rumbling guffaw. "Is that so, Dr Watson? How very surprising."

Gray looked as surprised as any of us. "Sherlock Holmes?" he asked, but it was clearly a rhetorical question.

"Tell us, Mr Gray," prompted Miss Hobbes, "what is the purpose of this machine, and for what reason have you been making these late-night excursions?"

"For them," replied Gray, trembling as he fought back tears. "It was all for them."

"This man is clearly disturbed," said Renwick, redundantly. It was plain for us all to see that Gray was suffering from severe shock.

"Speaking as a medical practitioner, it's clear this man needs rest and a chance to recover from the shock of this evening's events," I said, lowering my weapon. "I imagine we'll be better served by saving our questions until the morning."

"Very well," said Newbury. "May I suggest, Doctor, that you take this man into your temporary custody? I don't believe he represents any real danger, now that his machine has been rendered immobile. I have every faith that you'll be able to tend to his immediate medical needs, and I'm sure Mr Holmes would be only too delighted to hear that we've saved him a job." He delivered this with a wry smile on his lips, and I couldn't help sharing for a moment in his glee. After the manner in which Holmes had dismissed the whole episode it would give me no small measure of satisfaction to deliver Xavier Gray to his doorstep. I could imagine the look on his face.

"Very well," I said. "I shall escort Mr Gray to Baker Street immediately." I glanced at the wreckage of the submersible. "But what of this?"

"Oh, don't worry yourself with that, Dr Watson. I'll send for Sir Charles Bainbridge of Scotland Yard. His men will know what to do with the remains of this most remarkable contraption."

"Bainbridge?" I said, with a smile. "Then we have a mutual acquaintance." I'd worked with Bainbridge almost fifteen years earlier, during the Hans Gerber affair, and again on a number of other occasions during the intervening years. He was a good man, and an even better police inspector.

Newbury laughed again. "I'll be sure to give him your regards," he said. "Now, Doctor. Let us find you a cab. It's late, and we still have much to do. Our answers can wait until tomorrow."

"Very well," I said, helping Xavier Gray to his feet. "If you'll come quietly?"

The man nodded, hanging his head. "I will," he said, morosely. I decided to take him at his word, although I kept my revolver close at hand, just to be sure.

* * *

It was late when we arrived at Baker Street, gone midnight, but I was resolved to rouse Holmes from his bed. We'd passed the journey across town in silence, with just the creak of the carriage wheels and the clatter of horse's hooves to punctuate our journey.

Xavier Gray had remained slumped in the opposite corner of the hansom throughout, as if the life had simply gone out of him. I couldn't help feeling pity for the man, despite the events of the previous evening. I did not then know the nature of the horror that plagued him, but all the same I had some sense that he was carrying an enormous burden upon his shoulders. I decided not to press the matter, and respected his need for silence. Tomorrow, I would push for answers. Tonight I was close to exhaustion, and couldn't bring myself to coerce such a clearly disturbed man.

It was a bleary-eyed Mrs Hudson who came to the door of 221b, wrapped in a black shawl and wearing an exasperated expression. "Oh, Dr Watson. It's you."

"Indeed it is, Mrs Hudson. Please, forgive me for disturbing you at this unsociable hour."

Mrs Hudson gave me a resigned look. "And you think I'm not used to such shenanigans, Doctor? You did, after all, live with Mr Holmes for a number of years."

I grinned. "Is he home?"

"God knows," she said, with a shrug of her shoulders. "But I suppose you'd better come in. Your guest looks as if he's about to catch his death."

I decided not to disabuse Mrs Hudson of the notion that Gray was my guest. It wouldn't do to concern her with the truth that I was leading a wanted man – and a criminal, at that – into her home.

It soon became clear that Holmes was not, after all, at home. Nevertheless, there was little I could do but wait. I ushered Gray into the drawing room and convinced Mrs Hudson to return to her bed. I poured myself a whisky, deciding it would steady my nerves, and built up the fire in order to banish the chill.

All the while I kept my revolver close at hand, but Gray remained largely silent and subdued.

We'd been there for less than half an hour when I heard a key scrape in the lock downstairs. Footsteps followed on the creaking treads, accompanied by a gaily sung melody, "Tra, la, la, la, la." The footsteps halted outside the door. "Hello, Watson!" said Holmes, breezily, before the door had even been opened.

Of course, this was not a difficult deduction. Holmes knew Mrs Hudson's habits well, and that she would already be in bed. She would not have allowed anyone other than I to wait here for Holmes, and since it was evident that someone inhabited the drawing room – probably from the spill of light beneath the door – it had to be me.

The door swung open and Holmes' beaming face appeared in the opening. He was wrapped in a dark brown cape and was wearing a top hat. "Ah, I see you have a visitor?" he said, removing his hat and strolling boldly into the room.

I stood. "Indeed I do." I indicated the sorry specimen crumpled in the chair opposite. "This, Holmes, is Mr Xavier Gray."

Holmes looked from one of us to the other with a wide-eyed expression. "I… well… is it really, Watson?"

Xavier Gray glanced up at Holmes. "Dr Watson is correct, Mr Holmes. I am indeed Mr Xavier Gray," he said, his voice low and moribund.

"How extraordinary," said Holmes, "How very extraordinary." He seemed genuinely surprised by this development. He stroked his chin thoughtfully. "This business with the unusual beast?" he asked, after a short moment of reflection.

"Quite so," I said, proudly. "You were wrong to dismiss it, Holmes. It's proved to be the most remarkable of cases. The beast was in fact a bizarre, amphibious submersible being piloted by Mr Gray."

"Indeed?" said Holmes, without even a flicker of irony. "Well, perhaps I was wrong to be so dismissive, Watson. If it wasn't for your tenacity…"

"Don't mention it, Holmes," I said, with a smile. "So what now? I'm afraid we haven't questioned him yet regarding his motives. I fear he's rather in the grip of a severe case of shock."

Holmes nodded. "Very good, Watson. If I could prevail on for you for a short while longer, I'll send for Mycroft immediately. Of course, you're welcome to the spare room this evening, if you should wish it?"

The thought of my old bed reminded me of just how tired I was. By this time it was almost two o'clock in the morning. "Thank you, Holmes," I said, nodding in gratitude. "The spare room will be most appreciated."

I waited with Gray while Holmes bustled off to make the necessary arrangements. He returned a few minutes later, looking rather pleased with himself. "Mycroft will be here shortly. Now, Watson, if you'd be kind enough to pour Mr Gray a brandy?"

"What was that?" I said, somewhat startled. I'd been dangerously close to drifting off before the fire.

"A drink for Mr Gray, Watson. Make it a substantial one."

With a sigh, I pushed myself out of my chair and crossed to the sideboard. When I turned back a moment later, glass in hand, I was annoyed to see Holmes had helped himself to my seat, opposite our visitor.

"Mr Gray, I should like to talk with you," said Holmes, his voice low and even.

Gray seemed not to hear his words, or otherwise chose not to engage with them.

Holmes leaned forward in his – or rather, in my – chair. "I know what became of your family, Mr Gray."

At this the other man's demeanour seemed to alter entirely. He stiffened, lifting his head to stare directly at Holmes, who smiled calmly and waved at me to deliver the brandy. I placed it on the side table close to where Gray was sitting and retreated, moving round to stand behind Holmes.

"I didn't kill them," Gray said, gritting his teeth, and I was startled to see tears forming in the corners of his eyes as he spoke. His fists were bunched so hard by his sides that his nails were digging into the flesh of his palms, drawing little beads of blood. "Despite what they might say. I only wanted to protect them."

"I believe you," said Holmes, levelly. "It was immediately clear to me upon examining their remains that you were not to blame. Rather, it was the work of a criminal organisation, a network of thieves and robbers known as the Order of the Red Hand. All of their typical hallmarks were in evidence." He paused, as if weighing up his own words. "I'm very sorry for your loss," he added, almost as an afterthought.

Xavier Gray reached shakily for the tumbler of brandy I had provided for him and drained it thirstily, shuddering as the alcohol did its work. He returned the empty glass to the table, wiping his mouth with the back of his hand. "I tried to save them," he said, and his eyes implored us to believe him. "I tried to help. But I wasn't strong enough. I couldn't stop them. They held me back while they did it. They made me watch." He began to weep openly then, tears trickling down his pale cheeks. "And all for what? For a few measly pounds. I only wish they'd killed me, too. Then I wouldn't have to live with the memory."

Unsure of what else I could do, I collected his glass and poured him another generous measure. The story unfolding before me was not at all what I had expected.

"And so you decided to take matters into your own hands?" prompted Holmes, leaning back in his chair and making a steeple with his fingers.

"I didn't know what else to do," said Gray between sobs. "It was all I could think of. All of those machines, those weapons, just hidden there in storage, covered in dusty tarpaulin. No one would know. Those ruffians needed to pay for what they'd done."

Confused, I glanced at Holmes, who shook his head minutely to indicate that I should refrain from interjecting with any questions.

"So you took the submersible and set about searching for the perpetrators of the crime?"

Gray nodded. "Yes. I knew they wouldn't lie low for long. People like that never do. And so I made my nightly excursions in the stolen submersible, hoping to find them."

"In the very same location where your own family perished at their hands?"

Gray nodded. "Cheyne Walk. That's where they set upon us. I pleaded with them to stop. I tried to reason with them. I promised to give them everything if only they would spare the lives of my wife and children. But it was as if they were punishing me for only having a few pounds in my wallet. They wanted to make me pay, one way or another. And so I wanted to make them pay in return."

"It would never have been enough," said Holmes. "You would never have been able to live with yourself."

"You think I can live with myself now?" said Gray, burying his face in his hands. "I have nothing left to live for."

I hardly knew what to say or do. I'd seen men like this before, broken because of a grave loss. It was clear that Gray had been driven to do what he had because of grief, and that temporary, blinding madness it inspires.

I was still somewhat unsure of the full picture, but in listening to the conversation I had managed to piece together something of the story. It seemed to me that Xavier Gray had been the victim of a terrible, random crime, and that a gang of thieves had set upon him and his family in the street. His family had been brutally murdered before his very eyes, and as a consequence his mind had snapped. He had stolen the experimental submersible from − I assumed − the government facility where he worked, and had set out to seek revenge. It was a shocking tale, and I felt no small measure of pity for the wretch. I cannot say I wouldn't have done the same in his circumstance.

I jumped at the sound of a cane rapping against the front door, down in the street below.

"Mycroft," said Holmes, leaping out of his seat and disappearing to welcome his brother.

We remained silent for a moment. I heard Mycroft bustling into the hallway downstairs. "I'm sorry," I said to Gray, watching as he downed the remains of his second brandy.

"So am I," he replied, and I knew the words were not really intended for me.

Mycroft entered the room then, ahead of Holmes, and I once again found myself taken aback by the sheer presence of the man. He was heavyset, with an ample waist and a broad, barrel-like chest, and taller even than his brother. He looked decidedly put out at finding himself there at Baker Street at nearly three o'clock in the morning, and his forehead was furrowed in a deep frown.

"Watson," he said, levelly, by way of greeting. "I understand my thanks are in order?" His tone was business-like and clipped.

I smiled and gave the briefest of shrugs. "You're welcome," I said. "I did only what I felt was necessary."

"You did me a great service," said Mycroft, quickly, before turning to Gray, who was still sitting in the armchair opposite, clutching an empty glass. "Come along, Gray. It's over now."

Xavier Gray looked up to meet Mycroft's intense gaze. "Is it?" he asked, softly, before placing his glass on the side table and getting to his feet. "I don't think it shall ever be over."

Mycroft didn't respond, other than to place a firm hand on Gray's shoulder and to steer him swiftly towards the door. "Good night, Dr Watson," he said, without glancing back. "Until next time."

Holmes saw his brother and his charge into their waiting carriage, before returning to the drawing room, a sullen expression on his face. "A dark business, Watson," he said, quietly. "A dark business indeed."

"I'm just pleased that it's over," I said, stifling a yawn.

"Oh, I think for Mr Xavier Gray, Watson, the pain is only just beginning."

On that note, I repaired to my old room with a heavy heart, intent on a long and restful sleep.

The next morning I arose late to find Holmes had been up and about for hours. Indeed, I had my suspicions that, as I knew he was wont to do, he had not visited his bed at all.

"Ah, Watson!" he said jovially as I poked my head around the drawing room door. He was sitting with the morning newspapers, snipping away with a pair of silver scissors, taking cuttings for his scrapbooks.

"Morning, Holmes," I said, somewhat taken aback by his jollity.

"Come and sit down, Watson! We'll have Mrs Hudson rustle you up a late breakfast." The thought was most appealing.

"Tell me, Holmes, have you had word from Mycroft?"

Holmes nodded. "Indeed I have, Watson." He returned to his clippings.

"And?" I prompted, exasperated.

He glanced up from *The Times* with a mildly confused expression.

"Xavier Gray?" I said. "There are those of us still anxious to understand his story," I said, taking a seat opposite him. "As well as your role in the matter," I added, for in truth that was my real motivation.

Holmes set down his scissors. "Ah, yes. Of course. Xavier Gray, Watson, was a government scientist and spy. He was working on a number of highly sensitive projects in the area of mechanised warfare, when, a week ago, he suddenly disappeared."

"Disappeared?" I echoed.

"Quite so," replied Holmes. "His superiors were, of course, concerned for the man, and even more for the sensitive information he was party to. Had he defected? Had he been captured and taken prisoner? The usual means of investigation turned up nothing. His home had simply been abandoned, and his family were gone, too."

"And now we know why," I said, gravely.

"Indeed. But at the time, the men responsible for tracing him had been unable to turn up any evidence of where he might have gone. Mycroft feared he might have fled somewhere untraceable in order to sell his secrets to a foreign agency, taking his family with him. In desperation, he called on me to investigate."

"And?"

"I soon discovered what the others had, of course, missed. Gray's family – his wife and two young boys – had been horrifically murdered just days prior to his disappearance. It appeared to be the work of the criminal gang I spoke of, The Order of the Red Hand, a network of robbers and thieves who had set upon them in the street and cleared out their pockets before disappearing. The bodies were still lying unidentified in the morgue."

"But why did Gray believe he was under suspicion? Last night he was most anxious to clear his name when you raised the matter."

"Once I had discovered the truth about his family, the imbeciles at the Yard were quick to proclaim his guilt, despite my evidence to the contrary. They simply could not fathom why a man might flee in the aftermath of such harrowing events, unless he was himself the killer or somehow connected with the perpetrators."

"That's preposterous!" I said.

Holmes laughed. "An all-too-familiar story, I fear, Watson."

"One can hardly blame him for taking matters into his own hands when faced with that as an alternative. I should imagine any man in his position might have chosen to do the same."

"Grief drives people to do terrible things, Watson, as you well know."

"Indeed," I said, quietly. "What will happen to Gray now?"

"Most likely an institution, I'd wager. At least until he's had time to recover from the shock and torment that drove him to such extreme ends."

"Extreme ends indeed. I can only imagine that, when he attacked Sir Maurice, Miss Hobbes and I, he'd mistaken us for the very same criminals who had attacked and killed his family. Particularly when Newbury tossed a flare in his direction."

"I believe you'd be safe in that assumption," said Holmes. "I imagine he saw only what his shattered mind had conjured."

"And what of the Order of the Red Hand?"

"Ah," said Holmes, brightly. "Their story is far from over. We shall face the Order of the Red Hand again. I am sure of it."

"I have no doubt you're right," I said, knowingly. "Well, that's an end to a remarkable sequence of events, Holmes," I continued, with a sigh. "And a most satisfactory resolution. For both of us."

"Indeed," said Holmes, rising from his seat and crossing to the fireplace to search for his pipe and Persian slipper. "I believe the old adage, Watson, is 'to kill two birds with one stone.'"

"Quite so," I agreed. "It is almost as if…" I paused, hesitating to give voice to a nagging doubt that had been plaguing me since I'd woken that morning. "It is almost as if someone masterminded the entire thing."

"Really, Watson?" said Holmes, laughing. "You do have a tendency towards the fanciful."

"Hmm," I replied. "So where were you last night while all of the excitement was going on?"

Holmes smiled, returning to his seat and beginning to meticulously stuff the bowl of his pipe with shag. "A violin concerto. German. It was quite exquisite, Watson. The company was only in London for one night. It was truly not to be missed. Not under any circumstances."

"A violin concerto!" I exclaimed, astounded. "Really, Holmes!"

Holmes laughed. "Now, Watson. Breakfast!" he said, lighting his pipe and ringing the bell for Mrs Hudson. "There's a little matter I wish to discuss with you, regarding a missing jewel…"

The story of the Higham Ruby is a tale for another time, of course, and following the peculiar events of which I have just given account would seem entirely prosaic.

I sent word to Newbury that the matter had been successfully concluded and took pains to outline the story recited by Holmes, regarding Xavier Gray's unfortunate circumstances and the true nature of the mechanical beast we had fought. I received a brief note of thanks from Miss Hobbes, who explained that Newbury had been detained with other matters but wished to extend his thanks for the part I had played in proceedings, and to reassure me that the submersible stolen by Gray had been given over to the appropriate authorities.

It would be nearly two years until I once again encountered Sir Maurice Newbury and Miss Veronica Hobbes, in connection with the incidents I have previously set out in "The Case of the Five Bowler Hats". Events at that point would take a decidedly more sinister turn, and perhaps if I'd had the foresight I might not have wished so readily to find myself engaged in another mystery with that ineffable duo.

As it was, I'd found myself most invigorated by my association with Newbury and Miss Hobbes and knew that, should the circumstances again present themselves, I would most definitely enjoy the prospect of joining forces with them once again to investigate a mystery of the improbable.

Moreover, as I tucked into Mrs Hudson's excellent breakfast, I was content to know that for once in the long history of our friendship, I had been able to successfully surprise Mr Sherlock Holmes.

ABOUT THE AUTHOR

G eorge Mann was born in Darlington and is the author of over ten books, as well as numerous short stories, novellas and original audio scripts.

The Affinity Bridge, the first novel in his Newbury & Hobbes Victorian fantasy series, was published in 2008. Other titles in the series include *The Osiris Ritual*, *The Immorality Engine* and the forthcoming, *The Executioner's Heart*.

His other novels include *Ghosts of Manhattan* and *Ghosts of War*, mystery novels about a vigilante set against the backdrop of a post-steampunk 1920s New York, as well as an original *Doctor Who* novel, *Paradox Lost*, featuring the Eleventh Doctor alongside his companions, Amy and Rory.

He has edited a number of anthologies, including *The Solaris Book of New Science Fiction* and *The Solaris Book of New Fantasy*, and has written new adventures for Sherlock Holmes and the worlds of Black Library.

THE ADVENTURE OF THE LOCKED CARRIAGE

BY STUART DOUGLAS

My old friend Mr Sherlock Holmes long held the belief that the reading public had little need to know the intimate details of certain of our cases. Primarily, Holmes had in mind those rare occasions when he remained as baffled at the end of a case as at the beginning, but safe to say failure was not the sole reason for his – and my – silence. Some of our cases, in truth, were of a nature considered unsuitable for wider circulation than a brief sketch in my notebooks and a more detailed analysis in Holmes' archives.

But times have changed. As I sit here, an old man now, I can hear the clatter of motorcars outside in the street. Should I reach my hand out to the left, a wireless radio sits within reach, ready to transmit signals from all over the world, while to my right the telephone has been installed for so long that if feels like a commonplace, unworthy of note. Holmes himself is long gone, of course, and I myself cannot have a great deal of time left, the wonders of modern medicine notwithstanding. Perhaps this is the time to put on paper the last few unreported successes of the Great Detective's distinguished career. If not now, after all, then never…

It was (according to my notes) an overcast day in March when Holmes looked up from the newspaper he was busy slicing into pieces with one of my scalpels.

"Now this is interesting, Watson," he said, without preamble.

With a final flourish he slid the blade straight down the page and pinched out the article which had evidently caught his attention. I took it from his outstretched hand and read the text slowly back to him, as was then my custom.

A DISTRESSING MYSTERY

On Wednesday evening at approximately 6 p.m., a porter working for the Great Eastern Railway made a distressing discovery in one of the compartments being prepared for the return journey from Liverpool Street to Leyton station. A reporter for this newspaper discovered that the porter, Archibald Aberdeen, was alerted by a passenger wishing to join the train that the compartment he had attempted to enter was already occupied by a young lady, said lady apparently having fainted during her journey from Leyton. Being unable to rouse the seated figure, a local physician was called for and he, upon examination, declared life extinct in the unfortunate passenger. As the train was an express special, thus allowing no other passenger admittance to the compartment once the journey commenced, our correspondent understands that the police are satisfied that there is no reason to suspect foul play in this tragedy.

Not for the first time in our acquaintance I found Holmes staring at me expectantly, while I frantically attempted to ascertain the seemingly inconsequential fact which had piqued his interest.

I admit that I was a little irked by his air of condescension and determined to prove myself not entirely lacking in intellect. Unfortunately, nothing obvious suggested itself. "I'm afraid that I fail to see what intrigues you, Holmes. The unfortunate lady was in an otherwise empty, locked carriage on a swiftly moving express train and assured, therefore, of no company until journey's end. Given those circumstances, it cannot possibly have been anything other than natural causes. A tragedy, Holmes, but not a crime."

Holmes made a vague gesture with his hand, indicating neither agreement nor disagreement. "Perhaps," he murmured. He steepled his fingers in front of his face and closed his eyes for a moment. "But equally, perhaps not," he concluded, somewhat perversely I felt. He pushed himself from his chair with a characteristic burst of energy. "There is also the small matter of the porter, whose name I *almost* recognise, though from where I cannot say. Lestrade should be able to clear the matter up, in any case. Identifying a railway porter is a task even he should not find beyond him." And with that, Holmes threw open the door and was off, grabbing his hat and coat as he passed and gesturing for me to follow.

Later in life, Inspector Lestrade was pleased to admit that he owed a portion of his dazzling career to his relationship with Sherlock Holmes. In the early years of their acquaintanceship, however, he preferred, naturally if gracelessly, to stress his own solid police work and judgement of character and to skate quickly over any involvement by Holmes. Holmes, for his part, viewed Lestrade as competent enough for a policeman, though with a greed for popular acclaim which was anathema to my friend. These facts explained why Lestrade was always gracious enough to allow Holmes access to any case in which he expressed an interest. Nothing attracts public approval so quickly as success, I find.

So it was that within the hour we were ensconced with the inspector in his dusty Scotland Yard office, and the sallow-faced little man was checking a file for information on Holmes' behalf.

"No, Mr Holmes, the name Archibald Aberdeen rings no bells at all," he said, handing the file over to my friend and settling back in his seat, with a surreptitious wink in my direction. "Though since you can't actually say why we would know this gentleman, or even when or where we might have come across him, that's not entirely a surprise. What's your interest, if I might ask, Mr Holmes? As no one else could possibly have been in the carriage, we were intending to close the file on this case. Unless you have some particular theory as to the cause of the young lady's death?"

"Heart problems, possibly?" I ventured. The girl was young to suffer such a fate, but it was not unheard of, and the suddenness of her collapse argued against the more common ailments of the young.

"An excellent suggestion, Dr Watson! That was the very conclusion of the physician who examined the body. A weak heart, he said, which could have failed at any time. I must tell you, Mr Holmes, that a substantial amount of money was found in the carriage, in addition to shop boxes containing small items of feminine jewellery. In light of this, the matter is not viewed as a criminal one. To be honest, I can't see what interest you might have in the case at all."

"A substantial amount of money, you said?" asked Holmes, ignoring the rest of Lestrade's speech entirely.

"Nine ten-pound notes, no less, as well as —" He consulted the file again. "As well as one five-pound note, two pound notes, five shillings and a ha'penny, all discovered in the young lady's handbag."

"Not theft then," said Holmes. "And the young lady alone in a locked carriage the entire time. A corridorless express train, Lestrade, I think you said?" He nodded to himself in apparent confirmation. "Is there family?"

"There is. Within the hour her father was able to identify the poor lady as Miss Emily Williams, a respectable sort who lives — lived — with her parents in Putney. Miss Williams' fiancé, Mr James Hogg, had gone to the station to meet her and, not finding her there, had enlisted her father to help him search. The victim's body was discovered shortly after Mr Williams reported her missing to the police. There is a sister nearby, too, I believe. She was not involved in the search but a constable was sent round to break the news."

"The fiancé did not report it directly?" asked Holmes, without waiting for a response. "Not that it matters. Someone will always miss a respectable young woman."

"Nearly one hundred pounds!" I exclaimed, finally having a chance to speak. "What on earth was she doing carrying such a sum around with her? Where had she come from that she needed so much money to hand?"

Lestrade was, I believe, about to answer, but Holmes spoke first, irritation evident in his voice. "She was buying items for her wedding, Watson. That much at least is obvious, surely?"

I have remarked previously on my friend's astonishing ability to pluck facts from the seeming air, but I admit that this pronouncement left me dumbfounded. Before I could say anything, however, Holmes continued. "The money, Watson. From her father, presumably, Lestrade?" The inspector nodded in confirmation as Holmes went on, "Nine ten-pound notes, and a considerable amount of other denominations. Change, in other words, but given the amount involved, change from a selection of items, and with money enough left for further, more substantial purchases. The sort that an engaged young woman might make when preparing to set up a home of her own. Combine this with the fact that the young lady in question was returning by train from the shopping esplanades of the city, and that Lestrade mentioned items of jewellery, and the conclusion is inescapable. I need hardly add that either something caused her a great deal of distress before she boarded the train, or she had experienced second thoughts about her upcoming nuptials."

"Oh really, Holmes," I complained. "This is sheer conjecture on your part. There is no way you could possibly know intimate facts about Miss Williams' private life."

Holmes was in no way discomfited by my expression of doubt. "The lady returned with nearly all of the money she had taken shopping, Watson. Have you ever heard of a woman showing such self-control when shopping for her own wedding? Either she was forced to cut her trip short, or her heart was not entirely set on the expedition in the first place.

"No small love gift for her future husband either, you will note, Watson. I would hazard, therefore, that the two were not quite so close as one would imagine of a pair of young lovers. Further, she was on the half-past two special express train, not the later and more leisurely one. No, Watson, I think I am safe in stating that something led Miss Williams to abandon her plans and return home.

"Had she not done so, she might well have avoided the grisly fate which overcame her in that unfortunate railway carriage."

"Really, Mr Holmes, there's nothing to suggest a grisly fate," interrupted Lestrade, with asperity. "I've already said, nobody else entered the carriage, and as the train was a special express there was no possibility of anyone getting on at another station. Not to mention that the lady was found sitting in her seat, as calm as you like. She could not have been more secure in a locked and bolted room."

"Was anything disturbed?" I asked carefully.

"The lady was not… insulted in any other way, if that's what you're asking, Dr Watson," replied Lestrade with some embarrassment. "Her clothes were essentially intact, thankfully. In fact, with the exception of single glove, everything appears to be accounted for."

"What sort of glove?" Holmes asked, his interest obviously roused.

Lestrade consulted the thin file again and read out a brief description. "Dark blue lady's glove, right hand, lace at wrist, three small pearls on the back." He shrugged helplessly. "That's all we have I'm afraid, Mr Holmes. The other probably fell down the back of the seat or got missed by whoever picked up the carriage later. Nobody likes to hang about on a job like that, now do they?"

Evidently having heard enough, Holmes leapt to his feet. "Very well, Lestrade; if you will excuse us, I think we had best go and examine this peculiar carriage, which can cause a murderer to disappear into thin air. Come along, Watson!" he ordered as he pulled open the door and headed down the stairs.

I followed after him as best I could, with Lestrade's entreaty that there was no reason to jump to hasty conclusions soon lost in the air behind me.

As I walked alongside Holmes, he fired a series of questions at me. That he was not actually speaking to me was clear enough from the speed with which one question followed another and, more obviously still, from the way he answered the questions himself.

"Why did the killer not take the money in his victim's purse, Watson? Hmm, perhaps her bag fell under the seat, and he simply never noticed it. In the struggle, perhaps? But Lestrade said there was no struggle. Which does not necessarily mean there was no struggle, of course. Did Miss Williams sit quietly and allow herself to be slain? I think not, Watson. For that matter, how could she be murdered if no murderer could possibly have been present? I am temporarily puzzled, I admit it, Watson."

I took advantage of a brief break in this monologue to interject. "You're sure this is murder then, Holmes?"

Holmes stopped in his tracks and turned to address me directly. "Which would you prefer to believe, Watson – that a murderer extracted himself from a locked carriage in a moving train or that the lady's glove somehow managed the same trick by itself?"

That was hardly the question I was asking, I pointed out to Holmes with some acerbity. All very well to mock, I reminded him, but a young woman lay dead and, if Holmes was to be believed, her killer remained at large.

Holmes, to his credit, had the grace to look abashed. He was not a callous man, but he did tend, on occasion, to overlook the human element in his cases. "My apologies, Watson," he said, beckoning to a passing hansom cab. "I can conceive of no reason why Miss Williams should have removed a single glove, disposed of it in so comprehensive a manner and then conveniently and quietly died. Not to mention the small matter of Mr Archibald Aberdeen." He spoke to the cabbie and, as we settled ourselves, I asked him about our destination.

"Baker Street, Watson, where you will drop me off, then I think you should make a visit while I busy myself elsewhere. Lestrade says the unfortunate victim had family in the area of Leyton station: a sister. Go and speak to her, there's a good chap, and discover what you can about Miss Williams' state of mind recently. I have a feeling there may be something useful to be learned."

"And what of you, Holmes? Where will you be while I go calling?"

Holmes allowed himself a thin smile. "Oh, here and there, Watson," he said. "Perhaps even a trip to Aberdeen."

Miss Williams' sister, when I called on her, was a slight, timid creature who seemed surprised that I wished to speak to her about Emily, but determined to help, nonetheless. Would that I could have said the same of her husband.

A tall, painfully thin man with sparse sandy-coloured hair and an untidy moustache of the same colour, George Fellows paced up and down in front of his wife as though to barricade her against any threat from myself. With his long arms and legs flapping at each side, and his head bobbing forward and back in annoyance, I was put in mind of some carnivorous bird preparing for flight. Even after I explained that I was working with Mr Sherlock Holmes and the Metropolitan Police Force, Fellows regarded me with ill-concealed distrust.

"Why on earth would my wife know anything at all about the movements of her sister?" he spluttered. "As I'm sure the police are aware, Margaret and her family… do not speak."

I noted Fellows' slight pause and, turning to the lady in question, ventured to enquire the cause of the estrangement.

"My father does not approve of George," she replied. "He thinks –"

"That she married beneath herself!" Fellows interrupted. His face was flushed red with anger and, as he continued, his words tripped one over the other in his haste to spit out his fury. "That fool of a father of hers thinks that she would have been better marrying a clerk, not a mere sweep like me! A mere sweep! Me, who worked my way up from climbing boy, and now with half a dozen men working under me – aye, a businessman, no less! And as for Hogg, the precious clerk? A mealy-mouthed sycophant, ingratiating himself with the old man, turning Emily's head with his big talk, while the whole family looks down on honest working men."

He stopped to draw a breath. He was sweating and scarlet-faced, and pointed at his wife for emphasis as he repeated, "A mealy-mouthed sycophant that Margaret would never entertain. No, nor her noddy sister!"

Shocked though I was by the man's anger and lack of reverence towards the dead, there was little I could politely say in response. I had no wish to upset Mrs Fellows any further, even though her husband appeared to labour under no such compunction. She presumably believed her sister to have died of natural causes; who was I to disabuse her of that comforting notion? In fact, I was considering making my excuses when Mrs Fellows spoke again.

"There can be no harm in telling the truth now," she whispered. Then, gathering her courage, she continued in a considerably louder voice, "Yes, I did meet with my sister yesterday morning. It was when my husband was at work. She'd taken some money out the bank and wanted me to go with her, to do a bit of shopping, fill her bottom drawer for her." She stifled a sob and took a deep breath. "Oh sit down, George, please! Stop your complaining for a minute and listen to me."

As I remarked to Holmes later, the change in the woman was remarkable. I had taken her to be a timid mouse and her husband to be the bully who had cowed her completely. And yet with an abrupt wave of her hand she gestured at her husband to sit then turned back to me, with a glint of determination in her eyes.

"Please do not concern yourself with George's intemperate words, Dr Watson. It is merely the desire of a loving husband to stand for no slight, however small, against his wife. It makes him −" she paused, considering her next word "− stressful."

"You must understand that my father has always assumed that both of his daughters would marry someone from his own line of work. He has worked in the bank for thirty years, you see, reaching his present position on the board some ten years ago. He knows only bank staff and their families − he can imagine no better society, nor a better match for his children. So when I met George, and fell in love with him, it mattered little to my father that he is the proprietor of a successful business, only that he is not an office worker like himself. And so my father will not speak to me, now or in the future, and I have been cut from his will entirely, while Emily… well, she had her Mr Hogg, as respectable a clerk as ever earned a wage behind a bank counter.

"But that's not her fault, is it, Dr Watson? She can't help our father's prejudices any more than I can. Our mother is dead, and my sister's health is not good, so we meet up now and again, without telling anyone. Should my father discover our continuing friendship, he would cut Emily from his will as quickly as he did me, for all that he is in poor health himself nowadays and should be considering the world to come, rather than manipulating his children here on Earth."

Fellows had tried to interrupt several times during this speech, puffed up with righteous indignation, but his wife was a stronger soul than I would have credited previously, and she silenced him with a glance.

"Usually we would go window shopping around the big shops; no chance of bumping into either George or Margaret's fiancé outside Harrods on a weekday afternoon."

"And yesterday?" I prompted.

She nodded as though the day itself required confirmation. "Emily had taken everything from her savings account in order to purchase the sort of bits and pieces required by a woman on the verge of marriage. In fact, she had the money in her purse when we met up – one hundred pounds, would you believe? She gave it to me to hold, you know; I never had such a large sum in my hand before and perhaps never will again."

It was clear to me that Mrs Fellows was only maintaining her equilibrium by a minor miracle of feminine strength. Consequently, I tried gently to prise any remaining information from her as swiftly as I could.

"What did you buy, Mrs Fellows?" I asked.

"That's the thing, Dr Watson," she replied, shaking her head. "We didn't buy much of anything, really, though I tried to encourage her. Poor Emily complained that she was feeling quite unwell. She bought a necklace and a little silver bracelet, but nothing else. I was quite glad to bump into Mr Fraser, to be honest, so pale was Em—"

She broke down then, heavy sobs racking her body. Though I was keen to hear more, both of the victim's ill health and of this Mr Fraser, I could hardly interrogate a grief-stricken sister, even if I were so ill mannered as to make the attempt. Instead, I suggested that Fellows made his wife tea and, on that pretext, followed him to the small kitchen, where I alerted him to our suspicions regarding the death of his sister-in-law. His reaction was as unexpected as his earlier callous disregard. He blanched and stumbled a little, holding on to the back of a chair to steady himself. I admit that I was gratified at his depth of feeling, for part of me had been concerned at leaving a distraught woman in the care of such an unfeeling character. He asked if we had a suspect in mind. I was forced to admit that we did not, as yet, but reassured him that the investigation was in its early stages. As I made my farewells, I asked how well acquainted he was with Fraser.

"He's not a friend, if that's what you mean," he said, with a return of his previous ill humour. "Bill Fraser is an employee of mine – for the moment at least! He handles the paperwork, mainly. Between you and me, Doctor, he's a queer fish. Secretive, if you know what I mean, and inclined to fits of temper. It wouldn't surprise me if he'd engineered that meeting with my wife and her sister. I've always thought he had a thing for her. Turns my stomach to think of it, after what you just told me."

He showed me to the door, and the last I heard him say before it swung shut behind me was, "You should be speaking to Fraser! Imposing himself on two ladies like that!"

My meeting with the Fellows had taken so short a time that I doubted Holmes had returned to our rooms yet. I did not know what to make of the couple I had just met, but the station from which Miss Williams had begun her final journey was a short walk away; the opportunity to investigate was too great to miss, so I hastened in that direction.

Unlike the great stations of the capital, this suburban line boasted only two platforms and a single, small ticket-office, to which I repaired immediately on arrival. A heavyset, bespectacled guard in the uniform of the railway company smiled at me from behind the counter and asked how he might be of assistance.

As I had noticed in the past, mention of Sherlock Holmes opens all sorts of doors, and the guard proved more than happy to answer any question I cared to ask him. He shouted across to a colleague to cover for him and led me through a door marked "Employees Only", down a short corridor and into a surprisingly well-appointed staff lounge. As we took a seat, the guard introduced himself as Cedric Tyler and repeated his earlier query.

In all honesty, I wasn't entirely certain what I wanted to know. I hesitated as I tried out first one, then another question in my head, before finally asking Tyler if he had noticed anything unusual on the day Miss Williams was killed. I was aware that Holmes referred to this very question, when coming from Lestrade or Gregson, as "time-wasting chatter" but it had always seemed a reasonable opening gambit to me.

Another guard chose that moment to enter the room. Tyler called him over and described my interest in the case to him. It transpired that the guard – one Peter Nicholas – had been on duty on the day in question. Furthermore, he had seen the lady enter the carriage, and one strange event which occurred immediately thereafter. Obviously pleased to be the centre of attention, the guard described a disagreement shortly before the train commenced its ill-fated journey. It seemed that a gentleman had attempted to enter Miss Williams' carriage minutes before the train's departure but had been rebuffed in some way and had been forced to make a hurried exit. Odder still, the exact same thing had occurred moments later when the gentleman had attempted to join the next carriage along!

"And what happened next?" I enquired, but all the guard could say with certainty was that the gentleman had finally gained entry to a third carriage. No, he did not know the name of the gentleman, but yes, he would recognise him again. Indeed he would be happy to point him out if I cared to return at six o'clock that evening, for the gentleman returned from town at the same time on most days.

There being nothing else either man could add, I thanked them both for their time and followed Tyler back to the ticket office and from there into the station proper. As I boarded a hansom back to Baker Street I reflected that, even allowing for the old saw that the murderer often returns to the scene of his crime, this one would be incredibly foolhardy to return there every day at six.

On my return to Baker Street, Mrs Hudson informed me that I would have to go straight back out. Holmes had sent word that I should meet him at the station where Miss Williams had met her sad fate. I freely admit that I was not keen on doing so. It had been a busy day and the weather outside had taken a decided turn for the worse. The combination of the customary London fog and a steady downpour made a pipe in front of the fire a most appetising prospect.

But I could hardly let my friend down, and there was the poor dead girl to take into account. So without even stopping to change my jacket, I headed out into the rain.

Given recent events, I half expected the station to be closed, but then as now, money carried more weight than propriety, and the platforms and waiting room were busy with travellers. Typically, Holmes had failed to give a precise account of where he would be, and so I found myself leaning casually against a wall, scanning the passers-by for a familiar, if disguised, face. A group of giggling schoolgirls skipped past, then a very short woman, followed by a rush as a recently arrived train disgorged its contents onto the platform in front of me. As the mass of humanity flowed round me as though I were a rock jutting from the sea, I realised the futility of the exercise. Holmes could be any one of a hundred men in the crowd and I would be none the wiser, so great were his powers of disguise and deception. Not for the first time, I cursed his high-handed arrogance. In fact, I was muttering imprecations against him when a hand descended on my shoulder and a peculiar voice whispered in my ear, "Follow me, if you would be so kind, sir. There is someone of your acquaintance who wishes to speak to you."

The speaker began to push his way against the tide of the crowd, evidently and correctly assuming I would do as requested. From behind, the best I could say of him was that he was an elderly railway porter of slightly below average height with thinning grey hair. Holmes would not have been impressed.

The porter headed for a door set in the side wall of the station tearoom. I followed him in and took a seat at a table opposite Holmes and my strange guide.

Holmes' habitual elegant dress had been discarded in favour of a rough jacket and working man's trousers, topped with a cap which had seen considerably better days. His face, however, was unchanged and I was surprised at the simplicity of his disguise, if I could even call it that.

His voice at least was rougher than usual. "'Umble apologies for the cloak-and-dagger stuff, sir, but I've got me reasons, I can assure you. I 'ad the thought of examinin' the scene of the crime unobserved, but this gentleman –" he gestured towards the porter "– is an old Indian 'and, not, it transpires, one to miss an inquisitive stranger in 'is station. Not even one disguised such as 'ow I am just now. Corporal Archibald Aberdeen, meet my client, Mr Williams. Mr Williams, Archibald Aberdeen."

It was all very peculiar, but I had been in enough scraps and scrapes with Holmes to know when to play along. "How do you do, Mr Aberdeen?" I said, with a frown aimed in Holmes' direction, confident it could be construed in any number of ways by the porter. "But perhaps you could tell me what you have discovered to date, my man?" This last was aimed at Holmes, who merely smiled roguishly at my discomfort and took up his story.

"After serving under General Wheeler for many years," he explained, "Mr Aberdeen 'ere returned 'ome to find 'isself – you'll forgive me – fallen on 'arder times and forced to take employment where 'e could find it. So 'e's now a porter at this very station. A stroke of luck for us," he concluded, "for 'im it was as found the body. Beggin' your pardon, sir, for any unpleasantness this might cause you."

Aberdeen looked up and, at some signal from Holmes, began to speak.

"My part is straightforward enough, Mr Williams, sir, and quickly told," he began. "Your man here is correct that I am the one who discovered the lady, as it were. Your daughter would it be, sir?" he asked with a degree of tenderness and consideration I would never have expected. "My most sincere condolences. It is a terrible thing to survive such a loss."

I am not ashamed to admit that at that moment I would gladly have told the porter I was a fraud, for I could not help but feel the most appalling charlatan, accepting heartfelt commiserations for a loss not my own. The slightest of warning signs from Holmes caused me to hold my tongue, however, and as Aberdeen returned to his narrative, I leaned forward with interest.

"I'm sorry to say, sir, that there isn't much I can tell you. Nothing important, in any case. The door and window were shut tight, sir, so that from the outside everything seemed as it should be. The lady was sitting straight as a preacher on Sunday, she was, with her bag neat as you like on her lap. Even her little bonnet was sat pretty as you could wish for on top of her head. If her eyes had been closed you'd have thought her sleeping, you really would, sir. Not that I did, not for a moment. I could tell she was done for."

He leaned in close to Holmes, as though to prevent my hearing what he had to say next, but I could just about make it out. "This is not my first body, not by a long shot. But my first lady, if you take my meaning, native women not counting."

He leaned back again and continued at a more normal volume. "Nobody came out of that carriage before I went in, Mr Williams. I'd swear that on oath, if need be. I watched the engine from the moment it came out of the tunnel over yonder, you see, until I opened the door to the lady's carriage, and nobody went near it."

His voice tailed off weakly. "Such a pretty young thing," he said, then frowned. We sat – the three of us – in awkward silence for a minute or two, before Aberdeen announced that he must get back to work.

I thought for a moment that Holmes intended to hold him back, for he certainly stretched a hand out as Aberdeen stood to take his leave. But he evidently thought better of it and allowed the movement to turn into a gesture of farewell instead. Aberdeen all but saluted in return, and nodded politely to me with a murmured, "A pleasure, Doctor."

I was about to correct him but he left the tearoom without another word. Through the window I saw him take a luggage cart and, pushing it in front of him as an effective plough through the crowds of travellers, make his way towards a small building at the back of the station. He allowed the cart to come to rest to the side of the entrance to the building then pulled his collar up against the rain and moved out of sight.

Holmes sat back in his chair as the figure disappeared into the rainy station. "Mr Aberdeen is distressed and requires some time alone. And here –" he concluded, indicating an approaching boy "– comes someone bearing the reason for his distress, if I'm not mistaken."

The boy handed Holmes a folded piece of paper then disappeared into the crowd. Without long experience, I doubt that anyone else could have identified any emotion on Holmes' face as he read, but I was sure that whatever it contained, it had confirmed a suspicion already held. Wordlessly, he handed the note to me.

It was not, in fact, a note all, but rather a newspaper cutting. As Holmes explained that it had been fetched from his own archive, I recognised an artist's likeness, prominently displayed in centre page, of Archibald Aberdeen. Younger, granted, but unmistakably the same man. The text, however, was in a language I did not recognise, though it did bear similarities to some of the writings I had come across in Afghanistan.

I glanced up at Holmes quizzically.

"The clipping is from an Indian newspaper and not as well written as one would prefer, so I will summarise for you. Put simply, Aberdeen was suspected, some thirty years ago, of the brutal murders of a young native man and the man's intended wife. No charges were brought but this newspaper at least thought it a grave miscarriage of justice and campaigned sufficiently loudly for Aberdeen to be transferred out of the country."

"And we just let the man stroll out of here!" I protested, already rising from my seat.

Holmes was more sanguine. "Wait, Watson!" he cautioned. "There is little to link Aberdeen to the dead woman, nor should we assume the guilt of a man never charged of any crime, no matter what some colonial newspaper might once have had us believe.

"Aberdeen will not run in any case. He has no reason to do so, having no suspicion that this decades-old accusation is known to anyone but himself. Indeed, in spite of recognising the unusual name as soon as you read it out to me, I did not place it in its correct setting until I actually saw Aberdeen himself. And this newspaper clipping from my archive confirms my suspicions. I doubt there are more than three people in the whole of London who know of Aberdeen's story, and two of those people are sitting at this table. No, he will not run. But he will bear watching, I grant you."

With that, Holmes gestured to someone I could not see and the same boy who delivered the newspaper clipping re-appeared at my shoulder. A brief, hushed conference ensued and the boy departed in the direction of the rear of the station.

Holmes, now apparently satisfied, settled himself back into his chair. "Not that he is a man who would be difficult to find again, if need be. Archibald Aberdeen is not an overly observant man, I assure you, Watson, for all my recent flattery of him. It took me nearly twenty minutes of wandering round the station in as suspicious a manner as any amateur pickpocket before Mr Aberdeen finally spotted me. If that is the standard of scouts in Her Majesty's Army I am astonished we are not commonly trounced by our enemies! In any case, spot me Mr Aberdeen eventually did, and once I had established my bona fides as a private policeman working for the family of the dead girl, he was more than willing to chat freely." Holmes chuckled wryly. "I have observed that one rascal discovering what he believes to be another will be a friend and confidant from that moment on. Perhaps Mr Aberdeen would have been happy to speak to me regardless, but I think not. Railway people are an insular, clannish group and not always open with strangers.

"So it proved, in any case. Once Aberdeen believed he had caught me snooping about, not only was he willing to describe the scene of the crime in detail, he even provided me with its present location. It will have been cleaned, of course, but even so it may yield an item or two of interest. There is one theory in particular that I am anxious to test."

He brushed some crumbs from his jacket. "But first, what of the sister? Did she offer up anything of note?"

In the recent flurry of revelations, I had quite forgotten my earlier interviews. Quickly, I recounted my impressions of the Fellows and the interesting snippet of information from the railway staff. The grin that greeted this was unexpected in its ferocity, for all that I had thought that Tyler's story would interest him. Typically, Holmes refused to elaborate.

"I'm afraid to say that the carriage in question is being held in a siding at the station you so recently left, Watson. Shall we take the train back, and so sample the same journey as the unfortunate Miss Williams?"

STUART DOUGLAS

* * *

A train journey can be many things and can serve many purposes. In this new century, it can transport a man in luxury from Venice to Vladivostok, or it can be used to ferry a platoon of troops across the crater-filled ruins of France to their deaths. When Sherlock Holmes and I frequently criss-crossed London and the Home Counties on the trail of villainy, however, trains were slower, more basic and far less luxurious. The special express Miss Williams had taken was an oddity; the slow, noisy locomotive we took in the opposite direction was far more common.

We boarded at the run, just before it pulled away, and by sheer luck snagged an empty carriage, just as Miss Emily Williams had done before us. I pulled the door shut and sat down heavily as the engine jolted into action. Immediately, Holmes fell into deep thought, staring intently out of the window in silence. Generally, when Holmes becomes thus distracted while travelling I fall back on reading or updating my notes, but as I had not intended to take the train at all, I was entirely unprepared. As a consequence, I was forced back upon my own thoughts for the duration of the journey and I freely admit that I allowed my mind to wander as the train began to pick up speed.

After only a minute or two in the dark tunnel which appears to be a requirement of every English railway station, we emerged into a world of only slightly more light, as the train settled into its place on a sunken track cut into the very body of the city. Had I hoped to spend a pleasant half hour idly watching the countryside fly by, I was in for a shock, but fortunately I had lived in the capital long enough to know that greenery was in short supply, especially near railway lines. Consequently, the view of embankments covered in thick weeds and dusty grey grass was no surprise. Ahead, a gang of labourers were doing their best to clear some of the overgrown undergrowth, but it looked to be back-breaking work and unlikely to achieve much long-term success. As the train passed them, each man took a moment to look up and wave to the passengers. When I lifted a hand self-consciously in reply, Holmes started violently across from me.

"Holmes?" I said, with some concern, but he gestured impatiently for silence.

As soon as we arrived at the train terminus, he ran into the street and, waving down a passing hansom cab, ordered the driver to take him back to the very station we had departed so recently. As the cab pulled away, he leant out and shouted that he would prefer it if I did not examine the carriage myself.

"But perhaps a word or two with the mysterious Bill Fraser?" he shouted at the last, then pulled his head back inside and was gone.

Bill Fraser, when I tracked him down, was a small, slim man with a quiet, hesitant manner of speaking. He wore his brown hair trimmed short, almost to the skull, and his neat moustache was cut similarly close. When he spoke his hand invariably fluttered to his mouth, where his fingers spread out over his lips like the guard on a helmet. The impression of some form of nervous bird was unmistakable.

Fraser's room reflected its tenant in every respect. Tidy and spotlessly clean, I considered ruefully how different it was to my own lodgings. He politely bade me take a seat and, in response to a question about his meeting with Miss Williams the previous day, proved happy to talk at length.

"Our meeting was pure coincidence, Dr Watson," he began in a friendly tone. "It so happened that I had the afternoon off work and a couple of errands to run in the city, so I'd taken a train that morning and then spent about an hour engaged in shopping. I was actually thinking that I'd best be heading back, so you could have knocked me down with a feather when I opened the door to the last shop I had to visit and out walked Mrs Fellows and her sister. I mean to say, I didn't know that it was her sister, not having had the pleasure before, but I would have guessed she was family in any case, so strong was the resemblance."

I nodded my understanding. "And Mrs Fellows asked you to walk with them?"

"Not quite, Dr Watson. Mrs Fellows was kind enough to say hello and even to introduce me to her sister, but I could see she was in a hurry to be going. They had one or two small bags with them but it seemed that not much had caught Miss Williams' eye, for she said that they had been walking about the shops for several hours. In fact, she said that it was fortunate that her sister had accompanied her, as she – Mrs Fellows, that is – had far greater experience in furnishing a new home and had prevented Miss Williams buying many unsuitable items. Please believe me, Doctor, when I say that I would never have dreamed of imposing myself on them, but it so happened that Miss Williams noticed that I was carrying some sheet music, and asked about it."

He laughed, a little self-consciously. "I am teaching myself the violin and had just bought the score to the latest Gilbert and Sullivan operetta. Miss Williams, it turned out, had a similar fondness for their work and asked me to walk with them so that we might discuss our favourite sections. She was a fanatic for the earlier operettas, *Pirates of Penzance* for preference, she said, while I prefer their more recent work."

"When did you leave the ladies?" I asked as he fell silent.

"Why, I did not," replied the man in surprise. "At least not at the same time. Mrs Fellows began to feel unwell and suggested that they should cancel their expedition for the present. Mrs Fellows said she would walk her sister to her train, but Miss Williams was kind enough to say that she would be perfectly willing to have me escort her directly to the station, so that Mrs Fellows could more quickly get her herself home, before her illness worsened. So I hailed a hansom for Mrs Fellows, though she objected to being treated like an invalid, and then walked Miss Williams to the train station, where I left her at the gates, having no platform ticket of my own."

"And that was the last you saw of her?" I asked.

Fraser nodded. "It was. I only wish she had listened more to her sister. They – that is Mrs Fellows and Miss Williams – had been discussing the dangers of a single lady travelling alone on the railway, you see. They asked my advice and I told Miss Williams to be careful who she allowed to sit in the carriage alongside her, what with there being so many strange men about. Which seems so ironic now, when she died all alone in a locked carriage."

For a moment I wondered why Mrs Fellows had not mentioned this discussion when we spoke, then I remembered that the interview had broken off early and we had not covered the time after she and her sister had met up with Fraser.

I asked the man a few other questions, but he was unable to tell me anything of use to the case. We briefly discussed his employer (a good man, who worked hard and thought the world of his wife) and Mrs Fellows (who he claimed barely to know, beyond exchanging pleasantries), but he could suggest no person who might have carried out the assault on Miss Williams. I thanked him for his time and left.

It was early evening by the time I emerged. I could return to Baker Street and a well-deserved dinner courtesy of the redoubtable Mrs Hudson, which was undeniably a tempting thought. But it was only a short walk to Leyton station, and the guard, Nicholas, had suggested returning at six to interview the mysterious gentleman who had struggled to find a carriage on Miss Williams' train.

So it was that I found myself once more at the entryway to Leyton station. No less than earlier, the platforms and thoroughfares were thronged with people, bustling past with heads down, muffled against the cold fog, resembling nothing so much as a river in full spate. It seemed a hopeless task to identify one man in such an assembly, but fortunately Tyler happened to be passing as I stood irresolutely at the edge of this tide of London life.

"Dr Watson," the guard cried as he emerged from the throng. He explained that he was finished for the day, but would be delighted to point out the man I was looking for before setting off for home. He led me along the front of the crowd for a moment or two, then cut across them in determined fashion, an old hand in such matters. I followed more tentatively, apologising first to one side then the other, as our path disturbed the passage of commuters and caused various passengers to come to an unexpected halt.

We emerged from the other side into an area of comparative peace. Tyler gestured at a man walking towards us. His chin was held low and tucked into the top of a substantial scarf. As he also wore a somewhat shapeless brown hat, pulled down over his eyes, it was difficult to see anything of his features until he was almost upon us.

"Excuse me, sir!" said the excellent Mr Tyler, placing a hand on the man's arm. He stopped at once and looked up at us, expectantly. Now exposed, I could see that the man had a patrician look about him, with a strong chin, thin lips and a long, straight nose. His eyes, however, were his most prominent feature. They were pale blue and sparkled with such evident delight in life that I found myself warming to the man before he had said a word. When he did speak, in response to Tyler's introductions and mention of the trouble he had experienced finding a carriage a few days previously, his voice was a match for his face, a rich baritone with a hint of the florid about it. He had a tendency to speak at length with no apparent pause for breath.

"Why yes indeed! I remember it most vividly! It was very peculiar all round, in point of fact. But first! My name is Henry Clarendon, an actor by profession, and I am delighted to make your acquaintance, Dr Watson." He handed me his card and beamed at us both. "I make a point of keeping up to date with the activities of Mr Sherlock Holmes and yourself. I appreciate the drama of the thing most of all, of course, but the clever way that Mr Holmes comes to his conclusions are worthy of praise indeed!

"But let me think back to that day. I am currently appearing as Gloucester in a production of *Lear* – in fact I have just returned from the theatre – but I was not required for rehearsals that day so had been pottering here and there. Little antique shops, sellers of bric-a-brac, you know the sort of thing, I'm sure. Quite exhausting in its way, and so I had a spot of tea in a little cafeteria not far from the station prior to meeting a friend in town. I arrived at the station, saw that a train was shortly to leave and made my way to the platform." The actor's brow furrowed with indignation as he recalled the events of that day. "The first carriage I attempted to enter contained but a single young lady," he continued. "I made to move within but I had no sooner put a foot inside when the foolish woman began caterwauling as though I were Franz Muller himself! I removed myself with dispatch, let me assure you, gentlemen. I have no wish to be another innocent man pilloried in the newspapers for the crime of travelling alone in a carriage with a vaporous woman possessed of an overactive imagination!" The man's voice had risen to a near-shout by now, and in my medical opinion his face was dangerously flushed, which made the huge grin which next spread over his face surprising, to say the least. "But never mind, eh?" he boomed. "Never stay where you're not wanted is my professional motto, and it makes a dashed good one for other areas of life too.

"In any case, finding myself once more standing on the platform and the train in danger of leaving without me, I hurried to the next carriage along, flung open the door – and met with a barrage of abuse that, were I not a peaceful man, could well have led to the fellow within receiving the thrashing of his life. 'Blackguard' was the very least of the epithets cast in my direction, Doctor, but I decided discretion was the better part of valour and closed the door on the dreadful man. I then moved along to a third carriage, where a very friendly couple – from Grimsby, would you believe! – were happy to welcome me into their snug little abode. We wiled away the journey most pleasantly, I may say, with the two young people delighted to listen to a selection of my speeches from the Bard. So all's well that ends well, eh?"

He beamed at us from underneath his battered hat. "And now, if there's nothing else with which I can help you, gentlemen, you will have to excuse me. This fog does nothing for the vocal cords, and my voice is my instrument, when all's said and done." I had just enough time to obtain a brief description of the foul-mouthed passenger before he offered his hand and his business card, and with a hearty "Good day!" was swallowed up by the crowds, which even yet ebbed and flowed through the station.

I offered the same farewell to Tyler and, content in a day's work well done, made my way to the street outside, where I hailed a hansom back to Baker Street.

"Getting down to the train track on foot proved to be more difficult than I expected," Holmes began. We were sitting once more in our rooms in Baker Street, with the fire roaring and the fog and steady evening rain safely outside.

Holmes had returned some two hours earlier, still in his working man's clothes but covered in mud and dirt. He had immediately disappeared into his bathroom and remained there for some time, singing a soft aria to himself which I could hear through the door. When he returned to his chair by the fire he was once again Mr Sherlock Holmes. As he stuffed his pipe with his favourite rough shag tobacco, I regaled him with the tale of my meeting with Bill Fraser, before he in his turn described his activities that afternoon.

"The bank is fairly steep, and the late rain has caused it to become slick and dangerous underfoot. It was all I could do to slide down to the gravel path, and even so I admit to a slight stumble or two. I was glad not to be in finer dress, Watson, I can tell you. To discover then that there was no easy access to the tunnel from the station was a crushing blow, and one which might have stumped me altogether had it not been for the lucky happenstance of our old friend, Archibald Aberdeen, seeing what I was up to and coming to my aid.

"You must understand, Watson, that along each side of the tunnel runs a walkway for railway staff. After examining the carriage, it was my intention to take a stroll along one of these walkways and thereby effect a meeting with the workmen who have been clearing the wilderness at the side of the tracks for the past two weeks. Unfortunately, this particular station has locked gates barring just such access – to prevent the poor from sleeping under the bridge, I believe – and the entire walkway is enclosed in iron bars, creating a form of cage which would have left me standing foolishly in the drizzle, had not Mr Aberdeen fortuitously appeared at my shoulder."

At this point, Holmes leaned forward and pointed at me with the stem of his pipe. "We have misjudged that man, Watson, misjudged and maligned him. For one thing, it seems that Mr Archibald recognised me from the off, but chose not to speak, in fear of jeopardising our on-going investigation. Secondly, and more importantly, he had approached me at the tunnel mouth in order to explain the circumstances of his problems in Afghanistan."

From his uniform pocket, Holmes said, the porter had pulled a small etching of a native lady, dressed in the full ceremonial regalia of her people. This, he said, was the girl of whose murder he had been accused. She was engaged to be married to a local man, and he of course was a soldier in Her Majesty's Army; more even than Romeo and Juliet, theirs was a love which was doomed from its very beginning, and their every meeting a danger to them both.

And yet meet they did, Holmes continued, for over a year, stealing an hour together when they could, always a single misstep from discovery. Twice, Aberdeen claimed, he had had asked the girl to marry him and return to England as his wife, but each time she had refused, though she must have known that their secret liaison could not last forever. Sure enough, one day Aberdeen had gone to the abandoned temple which they used as a rendezvous and had discovered the girl's fiancé standing over her unmoving body, the rope he had used to strangle her still in his hands. Aberdeen had broken down at this point in his tale and Holmes, never a man comfortable with strong emotion, quickly finished recounting the story to me, eager to be done with it. In short, Aberdeen managed to overpower the man and revenge himself for the girl's death – surely a hollow comfort. Shortly after, he was discovered insensate on the ground by a passing patrol and taken into custody. Luckily, the army had believed his story, especially when it emerged that the native he killed had boasted of his intention to slay the woman who had dishonoured him.

"Whoever our killer is," Holmes concluded, "I am certain that it is not Mr Aberdeen."

Returning to his narrative, my friend described how Aberdeen unlocked the gate blocking the tunnel and bid Holmes to precede him into the gloom before them.

"As he and I walked along the narrow path," Holmes continued, "we had some difficulty keeping to a steady pace, so dim was the tunnel and uneven the ground underfoot. In fact, I almost missed something of vital importance because of it. At one point, I felt my foot slip on what I fancied was a damp rock or discarded rag and I stumbled and fell against the tunnel wall. Had Aberdeen not taken the time to check that I was unhurt, I might never have bothered to examine the object which had so nearly caused me to come to grief."

In his hand he held a crumpled lady's glove, dirty and soiled but recognisably the double of that Lestrade had described. One of the three pearls on the back of the glove was held in place by but a single thread and the stitching had come away a little at the junction of the thumb and the palm, but it was definitely Emily Williams' missing garment. I glanced at my friend's face as he held it out to me, but if this was a clue which shed decisive light on the case, it was impossible to tell. His brow was furrowed and his lips thinned in what I would have called barely repressed anger, had it been any other man.

"So it *was* murder," I said. Clearly no woman in her right mind would board a train and then almost at once remove and discard a single glove, never mind doing so immediately before suffering a fatal heart incident. I said as much to Holmes and, given an opportunity to demonstrate his intellectual powers, he shook his foul mood a little, though I could see from his manner that he remained uncommonly angered by something.

"Murder it was, Watson," he agreed, "and this glove tells us something important about the murderer as well as confirming the act itself. Do you remember what Aberdeen told us about finding the body?"

I nodded. "That the lady was sitting very properly in her seat, with her bag in her lap and her hands folded before her."

"And that the door and window were closed, Watson. Miss Williams is hardly likely to have opened the window, discarded her glove, and then closed it again. More likely, I would say, that she was at the open window when something came through it and knocked the glove from her hand – and whoever or whatever that something was, it closed the window afterwards."

"Something came *through* the window? On a moving train in broad daylight? Are you suggesting that something *flew* into the carriage?" I have always had the greatest respect for the intellect of Sherlock Holmes, but there have been times when I have found some of his theories more reasonably described as flights of fancy. This idea of a flying killer seemed to me to be one such theory.

"No, Watson! It – or rather he – did not fly into the carriage, he *climbed* in! While the train was going through the long tunnel just after leaving the station, the murderer opened the door by reaching in through the window, and then swung himself inside. Perhaps Miss

Williams saw him appear from nowhere and tried to keep him out by pushing the door closed, or perhaps there was a struggle in which the window remained open. Either way, in the moments immediately before her death, Miss Williams' glove was dropped out of the train and ended up in the weeds and dirt at the side of the track.

"I checked the carriage before returning home this evening, and I believe there is space on top for a man to have hidden and then carefully lowered himself down once the train was obscured from sight by the railway tunnel. There are footprints on the outside of the door, immediately below the window. Rather an oddity. One or two footprints as our killer swings himself down, gains his balance and reaches down to the door handle – that I can accept. But this is a collection of prints, one over the other, smudged and obscured, as though he hung there, braced against the door for some time. Which cannot be correct, for surely Miss Williams would have spotted him."

"Unless he was hidden in the next carriage along!" I interrupted with excitement. I explained to Holmes what Mr Clarendon had told me about being ejected from not one, but two carriages.

My friend was instantly alive with exhilaration. Leaping from his chair, he cried, "We have him, Watson! We have him!" I have rarely seen Holmes so delighted, though I was unclear just how much it helped to know that the murderer had come from the side rather than the top of the train. "Or very nearly," he amended in an undertone. "Knowing is not the same as proving.

"But wait – I have something else to show you, Watson!" He brightened, pulling a second object from his pocket.

The hypodermic syringe he carefully handed to me was damaged beyond any chance of future use, the needle snapped off and the plunger missing. I sniffed the end cautiously and was rewarded with an unpleasant though unfamiliar odour. "Have you tested this?" I asked, indicating the tiny amount of liquid still in the barrel.

Holmes nodded. "I have," he said, "and it is undoubtedly the poison aconite: a product, as you know, of a common garden plant and available still from chemists across the land."

I inhaled deeply in shock. Aconite poisoning was not a pleasant death, though it could be a quick one. The unfortunate victim would

STUART DOUGLAS

immediately have experienced numbness in her throat and difficulty in speaking, followed by a severe burning sensation there and along each of her limbs. Perversely, this burning sensation would have been accompanied by a heightened coldness in her extremities. A complete loss of control over her limbs would have ensued before her sight began to dull and her hearing fade away. Death could take place in less than five minutes (and leave no outward sign) if no help was available. And where was the poor woman to obtain help, locked as she was in a small railway carriage, with no exit and only her murderer for company? If I closed my eyes I could imagine him standing dispassionately over Miss Williams, lifting not so much as a hand in aid as she left this world in pain and terror and despair.

Seldom have I felt so nauseated or so revolted by my fellow man. "Where did you get this, Holmes?" I asked.

"After serendipitously discovering the missing glove, I continued on my original mission to speak to the labourers clearing the trackside. My intention had been to ask whether they had noticed anything as the train went past, but though they often wave, the speed of the train is such as to make any detailed observation impossible. They were, however, of far greater help with the second part of my mission. They had found a wild assortment of bits and pieces as they removed the undergrowth – old tins and discarded newspapers mainly, but here and there something more unusual. And amongst their most recent finds was the hypodermic you hold so gingerly in your hand. It could not have been lying in the weeds for long, for it had caught in the uppermost fronds of a clump of tall grasses and not yet fallen to the ground below. Once we find the man who threw this syringe from the train, the man in the next carriage along, then we shall have our killer."

He fell silent for a minute or two, staring into the fire. "How did your actor describe the man who so rudely lambasted him?" he finally said.

"Muffled and hatted, in a long coat with a turned-up collar. Which could be anyone."

I was painfully aware of the poverty of this description and fully expected Holmes to dismiss it offhand, but instead he seized on it avidly. "Perhaps so, but this man has seen the killer close to and may remember more with some prompting. You have his card still?" I pulled the card from my pocket and handed it to Holmes, who glanced at it then reached for his coat. "In any case, it is too good a lead to ignore. Come, Watson, there is still time tonight to speak to Mr Clarendon!"

Clarendon's room was exactly as I would have expected from our earlier brief meeting: unconventional, noisome and somewhat larger than life. It was dominated by an over-large though fine painting of one of the Christian martyrs displayed above an off-white plaster fireplace; the ascetic in the image was pierced with arrows and slumped forward from the tree to which he was tied. Open copies of the theatrical periodical, *The Stage*, were scattered on every available flat surface, alongside pencil-daubed scripts, pages of handwritten notes and, to Holmes' amusement, a much-thumbed copy of Mr Wilkie Collins' *The Moonstone*. It was cold in the room but no fire was lit, nor did Clarendon make any move to light one, instead contenting himself with sweeping an armful of detritus from one chair and inviting my friend to sit. I forestalled any similar assault on the flooring by indicating I was happy to stand.

I was surprised to see that Clarendon was grinning from ear to ear. Apparently unable to stand still, our host paced up and down before the cold fire saying nothing but smiling constantly, until Holmes broke the silence. He had barely uttered a word, however, when Clarendon burst into a more extreme version of the constant stream of chatter I had remarked on earlier that day.

"May I stop you there, Mr Holmes, and make a few introductory remarks myself? Listen to me – Mr Holmes indeed! Mr Sherlock Holmes, detecting in my very home! Wait until I tell people about this! In any event, Mr Holmes, I must tell you that I take a great interest in you and your cases, and consider you the preeminent detective in London today, far outstripping the likes of Hewitt and that foreign chap Dupin."

With that he strode forward and extended a hand to Holmes, who, with a little trepidation, took it in his own and submitted himself to a hearty shake.

"I thank you, Mr Clarendon," he said, "though modesty forbids my agreement with your judgement. I will, however, agree with you that Miss Clarissa McCarthy does not have the gravitas required to play Cordelia, and extend my hope that your financial fortunes will soon return to their previous even keel. I am sure that you will be able to obtain a new role very soon."

For a second Clarendon's face fell in almost clownish dismay, then the grin which had already threatened to split his face in two extended a further few inches as the man threw back his head in the loudest of laughter. "I hesitate to utter the cliché, Mr Holmes –" he managed between guffaws "– but how did you know all that?"

For all his pretence of annoyance at being treated like a magician, I knew my friend appreciated being asked to explain his observations, and so was not at all surprised when Holmes, after waving a self-deprecating hand, answered Clarendon's question in full.

"It is not beyond reason, Mr Clarendon, to suggest that a man with no fire lit on a cold evening like this is conserving his funds, although the rich brocade of your smoking jacket and the superior nature of the artwork on display hints that this is a temporary, or at least recent, condition. The fact that you have been drafting theatre reviews –" he gestured at the papers strewn around the room "– further supports the proposition that acting has not recently proven sufficiently remunerative. You mention Miss McCarthy in disparaging terms in the review topmost of the collection heaped on that occasional table, and I happen to have seen her play the title role in *The Duchess of Malfi* last month. She is, as you say, too jejune for the role. I surely need not elaborate on the circled job advertisements in the theatrical periodicals I can see all around?"

He waved a hand again to forestall any deluge of praise from Clarendon and was at once business-like.

"You told Dr Watson, I believe, that you were in rather a hurry that day?"

"Yes," the actor replied, "I was in danger of missing the train entirely, so was more put out than usual to be rebuffed not once but twice."

"And you told the good Doctor that the gentleman in the second carriage was entirely muffled and hatted so that no part of his face could be seen?"

"Exactly so, Mr Holmes."

"Was there any other thing you noticed about him, then, that might enable us to identify the man now?"

Clarendon took his time to answer, spending more than a minute in complete silence, his eyes closed, reliving the scene in his mind. Finally, he opened his eyes and shook his head. "Nothing, Mr Holmes; I can think of nothing else. He was tall, but not unnaturally so, otherwise I might have considered that his reason for wishing the carriage to himself. He had his legs stretched out when I entered, but there was still plenty of room for me, had he not immediately started shouting abuse and waving those long fingers at me like some demented spider –"

"Long fingers!" I exclaimed, as an image from earlier in the day came irresistibly to mind. But Holmes, as ever, was one step ahead.

"Thank you, Mr Clarendon. I would say that little detail – combined with others I have already had laid before him – will prove enough to convince Lestrade to arrest George Fellows and his wife, the victim's sister. I expect one will turn on the other quite soon after their arrest – the wife, if I am not mistaken. She believes herself to be more sinned against than sinning, after all."

Not for the first time, I stared at my companion in amazement. For his part, Holmes acted as though nothing exceptional had occurred. He merely shook Clarendon's hand, and informed me as he headed for the door that he would be happy to explain – once we had given Lestrade the last piece of this particular jigsaw.

As it turned out, it was the following morning before Holmes and I sat down together. Over breakfast, Holmes was happy to explain those elements of his thinking to which I had not been privy the previous evening.

"You must forgive me, my dear fellow," he began as he held the newspaper out to me, displaying as it did the headline FAMILY MEMBERS

ARRESTED IN RAILWAY MURDER! "I have been even more remiss than usual in sharing my thoughts with you regarding this case. In my defence I can only plead the fact that we have gone our separate ways more than is common over the past day or so."

Holmes' smile was such that I could not help but feel that he was toying with me. "The key to this whole affair is a simple one. All along everyone has referred to the location of Miss Williams' murder as a *locked* carriage. And of course, it is no such thing. The door to a railway carriage is closed tight, of course, but not locked, else there would be no way for passengers to leave in emergency – or indeed at their destinations.

"Thus, even before I carried out my examination, I had concluded that the murderer must have climbed into Miss Williams' carriage after the train had left the station. The carriage door handle merely required a sharp twist, and the killer would be inside. I had assumed that this would have been done in the open, given the darkness of the tunnel and the closeness of the iron railings to the side of the train, but when you mentioned that Mr Fellows had begun life as a sweep's boy, and so was used to moving in tight, dark spaces, I began to suspect that tunnels offered the perfect cover, at both ends of the journey. Finding the missing glove as I did simply confirmed my suspicions. George Fellows moved from his carriage to the next while the train was concealed by the railway tunnel, and there killed his victim."

I must admit to a certain grudging, if fleeting, respect for Fellows at that point. The thought of clinging to the side of a train thundering along in the darkness, and with deadly iron spikes only inches away, filled me utter horror. Whatever else the man might be, he was clearly no coward. But Holmes had continued speaking.

"Initially, I was sure that murder, not robbery, was the motive for this crime – and yet what killer would turn up his nose at a providential hundred pounds? Only one who had expectation of far greater remuneration to come, obviously. A woman who believed she would soon have no difficulty making her peace with her father and making her way back into his will. They would be united in grief, after all. Mrs Fellows would have little need for a mere hundred pounds then. Better that her husband leave the money and thus convince the police that nothing sinister could possibly have taken place. However, last night you raised an interesting alternative possibility."

My confusion was apparently obvious to my friend, for he sighed, "Mrs Fellows' reluctance to spend any money, Watson! Fraser remembered that Mrs Fellows had discouraged Miss Williams from making any substantial purchases. I had been working on the assumption that murder had always been the intention and the money left in place to deflect suspicion, but now the very opposite notion gained substance. Why would so much care be taken about one hundred pounds before the murder, and so little afterwards?"

I assumed the question was rhetorical, but Holmes apparently expected an answer. I shrugged helplessly and waved a butter knife at him to go on.

"Two different aims, Watson! Mrs Fellows expected a robbery only, and wanted as much of the hundred pounds to remain intact as possible. Evidently, Mr Fellows disagreed, but I very much doubt that Mrs Fellows intended her sister to die, or knew that her husband had a syringe full of poison with him. I suspect the original intention was for a quick robbery – in and out in the first tunnel, where in the darkness Miss Williams would not recognise her assailant as her brother-in-law. But one hundred pounds was not enough for George Fellows – not when there was an inheritance to step into."

"Is that the entirety of your evidence, Holmes?" I asked, for though I could not fault his reasoning, I remembered my vision of the killer standing over his dying victim and was determined that he paid the full price for his crime.

I think Holmes understood, for rather than bristling at my perceived lack of confidence, he was content to explain in further detail. "No, not at all, Watson, and you are quite correct to ask, for this was a clever and subtle crime. One, indeed, which we might never even have noticed had it not been for the wholly coincidental presence of the man Aberdeen. I fully believe that the Fellows would have escaped justice entirely had it not been for that, and one other unforeseen complication.

"Mrs Fellows did not expect to bump into Bill Fraser, nor was she prepared for the fact that her sister would so quickly find common ground with the man and invite him to walk with them. The plan called for the two women to spend the day together, with no other close witnesses, so that Mrs Fellows could ensure that as little money as possible was spent, and then guide her sister to a solitary train compartment. But Fraser prevented that, and neither she nor her husband were cunning enough to extemporise, nor experienced in lying.

"Mrs Fellows tried to shake Fraser off by feigning illness, but when it became clear that Miss Williams was happy to be escorted by him to the station, she made her excuses and, I suspect, rushed home in order to establish a rudimentary alibi. The original intention was presumably that Mrs Fellows would accompany her sister to the very door of her compartment, ensuring no other passenger boarded before the train left. She would then tell her husband that the coast was clear – for how else could he be sure that there would be no witness? The chance meeting with Bill Fraser put paid to that plan, which is why the footprints on the train door were smudged. George Fellows, having no word from his wife, must have held himself against the door while he checked his sister-in-law was the only occupant, rather than swinging over and through in one movement.

"As I say, I cannot *prove* one way or the other whether the initial intention was murder or simple robbery, but I believe I can say what actually transpired. Having committed his foul deed, George Fellows calmly returned to his own carriage while the train traversed the second tunnel – the one leading into the terminus – and was gone long before anyone noticed that the quiet young lady sitting in the adjacent carriage was dead."

There was a ghost of a smile on Holmes' face, as he sipped his tea. "And of course I did send word to Lestrade yesterday evening to check on Fellows' recent movements! You will not be surprised to learn both that his company is in severe financial difficulty – the sort that even one hundred pounds will not fix – and that he spent the morning loafing about near the station, before buying a ticket for the same train as Miss Williams. You may be more surprised to discover that Fellows was arrested wearing a set of cufflinks, engraved with the letters "JH" beneath: obviously a present from Miss Williams to her fiancé, James Hogg. He says that his wife gave them to him; she says she has never seen them before. It will not be long before one or other of them attempts to come to some sort of deal with the police."

Holmes paused for a second in contemplation. "Which means that, in this minor matter at least, I was incorrect. Miss Williams remained constant in her affections to the end. That may be of some consolation to the family."

And with that, Holmes turned his attention back to his newspaper, and his boiled eggs. I intended to write up the case for publication, but no matter how I tried I could not forget my vision of Miss Williams' dying moments, nor turn it into something suitable for an audience of my peers. But now, as the third decade of what I still consider the new century beckons, it seems a foolish delicacy on my part to remain silent and rob my friend of his success…

ABOUT THE AUTHOR

Stuart Douglas has worked in a toy shop, a zoo, a chocolate factory and on a farm, and now runs Obverse Books. Should he ever manage to appear in *Doctor Who* he will, therefore, have fulfilled all of his childhood ambitions.

THE TRAGIC AFFAIR OF THE
MARTIAN AMBASSADOR

‿୨ୄ‿

BY ERIC BROWN

There commenced in the spring of 1915 one of the most fascinating cases that my friend, Mr Sherlock Holmes, has had the fortune to investigate since the arrival on our planet of the Martians ten years ago.

We were relaxing in our rooms that morning, having recently solved the enigma that came to be known as "The Mysterious Affair of the Rosebury Diamonds". I was scanning *The Times* and my friend, as was his wont of late, was poring over one of a dozen tomes he had purchased from a bookseller on Charing Cross Road.

In 1906, shortly after the establishment of the Martian presence in London and other capitals around the world, my friend took it upon himself to learn the predominant language of the Red Planet. Almost a decade later, thanks to his diligence and exceptional powers of memory, he was practically fluent in that notoriously complex tongue. As a reward he had bought himself a complete set of the *Encyclopaedia Martiannica*.

Now I set aside my paper and glanced across at Holmes. He had taken a break from his studies and was filling his pipe.

"What are you reading about now, Holmes?" I enquired.

He flicked a hand at the open page. "A volume on the biological history of the Martian race," said he. "Fascinating. Did you know, Watson, that the gestation cycle of a pregnant Martian female is a little over three Terran years?"

"I must admit my ignorance in that area," said I.

"And were you aware, moreover... Hullo, and what's this?" he said, glancing across at the window.

The spring sunlight had been occluded suddenly, as if by a storm cloud, and as we strode across the room and stared out we beheld the reason. A Martian tripod, fully a hundred feet high, stood in the street outside.

"Curiouser and curiouser," Holmes commented, for a platform was descending from the underbelly of the cowled vehicle and riding upon it was a Martian.

Now, for all that the Martians occupy our planet in their hundreds of thousands, it is not an everyday occurrence that one of their number is seen, as it were, in the flesh. Their singular three-legged transportation devices might ubiquitously prowl the capital from Richmond to East Ham, and from Barnet to Croydon, but the creatures themselves show a distinct inclination towards privacy.

Not, however, this individual – for it stepped from the platform and trundled on its many puckered tentacles across the road and on to the pavement.

Holmes rubbed his hands together in delight. "Why, I do believe, Watson, that the Martian is making a beeline towards 221b!"

Indeed, the alien was hauling itself up the steps towards our front door. We repaired to our respective chairs and made ourselves ready for the audience. I was, I have no hesitation in admitting, more than a little excited at the prospect of the imminent meeting.

A minute later Mrs Hudson, appearing unaccustomedly flustered, burst into the room. "Oh, Mr Holmes!" she cried. "Would you credit it, but there's one of those 'orrible Martian creatures downstairs, and it said it wants to see you promptly!"

My friend smiled. "Then if you would kindly show the fellow up, Mrs Hudson."

"And leave its dreadful slime all over my new carpets?"

"I will personally pay for their cleaning. Now, I rather think that time is of the essence."

With an indrawn breath, Mrs Hudson departed.

Evidently our extra-planetary visitor, for all its many tentacles – or perhaps because of them – found the ascent of the staircase something of a trial, for it was a good five minutes before Mrs Hudson flung open the door and stood aside as the Martian shuffled into the room.

We rose to our feet, as the occasion seemed to demand, and I stared in fascination at our visitor.

We are all aware, from the many illustrations provided by our national dailies, of the appearance of the beings from the Red Planet. Now, however prepared I might have been, the sight of the creature in such close proximity provoked in me the contradictory emotions of fascination and repulsion, for the Martian was truly a hideous specimen of its kind.

It stood perhaps five feet tall, its shorter lower half consisting of six writhing tentacles most easily described as octopoid. Its larger upper section, or torso, however, bore no relation to that of any terrestrial creature, and this perhaps accounted for my horror.

Set into the oily brown skin of its torso was a quivering, v-shaped mouth and two vast, cloudy eyes. Strapped around its mid-section was a belt, fastened to which was a small black box.

However uncomely its appearance, it was nothing beside the revulsion I experienced as the creature's peculiar body odour wafted my way – a scent that combined the stench of putrid carrion with the sweet reek of rotting fruit.

Holmes, maintaining an enviable *savoir-faire* in the face of the noisome aroma, gestured the alien to a *chaise longue*, the only piece of furniture in the room able to contain its broad bulk.

The Martian sat down, arranging its several limbs across the brocade in a manner at once business-like yet prim. As we watched, the peculiar v-shaped mouth quivered and a series of rapid burbles, and not a few belches, filled the air.

"Mr Holmes, Mr Watson –" the tinny translation issued from a grille in the black box seconds later, "I am Gruvlax-Xenxa-Schmee, deputy ambassador to the British Empire, and I have come today to request your investigational services."

Holmes leaned forward, evidently excited, and it was a temptation beyond his powers of resistance to reply to the deputy ambassador in its own tongue. My friend gave vent to a horrible series of eructations which surely taxed the elasticity of his larynx.

The Martian flung several of its tentacles into the air and replied excitedly, "But you have mastered our language as no other Earthling yet, Mr Holmes!"

My friend laughed. "We should proceed, for the sake of my friend Mr Watson, in English." He turned to me and said, "I asked, Watson, as to the nature of the investigation."

Presently the creature replied, "I am afraid that it should remain undisclosed until you have agreed to accompany me to the ambassador's residence, where I will furnish you with all the relevant details."

Holmes harrumphed, not taken by such a stipulation. His curiosity, however, was piqued. He said to me, "This can be no little matter, Watson, if the ambassador himself requires our presence." To the Martian he said, "Very well, Mr Gruvlax-Xenxa-Schmee. Shall we hasten to the embassy?"

"We will avail ourselves of my tripod," said the Martian.

Holmes jumped to his feet. "The game's afoot, Watson," said he, and reached for his cape.

To stride the boroughs of London as if on the shoulders of a giant!

We sat ensconced in comfortable armchairs in the hooded cockpit of the tripod and goggled in amazement at the business of London passing to and fro far below. Tiny cars powered by the latest Martian technology beetled along like trilobites, and in the air the first of the flying machines, owned by intrepid – and wealthy – Earthmen buzzed about like insects.

The ride was over all too soon. What seemed like minutes later, we were deposited outside the Martian embassy in Grosvenor Square and ushered up the steps by the deputy ambassador. In due course we entered the sitting room of the penthouse suite and paused beside a polished timber door.

Without further ado Gruvlax-Xenxa-Schmee said, "I made

the discovery this morning, Mr Holmes. Beyond the door is the ambassador's bedroom, and it is my habit to enter at eight, once the ambassador has risen, to apprise him of the day's agenda."

Holmes fixed the deputy with an eagle eye. "And this morning?"

Gruvlax-Xenxa-Schmee reached a tentacle towards the door and turned the handle. The door swung open, and the Martian stood aside and gestured for us to enter.

Holmes stepped forth with alacrity, and a little more hesitantly I followed.

We were in a bedchamber dominated by a large double bed, upon which reposed the bulk of the Martian ambassador.

I did not require a doctorate in Martian medicine to ascertain that the ambassador was quite dead.

"Stabbed," Holmes opined, "by a sharp implement in the centre of its torso – the area in the Martian body where the major pulmonary organ is located."

Gruvlax-Xenxa-Schmee shuffled back and forth beside the bed, obviously in a state of great agitation or grief. "We have summoned our finest investigational team from Mars," it said, "but it will be several weeks before they arrive on Earth. Also upon that ship is the ambassador's life-mate, come to retrieve her partner's corpse for burial in the sands of our home planet."

I stood over the bed and gazed down at the dead Martian. Added to its usual odour was the obnoxious stench of escaped bodily fluids. I withdrew a handkerchief and covered my mouth and nose.

Ichor, sulphurous yellow and viscid, had leaked from the wound in its torso and pooled in the sheets around its bulk. Its vast eyes were open, and stared blindly at the ceiling. Its v-shaped mouth likewise gaped, as if emitting a final, painful cry.

Beside the bed was a small table upon which lay several envelopes, each one slit neatly open.

"At what time did you last see the ambassador?" Holmes asked.

The Martian replied, "At eleven last night, when he retired."

"And you say the door was locked?"

"From the inside, by the ambassador."

"Was he in the habit of locking his bedroom door?"

"The ambassador valued his privacy."

"I see," said Holmes. "I take it you had a spare key?"

"That is so. And I fetched it when the ambassador failed to respond to my summons at eight."

"And the key, deputy ambassador – is it kept in a place from where others might easily take it?"

"It is kept in an unlocked drawer in the bureau," it replied, gesturing to the adjacent sitting room with a quivering tentacle.

"How many members of staff would have access to the key?"

"Just four: two of my own people, and the two humans who work in the embassy."

"If you would kindly summon them forthwith for questioning, I would be most grateful."

The Martian shuffled from the room. Seconds later Holmes declared, "Hullo, what's this?"

In three strides he had crossed to the window, which stood open six inches. He lifted it further and peered out. I joined him; the drop to the gravelled forecourt below was in excess of forty feet, and no convenient drainpipe, wisteria or the like, clad the wall to provide suitable access.

Holmes stood back and contemplated the wall below the windowsill.

I saw what attracted his attention – a gouge in the wallpaper four inches beneath the sill, and an abrasion on the paint of the woodwork itself.

"But what could it be?" I asked.

"If the ambassador was in the habit of keeping his window open at night, and an intruder armed with a grapple and rope... You catch my line of reasoning, Watson? Then again, there might be an entirely innocent explanation for the marks."

I examined the wall more closely, and when I turned from the window Holmes was tucking something into his breast pocket, which he had presumably taken from the bedside table. There was an expression on his face which I have beheld many times before: the aquiline glint in his eye that betokened the fact that he had garnered what he considered to be a significant clue.

Before I could question him, however, the deputy ambassador returned.

"The staff are gathered and await you next door, Mr Holmes," it said.

"And you have been in the employ of the embassy for how long?" Holmes asked.

"Three years this May," replied the gentleman by the name of Herbert, a sallow man in his late forties with expressive, melancholy eyes and a straggling moustache. In a singular recapitulation of the physiology of his employers, Herbert had short legs and a stocky, barrel-like torso.

"And your position in the embassy?"

"I work as a... you might call it a scientific advisor to the ambassador and his staff. I liaise between the Martian scientists and engineers who visit our world with their wonders, and their opposite numbers on Earth." He spoke in an odd, high-pitched voice, with not a little trace of cockney in the vowels.

"And you trained at...?"

"The Royal College of Science, under none other than the great Professor Huxley himself."

Holmes smiled. "For a man of humble origins, Herbert, you have acquitted yourself remarkably well."

"Not too badly, if I say so myself – for the son of a draper," Herbert said.

My friend cleared his throat. "Now, to the matter at hand. In your time working in the embassy, have you had reason to notice any enmity being directed towards the ambassador?"

Herbert shook his head. "None whatsoever, sir. The ambassador is – was – well liked, by both Martians and humans. He was a wise and generous employer. I cannot imagine who might have done this."

"Are you aware of the political factions that exist amongst the Martians? We well know that there was political strife, not to say animosity, between certain nations before their arrival here."

The scientific liaison officer shook his head. "I know of certain political differences between the Martians, yes, but I was not aware that such differences existed between the ambassador and his staff, or any other Martians who had dealings with him on Earth."

"Very well. Now… we come to the business of what happened last night. Gruvlax-Xenxa-Schmee last saw the ambassador at eleven o'clock, at which time the ambassador repaired to his bedchamber and locked the door. It is my estimation that the ambassador died at some time between eleven and six or seven this morning… though I admit I am not an expert on matters of Martian pathology. Now, where were you between these hours?"

"I have a room in the basement of the embassy, sir. I retired at nine, where I wrote for two hours before going to bed."

"You keep a diary?"

Herbert smiled. "I write fiction," he said. "Though nothing of what I write finds favour with publishers' current tastes. Too fantastical," he finished.

Holmes murmured his condolences. "Perhaps what is needed in these fantastic times is a little more social realism," said he, then returned to the matter at hand. "And you rose at…?"

"Eight, as usual. It was then that Gruvlax-Xenxa-Schmee summoned me with the alarming news."

Holmes nodded sagely, regarding his long fingers splayed on the table-top before him, then looked up at Herbert. "And I take it that you know where the spare key to the ambassador's bedchamber is kept?"

"Yes, sir. In the bureau in this very room."

"To which you have access?"

Herbert nodded. "Yes, sir."

"That will be all, Mr Wells. Will you be kind enough to send in Miss West?"

Herbert opened the communicating door to be met in the threshold by a vision of striking loveliness, a woman I guessed to be in her mid-twenties, raven-haired, pale-skinned and serious. I noted that I was not alone in observing what passed between them: Holmes watched the couple as they gripped each other's hands and uttered what might have been reassuring words, before Miss West smiled bravely and strode with exceptional deportment into the room.

She seated herself at the table. "Mr Holmes, Mr Watson; it is an honour indeed to meet at last such illustrious upholders of the judiciary. I have followed your exploits with considerable interest, gentlemen."

Holmes smiled thinly. "In which case you will have no objections to aiding our enquiries?"

The slightest frown marred, for a second, the perfection of her alabaster forehead. "Of course not, Mr Holmes."

The interview that followed was the swiftest I have ever seen my friend conduct. It seemed barely two minutes from when Miss West entered the room to the time she swept out.

"If you could inform me of the position you hold in the embassy, Miss West, and the duration you have been here?"

She regarded Holmes with a level gaze, her vast brown eyes unwavering. "I am – was – employed as the private secretary to Yerkell-Jheer-Carral, the late Martian ambassador, and I have held the position for a little over six months."

"And your duties entailed?"

Was it my imagination, or did I see a flare of anger in those serene chestnut eyes? "What do you expect the duties of a private secretary to be, Mr Holmes? I arranged the ambassador's itinerary, dealt with his correspondence, interviews and the like."

"Would you say that, over the months you have held the post, you have come to know the ambassador?"

She frowned as she contemplated the question. "I am not sure that one is able to come to *know*, with any certitude, the person of an extra-planetary being."

"But did he seem, in your dealings with him, a fair employer?"

She shrugged expressively. "I had no… complaints."

"And between the hours of eleven last night and seven this morning, you were on the premises of the embassy?"

"I have an apartment nearby, but last night I was working late. It was after midnight when I left my office and made my way home."

"And when was the last time you set eyes on Mr Yerkell-Jheer-Carral?"

"That would be around seven, when I finished taking that day's dictation."

My friend then surprised me by saying, "Thank you, Miss West. That will be all, for now."

Miss West inclined her fine head towards Holmes and myself, then rose and hurried from the table.

She was almost at the door when Holmes asked, "One more question, if I might, Miss West?"

She turned. "Yes?"

"How long have you known the ambassador's scientific liaison officer, Mr Wells?"

"For a little short of six months," she replied.

"And how would you describe your relationship with him?"

Something very much like annoyance, or perhaps indignation, flared in her gaze. She said defiantly, "Mr Wells and I are engaged to be married, Mr Holmes," whereupon she turned and swept from the room.

For the next hour we interviewed the two Martian staff members, attachés who liaised on matters of state with the British government. They could tell us little about the ambassador, other than that they held him in high regard, were terribly shocked by his passing, and had little to vouchsafe on the matter of the political factions that had riven the Martian nations preceding their arrival on Earth. When asked if the ambassador had enemies amongst the many Martians in London, each responded with surprised sounds which their box-translators struggled to interpret.

In due course Holmes dismissed the second attaché and turned to Gruvlax-Xenxa-Schmee. "You might inform Scotland Yard of what has happened. And I suggest that you authorise your medical authorities to deal with the ambassador's corpse."

Gruvlax-Xenxa-Schmee waved a tentacle. "Inspector Lestrade is on his way as we speak," it said, "and the body will be removed just as soon as he has conducted his enquiries."

"And I wonder what good old Lestrade will make of the sad affair?" Holmes said in an aside to me. "Come, Watson, we have learned as much as is to be learned here. We continue the investigation elsewhere."

"And where might that be?" I asked as we took our leave of the embassy.

Holmes smiled thinly. "We are heading for Madam Rochelle's," he said.

I echoed the name. "But isn't that…?" I began.

"Indeed it is, Watson. Madam Rochelle's is perhaps the most exclusive brothel in London."

"I'm not at all sure…" I began as we paced down a narrow alleyway off the Strand, glancing over my shoulder to ensure that we were not being observed.

"Curb your fears, Watson. We have penetrated more insalubrious premises in the course of our investigations. Aha… this must be it."

A dark recess gave access to a door, upon which Holmes rapped with his cane. A second later the door opened and a thin face peered out.

My friend whipped a card from his pocket, showed it to the doorman, and stepped inside.

"Where on earth did you come by the card?" I whispered as I followed Holmes down a darkened corridor.

"Where else, Watson, but in the ambassador's bedchamber."

"Ah! So that's why you were looking like the cat with the cream," I said.

Holmes paused and turned to me. "Your powers of observation, Watson, are as acute as ever."

I huffed at this, then said, "And what else did you find in the bedchamber?"

My friend gave a short laugh. "I found nothing, Watson. That is, I did not find what I was looking for."

"And what might that have been?"

"The opener with which the ambassador had slit his letters."

"The murder weapon!" I expostulated.

"A brilliant deduction, my friend. Now, I think through here…"

He opened a green baize door and instantly we were assailed by loud music – Debussy, I thought – from one of the new-fangled Martian harmony-grams, along with the overwhelming reek of perfume and a sight to shock the most jaded of sensibilities.

Young ladies, in various stages of *déshabillé*, disported themselves around the room upon chesterfields and divans, courted – shall we say? – by their suitors. It was only then that the need for the perfume became apparent: several amongst the clients were none other than malodorous Martians, and it was an odd, not to say nauseating, sight indeed to see the ivory limbs of the young ladies entwined with the writhing tentacles of their otherworldly patrons.

"I never even dreamed…" I began.

Holmes commented, "Some Martians find our women irresistible, Watson."

"What shocks me is that some of our women succumb to their advances."

"Such is the tragedy of their circumstances," said Holmes with a lugubrious expression.

A scantily clad woman of middle years advanced upon us, smiling. "Welcome, gentlemen. If I might take your coats…"

Homes proffered his calling card and said, "If you would be kind enough to present this to Madam Rochelle, and impress upon her that we need speak to her about a matter of the utmost importance."

Two minutes later we were ushered into a highly scented and sweltering boudoir. A buxom woman, whose wrinkled flesh spoke of advanced years, sat upon what appeared to be a throne beside a blazing fire.

"Mr Holmes hisself!" she declared in a Hackney shriek. "Never thought I'd see the great detective on my turf, so to speak. Are you sure I can't tempt you with one of my more beautiful girls?"

Holmes maintained an admirable élan. "We are here to investigate a murder, madam."

"A murder? Who's been murdered? I assure you none of my girls –"

"I understand that none other than the Martian ambassador himself, a certain Yerkell-Jheer-Carral, was a frequent visitor to your establishment?"

"'Was' is right, Mr Holmes. The ambassador stopped coming here about six months ago, and I right miss him I do. The ambassador was a bit of a character, you see."

My friend considered her words and stroked his chin with a long forefinger. "That is interesting, and informative," he murmured to himself. "Now, could you tell me if any of your ladies are in the habit of visiting the ambassador at the Martian embassy?"

"What? And you think I send my girls out into the city? I protect my girls, I do."

"I am sure you do, Madam Rochelle," said Holmes. "I wonder if you can recall, when the ambassador visited your establishment, if he exhibited a preference for a certain type of lady?"

Madam Rochelle thought about that. "He liked 'em dark, Mr Holmes. No blondes for the ambassador. Dark and sultry was how he liked his wimmen."

Holmes thanked Madam Rochelle, assured her once again that we did not care to avail ourselves of the pleasures of her establishment, and withdrew.

We escaped the cloying confines of Madam Rochelle's and once again breathed the refreshing spring air of the Strand. Holmes made a beeline for a Communications Kiosk − yet another wonder for which we had to thank the Martians − on the corner of the Strand and Northumberland Avenue. "Excuse me one moment, Watson," he said, and squeezed his angular frame into the kiosk.

He stepped out minutes later and explained, "I contacted Mr Wells and Miss West, and arranged to meet them, in secrecy, on Hampstead Heath at six." He crossed the pavement and slipped into W.H. Smith's, emerging soon after to hail a passing taxi.

"And now?" I asked as we climbed aboard.

"To the Martian embassy," Holmes said, and within seconds we were hurtling through the streets of the capital.

* * *

An underling Martian showed us into the embassy and summoned the deputy ambassador.

Holmes asked if he might again examine the ambassador's bedchamber, and Gruvlax-Xenxa-Schmee escorted us up the stairs to the penthouse suite.

Holmes hurried over to the bed while I remained on the threshold with the deputy, stopped in my tracks by the foul stench issuing from the corpse. Holmes, for his part, seemed not to notice the aroma. With his back to me, he appeared to be searching through the late ambassador's inert tentacles.

"Aha!" he said at last, and turned on me a look of triumph.

Gruvlax-Xenxa-Schmee perambulated itself past me and into the room. It gave vent to a series of oesophageal belches which the box at its midriff translated as, "Mr Holmes, if I might enquire as to how the investigation proceeds?"

"I am happy to inform you that the case is solved," Holmes said. He stood beside the bed and gestured at the tangle of dead limbs sprawling across the counterpane. "My initial examination of the corpse failed to locate the implement which caused the fatal injury for the very good reason that it was concealed beneath the ambassador's forelimb."

Gruvlax-Xenxa-Schmee hurried to the bed and I, gagging at the stench, joined them.

I stared down at the tangle of tentacles and beheld, gripped in a suckered pseudopod, a bloodstained letter-knife.

The Martian spoke. "Are you saying, Mr Holmes, that…?"

My friend said, "My investigations led me, in due course, to an establishment at which the pleasures of the flesh might be indulged by those of little self-restraint. It is my painful duty to inform you that the ambassador was a frequent visitor to this establishment, where he developed a predilection for human ladies of a certain type."

Before me, Gruvlax-Xenxa-Schmee appeared to slump. "I was aware of his weakness," it said, "and more than once attempted to reason with His Excellency, to no avail."

"It is my opinion," said Holmes, "that remorse overcame the ambassador, and in the throes of self-recrimination, and guilt at his unfaithfulness to his mate – at this very moment travelling the gulf between Mars and Earth – he took his own life."

The deputy ambassador said, "A tragic affair, Mr Holmes…"

We took our leave, and, as we hurried across the square towards the taxi rank, I said doubtfully, "Suicide? But… how was it that you didn't find the letter-knife when you first examined the corpse?"

"All will be revealed in time, Watson. Have patience." He opened the rear door of the taxi and slipped inside. "To Hampstead Heath," he told the driver.

We came to the crest of the hill and stood in silence, all London spread before us. The sun was setting, and a roseate light bathed the capital. I made out familiar landmarks, St Paul's and Nelson's Column, and more recent additions to the city's skyline: the spaceyard in Streatham constructed by the Martians, and the stanchioned air-port for the new flying machines over at Bermondsey. Prominent across the city were the towering tripods, stilled now after the activity of the day, hooded and slightly sinister. Soon, when the sun went down, they would begin their curiously mournful and eerie ululations, the meaning of which was still a mystery to us humans.

"Who would have guessed, Watson, that in the last years of the nineteenth century, our world was being watched keenly and closely by intelligences greater than, and yet as mortal as, our own?" Holmes sighed. "Who would have guessed that, in time, they would cross the vast gulfs of space and settle our planet? If that first invasion had succeeded, if the microbes of this world had not fought off the invaders as successfully as any army, then life on Earth would now be under the yoke of terrible oppressors. Give thanks that a second, more altruistic Martian nation followed, who worked to cure the microbial disease that did for their cousins, and who brought a new, technological age to our planet. And yet, Watson…"

"And yet?"

"And yet, the Martians are an invading army still, for all their technological accomplishment and largesse, and they bring with them their own ignorance, and evil."

ERIC BROWN

He paused, his aquiline face plunged in melancholy introspection for a space, and then he roused himself and pointed. "Look, Watson, down by that oak. Mr Wells and Miss West, holding hands like the lovers they are. Shall we join them?"

We made our way down the incline and met the pair beneath the spreading boughs. Both looked suspicious, West's beautiful visage drawn and even paler than usual.

Wells stepped forward. "You said you had news…?" he began.

"The case is resolved," said Holmes. "We located the weapon."

At this Wells flinched. "Located…?" he echoed.

"It was concealed beneath the ambassador's tangled limbs," Holmes explained.

Miss West stared at him. "But isn't it curious that you did not find the knife when you first examined the corpse?"

"Not in the slightest," replied Holmes, "for the knife was not in situ when I first made my examination."

"What?" I cried.

"Then how…?" Wells began.

"I placed it there just one hour ago, when I entered the ambassador's bedchamber for the last time."

I stared aghast at my friend. "Do you know what you're saying, Holmes?" I expostulated. "Why… but that means the ambassador cannot have taken his own life!"

Holmes smiled, and turned to Mr Wells and Miss West. "That is correct, is it not? Would you care to explain?"

Miss West opened her mouth, quite shocked. "Why, I have no idea what you mean…"

"Come, my dear. I am quite aware of the ambassador's… predilections, shall we say?"

At this, Miss West broke down and sobbed. Wells embraced her, and it was a minute before she regained her composure, looked Holmes squarely in the eye, and said, "Six months ago, upon my appointment as the ambassador's private secretary, he made his feelings known. I was revolted, of course, though I was well aware of the… the tastes of some of his kind. The ambassador, for all his status, was not exempt from these depravities… and with increasing insistence he proceeded to press himself upon me. Last night he asked me into his room, ostensibly to dictate a last letter. However…" She sobbed, biting her knuckle. "Oh, it was horrible, horrible! His strength, his ghastly, overwhelming…"

Holmes reached out and touched her shoulder. "Please, there is no need to go on."

Wells interposed. In a trembling voice he took up the story. "I was passing the room, Holmes, when I heard Rebecca's cries. I fetched the key and let myself into the bedchamber, and what I saw there…" He shook his head bitterly, his expression wretched. "I was beside myself with rage, sir, and, blinded to the consequences, took up the letter-knife and… and plunged it into the horror's torso…" He looked up, defiantly. "I am not proud of what I did, but my love for Rebecca and my revulsion at the ambassador's vile actions…" He paused, then went on. "I opened the window and gouged a mark in the wall beneath, to make it appear that the murder was the work of an intruder. I then left the embassy and disposed of the knife in the Thames."

He looked up, staring Holmes in the eye, and said, "I do not regret what I did, for the animal had it coming to him, and I will face the consequences like a man. If you inform Scotland Yard of my actions, I will have my day in court."

Homes smiled at this, then said, "Well said, but it will take more than pretty rhetoric to persuade me that what you said is the truth of it."

I stared at my friend. "What the deuce are you driving at, Holmes?"

The great detective turned to Miss West, and said, "Well?"

Miss West faced the detective foursquare, thought for a space, and began, "I —"

Wells gripped her hand. "Rebecca…"

"No, Bertie," said she, "the truth is better out… You are correct, Mr Holmes, Bertie did not kill the ambassador in a fit of rage." She took a deep breath, then said, "*I* did… for when he pressed himself upon me, held me down with his tentacles and… and proceeded to… You must understand that I was beside myself with terror, and when

I saw the letter-knife on the bedside table, I reached out and grasped it and…" She stopped, almost out of breath. "I did what I did, Mr Holmes, in self-defence, but I too will face the consequences if that is what you feel right and proper."

Holmes shook his head. "As far as the authorities are concerned, both human and Martian, the affair is closed. The ambassador killed himself in a fit of remorse and guilt for his philandering with human women. The Martian judiciary will not arrive for another five weeks, by which time what evidence there is will be corrupted. While not condoning your actions, I understand the terrible fear that drove you to commit the deed."

"You mean…?"

"In my opinion you have suffered enough, Miss West. Naught will be gained by hauling you before the court, for while a human law might have sympathy with your plight, I cannot say the same for the Martian judiciary."

She stared at him open-mouthed, tears glistening in her eyes.

"If I were you," Holmes went on, "I would leave the embassy, turn your back on the terrible memories of last night and start anew. Your secret is safe with Watson and me."

Wells said, "Why, but I cannot thank you enough, Mr Holmes!"

Miss West stepped forward and placed a kiss on the detective's cheek. "Thank you," she murmured.

Presently we watched them step from beneath the boughs of the oak and, hand in hand, walk into the diminishing twilight of the Heath.

Back at Baker Street, Holmes lit his pipe and pulled upon it ruminatively. I stared up at the stars scattered brightly across the heavens and said, "You think they'll be all right, Holmes?"

"They have talent, Watson. I've read a little of Miss West's journalism, and very impressed I was. And maybe Wells' jottings will come to something."

For a time I was lost in a brown study as I pondered the coming of the Martians and the many wondrous, and not so wondrous, incidents their arrival had entailed.

We strode on in companionable silence as the darkness deepened around us, and at last, from all across London, near and far, there sounded the first of the tripods' strange and mournful cries.

"Ulla, ulla," they called dolorously into the warm night air. "Ulla, ulla…"

ABOUT THE AUTHOR

E ric Brown has lived in Australia, India, and Greece. He began writing when he was fifteen and sold his first short story to Interzone in 1986. He has won the British Science Fiction Award twice for his short stories and has published almost fifty books. His latest include the novel *Helix Wars* and the collection *The Angels of Life and Death*. He writes a monthly science fiction review column for the *Guardian* and lives near Dunbar in Scotland. His website can be found at www.ericbrown.co.uk.

THE ADVENTURE OF THE SWADDLED RAILWAYMAN

BY RICHARD DINNICK

As I have said before, from the years 1894 to 1901 inclusive, Mr Sherlock Holmes was a very busy man. It is safe to say that there was no public case of any difficulty in which he was not consulted during those eight years, some of them of the most intricate and extraordinary character, in which he played a prominent part.

Just such a case came to light in the autumn of 1898. Holmes had taken to rising late and breakfasting at a time more appropriate to luncheon. It was therefore at least mid-morning before he began his perusal of *The Times* that day. He had taken a seat at the breakfast table laid by Mrs Hudson and had yet to even speak a word to me in greeting or acknowledgement.

He was in the final throes of filing his pipe after dissecting a pair of smoked kippers when he turned to me.

"What do you think of London's underground railways?" he asked.

"Well," I said. "It is progress. To traverse the capital underground is a marvel. The working classes can travel in relative comfort and speed, can they not?"

Holmes sucked on his pipe and produced a cloud of blue-brown smoke that wafted up to the ceiling, causing a cloud level to form, caught in the sunlight coming in through the windows from Baker Street.

"No, Watson," Holmes replied at length. "They cannot. The

carriages and system are hot and crowded. The companies behind these 'marvels' continue to disembowel London, while at the same time congesting both parliament and the Queen's Highway. It has sometimes proved near impossible to take a hansom cab across some districts of the metropolis due to the earthworks along the thoroughfare. And now this!"

Holmes had become animated in a manner I knew meant that not only his interest but also his pique had been aroused.

"Now what?" I asked, rising from my chair.

"See for yourself!" He folded *The Times* neatly and handed it to me, tapping the relevant piece with two elegant fingers.

Between an item on Jewish anarchists and the new progressives of the Liberal Party I read:

RAILWAY WORK SUSPENDED BY FEAR OF GHOST

Work on the new Central London Railway has been suspended at Bloomsbury because workers say the tunnels are haunted. Construction of the deep-bore tunnel and its stations began last year but now workers have downed tools and some have simply not returned to work. A figure was seen in the tunnel where none could possibly have been and disappeared when the foreman went to clarify what the person was doing.

I looked at Holmes.

"A ghost!" exclaimed he. "Fascinating, is it not, how the mind of the common man turns to myth and superstition to explain something that appears inexplicable."

"And you are sure it is not a ghost…"

Holmes laughed humourlessly. "I realise that to your eyes I am a slugabed, Watson, but do not presume that my ability to spot mockery has been dulled by the lateness of my rising."

"No," I said in an appropriately contrite fashion. "I am sorry, Holmes."

"You know my methods and you know even better my distaste for the fantastical. Rational explanations are often improbable or even implausible and yet the supernatural is repeatedly called upon to make up any shortfall in data."

"Yes, Holmes. You have often said as much to me," I said and then did my best to affect an exact recitation of what might have passed for his motto or mantra. "When you have eliminated the impossible, whatever remains, *however improbable*, must be the truth?"

"Very good, Watson!"

"So you know what this ghost is?"

"I do not. But of one thing I am perfectly certain."

"And that is?"

"That the figure is most emphatically *not* a ghost."

Soon after, we were seated in a hansom cab, clattering our way across the capital from Baker Street and along Gower Street and thence to the site of the dig at Bloomsbury. Holmes sat in silence with his fingers in a steeple beneath his chin. I knew this to mean he was deep in thought and left him to his labyrinthine processes.

When we arrived, the excavation was dominated by a huge crane that had been erected for the removal of the detritus from the tunnelling far below. The site was encased by a wooden fence and the London traffic had to make do with the side streets around it. Several young men were collected under a nearby tree. By their dress and reading matter I assumed them to be students from the nearby University College London.

A wide, gated entrance allowed for the removal of earth from the digging and through it I could see two gentlemen holding a discussion. One was older and considerably taller than the other, with great whiskers that were greying at the edges. His younger counterpart wore a brown suit and a bowler hat of the same hue.

Holmes spoke briefly to the men, who smiled and nodded as I joined the group.

"We are indeed fortunate, Watson!" He turned to the first man. "These gentlemen are engineers engaged in the construction of the new railway – Mr Joseph Porter and his assistant, Mr John Earl."

"Excellent," I said, although I had not the faintest notion why Holmes was so excited.

"It is a most rum affair," commented Porter. His voice was deep and had me in mind of a music hall master of ceremonies. "As you may know, Mr Holmes, the Tube has not been without its share of strange occurrences."

"Oh?" I asked. Even if Holmes was apprised of these matters, I was not.

"When one is tunnelling or even using the cut-and-cover method of Tube construction, one may come across all manner of things in the ground," explained Earl with a nervous, staccato delivery. "Not least of which are plague pits and former graveyards unmarked on any map."

"This often spooks the men," confided Porter in a conspiratorial whisper, narrowing his eyes. "They are a superstitious breed. Hard working but willing to believe in any mumbo-jumbo that might cause them ill fortune or otherwise mean they might have a cursed life! Hardly rational."

"Indeed," Holmes commented.

"Did you see the ghost that the newspapers are reporting?" I asked. They both shook their heads.

"Old Tom said it was like a mummy!" Earl announced. "He told all the labourers about it and said it was a bad omen."

Porter frowned at him. "Poppycock!" he exclaimed. "Mummies, indeed."

"Well," said Holmes, gazing about. "We are very close to the British Museum. Perhaps we should enquire there if they have misplaced a pharaoh from the Egyptian Room."

Porter stared at him with an open mouth before realising Holmes was attempting humour. "Aha!" he boomed. "Very good, Mr Holmes. Yes. The Egyptian Room."

Holmes smiled beatifically, then leant in and spoke in a hushed tone. "Nonetheless, a trespasser in the tunnel cannot be a good thing," he said. "With your leave, Mr Porter, I should like to speak with the navvies and the foreman. They are the only true witnesses to this 'subterranean spectre' and I should like to establish what they saw for myself."

It transpired that the men in question worked on the tunnel at night and a different team of workers was employed during the day.

So far, because of the refusal to work on the site, no one had seen anything untoward for over a day now. Holmes asked for addresses for the men of the night shift and Mr Earl obliged by vanishing for a short period and returning with a handwritten list.

"We do not have all our workers' addresses," he confessed. "But I trust these should prove sufficient to your purposes, Mr Holmes."

The first stop we made was at a large and ungainly lodging house in Westminster, it being the nearest address to our point of origin. Two urchins were perched on the doorstep and, due to the manner in which their hair had been trimmed with what must have been blunt scissors, it was impossible to assign either child a gender. Holmes stepped between then and disappeared inside.

Upstairs we encountered several women and an old man who were clearly grieving. When we enquired as to the nature of their woe the old man informed us that his son had passed on that very morning. I gave him my sincere condolences, but Holmes cared not for such niceties and was already inside the lodging rooms, speaking with a young woman, asking how this tragedy had occurred.

Her name was Rusheen and in a light Irish lilt she explained that Sean was her cousin and had appeared "right as rain" two mornings ago. But after developing a nasty cough he had taken himself to bed – apparently very uncharacteristic behaviour for the young man. His "ma" had found him dead that very morning.

"And did he mention anything unusual he had seen at work?" Holmes asked.

"You mean the 'ghost'?" Rusheen asked in a hushed tone. "He saw it. Said it chilled him to his very core, it did. We even heard him screaming the previous night. We thought it was a nightmare."

"Brought on by the sighting?" I asked. "How did he describe it?" I was keen to erase the ethereal spectre I had in my mind's eye.

"He said it were a mummy, not a ghost," she said. "He saw it down the tunnel about a hundred yards or so. Said the figure was covered in bandages."

I looked at my friend, but he ignored my raised eyebrows.

"And did he say at what time this man appeared?" Holmes demanded.

"I think it was towards the beginning of the shift," Rusheen replied. Then she stared from me to Holmes and back again. "You're not police, are you?"

"No, madam, we are not," said Holmes, as if affronted by the very suggestion. "We are merely interested parties."

"We are sorry for your loss," I added. "We have come to pay our respects."

"He'd have been tickled to think a pair of gents such as you was paying their respects to the likes of him," Rusheen said, and managed a brave smile. Then she pointed through an open door to a room where furniture had been pushed back against the wall, allowing her cousin's body to be laid out.

"Come, Watson!" Holmes left the woman without a second thought and allowed me to move ahead of him into the small bedroom. "As thorough an examination of the cadaver as you can manage without defiling the poor unfortunate."

I nodded and approached the bed. Sean Finlay was approximately twenty-five years old and five foot eight inches tall with a comma of sandy hair. He had been readied for the afterlife and dressed in a black suit with pennies on his eyes. As I looked more closely, though, I could see that the eyelids were inflamed as if he had suffered from conjunctivitis. I also noted that his hands, which had soil or dirt beneath the fingernails, were covered in bandages.

We discussed these findings as we left the lodging house and walked down to Westminster to hail another cab.

"He could not have worked in tunnelling if his hands had been thus affected before he came off the shift," Holmes told me. "For how could he have performed his duties? No, the wounds were given to him or were self-inflicted between the early morning of Tuesday and last night."

"Yet, according to his family he remained in bed all that time," I added. "Do you think the cough pertinent?"

"All data must be assumed to be pertinent until it proves otherwise," Holmes replied inscrutably.

We took our third hansom cab of the day from Westminster to Bermondsey. Tom Stevens' address was far less salubrious than Sean Finlay's had been. This was a London slum of the worst kind and Holmes mused as to why a relatively well-paid navvy would still live in such a place.

We found the address easily but after Holmes had rapped on the front door with his cane several times, it became clear that no one was home. Holmes quickly ingratiated himself with an old washerwoman who was sitting on a nearby doorstep with a mangle and some linen. He returned several minutes later with a slight smile upon his lips.

"Mary over there informs me that she witnessed Tom come home two mornings ago. As far as she knows he has not left since, neither has he received any visitors in that time."

"Mary is remarkably well informed," I snorted.

"Never underestimate the powers of retention belonging to someone who is employed in repetitive work. Apparently she watches the entire world pass by her front door," said Holmes. "And thus she also knows that Mr Stevens returns home in the early morning, when it is his habit to leave his door unlocked until he goes to bed sometime around ten o'clock, for this is when he draws his curtains."

He tried the handle and the door opened a couple of inches. The smell assaulted us first, followed by a small cloud of disturbed flies. Lying on the floor of the narrow hall was the body of a man, possibly fifty years old.

"Tom Stevens, I presume," I said. Holmes nodded and immediately bent and pushed the deceased man's shirtsleeve up the arm that lay closest to us. I knelt and, taking a handkerchief from my pocket, held the man's hand in mine. It was covered in blisters of a sort I had never encountered.

"I hope this isn't plague," I said.

"Unlikely, Watson."

Then it struck me. "You said the door would be locked."

"A simple application of logic and a little conjecture," he replied. "When we arrived I wondered why a man who was remunerated sufficiently to leave the area and set up a new home in a better neighbourhood had not done so. The reason is sentimentality, Watson. The man probably grew up here, or close by, and the engineers had called him "Old Tom". Therefore, he was bound to be older than Sean Finlay. As I suspect that our railway workers have been poisoned and that the toxin is a slow-acting one, it would affect an older man more quickly than a younger one due to the fortitude of the latter's constitution. I surmised that Mr Stevens would not have survived long enough to lock his front door."

I shook my head in admiration.

"Now, we must bring the police into play," said Holmes, standing up. "I would like a thorough post-mortem performed on Mr Stevens and I suspect they would prefer us to do it at the mortuary."

The arrangements to have the body taken to Scotland Yard and my involvement in the examination took some time, but if there is one thing the inspectors of the Metropolitan Police know, it is to heed the requests of Mr Sherlock Holmes.

For his part, Holmes said he would return to Baker Street, and when I returned there at almost midnight, I went straight to bed.

The next morning I rose late and went in search of breakfast. Instead, I found our consulting room covered in scientific journals and copies of the Hansard from Parliament. I thought these two were interesting compatriots in Holmes' research. Of the great man, however, there was not a sign. I called out to him, but of course he made no reply. I suspected his mind to be totally focused on whatever task he had appointed himself.

A rapid search of the apartments unearthed Holmes at a table lined with bottles and test tubes. He was wearing goggles and gauntlets of some kind. He looked as if he were about to take to the skies and I said as much.

"You may be closer to the truth than you believe," he said absently. "Tell me about the post-mortem."

Holmes listened intently as I imparted my report. Robert Stevens had been killed by water on the lungs. He had second-degree burns on his hands, and his eyes – like those of Sean Finlay – showed signs of conjunctivitis. No poison as such was detected, although there were chemical elements that should not have been present.

"Just as I thought," he said, and stood up. "I think we should attend to our hunger."

As we breakfasted on sausages Holmes pored over *The Times* and, shortly after opening it, gave a triumphant "Ha!" He spun the paper round and slid it across the table.

The story of the haunted tunnel had graduated dramatically in the number of column inches, and now recounted the untimely deaths of ten more labourers the previous day, three days after they had stopped work. This was seen as further evidence of a mummy's curse and, just as Holmes had joked, the paper now married the bandaged figure with the proximity of the British Museum.

"I had expected more of *The Times*," Holmes said. "But this will force our unknown poisoner's hand."

"How so?" I asked.

"We must visit Bloomsbury once more," he replied.

As well as broadening his mind on the subject of chemistry and parliamentary procedure, Holmes had also managed to obtain a letter from Joseph Porter that gave him practically *carte blanche* at the Bloomsbury tunnel. He gave me the letter and asked me to meet him that evening at the site.

On the strike of six, I arrived at the double gates and presented my credentials to the night-watchman, who ushered me through to a rather ramshackle elevator. I asked if Mr Sherlock Holmes was awaiting me and was told that Mr Holmes had requested I descend to the tunnel to meet him there.

In the lift was a bent old man with a moustache sporting a thick and grubby coat, a similar scarf and a hat of charcoal grey. He touched his cap as I stepped in and then stretched past me to draw a safety lattice across the opening.

I rode the lift into the depths of London. It became increasingly warmer the deeper we descended, as if Hell really were an underground realm and we were dropping into its fiery furnace.

"Hot, ain't it?" asked the old man and gave a nasty, hacking cough. I wondered if he was in the early stages of pneumonia.

"Yes," I said, smiling.

"Why don' you loosen that tight collar o' yours?"

I bridled at the fellow's impudence, but then realised who it was that had addressed me. For the old man had straightened up, gaining a good few inches in height. His shoulders also rose, losing their slouch, and he removed the cap to reveal elegantly slick, black hair. "Holmes!"

"Good evening, Watson. Forgive my need for deception. I do not want our quarry to know I am here. Your presence will put him on his guard, I am sure, but mine might well deter him and he does so want to return."

"How do you know this?" I asked, but Holmes ignored the question. "What did your scientific and parliamentary endeavours unearth?"

"As there is patently no possibility of the dead roaming the tunnels of the Central London Railway and even less likelihood of that member of the netherworld having once been mummified, I thought it an obvious course to check the parliamentary records," said Holmes.

"To what end?"

Holmes smiled in the half-light. "Each railway line constructed beneath the magnificent metropolis of London has been the result of an act of parliament, suggested by those corporations engaged in the construction of such enterprises."

"I see," I said.

"My point being that any party that objects to the construction of these subterranean railways may avail themselves of the opportunity to make their feelings known to their Member of Parliament. Sometimes, depending on their rank and position, these persons can object in person by appearing at the committees held on the subject."

"And from this you have a list of suspects, I take it?"

"We have a list of those who objected to the Central London Railway," Holmes said.

The lift reached the bottom of the shaft and Holmes pulled on a lever, bringing the elevator to a halt. He pulled the cage-like door open and we stepped out onto the slightly damp ground. Then the great detective reached behind him, back into the lift, and set the lever in place once more. Immediately the cage started on its return to the surface.

"Why have you sent it back to ground level? How are we to escape if there is a killer down here?"

"This is not the only way down. It cannot be," said Holmes.

He marched off towards the main tunnel, and we found it surprisingly easy to see for there were lamps at regular intervals. To our right was the much wider and taller construction of an iron-lined tunnel that was to be a station, one I was later to learn was going to be called "Bloomsbury" until "British Museum" was deemed a better designation.

Considering there were no works being carried out on the line due to the lack of navvies, there were more sounds in the tunnel than I had expected. I have to confess that even as a man who has seen action – not only abroad in military service but also in the pursuit of justice here in England – I found myself unnerved in the extreme.

Holmes, naturally, seemed spectacularly unaffected by the echoes of what must have been water dripping, or the strange metallic sounds of physical contraction or expansion by the ironwork. Despite the uncommon heat, I shivered.

The scene was not as I had been expecting. There were no tracks laid and no evidence of a platform. At the eastern end there was a collection of heavy machinery and what looked like a ring of metal where the tunnel mouth should be.

"That is the tunnel shield," Holmes said. "It protects the workers from collapse and allows the iron framework for the tunnel supports to be laid as the tunnelling progresses. It was originally the invention of Brunel, now ameliorated by other engineers for this exact purpose."

An iron and wooden chute had been placed before the metal shield. It had earth and stone as well as other detritus resting upon its slatted belt. It looked as if it should move, transporting this debris to a cart that was then transported back to the shaft we had descended so that it may be removed completely.

There were tools and other general building paraphernalia that

I could not pretend to understand. I knew what they were: several lengths of rope, some barrels of grease and other substances, a packing crate of rags and strips of cloth and some spare chains. I had no idea what they were all for, however.

Holmes began to whistle tunelessly as he examined the digging equipment.

"So," I said, casting a nervous look back down the half-lit tunnel. "Tell me about the petitioners against the Central London Railway."

Holmes stopped whistling and took a pickaxe from where it rested against the wall. He began to swing his implement at the rock face.

"Some of the most influential and important personages of the day," he said. "Bazalgette, for one."

Sir Joseph Bazalgette had been responsible for delivering London from the infamous "Great Stink" in the middle of the century as a result of his vision and determination to build the best network of sewers the world had ever seen. He had died in 1891.

"Yes," replied Holmes when I remarked upon this. "That rather does rule him out as a suspect, does it not?"

Holmes went on to tell me that numerous people and public bodies had complained about the building of the railway, perhaps most notably both the Dean and the Chapter of St Paul's Cathedral. As with most property owners, their concerns lay in subsidence.

"I daresay they are not the first of the priesthood to bemoan the undermining of the very foundation of the church," Holmes said with uncharacteristic jocularity. I enjoy a good pun but did wonder at the questionable taste and possible blasphemy of this one.

"The City Corporation also objected," my friend concluded, "as did the newly formed London County Council, although theirs was a more interesting objection than the others: theirs was a political objection. They wanted the working man to be catered for and believe all railway owners to be only interested in the wellbeing of the well-heeled."

"Hardly cause for murder," I said.

"To you or I, yes," replied Holmes, hitting the rock face repeatedly. "But to men who believe passionately in a cause? Perhaps not. Or perhaps our poisoner was not intent on murder…"

I frowned at this and was about to form another question when we both heard the unmistakeable sound of footsteps.

"I doubt any mummy, ghost or other ghoul would make so heavy a footfall!" he whispered over the sound of his digging. Then he stopped and mopped his brow with what I recognised was one of his scientific gauntlets. He then proceeded to put on the gloves as calmly as if he were about to take a stroll in Regent's Park.

I bent down, pretending to tie my shoelace, and in so doing caught a glimpse of the figure illuminated by one of the tunnel lamps. It was as Sean Finlay had described it to his cousin: not ghostly at all but covered almost entirely in gauze bandages – most alarmingly around the head and especially the nose and mouth.

I swallowed hard and reached instinctively for the revolver secreted in my jacket. Before I could draw the weapon, Holmes stooped and picked up one of the containers of what I took to be grease for the machinery.

"I know what this is!" he called out loudly. "And why you have returned for it."

I turned to see that our erstwhile mummy had stopped almost thirty feet from where we stood, flat against the wall and frozen by indecision. Holmes started running towards the intruder, who finally elected on fleeing, spinning on his heel and sprinting away down the tunnel at an impressive rate.

"Watson, your revolver," called Holmes, haring along the tunnel after the bandaged man. I withdrew my firearm, broke it to check each chamber had a round within and then cracked it back into place.

I ran the length of the oversized stretch of train tunnel, but ahead I could see no sign of the mummy. Instead, in the darker, narrower section beyond, Holmes was standing, gazing up at an angle. I arrived to see an alcove dug into the side of the main bore that bent to the right, hiding a shaft not wider than a card table with a line of metal rungs that disappeared into the darkness.

"Ventilation," said Holmes. "The workers need to breathe, and so will the passengers!"

"Why did no one mention this?"

"You see how far the rot of superstition can spread, Watson?

No one thought of this because ghosts and mummies have no need of air!"

"Why a mummy, though? I do not understand the need for such a costume!"

"Did you know that one of the engineers on this line is president of the Egypt Exploration Fund?"

I looked at Holmes. "You're not serious, Holmes."

"That is a fact," he replied. "Another is that a second engineer is the man who designed the vessel used for transporting Cleopatra's Needle here in 1877."

"You think there is a curse?"

"A mummy's curse? Really, Watson." He looked disappointed in me. "Again, I am merely showing that coincidence is indeed rife and the dedicated detective cannot be swayed into thinking it any more than part of life's highly original tapestry."

"Incidentally, should we not be chasing the fellow – whoever he is – up that ladder?"

"No," said Holmes. "I took the precaution of asking our friends at Scotland Yard to post two constables at ground level in case of just such an instance. We need only remain here to ensure he does attempt to retrace his steps."

My revolver saw no active service that night. We clearly heard the man emerging at the top of the shaft only to be met by a pair of bobbies. We then summoned the lift and returned to the surface so that Sherlock Holmes might complete his enquiry.

Holmes retrieved his more usual attire from a bag at the site office, and we took a cab to Scotland Yard. There we met a baffled young inspector called Pike, who told us what his constables had done upon apprehending the figure making his way up Montague Street.

According to them, he had not been completely covered in gauze but wearing a fencing outfit. Only his head and hands had been bandaged. Holmes nodded as if all this made perfect sense. He then asked if he could see the man.

Inspector Pike took us into a cell where a youth lay on the bed, his eyes red with tears. He didn't look like the type of man to kill ten men, but then I was constantly surprised by man's inclination to the nefarious.

"He won't give his name," said Pike as we stood over the young man.

Holmes sat beside the young man and spoke quietly. "I take it you are a student at University College London?"

The boy looked up at Holmes. He nodded mutely.

"And a follower of Viktor Meyer as well as, perhaps, Robert Owen?

The boy sat upright. "How did you know –"

"About the German chemist? I can only assume you have read his paper on the combination of chloroethanol with potassium sulphide, combined with the treatment of thiodiglycol with phosphorus trichloride."

"What does all that mean, Holmes?" I asked.

"It is a powerful combination of chemicals that results in skin irritation, blindness, burning and – if inhaled – could produce water on the lungs."

"Tom Stevens!" I exclaimed, realising the link.

"Precisely," said Holmes.

"I didn't mean to kill those men," said the boy.

"Give us your name," said Holmes. "It would be the easiest thing in the world for the inspector to call upon University College and make enquiries as to any absent students. I suspect there would be only one."

"Edward Hughes," he said, casting his gaze to the floor.

"Well, Edward Hughes," said the inspector. "You are under arrest for the murder…"

"Not murder, Inspector," Holmes said, holding up a hand.

"If you undertake an inspection of the tunnelling equipment beneath Bloomsbury you will find it in an unusual state of cleanliness. Mr Hughes here returned to clean the chemical solution from the machinery as soon as he learned of the workers' deaths."

"I did," said Hughes in a small voice. "I wished to prevent any further harm…"

"So, manslaughter," said Inspector Pike.

"But why were you dressed as a mummy?" I asked.

"As had been ascertained by the German chemist, it was best to wear gauze to protect the eyes, nose and mouth when handling the chemical monstrosity he had concocted – no doubt using the chemicals and apparatus afforded you by the University laboratories."

Hughes nodded again. "I placed but a small amount on the digging mechanism. It was meant to incapacitate the men, not... kill them."

"Indeed," said Holmes. "But in the handling of noxious chemicals one must be more scientific in one's measurements than 'small amount'."

Hughes started weeping once more.

"That's the method," said the inspector. "What about the motive, Mr Holmes?"

"Mr Hughes here is a believer in socialism – probably his most cherished dream is of a utopian socialist society – hence a follower of the thinker Robert Owen, who was a staunch supporter of workers' rights and the idea of municipal ownership. With the building of the line suspended and the men injured it would appear that not only could private enterprise not deliver the railway in a timely and unhindered fashion, but that they also had a disregard for their workers' safety."

"Yet the arrow fell far from the target," said Inspector Pike, gazing dispassionately down at Edward Hughes. Then he ushered us from the cell, leaving the man to his guilt and his tears.

"I do feel for him, somewhat," I said as we stepped onto the Embankment once more, "I realise he has caused the death of his fellow man, but he was seeking a greater good, surely?"

"The ends can never justify the means, Watson," he said, looking at me with a clear and penetrating gaze. "We must battle that kind of thinking. For if that philosophy should triumph, then our humanity will have become as deeply buried as that infernal railway."

ABOUT THE AUTHOR

Richard Dinnick is a writer of scripts, novels and comics. He writes audio drama scripts for franchises such as Doctor Who, Stargate, Sherlock Holmes and Sapphire & Steel and the online phenomenon Moshi Monsters. He has also acted as script editor and assistant producer on a range of *Sherlock Holmes* audio dramas.

His first novel *Alien Adventures* was published by BBC Children's Books in 2010 and he has since gone on to write books and short stories for Penguin UK, The Black Library, Running Press and Snowbooks.

He has also written comic strips for IDW and BBC Magazines and his first original graphic novel will be published in 2013.

THE PENNYROYAL SOCIETY

BY KELLY HALE

Now pennyroyal, well, any girl can find that growing wild. And rue! Goodness, that's been used for ages. Hamlet's Ophelia knew all about rue, though it didn't do her much good in the end, poor thing. A spoonful of the seeds of Queen Anne's lace taken each morning will prevent a woman catching pregnant at all. Dittany, birthwort, willow bark, juniper, asafetida, angelica, tansy, filix fern. Some alone, some mixed with others. In pills or pessaries, douches or tinctures. Add a charm or recitation if you think it helps. Prayers to our Blessed Mother. Those never hurt a woman neither.

D octors were, in general, not sympathetic to women in these matters. Agnes knew this for a fact. They had all stood against her mother in court, priggish and self-righteous. She had little hope this one would be different, and he didn't prove her wrong. His mouth was set, features stern; the sort of piety that comes with the privilege of his gender and the smug certitude of those in his profession. Still, she could tell he hadn't spent much time on his knees in prayer, not like a woman with four little mouths to feed and another growing hungry in her belly.

No. Dr Watson was not a church-going man. Neither was the detective. But then, he did not pretend otherwise.

She cared not a whit what these men thought of her at any rate. She'd come here because of Millie. *For* Millie.

Mr Sherlock Holmes leaned forward, the better to aim his cleverness at her problem, she supposed. And indeed, his head led the charge, the rest of his body following after, all sharp angles and elbows. Fingers like little soldiers stood at attention beneath his chin.

"Was the entire group bound over and then released *en masse?*" he asked. No preambles or social niceties for him.

"The women with children at home were lectured at some length and then dismissed with only a warning," said Agnes, adding, "which was a kindness, I suppose."

"I'm certain the ladies' husbands appreciated the forbearance of the magistrate," Dr Watson said. Then muttered under his breath, "Though I cannot imagine what yours is thinking."

"Nor can I," she replied, "since he is no doubt sharing those thoughts with his mistress in Buenos Aires."

She regretted the outburst immediately. *Ah, of course,* his expression read, *that explains everything.* A sharp eye-dart from the detective and the doctor murmured an apology – of sorts.

Mr Holmes resumed his enquiry. "So, women with children at home were released. You and your friend were not."

"That's correct, sir, yes. I and several of the unmarried ladies were made to wait until after the magistrate had luncheon." She made no mention of the fact that they were all made to wait though they'd had no food or drink since before their arrests the previous day.

"And Miss Barnett was with the group at that time?"

"She was. After the magistrate heard our cases, I was bailed. The others were released on their own recognisance. Millie – Miss Barnett – agreed to hold my belongings while I was detained."

The detective sniffed at that, two little inhalations, like a dog after a particular scent. In some other circumstance Agnes might have laughed, it was so odd. "These belongings," he said. "Describe them in detail, please."

She folded her hands upon her lap, wondering how much detail he needed, how much she wanted to give. Even now, looking at the worn places in the fabric of the skirt she wore, how the pile of the fustian was compressed or bare enough in some parts to see the twill weave beneath, the little burn holes –

He had not mentioned a fee as yet.

"She had my jacket," Agnes began, "a russet-coloured wool, trimmed in brown plush with buttons covered in the same fabric. Quite plain save for a variety of pins upon the breast – slogan phrases from our cause, mostly. Grey kid gloves in one of the pockets. My hat – do you wish to know the style of it?" Most men were not well up on women's fashions, but he gave a terse nod. "Flowerpot, or three-storey hats you may have heard them called, in brown felt with a slightly crushed crown, a red silk band and cockade, and a turkey feather. I believe the hatpin was still in it – plain stick, cone-shaped end. Also, she held the Gladstone bag in which we'd carried the – the pamphlets and other items that had been confiscated. The bag was quite old and battered, brown leather with one broken buckle strap. Thankfully I had my pocketbook in hand so as to pay the bond or she might have had that with her as well."

"When did you come to realise Miss Barnett was missing?"

"Almost immediately. Or at least, I felt something was wrong as soon as I saw she was not outside with the rest of our group. I – I'd assumed she'd gone into the street to wait for me with the others. They'd assumed she'd stayed inside with me as a show of her support."

"You've not seen her since?"

Her throat constricted and she found she couldn't speak to answer. She shook her head and snatched at the handkerchief tucked into her cuff, mortified by her tears, angry that they were witness to it.

The gentlemen gave her a moment to compose herself. The doctor perhaps would have given her more than a moment, but Mr Holmes seemed to feel a moment was quite long enough, and he proceeded apace with a touch of impatience in his voice. "None of your associates recalls seeing her leave the premises. What of the police at the doors?"

"We asked, of course. The constables claimed not to have seen her go back inside either. We walked round the station, calling out to her, and even went as far as the hospital before returning. Miss Phelps convinced a few policemen to search for her inside."

"But they didn't find her," Dr Watson said.

"Do you think I would be here if they had?"

"Mrs Despain."

Her head snapped towards Mr Holmes, his voice and the calm, clipped manner in which he said her name cautioning her to civility. "Yes, well, they claimed they *had* searched for her, though I cannot be certain of it. They were not inclined to do us any favours, you understand. I then went to our rooms in Minerva Street −"

"The rooms you and Miss Barnett share?"

"Yes. The Pennyroyal Society keeps offices above a small jobs printer, and our rooms are there as well. But she hadn't returned to them. I went back out, enquiring after her, asking if anyone had seen a young woman meeting her description, but if anyone had, they were not forthcoming. I stayed out well past it being entirely safe, and when I returned I discovered our rooms had been ransacked."

"Was anything missing or stolen?"

"The culprits seemed more bent on wanton destruction."

"Wanton destruction is often used to cover up a search. They were looking for something."

"I − I don't know what it could have been. They destroyed anything of value…"

Whatever he saw in her hesitation must have prompted his next question. "Why were you the only one bailed, do you suppose?"

She fixed her eyes on the handkerchief in her lap, twisting and untwisting the delicate linen. "I − I'm not sure −"

"You were the only one charged with an actual crime. All the other ladies were issued warnings or charged with civil infractions. Yet I was given to understand you were not the only person handing out the prohibited materials. Nor did you organise the demonstration."

"I am the author of the information in the pamphlets."

Dr Watson made a sound suspiciously like "harrumph".

"I've seen the pamphlets." Holmes pressed on. "There is no author's name given for precisely that reason, so that no one person would have to bear the full burden of the law. Why would you confess?"

"I didn't. Perhaps I was charged because Mrs White wasn't there. She'd taken ill. I'm her… second-in-command."

The doctor added a derisive snort.

"*Watson*," Holmes warned, "enough. You've made your opinion quite clear."

"I don't think I have! Women with no medical training whatsoever are marching about the East End prescribing risky contraceptive concoctions and dangerous abortifacients. The poor would be better served – and safer, I might add – being schooled in the discipline of abstinence." He'd clearly given up any eschewals of propriety and spoke now as if there were not a woman in the room.

This suited her fine.

"Oh, abstinence," she replied. "Yes, quite right, because men of all stations in life are so very good at *that*. And who must bear the burden of this lack of restraint –"

"You cannot blame men alone for that lack of restraint, madam. Women of the lowest order are on offer twenty-four hours a day in some parts of this city –"

"I would challenge *you* to live on three shillings six pence a week doing intermittent slops work and still remain virtuous!"

A loud bang rattled cups and saucers and set the biscuits dancing on the plates. Startled to silence, both parties turned to the source of the sound, at which point Mr Holmes ceased pounding his fist on the table.

"We've gone off the rails. *A bit*," he said, looking pointedly at each in turn. He righted a cup, flicked a glance at the doctor. "I am somewhat surprised at the frank nature of this discourse, Watson. You tend to be more circumspect in front of a lady. I do hope you're not suggesting Mrs Despain is anything less than a lady?"

"Of course not!" Watson sputtered.

"Good, good. Her mission does not preclude her honour. I *myself* am wholly uninterested in reformist notions of social justice or the rights of the poor to practise family limitation. I am – and I hope you are with me in this, Mrs Despain – primarily interested in the disappearance of Millie Barnett." He gave her a tight smile possibly meant to reassure her, though rather cool for it. "However, the subject matter does bring a point to bear upon your situation, and perhaps to the circumstances of Miss Barnett's disappearance."

"Pray enlighten me," she told him, still seething.

"Is there a possibility you were singled out for harsher treatment because of your mother's notoriety?"

Ah, and there was the trap sprung and her foot caught. Prevarication would avail her nothing with this man, and there was no use in pretending ignorance. "I will not discuss my mother with you, Mr Holmes."

"Then I fail to see how I can be of assistance."

"Why?" Watson asked. "Who is her mother?"

"My mother can have little to do with this, surely?"

"Miss Barnett had *your* belongings in hand when she disappeared. If someone believed her to be you, well, considering the cause you have taken up, so similar to your mother's…"

"Who is her mother, then?"

"*Must* he be here during our *entire* consultation?"

Sherlock Holmes blinked, unmoved by plea or protest. "He has knowledge I lack."

Watson eyed his associate warily. "Do I now?"

"You are both a doctor and a married man and therefore have practical experience and medical expertise I do not in regards to the, er, *remedies* the Pennyroyal Society advocates and distributes in the East End."

It was Agnes's turn to scoff. "My mother had more understanding of nature's own remedies in her apron pocket than most doctors have in their entire heads."

"Yet your mother is in prison. The remedies in her apron pocket led to a woman's death."

"Maryanne Sallow's husband didn't want another child and he didn't want *her*. He gave her too much. He *killed* her. He should have gone to prison, not my mother!"

"So you claimed at her trial, though you could not provide proof of his intent, as I recall."

"Dear Lord!" Watson interjected. "Are we talking about Louisa Gillespie? Mrs Gillespie? Mother Lou, the baby-killer?"

* * *

Agnes fled the sitting room of 221b Baker Street with scarcely any recollection of what was said after the damning appellation. She was nearly at Aldersgate before she realised how far she'd walked fuelled entirely by outrage. And still she could not let go of it.

Her mother was not a baby-killer! Her mother had delivered more living infants to the poor women of Whitechapel and Bethnal Green than any doctor on any ward in any charity hospital *anywhere*. And unlike those doctors, she told women how to keep from having more or how to relieve themselves of the burden of another. Charlie Sallow had killed his wife with pills intended to expel a *dead* foetus. Pills made by Louisa Gillespie for that purpose. Her poor mother, so disheartened by the death of Maryanne, had said and done little in her own defence. Serving a ten-year sentence at Holloway even now while Charlie and his new wife kept a little sweet shop off Tottenham Court Road.

Her righteous anger was not lessened any by finding a rough man waiting in her lodgings. After squealing like a frightened little girl, she quickly realised who it was and wanted only to punch the ugly smirk off his face. "How did you get in here? Who let you come up?"

"Keep your voice down," he urged, though the sound of the printing press below would cover any noise they made. There was no one in the offices out front. He could murder her right now and her cries would not be heard above the din below, which he knew full well. "Anyway, no one saw me."

"Are you responsible for this?" Her arm swept a tense and jerky arc encompassing the wreckage.

"Ah, no. Beaten to it." His boots crunched the shards of broken glass, stirring up puffs of powdery chemicals and the scent of crushed herbs as he had a look around. He scratched at the back of his neck. "Blimey, someone has it in for you lady reformers, haven't they?"

But the Society offices had not been touched. This seemed a much more personal attack. Pointed, direct. She picked up the broken microscope from beneath the workbench with two hands and an unladylike grunt, cradling the weight of it in her arms as if it were a sleepy baby. "I would have thought you'd be busy deciphering code by now, Mr Murphy."

The grin was stuck to his face like a plaster but his jaw was working on an emotion altogether less cheery. She'd seen enough of the criminal element to know that, although he had the look down, he wasn't one himself, strictly speaking. She didn't know his real name, or his rank or title, and she didn't care to.

He cocked his head, sizing her up. "Hard to do without the encryption key you promised, Mrs Despain. Where is it?"

"What do you mean? Don't tell me you've lost it already?"

Mr Murphy sighed like a man who sorely missed the much simpler negotiations required of breaking heads with truncheons. "I'm only giving you this one warning, right? So if you have crossed us, it will not go well for you or your dear mother. She'll stand no chance of a commuted sentence nor even parole, should it be considered. And do believe me when I tell you I shall most happily send you to the same hell, if it comes to it."

"But – but I don't understand. Your men searched the bag, didn't they? At the station?"

"And they found nothing but those disgusting tracts you publish."

"No, no, it was – there was a playbill, a playbill from Beecher's Music Hall printed on that very press downstairs! The bag has a false bottom –"

His sudden intake of breath and the expression on his face told her everything. They'd missed the false bottom entirely.

Oh dear God. Millie!

"Millie still has it, my friend Millie, she has the bag!"

The man huffed out a sigh. "Well that's a sorry piece of luck. Damned sorry! Pardon my language."

"She's gone missing. You have to find her! You must begin a search immediately. You must –"

He pried her fingers from their twisting grasp on his lapels and shoved her away, not hard, but enough so that she stumbled back, off-balance, only righting herself in time to keep from falling onto the dangerous debris that littered the floor. Panting, chin thrust out, Agnes tried to keep her voice sure and her lip from trembling. "You think the Fenians are the only ones that plant bombs? You'll have more than just another riot on your hands if you don't find her."

"If they've not found her already," he said. "Mayhap they took her thinking she was you."

The words were a chilling echo of those uttered by Sherlock Holmes. "No," she said, and then again, as if repeating it could make it true.

"Not as well in with Hyndman and his revolutionary lads as you led us to believe, are you, Mrs Despain? Or maybe they know your friend *isn't* the mole in their midst, and they're hoping to draw you out and us after. Let me tell you now, we won't be doing that. I'm thinking we'll find it necessary to shut this operation down. We've got other moles in holes." The phrase amused him and he gave a little chuckle before pulling his cap low over his eyes and fastening up his jacket. Pushing past her, he headed towards the tiny bedroom under the eaves.

"You can't just leave!" she cried, rushing after him. "What about my friend? She's innocent, she knows nothing of this."

"Well, I'd be more concerned about my own welfare, were I you."

"You will offer me no protection, either?"

"We offered you what you asked for, if you succeeded, and you wanted only the one thing."

Yes. *Then* she'd only wanted her mother's freedom. Now…

"It's hardly my fault your men are idiots!" She waded through feathers, straw, piles of cotton wadding, to grab his arm and make him stay, make him do something! He jerked out of her grasp. "I did everything asked of me," she said, forcing the next word out between her teeth. "Please."

He paused, one leg dangling out the window as he considered. "I suppose if you can recover that cipher-key you might save your friend and see your dear old mum back home. I hope you can. I hear the poor woman's taken a turn for the worse." He smiled. "We will, of course, disavow all knowledge of you, should you be caught."

He touched the bill of his cap in farewell and then was gone. She heard the scrape of his boots on the ledge and a thud as he dropped to the narrow passage below.

* * *

Standing amidst the ruins of Millie's little makeshift laboratory was a crushing reminder of all Agnes had lost in the past two days. Poor Millie had been building her lab long before Agnes met her, but once they *had* met and knew their interests and missions overlapped, much of their combined income had gone into acquiring those items necessary to Millie's research. Whatever small profit was made from selling the herbals (and Millie never knew that the bulk of this profit came from women employed in certain houses in the Mile End Road and elsewhere) went to furnish the lab. They had a tincture press, distillation apparatus, two Bunsen burners, one naturalist's microscope and one binocular microscope, beakers, retorts, measuring cylinders, crucibles, an autoclave, droppers, pipettes, spirit jars, bottles of solvents and packets of chemicals, as well as hundreds of apothecary jars filled with roots, bark, leaves and fungi.

All of it gone now, destroyed. This destruction, utter and absolute, shocked Agnes to her core. So vicious. So *personal*. Not only the lab equipment smashed but also the tea things and the kettle, the soup pot, and the chamber pot. There wasn't a stitch of clothing left that hadn't been ripped, slashed or ground into the broken glass with a large boot. The bed was ruined as well, the ticking violently shredded, wadding strewn about and, insult to injury, the culprits had soiled it with urine – their own, she suspected.

And now, though she'd fully intended to make a dent in the mess with a broom and dustpan, the heavy weight of her loss bore down upon her. The despair at her predicament, and her dread over the fate of her dearest, most stalwart friend conspired to deplete her and, finally, to defeat her. She had energy only enough to clear a bare place on the floor before lying down, her body curled around the broken microscope. Shattered and hopeless, she began to weep.

Sometime later, she awakened. It was pitch dark. The printing press on the main floor had shut down for the night and though it always groaned a bit as the machinery settled, the sounds that awakened her were the subtle, furtive movements of someone in the offices out front, quietly opening desk drawers and shuffling papers about.

She sat up slowly, straining to listen, heart thundering beneath her breastbone. Her limbs screamed at her to run, run, for God's sake, run! Her leg jerked unbidden, boot colliding with bits of glass.

The intruder stilled. She knew he was listening just as hard as she was, and she pressed both hands over her mouth to stifle the ragged sounds of her own breathing. The inner door to the office squeaked open and stealthy footfalls traversed the narrow passage towards her. A wavering, unsteady light showed beneath the door, creeping farther into the room with each creak of the floorboards. The door handle moved, dropping slowly.

Agnes flung herself against the door. Mad, crazed with terror, she screamed and raged and shouted, threatening murder and damnation, pounding her fists on the wood, kicking at it as if she could kick through it to the wicked man on the other side. Finally, breathless, panting, hands aching, scraped and bloodied, she turned her back to the door and let her body slide to the floor. "There's nothing left, you cur," she sobbed, her voice raw, "you've taken everything."

A long pause, then –

"Mrs Despain?"

Sherlock Holmes fetched her brandy, barley water and a meat pie from the Black Penny Tavern. He lighted the lamp in the tiny offices and bade her refresh herself while he took his own lamp in to examine her rooms and search for evidence. Drained and numb, she had little enthusiasm for anything, let alone a greasy meat pie from the Black Penny. But the barley water soothed her throat and, after a few minutes, the brandy soothed her nerves. The ache in her hands and wrists from hitting the door dulled with each swallow.

Half an hour at least had passed before he returned with a large notebook in hand. She gasped at the sight of it, seeing the worn and curled edges, the card cover stained with tea and the odd solvent – exactly as Millie had left it. Before she could ask he said, "It most likely fell behind the workbench before the destruction began. Had the culprits known of its existence, it would not have been spared."

"Do you think Millie's laboratory was the target?" Very few people even knew of it, and if it was the target, why lay waste to everything else?

He placed the notebook carefully on the desk, eyes fixed upon it, his expression undecipherable. After a moment, he emitted a sound of self-admonishment and laid his hand upon the book, giving it an oddly affectionate sort of pat. "There are very... unusual formulas written in this book."

Agnes took another sip of brandy, well, more of a gulp really, uncertain how to proceed or how much to share. One needed to tread carefully. Men often felt proprietary in matters of science, she'd noticed. "Millie has been trying to isolate the compounds which are similar or common to each of my mother's herbal remedies. She hopes to formulate something with a more precise dosage and certainty of outcome. Or so she has explained it to me. I'm not well versed in chemistry."

"Not many women are. Still, I had wondered when you came to me. The skirt of your frock shows chemical burns, a scattering of tiny holes at the knee and hem, yet you've no marks on your hands." He held out his own hands and she could see the tiny scars on the backs of them, much like Millie's own.

"So you are also a chemist? You understand what she was attempting?"

"It's − it's quite... bold." He avoided meeting her gaze and she wondered at that.

"My mother says nature provides solutions and medicines for all ills." He gave a distracted noncommittal grunt, having returned to flipping the pages of the book. She watched him, saying, "Most of my mother's remedies have been used for thousands of years."

"I know. Dioscorides wrote about them. Pliny as well." He glanced up at her sharply. "Did Miss Barnett have access to a copy of the *Tractatus de vertutibus herbarum* by any chance?"

"Oh goodness, I've no idea. Probably. She has loads of old books like that. Latin, Greek, German − oh Lord! Her books!"

"Really, Mrs Despain. Have you only just realised those are missing?" He sounded horribly disappointed. "I did ask, if you'll recall."

"I wasn't thinking clearly at the time."

"Yet you were cunning enough to evade certain questions."

"I think my reasons for not wishing to discuss my mother were well founded, given the reaction of your associate."

"I asked why you alone were charged with a crime. I offered a possible reason having to do with your mother. It was not, however, the actual reason, was it? So I'll ask you again. Why were you charged and then separated from the other women?"

A breath shuddered out of her. "They thought I – they must have believed I still had something they wanted."

"Who? The CID? The Special Branch?"

She rocked forward with a low moan, covering her face with her hands as fresh tears overwhelmed her.

"You must trust me now, Mrs Despain."

"No," she cried, shaking her head, "no, I mustn't. I can't! Millie's in terrible danger because of me. I cannot put you in danger as well."

He chuckled softly. "Well, though I appreciate your concern, I can assure you I'm quite able to take care of myself in that regard. In fact, I believe I am much better equipped to handle the danger –" Her head shot up at that and he growled in frustration. "Oh, for heaven's sake, don't look at me so. It is not an insult to your self-sufficiency. Look around you! You're in well over your head. Surely you realise that?"

In the next instant he was crouched before her chair, hands grasping the seat on either side of her. She could feel the tension vibrating in his arms as he urged her to look him in the eye. Finally, she did.

"I can help you, Mrs Despain. Let me help you."

Her husband, Mr Henry Prosper Augustus Despain, was a proud Marxist. He had been a member of the SDF and then of the Socialist League even before he met the Argentine woman and abandoned his wife to start a revolution elsewhere. Agnes suspected this urge to fight for the workers in another land also had something to do with the Argentine woman being all of nineteen and she, his wife, thirty-eight. Still, his friends in the movement were her friends as well, and she went to their meetings, edited columns for their publications and encouraged the small female membership to join her mission to free poor women of the burden of too many children. But she would never have come to the attention of the Metropolitan Police Commissioner or the CID were it not for her mother's trial and the nuisance she'd made of herself during it, demanding investigations, and presenting evidence they chose to ignore.

"My mother had been in prison for six months when they first approached me. They said they could get her sentence commuted if I would agree to collect and pass along information on certain members of certain groups. This was early last year, before I'd met Millie. I never had much to offer them, you understand. The Socialist League is not particularly secretive, and the SDF has so much infighting amongst the various branches that nothing whatsoever gets done – unless there's a riot, of course. It wasn't until the anarchists started up, with their targeted acts of sedition, that I was informed I must deliver something substantial or the deal was off."

"And you did," Holmes said. "The Gladstone bag?"

She nodded miserably. "It had a false bottom. There was an encryption key hidden within the text on a playbill. But the police missed it completely when they searched the bag." He made a rude sound indicating what he thought of the police. She raised her head from the pillow of her dejection – folded arms on the desk – and said, "There are hardened men amongst the anarchist factions, Mr Holmes. They wouldn't hesitate to harm a woman if they thought their cause betrayed."

"Hhmm," was his only comment. He was examining an object held between his fingers, turning it back and forth in the low light of the desk lamp. It appeared to be a man's cufflink. How he had found such a thing in all that wreckage and by the light of a single lamp she could only imagine. He pushed it across the desk to her, his expression impassive, though she suspected he was keen to get her reaction. She took it in hand, peering close with the aid of the lamp. It was the sort of cufflink with the long stud attached. The cuff button itself was a large rectangular shape with a lithograph of an estate house or great hall set under glass, and framed in bronze. She handed it back. "Nothing I recognise."

"Yet, oddly enough, I *do*." He gazed at her thoughtfully. "I had no opportunity to ask before, but did you attempt to contact Miss Barnett's family?"

She shook her head. "Millie never spoke of her relations. She did not want to speak of them, and put me off if ever I tried to bring it up."

"This," he said, holding the cufflink up to the light, "is an image of St John's College, Cambridge. A don of that college is a renowned chemist and was one of my teachers when I attended university. In fact, I believe Miss Barnett and I may have had the same teacher of chemistry."

"Millie did not attend university, Mr Holmes!"

"Oh, she didn't have to." Before Agnes had time to react to that statement he said, "Whoever destroyed Millie's laboratory, they were very careful of the caustic chemicals. I found evidence that most of those were packed and removed along with the books before the real destruction even commenced."

"So I should be grateful they didn't do more damage?"

"You should be grateful your friend is *not* in the clutches of anarchists," he said, then muttered under his breath, "though perhaps no better off."

"What do you mean?"

"Family, Mrs Despain. Family." He bounced the cufflink in the palm of his hand a few times before tossing it high into the air and catching it neatly behind his back. Seeming thoroughly pleased with himself, he'd slipped it into his pocket when Millie's notebook caught his eye again. His fingers flexed and curled into his palms. She pulled the book towards her across the desk.

"So… you think her family found her and took her away?" She should have felt some relief at the idea, but when she thought of all the equipment, how much it had cost, and the hostility behind its systematic destruction, she was filled with a sick dread.

"It is one possibility," he said as he gathered up his jacket and made to leave. "Have you another place to stay? It will be difficult to find a reputable hotel or lodging house at this hour but I can arrange for you to stay with Dr Watson and his wife –"

"What? No! I don't even like the man. I could hardly impose upon his wife." She picked at a loose thread on her skirt. "I want to be here in case she returns. Anyway, I've slept in this chair before." She took an old lap rug from a pile on top of the letter cabinet, unfurled it and demonstrated how cosy it would be.

He hesitated a moment, then nodded. "I shall be in contact as soon as I'm able."

"Mr Holmes," she called after him. "I – I'm afraid I shan't be able to pay for your services for some time, but if you keep a tally of your expenses –"

"Good night, Mrs Despain."

Two days passed with no word. On the morning of the third day, as she was preparing to send him a telegram, Mr Holmes came to call. He was dressed as a gentleman instead of a thief, but with a certain funereal air that made her heart sink. He had the Gladstone bag.

He placed it on the desk. She stared at it, tears prickling the back of her eyes. "You didn't find Millie."

"The situation is rather complicated. May I sit?" he asked. She didn't answer, looking away from him as if not seeing him would make whatever news he had easier to bear. He pulled out the chair opposite her and sat anyway. "I have found her. She's alive, though the circumstances are not pleasant."

"Oh God. She's not been injured or interfered with, has she?"

"No, no. Nothing like that. My suspicions were confirmed. It was her family that took her."

"Against her will!"

"Yes. So it would seem. Dr Esau Barnett of St John's College is Millie's father. He sent her brothers to collect her from the police station discreetly and it was they who destroyed her laboratory. I'm very sorry, but as she is unmarried she is legally in his charge. The books Millie had in your lodgings were taken from his private library. *Stolen* by her. One, the *herbarum*, was printed in Venice in 1499. It's worth a small fortune."

"But he wouldn't send his own daughter to prison, would he?"

"No. He has sent his own daughter to the District Lunatic Asylum in Cambridge instead."

She sat with that for a moment, then jerked open a drawer next to her knee. Millie's notebook was slapped onto the desk. "Is this insane? You called it unusual, but there was reservation in your tone, a touch of unease. I am not a chemist. Was it mad, what she wrote here? What she was trying to do?"

"Not mad. No, not at all. Bold. Ambitious. A bit… unnerving." He shook his head, embarrassed. "That tone you heard from me? The sin of envy, I'm afraid."

She pulled the Gladstone across to her.

"It's not there," he said quickly, even as she fiddled the catch to reveal the empty compartment hidden in the bottom.

"Are you about to betray me, Mr Holmes?"

He huffed a sigh. "I've not taken you for a fool yet, Mrs Despain. Don't make me start now."

"Then what have you done with it?"

"It's in a safe place."

"What do you *intend* to do with it?"

"Negotiate a deal far better than you ever would have got from the CID, trust me." His eyes shifted sideways, avoiding her gaze. "You have no idea what you had there, Mrs Despain, and *they* would have even less." He reached across the desk to grasp her hand. "*Trust me*," he repeated, and this time his grey eyes locked to hers.

The following Monday she received a letter delivered by hand:

Mrs Despain,

Enclosed you will find a ticket to Liverpool, and three more for passage to America on the RMS *Umbria*. Money has been wired to the Cunard Line shipping office and will be held in your name. It is not a great sum, but will provide enough for the journey and for moderate lodgings for you and your companions upon your arrival in New York. Your mother will join you shortly before departure, and, if all goes according to plan, a young lady by the name of Miss Ada Mercy will join you as well. If she does not arrive in time for the scheduled departure then I will have failed in securing her release. It is, nonetheless, vital that you depart as scheduled with or without her. This is a matter of your own safety and that of the security of the British Empire.

I urge you to make haste upon receiving this letter, and if you would be so good as to dispose of it after reading it. The stove in your office would suffice.

Yours,
Sherlock Holmes.

"Have you seen this? Did you have something to do with it?" Watson asked, sweeping into the sitting room and pointing at a column of print in the newspaper. He looked to have come all the way from Kensington in order to shake said newspaper in the face of the indolent man reclining on the sofa.

"Possibly," the detective said, "though hard to tell as I have no idea what it is you're pointing at there."

"Charles Sallow has confessed to the murder of his first wife! Apparently new evidence has come to light –"

"Oh. Yes. That. I may have had a hand in it." The tone was offhand and dismissive, but his lazy, self-satisfied smirk gave him away.

"Astonishing."

Holmes snorted. "Hardly. Much of the evidence was still in a cardboard box in Scotland Yard. I merely… assisted in obtaining a confession is all."

Watson sat and poured himself a cup of tea. "Ah, well then, Mrs Gillespie will be out of prison soon and back to her old tricks."

"She's long gone, Watson. You needn't worry about her doing unsavoury business in our fair city."

"Good," he said.

Mrs Hudson's girl rapped on the door just then, but didn't wait for permission before coming in and – rather insolently, Watson thought – dropping the morning post on the floor next to the sofa. Holmes rolled over and pawed through it. Extracting a packet covered with postmarks, he rolled onto his back again, squeezing and feeling and prodding the thing before tearing it open with a whoop of glee.

"What have you there?" Watson asked. The packet's contents looked to be a rather ordinary book, curled and worn about the edges, hardly worthy of such a display.

"Treasure!" Holmes exclaimed. He leapt from the sofa full of renewed vigour. Watson, having not lived with the man on a daily basis for a time, had forgotten the sorts of extremes his moods could take from one moment to the next. And yet he rarely saw this one, even then. This was joy.

"Really?" he said, baffled that the cause of it could be a tattered notebook. "It doesn't look like much."

"This?" Holmes cried, brandishing the book aloft like a trophy. "*This*," he repeated, carrying it to the table upon which his new Henry Crouch binocular microscope sat regally. "This, my friend, is payment in full."

He rubbed his hands together with a maniacal grin.

ABOUT THE AUTHOR

Kelly Hale lives in a crazy little place called Stumptown, America, where the streets are paved with espresso beans and the rubbish recycles itself. Her short stories have been featured in several print anthologies and a couple of online literary journals, and her novel, *Erasing Sherlock*, won a literary prize way back in the year 2000. There was a giant novelty check involved.

THE PERSIAN SLIPPER

BY STEVE LOCKLEY

For as long as I have known my friend Sherlock Holmes, he has kept his tobacco in the toe of a Persian slipper on the mantelpiece of 221b Baker Street. It is not the only one of his possessions that has intrigued me over the years, but the idiosyncratic use of this object as a receptacle for his tobacco made me more curious about this than anything else he owned. I asked him how he came by it once but all he said was, "I was given it, but that is not the question you should be asking." I fell silent after that as we both enjoyed time with our pipes, still none the wiser but with an extra puzzle to ponder over. Why should that be the wrong question? And if it was, what was the correct one? It was a long time before I learned more about the slipper and he finally told me what question I should have asked.

Holmes was standing at the window and looking out into the street while I read the morning edition. I found little of interest in there but knew that Holmes would find something out of the ordinary, even if he disregarded the major issues of world affairs. He had been looking out of the window every fifteen minutes, as if he was unable to settle to anything.

"I believe we are about to have a visitor," he announced eventually, only moments before we heard the front doorbell ring. He strode through the door to the landing and shouted downstairs. "Send him straight up, Mrs Hudson!"

I folded my newspaper to the sound of footsteps on the stairs while Holmes returned to the centre of the room, pacing in time with the rhythm until at last the man stepped through the open door.

"Mr Holmes?" the man asked tentatively.

"Please come in," my friend replied, stepping forward to shake our visitor's hand, a warmer welcome than I had seen him give most of our guests. Holmes indicated a vacant chair, but as the man began to speak Holmes raised a hand to silence him. I was prepared for one of Holmes' tricks of deduction but the young man seemed a little uneasy at the detective's manner.

Holmes slumped into a chair and sat in silence as he examined our visitor. The man ran his fingers around the rim of his hat which he held in front of him.

"The question is —" said Holmes, at last, as Mrs Hudson bustled into the room with a tray and interrupted him before he could say what the question was. "I didn't ask for tea, Mrs Hudson," he snapped a little too sharply to our housekeeper

"You don't ask me to do a great number of things, Mr Holmes, but if I didn't do them this room would be an even bigger mess than it is now."

Holmes said nothing, but the smile that played across his lips was forced. It was true that she did a great deal that Holmes took for granted, rarely with any show of thanks, and I knew that it would be hard to find anyone as tolerant of his behaviour as she was. She clattered the teacups as she placed the tray down and left the room without another word.

"The question is," Holmes repeated, as if there had been no interruption, "Are you Yousef or Iqbal?"

"Then you remember me?" the young man said, placing his hat on the arm of the chair.

"I remember two small boys who constantly demanded their father's attention. You have changed a great deal."

"I was only seven or eight years old when I saw you last. I can't say that I remember you, but my father has spoken of you many times."

"Six. You were only six."

"Ah, then my brother Yousef was correct."

I looked to Holmes in the hope that he would shed some light on the exchange, but he avoided my gaze.

"And your father is gravely ill."

"How did you know?" The young man could not contain his surprise, but I knew that Holmes would explain his reasoning.

"Had your father been well he would have come to see me himself. If he were dead then the signs of mourning would have hung heavy on you. There is enough concern for you to call for my assistance, so please tell me how I can help."

"As you have rightly guessed, Mr Holmes," the man began, though he looked startled at Holmes' snort at his choice of words, "my father is severely ill and needs you. He has refused the assistance of any doctor and only speaks your name. He raves much of the time, claiming that the djinn has returned and that only you can help. It is nonsense, I know, and I fear that he is losing a grip on his mind, Mr Holmes, but the least I can do for him is to try and follow his wishes. Please forgive me."

"There is nothing to forgive," said Holmes. "Do you still have the shop at the same address in Cheapside?"

"We have been there since we arrived in England, Mr Holmes. My father is a skilled man but he has never earned enough to secure us better premises. I have other errands to run in the city and will not return home until later today, but my brother is with him and will be expecting you if you decide to call."

"Of course we will, my dear boy. I hope you don't mind if I bring Dr Watson along with me?"

"Not at all. I am sure that my father will welcome any friend of yours, Mr Holmes."

The man left despite my offer of tea and, rather than risk the wrath of Mrs Hudson, I poured Holmes and myself a cup, but he was in no mood for refreshment. "There is not a moment to lose, Watson. A man's life might be at stake."

"As long as you promise to fill me in on the way," I said, taking a single swallow of the still-warm liquid.

"Of course, Watson, but remember when you once asked me about the slipper I keep my tobacco in?"

"Of course. You said that I asked the wrong question."

"Hah! And have you worked out what the question should have been?"

I shook my head and waited for him to enlighten me.

"The question you should have asked was not who gave it to me, but what became of the other slipper." He then fell silent once more until we were in a cab and heading towards Cheapside.

"Did you recognise him?" I asked.

"On the contrary," Holmes said, without turning his gaze from the outside world that passed by the window. "I had no idea who he was until a few moments after he came into the room, and even then I did not know which of the brothers he was."

"Well it sounds as if it is a long time since you saw him."

"Half a lifetime ago, Watson, I saved Iqbal's father's life and he gave me a gift. A pair of Persian slippers he had made with his own hands."

I waited for a moment, desperately wanting to know more but reluctant to force the issue. My friend was silent, though, and I knew that I would have to tease the information out of him. "So what became of the other slipper?" I asked eventually.

Holmes turned towards me and I knew he had been waiting for me to ask the question, even though he had already given it to me. "I gave it back to him and told him that if he ever needed my help, all he would need to do was send it to me and no matter where I was, no matter what I was doing, I would drop everything and go to his assistance. He did not realise it but by asking for my help he had saved me from the Black Dog that haunts me. It may have been a little fanciful, but at the time it seemed the right thing to do."

"Then why didn't the young man bring it with him?"

"Oh but he did, Watson. It was in his pocket. Did you not see the bulge in his coat? When you have held an object as often as I have held that slipper you would be able to identify its brother in the dark. His expression changed when he saw my own hanging from the mantelpiece, and that more than anything convinced me of who he was."

"Then you had no idea…"

"I knew when I shook his hand that he was a leatherworker. The calluses on his hands are different, he stoops at the shoulders from bending over his work and there was the slight odour of the tannery about him. His features marked him out as a man from the Levant but his accent belonged to someone who had been raised in this country – though he spends much of his time with someone who was not. When he glanced at the slipper and I saw the bulge in his pocket I knew that it had to be one of the boys now fully grown."

"But there were no clues as to which one it might be?" I tried to be flippant.

"They are identical twins, Watson."

He said it in a matter-of-fact way, but I knew that he was pointing out the folly of my attempt to find any shortcomings in his reasoning.

The shop was set into a terrace of houses, with the window of the front room given over to a display of gloves and belts that the residents of that district were never likely to be able to afford – and yet it was clear that the business had been there for many years. A bell rang as Holmes pushed the door open and led the way inside. Three benches were pressed close together in one small room, and while there was work in differing states of completion, there was no one being industrious at that moment.

"I'll be there in a moment," a voice called from up a narrow flight of stairs. Holmes said nothing, but looked around the room as if reminding himself of how things had once been, looking for changes or things that had remained the same. Eventually the sound of heavy-soled shoes came clattering down the staircase. The man that emerged into the room was as alike the one who visited Baker Street as two peas in a pod. It was hard to believe that it was not the same man.

"Yousef," Holmes said as the man looked at us.

"That's right." It took him a moment to realise who my friend was, but then he shook his hand warmly.

"My friend, Dr Watson."

The man nodded in acknowledgement and we exchanged the

briefest of handshakes. I tried to identify the calluses that Holmes had referred to, but to me they felt the same as any other working man. "My father won't see a doctor, I am afraid."

"But he will see me, or you would not have sent for me."

"Of course, Mr Holmes. Perhaps you can get him to open the door. I've just been up to see if he wants anything but found his door locked."

"Does he usually lock his door?"

"He has started to recently. He seems to be afraid of something, but we cannot understand what."

"Then take me to him, and Dr Watson will follow. We need not alarm him any more than absolutely necessary."

He led the way up the narrow staircase to the upper floor. What little light there was came from a window on the landing, but even that was enough to reveal the peeling wallpaper and the air of neglect. This was a place where almost every waking moment was devoted to working and eating with little time for anything else. There had been no mention of a wife or mother and I drew the conclusion that there had been no feminine presence in the house for a very long time. This was the home of a man who had raised two sons on his own.

We turned left at the top of the stairs and I held back as Yousef tapped on the bedroom door. "Father? You have a visitor. Mr Holmes has come to see you."

There was no response.

"Is there another key?" Holmes asked, trying the door handle himself to no avail. The young man shook his head and Holmes eased him to one side. He tested the strength of the door with a push of his shoulder and then, despite the young man's protestation, he gave a single hard kick at the lock. To the sound of splintering wood the door gave up all resistance and swung inwards.

"Watson, quickly," Holmes said, and stood to one side so that I could see the figure of a frail old man dressed only in a nightshirt, lying half in and half out of the bed.

I pushed past Yousef to get to his father, but even before I reached him and despite the meagre light that crept through the thin curtains, I could see that we were too late. I had seen the lightness of skin around the face, the tightening of muscles to create the rictus grin on his mouth; it left a man with the look of abject terror that would be enough to haunt anyone's nightmares. I searched for a pulse even though I needed no confirmation that the poor man's soul was no longer in this world.

"I'm sorry," I said. It was the platitude that sprung to the lips far too easily. "It was probably his heart."

Holmes stood over the corpse, but his eyes were not focused on it; they darted across the scene, looking for something.

"If there is nothing you can do for him then perhaps it is my turn." Holmes ushered me out of the room and I urged Yousef to follow. "He wanted my help and I will try to give it."

Yousef reluctantly led the way back down the stairs and into a tiny kitchen at the rear of the house. He started to busy himself with making tea, but it was only so that he had something to do. We talked about nothing in particular while we waited for Holmes. There were questions I wanted to ask but I did not want my friend to have to repeat them when he had finished looking for whatever had caught his attention. We did not have to wait long for the sound of him returning down the stairs.

"Had your father been ill for long?" Holmes asked as he joined us.

"A few weeks," the young man replied. "His health deteriorated gradually at first, but he became worse in the last few days."

"Your brother said that he had been talking about a djinn."

"He talked about a lot of things, but he did say that his sleep was often broken by nightmares."

"Has you father had any visitors recently, people you did not know?"

"There are always tradesmen calling to see us."

"But have any of them gone upstairs? To your father's bedroom?"

"Of course not, why would they?"

"Why indeed," said Holmes.

"Iqbal said that he was angry after a man came to the shop, but that was nothing new. The man was Greek and that was cause enough for my father to lose his temper."

Enmity between Turks and Greeks came as no surprise to me and immediately put me on my guard. But why would Holmes want to know if someone had been up to the old man's room?

"What did the Greek want?"

"I wasn't here, but Iqbal said he was selling something from door to door. Candles, I think."

"Candles?"

"Or matches. Something like that."

"Did your father buy anything from him?"

"Of course not. He did well to stay inside the shop as long as he did."

"Watson, perhaps you could help Yousef with the practicalities and I will see you on your return to Baker Street."

As he was about to leave, Iqbal returned, but Holmes slipped away without another word, leaving me to witness the exchange of bad news between one brother and the other.

I entered our rooms in Baker Street to the odour of chemicals and tobacco smoke. "Ah, Watson, sorry I had to leave you to deal with the practicalities but there was a matter that needed my attention."

"More important than offering comfort to the sons of an old friend?"

He ignored the comment and examined a candle he had secured with molten wax to one of Mrs Hudson's best saucers, then checked his pocket watch. As the flame flickered he crossed to the windows and drew the curtains closed in a single fluid motion.

"What are we waiting for?"

"Just a moment," Holmes said, delighting in the spectacle he was about to unleash. The flame changed colour for an instant and an explosion of hues filled the room. I stepped back in surprise, almost stumbling into one of the chairs, as the colour bloomed and the shape changed before disappearing as quickly as it had burst into life. Holmes wet his finger and thumb and snuffed out the remaining glow of the wick with the slightest of hisses.

"What was that?"

"Nothing that would be difficult to obtain and easy enough to work into a candle, so that the time of release could be controlled.

Were you not a little surprised that the bedroom curtains were closed during the day and a candle was burning in the night stick?"

"I have to confess that I did not notice."

"Of course you didn't, Watson, you were concentrating on your patient. This was the djinn that my old friend saw."

"*Timeo Danaos et dona ferentes*," I said, inspecting the candle a little closer, hoping that it was not about to explode into life again. Holmes said nothing and I could see that I had stumbled upon one of the gaps in his knowledge, but he was unwilling to acknowledge it.

"Beware of Greeks bearing gifts," I said. "It's Virgil, from *The Aeneid*."

"I know, Watson. My grasp of the classics may be limited but even I am familiar with that particular piece of Latin. I just could not understand why you chose to quote it."

"I had assumed that the candles came from the Greek salesman who visited the shop."

"Of course you did. And that was what we were meant to think, my friend."

"You already have the solution to this puzzle?" I was astounded, as I so often was.

"Almost, though I have one question left that needs to be answered."

"And what is that?"

"Why?"

"But who? Isn't that more important?"

"Not at all, Watson. I've known the answer to that particular question for some time."

By the time we returned to the tiny shop the body of the old man had been dressed and laid out on the bed ready for the undertaker. I have seen enough death in my time to be able to separate the idea of the person that had lived and died and the body that is left behind, but that did not stop it feeling strange when Holmes insisted on re-examining the room as if the body was not there.

He crouched at the door, brushing aside some of the splinters caused when he had kicked it open, and ran a finger across the brass escutcheon that protected and defined the keyhole. He perched on the edge of the bed and the body shifted slightly as he put his weight on the mattress. One of the twins gave a sudden intake of breath, though I was not sure which one. Holmes stared at a patch of wallpaper and tilted his head to one side to mimic the view the man might have had while lying in his bed.

The two brothers stood in the doorway as Holmes worked, though neither of them seemed comfortable with what they were seeing. At length Holmes appeared to discover what he was looking for and rose from the bed. He reached into his pocket and produced a key which he handed to me.

"I took the liberty of picking this up earlier. This is the key that was on the inside of the lock, but remember how easily it fell to the ground when we forced the door open? Was that likely to happen if it had only recently been turned to lock the door? Wouldn't it have been left in place ready to unlock the door again? Try it."

I slipped the key into the lock and tried to turn it, but the mechanism did not budge. "It won't work."

"Of course not. It's the wrong key," Holmes said.

"But it was in the door."

"Naturally. It was there to make us think that the door had been locked from the inside. A thread had been looped around this to pull it into the hole from the outside after the door had been locked."

"Is that even possible?" I asked, staring at the key which I had withdrawn from the lock.

"Evidently. There are even some fragments of the thread caught in the lock if you look carefully enough."

"Then there is no doubt that it is murder?"

"Of course not. And it was obvious from the start who it was and why I was called upon on the very day the crime was committed."

I heard the bell ring to signal the opening of the shop door, followed by the sound of several pairs of feet entering.

"I'll go," said Iqbal.

"There really is no need," said Holmes. "I told Inspector Lestrade to come straight up."

I said nothing. Holmes would never alert the police unless he was sure that the criminal could be delivered directly into their custody or needed the additional manpower his men could supply.

"Inspector?" asked Yousef. "What is this all about?"

"I'm afraid that your father was murdered."

"Murdered? Who by?"

"The Greek!" said Iqbal. "It had to be that damned Greek."

"There was no Greek salesman," Holmes said. "That was just to set us off on the wrong track if I discovered that this was murder rather than death by natural causes."

"But Iqbal saw him. He said he had to throw him out."

"Of course he did. But did anyone else see him? I asked some of the neighbouring shops and none of them received a visit from a Greek, but they did buy candles from a man who was selling from door to door. Your father once had an enemy who was Greek, who I helped deliver into the hands of the police, and it suited your purposes to have a mysterious stranger who could be held responsible for initiating your father's death."

All eyes were on Iqbal but this still did not make sense to me. Why would Iqbal want to kill his father? Then I realised that this was exactly the question that Holmes wanted the answer to himself.

Yousef could clearly not believe what he was hearing. It was hard enough for him to take in the fact that his father had been murdered.

"If Mr Holmes is convinced that you killed your father then I am sure he can prove it. He would not make allegations without evidence to support his claims," said Lestrade.

"You have nothing on me," Iqbal said, as Lestrade took hold of his arm and eased him into the grasp of one of his constables.

"On the contrary. Why did you come to me and talk about how your father had met me many years ago? You reminded me of a debt I owed him, and yet your brother did not seem to have the same recollection. Only you met the supposed Greek salesman, who not even your neighbours saw. But the most telling evidence remains on your sleeve."

Iqbal glanced at the cuff of his jacket and I caught sight of a discoloured patch in the cloth.

"When you came to Baker Street I detected a slight waxiness when I shook your hand, then I saw the patch on your jacket. While I had no idea of what it signified to begin with, it puzzled me. Once there was mention of an argument with a door-to-door salesman I knew that it was important. Claiming that the salesman was Greek was bound to raise my concerns; after all it was a Greek man that had threatened your father's life when I first met him."

"He rarely spoke of him," Yousef said, interrupting Holmes. "The Greek man. Who was he?"

Holmes paused for a moment. It was clear that he knew the answer but seemed to be considering whether he would reveal the information. "His name was Andreas Palandrou. He was your mother's brother. He was convinced that your father was responsible for your mother's death by stealing her away from her family and came looking for him. He planned to kill your father and take you both back to Greece with him."

"I had no idea," said Yousef. "He only told me that he had met you when Dr Watson's stories began to appear."

"He gave me this," Holmes said, producing the slipper from his pocket and handing it to the young man while his brother struggled in the arms of the police officer.

"My father has one like this tucked away in a drawer somewhere. I always thought it strange that he should keep an odd one. Perhaps it was to remind him of the kind of work he used to be able to do. Now we make gloves, but at least that requires more skill than the kind of work my brother would have us do," said Yousef, turning the slipper over in his hands.

"And what would that be?" Holmes asked.

"Knee pads for miners and back protectors for coal delivery men. Leatherwork for industry."

"And is there much demand for those items?" Holmes had never seemed that interested in the day-to-day activities of manufacturing before, but he clearly knew that this was important to the brothers.

"I have orders that would earn in six months what we normally make in three years," said Iqbal. "But my father would not entertain the idea. He was afraid of risk. We would have to expand into bigger premises, but the business would be there for us for a long time. We would not have to work as hard or live from hand to mouth."

"I doubt that very much," said Holmes. "This was a man who risked everything for the woman he loved, for the two sons who were everything to him and for a young man he barely knew. If he was afraid of anything, it was of the threat appearing again. I suspect that he feared success would bring his name to the attention of people he would rather not know of his whereabouts."

"He was weak."

"And you thought that was good enough reason to kill him? Your father had a weak heart and I suspect that you made him weaker with the use of gradually administered poison. So much so that a shock to the system would prove fatal. He was already afraid of the very idea of a Greek coming after him, and you fuelled that fear. I suspect that you told him the candles came from this imaginary Greek when he was too frail to even get out of bed. You closed the curtains and lit the candle and locked the door behind you, pulling a similar key into the hole to make it look like he had locked himself in. And then you came to see me to plant the idea that he was afraid a djinn had been sent to kill him."

The man said nothing more before the police led him away. He was close to admitting everything, I had seen that look often enough. Lestrade would not have much difficulty in getting the confession he needed. I had rarely known a man capable of killing the person who had raised him in such a calculated way.

Yousef gave the slipper back to Holmes and thanked him, saying that any debt had been repaid many times over. I was not convinced that Holmes felt the same. There was something about his demeanour that suggested failure, but we both knew that the old man was most certainly already dead by the time that Iqbal came to visit us in Baker Street.

He had done everything he could and that was all that was possible. Nevertheless, in the dark days that followed, I was glad he turned to his violin instead of the seven-per-cent solution.

ABOUT THE AUTHOR

Steve Lockley is the author of around a hundred short stories, including a couple of contributions to *Doctor Who* anthologies, along with a handful of novels and novellas. His next novel, *The Sign of Gla'aki*, co-written with Steven Savile and due to be published by Fantasy Flight Games in 2013, sees Harry Houdini and a young Dennis Wheatley caught up in a world of Lovecraftian horror.

With Mike O'Driscoll, Steve was awarded the British Fantasy Society Special Award in 1995 for their work on the horror convention Welcome to my Nightmare and he has served as a judge for the prestigious World Fantasy Awards. Steve lives in Swansea with more books than he can ever hope to read.

THE PROPERTY OF A THIEF

BY MARK WRIGHT

There have been times in my long association with Sherlock Holmes when I have seen my friend perform great service to a wide variety of individuals and organisations. Lords, ladies, servants, members of parliament, kitchen maids, draymen, theatrical entertainers, heirs and heiresses number amongst those he has pulled from the brink of ruin and disaster. From the darkest recesses of the London underbelly to the highest authority in the land, Sherlock Holmes is blind to the boundaries of status. If he deems a problem worthy of his singular attention, he will apply himself with vigour and fortitude.

I have always remained fiercely protective of my association with Holmes; not through selfish reasons, of course, but to sway those acquaintances that would seek to make currency from that association for personal gain. It therefore pains me that I have, on but one occasion, availed myself of his services as a personal favour to others. But not once did he falter from the path in the same diligent manner as he would in service to any other caller to 221b Baker Street; and blast it if he didn't approach the whole sorry affair with some amusement, mostly at my own expense.

"No, no, Watson, you must go!" said Sherlock Holmes. His long legs were stretched out before him, feet placed on the breakfast table in a manner that would surely bring forth the wrath of Mrs Hudson.

The tie of his open silk dressing gown trailed on the floor and he was wreathed in a blue fug of cigarette smoke.

"Are you sure you won't accompany me?" I asked.

"Ha!" exclaimed Holmes, throwing his head back and taking a long draw on his cigarette. It was the answer I had expected, and was an unequivocal no. The invitation to which Holmes was declining to attend was a weekend gathering at the stately home of Cunningham Hall on the Kent border. It would no doubt be a tiresome business. Politely stiff small talk over drinks, an attempt to throw oneself into the evening's social activities, and apparently on Saturday afternoon there was to be some cricket. A visiting team of some repute would be going into battle against a local side.

I was only going for Mary's sake; if only she could know it, I thought with a sad smile. James and Elizabeth Cunningham had been acquaintances of my late wife, who we had seen together once or twice prior to her passing. Since my inevitable return to the Baker Street rooms I invariably shared with Sherlock Holmes, they had continuously attempted to coax me to one of their frequent weekend gatherings. I was at the juncture where to decline yet another kindly invitation would border on impudence.

"But Watson," said Holmes, removing his feet from amongst the remains of breakfast, "you simply must go. The country air will do you the power of good." He rose and moved towards a bookcase, eyes darting keenly in the search for a particular volume. I didn't think for a moment that my friend had given any thought whatsoever to the restorative powers of a country climate, but it was to his credit that he was trying.

"If you're sure…" I began, but my half-hearted plea was waved away without a backward glance, cigarette smoke wafting around him in languorous curls.

I puffed out my cheeks and made towards the door. A triumphant "Ah!" from the vicinity of the bookcase indicated success in locating the errant volume and Holmes began his return orbit to the table. He absently extinguished the cigarette into a plate of cold kedgeree and glanced up.

"You off?"

"Ah, yes," I replied, feeling a little awkward at this parting. "Till Sunday, then."

"Hmm." He nodded, returning to his reclined position at the table, book already open, my presence seemingly forgotten. There would be no further words that morning, so I made a swift exit, not at all looking forward to the social ordeal ahead.

I retrieved my baggage from the hallway, bade Mrs Hudson farewell and stepped out onto the bustle of Baker Street. Here it was an easy matter to hail a hansom cab for the jaunt down past Hyde Park to Victoria station. Within the hour I was pulling away from the foetid press of London and was soon speeding on towards the Kent countryside.

It was a bright May morning and my mood started to lift the further from the metropolis the train carried me. Perhaps Holmes had been right about the country air after all.

I must have dozed off, as it felt that just minutes later the train shuddered and steamed to a halt aside the platform at Cunningham Halt station. These small country branch halts were such a curiosity to me, and I had seen many in my travels with Sherlock Holmes. I stepped onto the platform, blinking into the sunlight, and with my weekend valise, made my way out front.

Five carriages were awaiting the train's arrival. Several other guests destined for the Cunninghams had been on the train and I was thankful we hadn't happened to be sharing carriages. There would be enough awkward conversation to come over the next few days; it was a relief to postpone them for a while longer. But that moment was now upon me. As baggage was placed atop the carriage with the driver, I found myself sitting opposite a perfectly affable married couple who were keen to tell me about their modest property in Eaton Place. I vowed at that moment, as one must from time to time, to make the best of it as we clattered our way on to the hall.

Cunningham Hall was modest by the standards of country houses of the time. James had inherited the estate in the way these things happen, taking his responsibilities to the family seriously. The frittering away of vast sums, as seemed to be the modern vogue, was not for him. Mary had come to know James when he was making his way in the world, independent from his father, and he had learnt valuable lessons along the way. The family fortune – such as it was – was invested sensibly, and James was proving a popular master with staff and tenants alike.

The five carriages perambulated their way up the main drive to the house, which nestled against an attractive backdrop of undulating green. As their guests alighted and baggage was whisked away by efficient and smartly dressed staff, James and Elizabeth greeted their new arrivals.

"John," declared James warmly, taking my hand, "delighted you could come!" I returned the greeting. He retained the same tanned, handsome features that defied the passing years, but he was perhaps filling out the well-tailored waistcoat a little more snugly than before.

Elizabeth, as pretty as ever, kissed me gently on the cheek. "John." She glanced at James and then, curiously, peered around me to the carriage I had just stepped from. "Is… is Mr Holmes not with you?"

I rankled at this. "I'm afraid Holmes was indisposed in London." It was a terser statement than I'd meant.

Elizabeth's face fell. "The invitation was intended for both of you."

"I realise that, but Sherlock Holmes is never well disposed at being summoned to a particular time or place, unless on the most urgent business."

"But –" Elizabeth began, stopping short as James stepped between us.

"Elizabeth, leave the poor man alone. We're just delighted to see you, old boy." He looked pointedly at his wife. "Aren't we, darling?"

Elizabeth's face softened, any trace of disappointment fading. "Yes –" she smiled "– of course. You've been a stranger too long. We do miss Mary so terribly."

"As do I."

James ushered me skilfully towards the main door of the house. "Of course. So, tell me, how have you been?"

With that, I was whisked into the comfort of Cunningham Hall, any trace of unpleasantness extinguished in a trice.

* * *

One of the many reasons I tended to avoid gatherings of this nature was the seemingly long periods with nothing to do. Friday afternoons seemed to go on forever as others arrived and settled in, took in the lie of the land and scoped out their fellow guests. There was something of the military operation about these affairs, master tacticians preparing to go into social battle.

I chose to see out the afternoon in my comfortable guest room, taking the opportunity to enjoy the respite from the usual rhythms of life. I looked out from a window bordered on either side by trailing ivy onto the grounds that swept away from the rear of the house, where well-tended lawns dropped down to a small lake. In the distance, through the trees, I spied the pristine white lines of a marquee, where I guessed the cricket match was to take place tomorrow.

I sighed wistfully, wishing for half a moment that Mary were here. She always made occasions such as this more bearable. But the words of Sherlock Holmes came rushing back to me, as they frequently did: *"Watson, there is little virtue in wishing for things that cannot be."* Those words had made me angry at first, but I eventually came to realise they were as close to an expression of sympathy and understanding as Holmes was ever likely to give.

I turned from the window and dismissed the black mood as quickly as it was upon me. I had already decided to avoid afternoon tea. Instead, I settled down in an armchair to enjoy an hour or so lost in the pages of a book.

Bathed and dressed for dinner, I emerged from my room just as the pre-dinner gong sounded. I took a deep breath, relieved that I could still comfortably fit into my seldom-worn formal dinner wear, and descended the wide staircase. There was already a hubbub of conversation as other guests gathered for drinks in the sumptuously appointed reception room. I suddenly realised I was famished and eagerly looking forward to dinner.

"John, I thought we'd lost you," said Elizabeth as she took my arm as soon as I entered, guiding me into the social melee with the grace of an experienced hostess.

"Not at all, just enjoying the peace and quiet. You look beautiful." And she did. "The tiara sets everything off perfectly."

"This?" She raised a hand to gently touch the diamond-studded piece that adorned her hair. It was elegant, but understated. "A birthday gift from James's father shortly before his death."

"Well, it's quite delightful."

"Thank you, John," replied Elizabeth conspiratorially, instantly making me the centre of her world for those few moments. "Let's get you a drink and then I can introduce you around."

A few minutes later I was holding a glass of sherry, being ushered from one gaggle of guests to another. It was futile to resist – and to her credit Elizabeth did not once introduce me as the associate of Sherlock Holmes, as I had feared she would. Across the room I spied James holding court. He glanced over and gave me an encouraging smile.

It would be naïve to think that at least a handful of guests wouldn't know my name and of my connection to the well-known consulting detective, but for once I seemed able to enjoy being just plain old John H. Watson, MD.

I felt the press of Elizabeth's hand on my arm once more, pulling me inexorably deeper into the room. "John, there's somebody who's simply dying to meet you." My heart sank. I had thought too soon. "Arthur…"

At this, a gentleman standing with his back to me turned nimbly away from the knot of party guests he was talking to.

"Please," this newcomer said, breaking into a smile as he took my hand and began to pump it up and down. "Call me Raffles."

This Raffles had the easy, confident manner of one used to social graces. It did not take Sherlock Holmes' powers of deduction to see a public school upbringing behind the handsome, chiselled features, neatly parted dark hair, tall frame and formal white-tie evening wear. Elizabeth stood between us, glancing from one to the other with an expression of great expectation lighting up her face.

"Pleased to meet you." I returned the greeting. "I'm John –"

"Dr Watson!" declared Raffles, attracting curious glances from around the room. "I know exactly who you are. Can't get enough of your writings."

There it was. "Oh. You've read my work," I managed stiffly.

"Every word. Fascinating stuff!"

"Well," I began, somewhat defensively, "I understand they are popular in certain quarters."

"You are too modest, Dr Watson." The fellow's eyes twinkled mischievously. "But I can see I have embarrassed you. My apologies."

"Oh, well. I... There's no need, really," I blustered, disarmed.

"Oh, Arthur, I cannot trust you, can I?' said Elizabeth good-naturedly.

"Probably wise," said Raffles.

"Arthur is with the Gentlemen," said Elizabeth.

"I'm sorry," I asked, "the who?"

"The Gentlemen of England," continued our hostess, as if no further explanation was required.

"I sense you're more of a rugger man, Dr Watson?" enquired Raffles, and realisation dawned.

"Ah, the cricket match."

"Arthur is quite the star spin bowler," explained Elizabeth. "The Gentlemen have come down to give the local side a bit of a thrashing."

Raffles grinned. "Let's not be too hasty." He looked around the room. "Bunny," he called out, waving. A fellow dressed in similar attire to Raffles wandered over from where he seemed to be staring in rapt fascination at a portrait of one of James's ancestors. There was something of the hangdog about him as he sauntered over and smiled weakly. He was marginally shorter than Raffles, his hair parted in an approximation of his friend's groomed style, but thinner and unkempt.

"Hullo," he said, nodding.

Raffles made the introductions. "Bunny Manders, John Watson."

"Pleasure," I said, shaking hands with the newcomer.

"Bunny tends to knock around with me, old school pal and all that."

"Hmm," was all Manders seemed able to muster.

For a moment, it seemed an awful, awkward silence was about to expand around us, none of us knowing quite what to say. I saw Manders positively breathe a sigh of relief when the gong for dinner finally sounded.

"Well, there we are," said Raffles.

"Indeed," I joined.

"Yes, I'm famished," said Manders, immediately placing a hand to his mouth. "Oh, sorry. That was…"

"Shall we?" suggested Elizabeth, expertly covering the chap's social misdemeanour and guiding us through to the dining hall along with the other guests.

Dinner was a convivial affair, and with the fortification of a glass of excellent red, I began to relax and enjoy the company of those around me. I was seated up with James, and found myself next to a charming young lady whose father was something in the overseas trade business.

Elizabeth held court further down the table, Mr Raffles seated to one side, Bunny Manders opposite. Every so often, Raffles would glance in my direction, nodding amiably in acknowledgement. I smiled awkwardly back, and continued my conversation.

Dinner over and done with in painless fashion, there were the usual post-repast rituals to be observed, and I am loath to admit I did enjoy a rare cigar and glass of brandy. However out of practice I was within the social milieu, I like to think I judged a juncture to retire that was neither too early to be considered rude, nor too late to outstay one's welcome when the host simply wants to go to their own bed.

I awoke feeling surprisingly refreshed, sunshine bisecting the room through a chink in the heavy curtains, bringing with it the promise of a fine day. Even the prospect of an afternoon of cricket couldn't dampen my spirits, and I must confess at this point to a curiosity over this Raffles fellow. He seemed a thoroughly decent sort and I was hoping to talk some more with him over the course of the weekend.

At breakfast I found Raffles's associate, Manders, casting a lone figure as he picked unenthusiastically at some kippers. I joined him. At this he seemed to perk up. Where last night I had dismissed him as a harmless buffoon, I divined he was possessed of a sharp wit, albeit with an outlook on life that leant towards the bleak. But he was affable company, and we found we held some common interest – he had taken to writing himself, and we fell into discussing craft and technique, such as we both possessed.

I found myself rubbing along well enough with Manders for most of the day, and he was happy to accompany me on a turn or two around the cricket pitch that afternoon.

"Oh, he's very good," he said of Raffles, who I spied for the first time that day leading the Gentlemen out onto the field for the first of the afternoon's play. Manders entered into a garbled explanation of the status of the Gentleman as first-class amateurs in the game, in relation to the more professional standings of the so-called Players, but it was lost on me, as I suspect it was him. My dislike of cricket came not from ignorance of the rules – I understood them perfectly well – but from the interminable length of time each match took to play out. With a smile I recalled Holmes' succinct essay on the subject, of few words and strictly not for print, and determined to enjoy this brief exposure to the game.

On the basis of the afternoon's play, the reputation of Raffles as a spin bowler was quite correct. He took six wickets in quick succession, keeping the enthusiastic local side to a minimum of runs, which were then matched in short order as the Gentleman went in to bat. Raffles himself added a hefty number to the total.

"That was quite the performance," I begrudgingly told him over refreshing lemonade in the marquee following the end of play.

"Too kind, Dr Watson," said Raffles, as relaxed as ever. "Cricket is as much founded on luck as it is skill. There are more worthy challenges in life."

"You're staying for this evening's festivities?"

"Oh yes, wouldn't miss James and Elizabeth's shindig for anything. Would we, Bunny?"

"What?" said Manders, who had reverted to the ill-at-ease fellow I had met last night in the presence of his friend. "Oh yes. Wouldn't miss it."

"I'm afraid, Dr Watson, I shan't be able to let you off the hook much longer," said Raffles, a sly glint in his eyes.

"Whatever do you mean?" I replied warily.

"I will be demanding to know at least a little of your adventures with Mr Sherlock Holmes before the weekend is out."

I sighed, relenting with a weak smile. "Very well, I am at your disposal this evening."

"Excellent!" exclaimed Raffles. "One's life is so dull. We all need vicarious pleasure from time to time. Eh, Bunny?" At that, he slapped his companion on the back, causing him to cough and splutter into his lemonade.

And discuss we did.

Much of that Saturday evening has been lost to the more pressing events that would soon overtake them in my memory. However, the more informal evening of entertainment provided by James and Elizabeth was punctuated by a not-unpleasant conversation with Mr Raffles on my activities alongside Sherlock Holmes. He quizzed me at length on the case of "The Sign of Four", which he declared a favourite and had reread many times, and was in awe to hear first hand the tale concerning the giant rat of Sumatra. It still chilled me to this day, but I was happy to recount it with little coaxing.

Raffles maintained his unflinching admiration for Holmes and myself. "I am but a malingerer, a tedious man of leisure who would give much to experience even a little of the danger you have found yourself in."

"I believe Holmes would have it that my colourful style makes too much currency from that aspect of his investigations."

The evening was soon over, a pleasant soiree of good company and good food, and I now felt foolish for any apprehension preceding my arrival. Raffles excused himself surprisingly early, with a promise to renew our acquaintance in London, and it was only then I realised the unfortunate Manders had been absent for much of the evening.

I spent something short of an hour in the company of James and Elizabeth, who had been such excellent hosts, and I vowed to myself

I would make more effort in the future to see them. Then I, too, took my leave, making my way up the wide staircase.

Within a few minutes I was nestled once more in the comfortably apportioned bed, sleeping the sleep of the innocent.

"John."

I felt a hand shaking me awake and an urgent voice hissing in my ear. "John, wake up!"

I opened my eyes to find James standing at the side of the bed, holding a lamp above his head, although pale dawn light was creeping in around the curtain edges. "James?" I mumbled, disorientated. It felt just minutes since I had fallen asleep. "What is it?" And then I was bolt upright in bed, fearing the worst. "Elizabeth?"

"Lizzie's fine." His face was grim. "You'd better come."

I wrapped my robe about myself and, bleary-eyed, followed James from the room, down the main staircase and into the drawing room. I was not quite prepared for the scene before me.

Elizabeth sat, her entire frame devoid of the usual vigour. She looked up as I entered, her eyes red-rimmed from crying, then looked away to the rear wall which was lined with books. Except a small square of books had seemingly been removed – or rather slid aside, and then it became clear. It was a hidden panel, released by a catch or some such, revealing a safe – the heavy door of which was wide open.

"It's gone, John," said Elizabeth in a quiet voice. "My tiara. Taken."

I didn't know what to say. James went to Elizabeth's side as tears shone in her eyes. "There," he soothed, "don't upset yourself."

"Dr Watson, is it?' A uniformed police sergeant had been peering into the safe as I entered the room. He now turned towards me.

"Yes," was the only acknowledgement one could give to such a question.

"Sergeant Cope is with the local constabulary," explained James helpfully.

"Bad business, this. And early, too," he added, a touch indignantly, perhaps at the injustice of being wrenched from his bed at such an ungodly hour.

I stepped forward to get a closer look into the safe. "Was it just the tiara that was taken?" Elizabeth nodded. Both her and James were looking to me expectantly.

"What are your thoughts, Sergeant?" I enquired.

"Well, I don't rightly know, sir." With that, Cope lapsed into silence and continued to peer ineffectually into the safe.

"James," I heard Elizabeth whisper.

"Yes, all right, Lizzie," he said placatingly, squeezing her shoulder. "Ah, John, old man…" He ushered me from the drawing room and out into the main hall. "This has all been a bit of a blow, Lizzie's devastated."

"Yes, I can see," I said, affecting an air of sympathy.

"Aside from some cove creeping around the house of a night, that tiara was a gift from my late father. Money aside, there's the sentimental value. We were wondering…"

That sense of expectation I had felt a minute earlier blossomed further.

"The chances of getting a detective up from London before Monday are zero," James continued, "and the trail will be stone cold by then. These local bobbies are not the brightest of buttons…"

"James," I started, suddenly conscious of where the discussion was headed, but he cut me off with a pleading look.

"I hate to ask, we both do, but…"

"Watson!" said Sherlock Holmes as he stood framed in the doorway of Cunningham Hall, the brightness of the Kent sunshine contrasting starkly with the neat dark suit he wore.

"Holmes," I managed to mumble in greeting through a sudden yawn.

"You look terrible. I thought you'd come down here to relax."

We were several hours on from the moment James had wrenched me awake; since then there had been urgent conversations, excursions to the local post office to rouse postmistresses from beds, special telegrams to London and hasty breakfasts, all finished off with anxious hours of waiting.

"I feel dreadful at having dragged you down here, and as a personal favour, too," I said, feeling the need to apologise, but Holmes waved me away with a raised cane.

"Think nothing of it. There was a certain difficulty in arranging a train down to Kent at such an early hour, and on a Sunday, but a minor inconvenience at most."

I was woefully embarrassed that I had acquiesced to James's request that I summon Holmes immediately to tackle the matter of the theft. I had expected intransigence. But it was nearly noon on Sunday, and here he was. Pristine and, I noted with apprehension, bristling with enthusiasm.

"It's a terrible business," I said as we entered the house, my voice echoing in the hallway. A strange hush had descended on the house, despite the fact the local constabulary had not yet permitted any guest to leave.

"Yes, yes," said Holmes. "Let us get straight to the matter in hand."

A small welcome delegation awaited our entrance into the drawing room. James rose immediately from Elizabeth's side, who I was pleased to see more composed after the earlier shock. "Mr Holmes," he began, "please accept our apologies for dragging you all the way down here. And please, don't blame John, we did rather put upon…"

Holmes smiled thinly. "I only blame Watson for anything in the most trying of circumstances," he murmured, glancing at me with the conspiratorial look I had witnessed so many times throughout our friendship.

Introductions were made, but Holmes' eyes were already darting to every inch of the room, the personalities before him secondary to this new game he had been presented with. He affected a modicum of charm and sympathy towards Elizabeth, but Sergeant Cope was dismissed with nary a look. Curiously, Bunny Manders was present, sitting unobtrusively in a chair to the side. I nodded in his direction and he smiled back, with his usual hangdog, out-of-place expression.

"Mr Holmes." A clear voice rang out from the back of the room, breaking through the hush. I was taken aback to realise that A.J. Raffles was also present, his tall, lean frame emerging from a patch of shadow. He must have been standing stock-still for me not to notice his presence. "It is a rare honour to finally meet you."

"I'm sure it is," replied Holmes, eyes focused on the safe rather than the newcomer.

"Ah, Holmes," I said, "this is Mr Raffles."

"A.J. Raffles at your service." Raffles positively beamed at Sherlock Holmes.

Then I saw something that would have eluded even the sharpest observer in the room; I only did so as a result of many hours spent observing Sherlock Holmes at work. A flash of the eyes, a split second moment, but Holmes *looked* at Raffles. His eyes darted from the safe, fixed on Raffles, then his attention was singled back to the safe. It was a scant moment, but for a mind like Sherlock Holmes', that glance would have provided a lifetime of opportunity.

"Now," he said, taking a further step towards the safe, eyes narrowed. "I think it's time you told me everything."

Holmes listened intently as the story of the tiara's theft was related in detail, starting with the arrival of the weekend guests and finishing with the discovery of the open safe by an early-rising maid that very morning. James and Elizabeth were exhaustive in their detail, but Holmes thrived on facts. I punctuated events with salient information, while Raffles and Manders stayed supportively silent throughout.

"I will do what I can, though I fear this may not be much. I should not wish to raise expectations unduly." Holmes' words seemed to cut both James and Elizabeth. They said nothing, but I could feel Elizabeth's disappointed eyes on me, silent accusation radiating out from her.

Blithely unaware of the disquiet his last statement had caused in my hosts, Holmes got down to work. He examined the safe in great detail. He gently nudged the small, yet heavy, door back into place with his cane, scrutinising the combination and lock. He sniffed once, then began to walk backwards, placing his feet carefully down as his eyes swept over the polished wooden floorboards.

With his back almost at the door, he rose up to his full height and gave the room one final look. Those present gazed back, seemingly incapable of taking a breath. Raffles was leaning forward over the back of the chair that his associate reclined in, watching events unfold with rapt fascination.

"Watson," declared Holmes, whirling round like some dervish and exiting the room. I shot an apologetic glance to those assembled, and followed – as I had on many occasions.

Holmes was already halfway up the wide staircase, stooped low and holding his cane in hands clasped behind his back, when I emerged into the hallway. We proceeded up the staircase, along a hallway and up yet another staircase. All the while, Holmes was hunched, taking in every detail, every errant thread or scuff. I sympathised with the staff going about their business, forced to leap aside as the inexorable force of Sherlock Holmes swept down a corridor; or the guests, detained by the inconvenience of theft, jumping back in alarm as they emerged from their room – it certainly wasn't every day that the world's greatest consulting detective glided by your bedroom door.

By and by, I found myself following Holmes out into the fresh air through a convenient side door; and so our perambulations continued around the side of the house. He paused briefly at the rear of the property and peered up towards a window framed by trailing ivy, glanced down at the ground, then continued on his way. Soon we had come full circle.

"Well?" I asked hopefully as we stepped back into the house, but Holmes remained silent on our way back to the drawing room.

The group awaiting our return had seemingly not moved in the time we had been absent; eager looks awaited us on our entry to the room. I remained standing while Holmes eased his thin body into a chair. He steepled his fingers before his face and looked at each person in turn. Eventually he spoke.

"I fear," said Sherlock Holmes, "that I have nothing encouraging to report."

Expectation deflated from the room like a child's balloon, the colour draining from Elizabeth's face.

"I can find no evidence to suggest forced entry," continued Holmes. "Either the thief is possessed of such skill that they leave no trace of their insertion into the house – highly unlikely – or the thief is still amongst you."

James was on his feet. "Are you suggesting that one of our guests is responsible for the crime? Preposterous!"

"I never suggest. I merely present facts."

"The staff," said Elizabeth, fighting back tears. "It must have been one of the staff!"

"Do you have any reason to suspect any member of your household staff?" enquired Holmes.

"No, but…"

"Then you should not." Holmes spread his hands wide. "It is a common malpractice of the upper classes to rely on cliché when presented with absolutely no evidence."

I saw James's face colour with anger, his hands balling into fists. "How dare you!" I thought he was going to hit Holmes and I tensed, preparing to step in between, but Raffles beat me to it.

"Come now, James. You asked for Mr Holmes' assistance, and he is giving it willingly. Nobody is at fault because the facts are not as you would wish them to be." Raffles' even words had a calming effect.

"Yes, yes of course. You're right, Arthur. My apologies, Mr Holmes."

I attempted to break through the hot, tense atmosphere that now pervaded the room. "What do you suggest, Holmes?"

"There is only one course of action open to us, I fear."

"Which is?" asked James. Holmes looked directly at him.

"You must search the belongings of all your guests."

A stunned silence replaced the tension. "What?" blurted Elizabeth, now rising in shock to stand side by side with her husband.

"That's quite impossible," maintained James.

"Quite clearly it is not impossible. Your guests have belongings. They can be searched."

"I agree with Mr Holmes, I'm afraid," joined in Raffles, causing a startled Manders to sit up.

"I say, Raffles, steady on," he exclaimed.

"No, no, Bunny. It's quite correct, and the only way to be sure. Isn't that, so, Mr Holmes?"

Holmes inclined his head in agreement.

"You see? I will happily subject myself to a search, and so will Bunny." Raffles smiled amiably.

"We will?" asked a confused Manders. "Yes. Yes, I suppose we will." He sank back into the chair, crushed.

"But our guests, the explanations…" pleaded Elizabeth, the prospect of social embarrassment seemingly more devastating than the theft of her tiara.

"I have no personal connections to any of your guests, bar one, so kindly lay the blame for this intrusion at my feet," said Holmes, still reclining in the chair.

James sighed and with a look to Elizabeth, capitulated. "Very well."

Holmes jumped easily to his feet, clapping his hands together with a sudden injection of energy. "Sergeant Cope?" The representative of the local constabulary looked surprised to be called upon. "If you could rouse your men, we should be able to have this taken care of with the minimum of fuss."

"Yes, sir," said the portly police officer, almost standing to attention before bustling off, clearly happy to have something of import to attend to.

As Holmes had alluded, the process of searching the belongings of the houseguests was a simple and quick affair. They were, for the most part, already packed, having had several hours of indolence in which to assemble their possessions into an array of valises and weekend bags.

"If they have nothing to hide, they will not object," Holmes said in an aside to me, and he was quite correct. As the guests had effectively been under house arrest that morning, they were more than happy to cooperate with the search if it hastened their departure. All apologies from James and Elizabeth were waved away with good grace and humour as they lined up outside the dining room to present their various items of luggage for appraisal.

I stood side by side with Holmes, watching as the sergeant carried out the search, opening each case and dismissing the owner when each new bag failed to bring forth the stolen tiara. James held Elizabeth's hand, his wife growing more anxious with each new bag.

Raffles and Manders came in together, both dressed for the off.

"Here we are," said Raffles breezily, "all ready for inspection. You first, Bunny."

Manders' voice trembled with nervous energy. "Um, yes. Of course." He placed his modest valise on the table before the sergeant, his eyes twitching as he watched the policeman rummage through his belongings. He breathed a sigh of relief when the sergeant shook his head, but then looked even more distressed when Raffles presented his own baggage with a friendly grin.

"I do apologise for the state of my clothes, I'm terrible at packing. Elizabeth tells me I just need the love of a good woman to take care of that stuff." This coaxed a smile from Elizabeth. But standing beside him, Manders looked positively ill as the latches were released on the case.

Holmes had remained still throughout, but as the sergeant's pudgy hands worked their way through the case, he lent forward. Manders looked to be barely breathing, and I thought he would faint clean away as the policeman opened Raffles's washbag and peeped within. The sergeant closed the bag, turning to Holmes and shaking his head. Manders breathed out heavily, all tension leaving his body. Holmes nodded once at the sergeant, and if I didn't know better I'd say the ghost of a smile played on his lips.

His case secured once more, Raffles proceeded on an enthusiastic promenade of the room, giving out fond farewells and all his hopes for a happy outcome to the present situation. He stopped before Holmes, the two men facing each other. Raffles smiled. "Mr Holmes."

"Mr Raffles," said Holmes, simply.

"And Dr Watson," said Raffles, moving to me, taking my hand. "Yours has been a rare pleasure, and I shall hope to renew our acquaintance quite soon."

"Yes, I should like that," I replied. And I meant it. I liked the chap immensely, and Mr Manders, despite his awkwardness, had a certain charm.

Then the two men were gone, off back to London by whatever means was available to them.

* * *

I would like to say at this juncture that the matter of the stolen tiara was resolved quickly and satisfactorily. That was not to be the case.

There were still a few guests whose baggage was yet to be searched, but as each of them arrived in the dining room to lay bare their belongings, it was becoming increasingly doubtful the item in question would be miraculously brought forth. And so it was with a great lack of enthusiasm that Sergeant Cope hunted through the final item of luggage, then shook his head to indicate the negative outcome.

Elizabeth sat immediately, retaining her composure, but clearly shaken by the outcome.

"I am so terribly sorry," I soothed, but it felt an empty gesture. Why I felt the need to apologise I wasn't quite sure, but it was offered nonetheless.

"It's not your fault, John. Thank you. And thank you, Mr Holmes."

Holmes appeared unperturbed by the outcome, as if it were expected. "My sincere apologies. The facts, in this case, have done a disservice and I am afraid I have nothing further to offer."

Holmes appeared remarkably sanguine about his lack of success. "I suggest at this point you place yourself in the hands of Sergeant Cope and the local constabulary. I am sure their policing skills are beyond reproach and this unpleasant matter will be resolved very soon."

At this the sergeant puffed out his chest in pride, missing any sense of irony laced into my friend's words.

I offered to stay down in Kent for a further evening, but James and Elizabeth would hear nothing of it, insisting they'd like to put the whole thing behind them and get back to normal. If we didn't delay, there would be a train back to London that we had a chance of catching.

Holmes accompanied me to my room to retrieve my luggage. "Watson, I fear I have done you an injustice before your friends," he said, arms placed wide against the window frame as he peered out onto the grounds.

"No," I replied quickly, "I have done *you* the injustice. Calling you down here on a personal whim. Quite unacceptable."

"You have rendered unswerving personal service over many years of friendship. It speaks highly of your character that you feel embarrassed to have called on my services for personal reasons."

I put my jacket on and hefted my valise from the bed. "Shall we?" I asked.

"Indeed," said Sherlock Holmes, turning from the window.

There was a hurried and awkward farewell in front of the house. James and Elizabeth were somewhat deflated, as would I have been, but clearly the disappointment stemmed from the failure of Sherlock Holmes to conjure forth the stolen item. They were simply too polite to say. I was keen not to sully our relationship for the sake of Mary's memory, and promised a return visit to Cunningham Hall later in the summer.

The carriage delivered Holmes and I just as the train was heaving into the station, and we were soon comfortably appointed in a compartment and chugging back towards London. I caught myself dozing, and suddenly realised how tired I was. I let sleep take me, leaving Sherlock Holmes gazing out at the passing countryside, that ghost of a smile still playing on his lips.

It was a pleasure to arrive back at Baker Street – it usually was – especially as there was soon a fortifying cup of tea provided by Mrs Hudson to restore jaded spirits. I let myself sit a while and enjoy a moment of calm. Even Holmes seemed content to just idle in his chair; it was also possible he was deep in thought. One never could tell. He gazed straight ahead, a cigarette in one hand, the other hanging limp to the side of his chair.

Feeling refreshed, I left Holmes to his thoughts and decided to unpack. Placing the valise on the bed in my room, I stooped forward to release the catches. As I opened the bag, I cried out and almost jumped back in horror.

Perched atop my washbag was a diamond tiara.

Elizabeth Cunningham's diamond tiara.

A laugh caused my head to snap round. Holmes stood leaning with casual grace against the doorframe, smoke curling away from the cigarette held up to his mouth. He laughed again, a deep, joyous laugh, before turning about to walk into the sitting room.

"Holmes!" I shouted, stalking after him. "What is the meaning of this?" And damn it to hell if he didn't just keep on laughing. He threw his head back and laughed long and hard. Incensed, I strode back to my room, returning with the tiara clutched in my hand.

"This is no laughing matter, Holmes! *This*," I said, holding the tiara up high, "is a stolen item! And it is in my valise!"

Holmes managed to bring his laughter under control. "Forgive me, Watson, but somebody has played a marvellous practical joke, and it has quite tickled me."

"I am glad you find it so funny," I said with some indignation.

"There was serious intent behind this. Somebody set out to steal the item, but it has been executed with a certain amount of style and wit. Completely transparent from the start, but humorous nonetheless."

"Explain!" I cried.

Holmes leant back, fixing me with a steady gaze. "It all hinges on the irreproachable reputation of John H. Watson, MD."

"Me?" Now I was thoroughly perplexed. I sat on my own chair, gently placing the tiara on the table, afraid it could to shatter into a thousand pieces.

"A robbery has taken place. A criminal act, but the details of how that occurred are sideplay. The thief is clever and experienced. I imagine it was the matter of a moment to gain access to the safe and purloin the item. Barely worth my attention."

"Go on."

"The style of the act is inherent in what happens next. The thief could have simply vanished into thin air, but their absence, as I am convinced it was one of the houseguests, would have aroused suspicion. The theft of the item was bound to be discovered sooner rather than later, leaving the problem of couriering it from the house."

"But every bag was searched."

"Every bag, except yours."

I opened my mouth to speak, then paused to consider. Holmes was quite right. At no point in proceedings had any suggestion been made to place my own baggage under scrutiny. I looked at Holmes, agog.

"Who would dare suggest the baggage of Dr Watson, the famed and trusted associate of Sherlock Holmes, be searched in pursuit of a thief? Your honour and integrity are beyond question."

I coughed back sudden embarrassment at these words, unsure of what to say. "But that's…"

"Quite brilliant," breathed Holmes with rare admiration. "And our thief in the night would have been counting on that, planning their enterprise around that very reputation. There was risk, it may not have worked, but every thief must factor in a certain amount of random chance and uncertainty in their schemes."

"But who would do such a thing?" I spluttered, indignation getting the better of me again.

"We shall know the answer to that quite soon, I should think. But there is more to this than meets the eye."

"We must return to Kent," I insisted. "Return the tiara, or at least telegram to let the Cunninghams know we have it."

"No, no, Watson. For then we would be prevented from learning the identity of the culprit. And I should so like to meet them."

"You mean, they'll be coming here? To retrieve it?"

"Why go to the trouble of stealing such a trinket if the ultimate aim is not to possess it?"

"But that would be madness!" I said, pacing from my chair to the table and back again. "Breaking into 221b, of all the –"

"Watson, calm yourself. It is a further mark of the audaciousness – or arrogance – of our thief. The dividing line between the two is a thin one."

"Then what must we do?"

Holmes rose and walked across the sitting room to claim another cigarette. He turned as he struck a match to light it. "We have some dinner. And then we wait."

The sitting room at 221b was wreathed in darkness, the only illumination coming from the pale moonlight falling in a slanted shaft through the windows. Sinister shadows choked the familiar room, transforming it into a nightmarish landscape as the paraphernalia of Holmes' various pursuits were pulled out of shape.

My friend was seated in his armchair, as still as a statue. The only signal he was even awake was the glassy, cat-like sheen of his eyes.

I had been sat in the comfort of my own chair in such a fashion for some time, and it was now the early hours. My mind and body yearned for sleep, but Holmes insisted there was yet a game to be played out before the sun rose once more over London.

On the dining table sat the tiara, the cause of all the weekend's trials. I sighed and returned my thoughts exclusively to the vigil at hand.

Scant minutes later I was sure I had heard a movement to my left and behind Holmes: the door to my own room. Yes! There it was, the scrape of wood on wood. At that very second I would have gone crashing through the door to tackle the blackguard before they could even place one foot down, but Holmes raised a hand in a placating manner. I forced myself to sit back, subjecting the arms of the chair to unnecessary force.

A floorboard creaked within; the intruder was now firmly inside the walls of 221b. How Holmes could remain so calm was beyond me. Seconds later the door to my room eased silently open, and I sensed rather than saw the shape of a figure creeping into the sitting room. I remained as still as possible, awaiting the signal from Holmes. But when?

The dark silhouette padded stealthily behind the armchair in which Sherlock Holmes was seated. The figure paused, then after a second, made straight towards the table. A gloved hand reached out towards the waiting tiara.

"Now, Watson!"

At that I launched myself from the chair, diving bodily towards the intruder, knocking their legs from beneath them in a neat tackle. With an anguished squawk, the figure went down like a sack of coal. They writhed terribly, but I was able to wrench an arm round behind them. "Ow!" screamed the figure as the threat of dislocation persuaded them that any movement was to be discouraged.

A match rasped; a moment later the room was bathed in light as Holmes lit one of the gas lamps ranged around the walls. "All right, you have me," a muffled voice protested. "You have me, I shan't give you any more trouble." I hauled the interloper to their feet and turned them roughly to face me.

"Manders?"

I had to look twice, but there was no mistaking it. Standing before me, blinking sheepishly in the sudden light, was Bunny Manders! I have to say, he was the last person I had been expecting!

"Mr Manders, a pleasure to renew our acquaintance," said Holmes cheerfully. "Can we offer you anything? A tiara, perhaps?"

"Oh, very funny," frowned the unfortunate cove.

"What have you got to say for yourself?" I demanded, pushing the fellow down onto my chair.

"Absolutely nothing," he said, affecting a petulant defiance that had not been present before.

"I imagine the police will have a few things to ask you," I said.

"I imagine they will."

"A brilliant plan, Mr Manders, quite brilliant. And it nearly succeeded." Manders looked sullenly back at Holmes and stayed silent.

"What are we to do with him, Holmes?"

"It is perhaps a touch early to be bothering those tireless bastions of law enforcement. For now, we should restrain Mr Manders until such time as we can avail ourselves of the services of the nearest police station." Holmes moved to light another gaslamp. "There are handcuffs on the window ledge, Watson, if you would be so good?"

"With pleasure." As Holmes watched our guest, I moved quickly to the window to retrieve the shackles. A movement outside caught my eye and I glanced out onto the darkened Baker Street to see a uniformed police constable perambulating his way along the road. A beat bobby walking fearlessly through the night, lamp held aloft to light his way.

"Holmes, there's a bobby out there. That's a stroke of luck."

"Indeed it is. Quickly, Watson, before they have passed from sight."

I positively ran from the room and charged down the staircase, safe in the knowledge that Mrs Hudson was so acclimatised to the comings and goings of her gentleman charges that she could have slept through the Boer War. I unlocked the door and stepped out onto the street.

"Constable," I called out, jogging towards his receding form. The cloaked officer turned at my voice, pointing the glow of his lamp in my direction and peering at me as I approached.

"Is there a problem, sir?" he asked, the guttural voice matching the heavily whiskered features and corpulent frame.

"Yes, Officer, if you can come please, there has been a break-in at 221b Baker Street."

"Very well, sir," he said, scratching at an impressive sideburn, "lead on."

The officer didn't seem in much of a hurry as I led the way back to 221b. I desperately wanted to urge him along, but sometimes you just couldn't hurry the law. Eventually we emerged back into the now fully lit sitting room, the heavy breathing of the officer marking his progress up the stairs.

"Officer, and just in the nick of time," declared Holmes enthusiastically on our arrival.

"Indeed, sir," responded the officer. "Mr Holmes, is it?" Holmes nodded. "Pleasure, sir. Dr Watson 'ere has just been explaining what has occurred." He turned to Manders, still seated, but now cuffed. "This the intruder?"

"Indeed it is, Constable," I confirmed.

"Oh dear, oh dear, we are in trouble, aren't we, sir?" said the constable, looking down at Manders disapprovingly.

"Yes," replied the villain quietly. "I suppose I am."

The officer pursed chapped lips. "If it's all the same to you, I think I should take this gentleman off your hands and get him safely locked up in the nearest station."

Holmes nodded in ready agreement. "I do think that would be wise, Constable."

"I'd be grateful if you two gentlemen could come along to the station first thing in the morning, and we can take down particulars at the appropriate hour."

"Of course, anything we can do to help."

"Right you, on yer feet," the officer said to Manders, who, with his hands cuffed, was forced to wriggle this way and that until he eventually struggled to his feet. It would have been comical in different circumstances.

"You should be ashamed of yourself," I felt compelled to say as the officer placed a firm hand on Manders' shoulder and led him towards the door. He looked at me with sad, weary eyes as he passed.

"Watson, could you get the door?" asked Holmes.

Happy to oblige, I stepped ahead of the officer and opened the sitting-room door.

"Much appreciated, sir," said the constable.

"Oh, Officer?" Holmes called out just before he reached the door. The constable turned to Holmes.

"Sir?"

"I do think it would be safer if you took the tiara," said Holmes, picking it up from the table and holding it out to the policeman. "For safe keeping until it can be returned to its owners. I'm sure it will be more secure in a police station than in my sitting room."

The officer paused, looking at the tiara as it glinted in the light of the lamps, before taking it from Holmes. "Right you are, sir."

The matter seemingly concluded until morning, the constable began to push Manders towards the door once more.

"Tell me, Officer," said Holmes airily, "how is Inspector Leach?"

"Inspector Leach, sir?" the officer replied, still moving towards the door. "Very well, as I understand it. Very well."

"I am glad. Do pass on the regards of Sherlock Holmes."

"Of course, sir."

The officer was almost at the door, the silent Manders ahead of him, when I saw Sherlock Holmes' posture change, his whole body tensing for action. "Watson, quickly, the door!"

I had learnt over the years to seldom question the requests of Sherlock Holmes, and as the constable shoved Manders ahead of him as he himself leapt for the door, I slammed it in their faces and stood firmly in their way.

Manders turned to the constable. "What are we going to do?" he demanded.

The officer looked left and right, his cape flapping; then, with an exhaled breath, he stopped and smiled through his whiskers. He turned to face Holmes. As he did, he seemed to grow by two feet. "When did you know?" he asked in a smooth voice, devoid of the guttural London tone of the bobby.

"Almost as soon as I arrived in Kent," conceded Holmes, which did nothing to alleviate this confusing turn of events.

"There is no Inspector Leach, is there?"

"Only up here." Holmes smiled, tapping his temple.

"Will somebody please explain what is going on!" I demanded with raised voice.

"Apologies, Dr Watson," said the policeman amiably. "The last thing I'd want to do is cause you any further distress."

The constable removed his helmet and placed it, along with the tiara, on the table. "Stole this from a policeman up in Cambridge years ago," he went on, "back when those kinds of japes were all the rage."

The policeman began to pull at the whiskers on his face. Astoundingly, they came away in his hands, and seconds later I was astonished to find myself standing before A.J. Raffles. "I told you we'd be renewing our acquaintance very soon." He smiled.

"You blackguard!" I said. "You thief and blackguard!"

"Guilty as charged," said Raffles as, without invitation, he dropped down into an armchair. Manders remained standing, a sheen of sweat glistening on his forehead.

"I must congratulate you, Mr Raffles. An audacious scheme. Doomed to failure, but audacious all the same."

"From you, Mr Holmes, I take that as a compliment."

"Not a compliment. Just facts."

Raffles nodded graciously to this.

"How could you?" I asked, my rage threatening to bubble over. "Poor James and Elizabeth. You were their guest!"

"Elizabeth will have her trinket back, no real harm done. And you must admit, it livened up a rather tedious weekend."

The impudence of the miscreant quite stunned me into silence.

"Besides," continued Raffles, sitting forward and eyeing the tiara, "this was not the prize."

"Then what was?" I demanded, as confusion continued to reign in the sitting room.

"I was," said Holmes, who seemed to be enjoying himself immensely as he sat opposite Raffles in his own armchair.

"I suppose my scheme was somewhat transparent."

"Yes. But most amusing."

"Aren't you interested in how I did it?"

"I fear an honest answer to that question may cause offence," said Holmes. At a look from Raffles, he waved a hand dismissively. "A fragment of ivy leaf cut by the heel of a boot below Watson's window was as a flaming beacon. I have little interest in the sordid creeping around of a country house at night, but I'm sure your Mr Manders could turn the events into some form of entertaining prose."

I glanced over at Manders, who was still cuffed. He gave me a wan smile, and I couldn't help but hold some kindred feeling for him as Holmes and Raffles continued their conversation.

"One question," began Holmes.

"Anything."

"If you were so desperate to make my acquaintance, why not just make an appointment?"

Raffles smiled that easy, relaxed smile. "Where would the fun be in that?"

Holmes sat back, considering, as if the notion of doing something for fun had rarely occurred to him. "Hmm," he mused. "And now you have engineered a meeting, what, may I ask, are your conclusions?"

"It's been most illuminating. You do not disappoint."

Holmes rose. "Cigarette?" he asked, but Raffles declined. "Forgive me if I indulge, won't you?"

"Go ahead," said Raffles amiably. I couldn't credit this. They were talking like two fellows in a gentlemen's club. "What happens now?"

"Now?" countered Holmes. He considered, then shrugged. "You are free to go."

"What?" I exploded.

"What?" exclaimed Manders.

"To mirror the sentiments of our associates," said Raffles, "do explain. Please."

"I know of you, Mr Raffles. You are a thief, but you have a reputation. A reputation that interests me. You do not always steal for personal gain."

"But Holmes, you can't!" I was on the verge of apoplexy.

"In this case," Holmes continued, "I do not see that much harm has been done. Certainly no more a misdemeanour than stealing a policeman's helmet." At this I snorted. Manders stood with mouth agape as he listened to the conversation.

"This is unexpected," said Raffles, rising to his feet. "You are a fascinating and complex individual, Mr Holmes." Mr A.J. Raffles faced my friend Sherlock Holmes. "Tell me, are you a Gentleman or a Player?"

"Neither. I find subscribing to forced metaphors a tedious pursuit. Especially when they relate to cricket."

"Just the answer I was expecting."

"Holmes, I beg you…" I blurted. "He is a criminal."

"Yes I am, Dr Watson. And one day I shall be brought to book. But for now, I sincerely apologise for any inconvenience and distress I have caused you. I do hope we will meet again."

Raffles turned, this strange contradiction in a policeman's uniform, and made once more for the door, and, on this occasion, freedom. I felt quite powerless to prevent his departure, as if in the grip of some wider narrative of which I was but a small part.

"Come along, Bunny," he said to his associate as he opened the door. "We'll see ourselves out." With a brief nod to Holmes, he vanished.

Manders held out his still-cuffed hands in supplication to Holmes. "Could you…"

"I do apologise," said Holmes dismissively, "I appear to have mislaid the keys."

I almost laughed out loud as the poor fellow's face fell yet again. "Bunny!" Raffles shouted from the stairway. Manders shrugged apologetically, then shuffled out through the door after his companion.

A minute of silence passed in the sitting room, neither Holmes nor myself speaking. I wandered over and closed the door, standing with my back to my friend. I could stand it no longer. "Holmes, you are quite impossible," I shouted, wheeling round to find him looking expectantly at me. "Tonight, you have let a common criminal and his accomplice go. They have committed a crime!"

"Sometimes a crime goes unpunished for good reason, Watson."

"What does that even mean?"

"It means," said Holmes, after some consideration, "that there is more to Mr Raffles than a mere common burglar. There are, I feel, further games to be played."

"But what about the tiara? How do I explain to James and Elizabeth…"

"Fabricate something. Your writing is testament to your skills in that discipline. Investigations continued in London, you were on the trail of the master criminal, a thrilling rooftop chase to their lair. They escaped in a death-defying leap into the Thames, but you were able to retrieve the tiara at great personal danger."

"A lie," I said, my heart sinking as I sat at the table, looking gloomily down on the tiara where Raffles had left it.

"Exaggeration, Watson, exaggeration!"

"What would Mary say?" I wondered, aloud.

My friend struck a match and it flared, illuminating his features in momentary sharp relief. His cigarette lit, he extinguished the match. "Mary was always a pragmatist, and would have seen that you did your level best to save your friend's embarrassment, and above all, tried to help them."

"By summoning you from London on a mission of personal service to prevent their property falling into the clutches of a thief."

As the dawn light began to creep through the windows of 221b Baker Street, Sherlock Holmes drew thoughtfully on the cigarette, blowing smoke high into the air. "Ah, Watson. Sooner or later, *everything* becomes the property of a thief."

ABOUT THE AUTHOR

Mark Wright is a writer, journalist and producer who has written for many brands including *Doctor Who*, *The Sarah Jane Adventures*, *Highlander* and *Blake's 7*. He has written audio dramas, comic strips and novels and is a regular contributor to *Doctor Who Magazine*. For Big Finish productions he is the producer of the original science-fiction series *Graceless* and the co-producer of *Iris Wildthyme* and with Cavan Scott has contributed to the company's *Doctor Who* and *Blake's 7* ranges many times.

Mark has recently turned his attention to the stage, with his short play, "Looking for Vi", being selected as a finalist at the Off Cut Festival 2011. At the end of 2012, shooting began on a film adaptation of the play, which will premiere in 2013. He lives in Yorkshire with his family.

WOMAN'S WORK

∽ා৫∾

BY DAVID BARNETT

Mrs Martha Hudson had carefully excised the pages from
the latest number of *The Strand Magazine* with a sharp
pair of scissors and had commenced pasting them with
flour and water into a scrapbook already bulging with similar
cuttings when the bell rang three times in the cool stillness of the
kitchen, signalling that there was someone calling at the door of
221b Baker Street.

She wiped her hands on her starched apron, filed the scrapbook
away in her carpet bag, which always hung beneath the butcher's
block preparation table, and went to adjust the gas flame under the
lamb stew she had just put on the stove; dinner was many hours
away but the visitor was most likely bringing a conundrum or an
enigma – something to interrupt her carefully planned schedule for
Mr Holmes and Dr Watson, at any rate. That was why she more and
more often opted for stews of an evening, especially as the nights were
drawing in: they were less likely to spoil as her tenants and charges
allowed themselves to get wrapped up in whatever mysteries seemed
to be increasingly landing upon the doorstep. The bell sounded
impatiently again.

"I'm coming, I'm coming," Mrs Hudson muttered under her
breath, catching sight of the broom leaning against the range. She
had been intending to brush the small back courtyard before dinner.

She hoped whoever was now ringing the bell for the *third* volley of shrill chimes was not going to overly divert her from her work.

It was, as she might have guessed, Inspector Lestrade, bearing a parcel wrapped in newspaper that gave off a most disagreeable odour.

"Is himself in?" asked Lestrade, his moustache twitching, his ferrety-black eyes shining like pinpricks beneath the brim of his derby.

Mrs Hudson opened the door wide to allow the inspector entrance to the hallway. She had beeswaxed the woodwork just this morning; the smell coming from that package was already wrestling the scent of her hard work to the carpeted floor and beating it into submission.

"Fish, Inspector? I already have a lamb stew on for his dinner."

Lestrade tapped the side of his not inconsiderable nose. "I doubt he'll want to eat this, Mrs Hudson, but I am rather hoping he might *devour* it, *digest* his findings and *polish off* the mystery attached to it."

"No doubt to help tip the scales of justice in your favour," nodded Mrs Hudson, taking Lestrade's coat and hat.

He looked at her quizzically, then shrugged. "Are they in the parlour?"

Mrs Hudson rapped on the parlour door and cleared her throat as she swung it open; one never quite knew what they might find in any of the rooms of 221b Baker Street, so it was always best to telegraph one's entrance. At one time she would have been surprised to find her lanky, hawkish tenant standing in his slippers and robe, arm outstretched and holding a rapier with its business-end at the throat of the perpetually perplexed-looking Dr Watson, but not any more.

"…thus you see, Watson, that a left-handed swordsman could not have comfortably severed the left ear of his victim unless he used an anti-clockwise flourish of the wrist, which we are told he did not but rather, in most expressive language, employed a most definite *downward slash*."

"Bravo, Holmes," said Watson through his walrus-like moustache, gently moving the point of the rapier away from his throat with the palm of his hand. "Now I don't need to read the rest of that mystery story."

"The perpetrator is a dreadful hack, anyway," said Holmes. "But my finely attuned senses tell me we have a visitor with a mystery of his own... of a rather *squamous* nature."

Lestrade nodded and laid his package on the coffee table. The stench became even more pronounced as he unwrapped it, to indeed reveal a fish, perhaps twelve inches from nose to tail, its dark scales dappled with white. Its eyes were glassily blank and a long slit had already been carved in its underside. Holmes regarded it intently, then closed his eyes.

"Salmon?" he said hesitantly.

Mrs Hudson coughed, her sudden expectoration sounding something not unlike C*har! Char!*

"Ah, but wait..." said Holmes. "*Salvelinus leucomaenis,*" he murmured after a moment, his steely eyes snapping open. "*Commonly* known in England as white-spotted char, though not entirely a *common* fish." The detective bent forward and sniffed. "Dead for some time, I fear. You were not hoping to extract a confession from it, Lestrade?"

Watson chuckled. "More likely, he wishes us to catch the murderer!"

"Murder most foul!" exclaimed Holmes. "At least going off the smell of the damned thing. You have a mystery for us regarding this fish, Lestrade?"

"I do," said Lestrade stoutly.

"Then the game's afoot!" said Holmes, laughing delightedly, but to blank looks from the gathering in the parlour. He sighed. "It is a *game* fish, you see. And in length about *twelve inches*."

"Ah, the *game* is a *foot*!" said Watson, clapping his hands. "Oh, you are clever, Holmes."

Holmes smiled, and Mrs Hudson cleared her throat. "Will you gentlemen be requiring any refreshment?"

"Tea, Inspector Lestrade?" enquired Holmes. "Or something stronger...?"

Lestrade eyed the brandy decanter on the sideboard. "Oh, perhaps something a little more warming..."

As Watson went to do the honours, Mrs Hudson nodded. "I'll be in the kitchen, then."

But as she closed the parlour door behind her, she paused then put an ear against the woodwork, listening intently to the voices within.

* * *

"Yesterday afternoon," said Inspector Lestrade, finishing his brandy and offering his glass to Watson for a refill, "this was dropped off at the Commercial Road police station along with a letter signed by one Melvin Jacobs, informing us he had just purchased it from Billingsgate Fish Market."

"He purchased it himself? Has he no housekeeper? Or wife?" said Watson, sitting down with a fresh brandy.

"Presumably he is not of a position to employ a housekeeper," said Lestrade. "And the letter said his wife is laid up with a very mild case of typhus."

"Our Mr Jacobs lives in Aldgate," pronounced Holmes. "He is a member of the Jewry, and practically destitute."

"How on earth can you know that?" said Lestrade. "As it happens, he didn't put his address on the letter…"

Holmes sat back smugly. "Jacobs is a Yiddish name, of course. And there was an item in the newspaper about a typhus outbreak near the Aldgate synagogue. You said yourself he cannot afford a housekeeper, and he was not working on a Friday, so without a proper paying situation. Enough money, though barely I surmise, to purchase a fish to be served *gefilte*, as is the Yiddish tradition, on the Jewish Sabbath – Saturday, which is today."

"Genius," said Watson, sipping his brandy. He pointed at the fish. "Though it's not on his table. What's wrong with it?"

Lestrade procured a pencil from his inside pocket and poked it into the slit along the length of the fish's belly. "He began to prepare it, all right. Then he found this…"

Beneath the skin was an even more glittering prize. Along the length of the fish's innards were gems and jewels – two diamond rings, a ruby on a golden chain, garnets, a brooch, emeralds…

"A veritable treasure trove!" exclaimed Watson. "That fish has been eating well!"

"Better than Mr Jacobs, I'll warrant," said Holmes.

But Lestrade had not finished. He flipped over the fish with his pencil, the booty within scattering along the newspaper wrapping, to reveal a deep x-shaped scar on the previously hidden flank of the char.

Holmes leaned forward, his eyes narrow. "Not a process of the gefilte method of preparation, or certainly not one I have heard about," he said.

"A mystery, indeed, and one which I thought might whet your appetites." Lestrade nodded.

"Moreso than the fish," said Watson. "Having said that, can we keep hold of it?"

Lestrade shrugged. "I don't see why not, for a day or two."

"I'll get Mrs Hudson to put it on ice in the pantry," said Holmes. "We'll keep the gems in our safe."

"Excellent," said Lestrade, standing. "Then I'll bid you gentlemen farewell, and look forward to your thoughts."

Watson rang for Mrs Hudson to see Lestrade to the door, and when the inspector had left, Holmes called for his housekeeper to enter the parlour.

"What do you make of this, Mrs Hudson?" he said, indicating the char.

"Nice bit of fish, or it was," she said, sniffing. "You don't see white-spotted char often. A little past its best, mind."

"Ever seen a fish stuffed with gems?"

She shook her head, studying the jewels spilling out of the char. "Can't say as I have, Mr Holmes."

"Put it on ice for us, Mrs Hudson. Watson, put the gems in the safe. I think we need to cogitate upon this mystery."

When the housekeeper had gone, and Watson had locked the safe, the doctor said, "Is this a two-pipe problem, Holmes?"

The great detective settled back into his chair. "Something a little stronger, I think."

Watson unlocked the wooden cabinet by the bookcase and pulled out two glass vials. He waggled them both at Holmes. "Morphine or cocaine?"

"Morphine, I fancy. Aids the mental processes somewhat."

Watson locked the cocaine away and handed the vial, and a small syringe, to Holmes. "Very good. While you're, ah, cogitating,

I think I'll have a small nap. See if inspiration strikes."

Half an hour later, there was quiet over the parlour, save for the gentle snoring of Dr Watson and the fevered, low moans of Sherlock Holmes.

In the kitchen, Mrs Hudson rifled through the store where she kept old newspapers for bunching up and aiding with the lighting of the fires in 221b Baker Street. It had been a warm autumn so there had not been as many blazing hearths as the previous year, and she also burned the oldest dated ones first, so the number of the *Illustrated London Argus* which she was looking for had not yet been despatched to the fireplace.

There it was, the early edition from four days ago. She took it to the worktop and flicked through until she located the item she was looking for.

It was a small piece headlined THEFT OF PRICELESS JEWELS FROM LADY MORRIS HOLIDAYING IN PARIS, and told in florid language how the head of one of London's most affluent and established families had been holidaying with her son and retinue in the City of Lights when persons unknown struck at their hotel room, making off with a range of highly valuable and irreplaceable gems and jewellery items.

The report listed some of the items that had been taken: "Two diamond rings, one of them given to Lady Morris upon her engagement to Lord Morris of Fife, sadly deceased these five years; a gold necklace with a ruby stone; an emerald necklace; two garnet rings and a mother-of-pearl and gold brooch."

Stolen in Paris, and ending up in the belly of a white-spotted char at Billingsgate Market? They were well-travelled jewels, and no mistake. Mrs Hudson carefully folded the newspaper to display the news item and crept into the parlour, where Dr Watson was snuffling into his moustache and Mr Holmes curled, foetus-like, in his chair, his feet jerking as though he was a dog a-dream. Mrs Hudson tutted softly and removed the syringe from his forearm, placing it with distaste upon the salver with the brandy. She would never understand Mr Holmes and his chemical addictions. Mr Hudson – God rest his soul! – had always said, before he lost his life on that African field, of course, that a stout ale and the occasional whisky at Christmas should be enough for any man. He wouldn't have liked her mingling with these cocaine and morphine types. But Mr Hudson was long gone, and Mrs Hudson had to make ends meet, and if that meant renting out half the building (and re-badging the two halves 221a and 221b for the benefit of the Post Office) to the likes of Mr Holmes, and keeping house for him and Dr Watson, then so be it. She had to confess, she'd never had as much *fun* before she took on her tenants, not since Mr Hudson had died. So let them have their little foibles.

Dr Watson, as though sensing another presence in the parlour, began to snort more loudly. Quickly, Mrs Hudson placed the folded newspaper into the long, slim fingers of Sherlock Holmes, then stole out of the room, closing the door quietly behind her.

"Great Scott, Watson, I think I might have stumbled upon something!" exclaimed Holmes as Mrs Hudson laid out afternoon tea.

Watson harrumphed and sat bolt upright. "Just resting my eyes. What is it, Holmes?"

The detective produced the newspaper with a flourish. "Mrs Hudson, did I come into the kitchen while I cogitated?"

"I believe you did, Mr Holmes," she said. "You were looking in the bin where I keep the old papers. I asked if I could help but you were quite single-minded."

"Something must have occurred to me," said Holmes. "Look, Watson! This description of the jewels stolen from Lady Morris in Paris. Ring any bells?"

"By Jove, Holmes, they are the exact gems found in that blasted fish! Then we know who they belong to… but how did they get from Paris to London?"

"Imagine…" said Holmes, rising from his chair. "A thief, or thieves, common Parisians… they steal into Lady Morris's hotel room, loot her jewellery box, and flee… they make their way to the Seine docks – all dark doings are conducted at city docks – to sell on their haul… a fight ensues between the ne'er-do-wells – no honour amongst thieves, Watson! – and the jewels fall into the river, to be swallowed by a passing white-spotted char!"

Watson frowned. "Is that *probable*, Holmes?"

Holmes peered down his nose at the doctor. "I have said more than once, Watson, that when you have eliminated the impossible, whatever remains, however improbable, must be the truth."

Watson reached for his tea. "I dare say you're right, Holmes. It's just… well, we haven't exactly eliminated much so far, impossible or otherwise."

Holmes glared at him. "And you have a more suitable hypothesis?"

"Well, not as such…"

"Then let us away to Lady Morris, to return her jewels. Mrs Hudson, we shall be back for dinner and that wonderful lamb stew I can smell bubbling on the hob."

"Very good, Mr Holmes," said Mrs Hudson. That would just give her enough time for an errand of her own. To Billingsgate, before the fish market closed for the day.

"Now then, Mrs H., what can I do for you today?" Herbert the fishmonger was as broad as he was tall, ruddy of complexion and smelled perpetually of his stock in trade. Mrs Hudson wondered how his wife put up with it. "Bit of cod? Hake? Some lovely haddock just come in."

"I might be in the market for a nice white-spotted char," she said, clutching her ever-present carpet bag.

Herbert rubbed his broad chin. "White-spotted char? Now there's a fish. Not seen that for a while. Shockingly expensive, that is. Your Mr Holmes developed what we might call a sophisticated palate?"

"He likes his luxuries, now and again," she said. "So you don't have any, as a rule?"

Herbert shook his head. "To be honest, not had anyone offer me any, nor ask for it. On account of the cost, like. Have you tried up Covent Garden?"

Herbert was the sixth fishmonger she had tried at Billingsgate, and every time it was the same answer. Not a piece of white-spotted char to be had, nor had there been for some time. How surprising, then, that Melvin Jacobs had managed to buy one from Billingsgate just yesterday. Or so he said.

"Covent Garden?" asked Mrs Hudson.

"Oh, aye, there's a very posh little place up there, does all kinds of fish you won't get here in Billingsgate. Very snooty. For the la-di-dah folk. Now, are you sure I can't tempt you with a piece of this hake?"

The shop in Covent Garden was indeed very la-di-dah. It went by the name of Highfield's, and as well as fish it sold pickled goods and dried meats of a most exotic nature: salamis and German sausage, olives and big beef tomatoes. The woman with the long nose who presided over the clean, bright counter regarded Mrs Hudson somewhat sniffily as she entered, heralded by a tinkling bell over the door.

"Do you sell white-spotted char?" asked Mrs Hudson pleasantly.

The woman waved her hand at the display of fish upon a bed of crushed ice. "We do. How many would you like?"

Mrs Hudson looked at the prices and blanched. Perhaps Mr Jacobs wasn't as destitute as Mr Holmes' intuition suggested, if he was buying fish at these prices. She said, "Did you sell one to a chap yesterday? Party by the name of Jacobs?"

"I couldn't say who I sold them to. He doesn't sound like one of our regular clientele, but we have many, many customers. Why would you want to know?"

Mrs Hudson made her excuses and left, pausing in the street. Why would Jacobs have travelled to Covent Garden for a piece of overpriced fish? The daylight was fading and she decided she'd better get back to Baker Street before the gentlemen did. One more errand, though... just around the corner were the offices of White Horse Transport and Travel, the operators of the passenger line which had taken Lady Morris to Paris and back.

Mrs Hudson presented herself at the travel desk and murmured to the clerk, "I do hope you can help. I work for Lady Morris and... well, she's had a lot on her plate recently. You might have heard..."

The clerk, a young man with sprouting sideburns, glanced from side to side. "Terrible business, yes. How can I help you?"

"Just for the purposes of organising her bills... as I said, the Lady has been most upset and has been unable to locate her passenger manifests for the outward and return journeys. It's for extra payments to the staff who attended her..."

"Of course," said the clerk, nodding, and swiftly located the documents. "Do tell Lady Morris that all at White Horse wish her the speediest of recoveries from this shock."

Waiting for a cab to take her back to Baker Street, Mrs Hudson inspected the manifests. Just as she had thought. Now she had just to hope that one of those Baker Street Irregulars was hanging around up to no good in Marylebone.

"I must say, I thought Lady Morris might have been a *tad* more pleased at us returning her lost property," said Watson.

"I suppose that's the upper classes for you," said Holmes. "Find it difficult to show their emotions."

"This is dashed good lamb stew, Mrs Hudson," said Watson, ladling another helping into his dish. "Dashed good."

"Very warming, is lamb stew," acknowledged Mrs Hudson as her tenants ate a hearty dinner. "However... all that business got me thinking. I was sure I had a good recipe for white-spotted char somewhere."

"Probably in that carpet bag you cart around all the time," said Watson. "Heaven knows what you keep in that thing."

"A mystery we shall never solve, Watson!" declared Holmes, dipping bread into his stew.

"I did find it, but..." said Mrs Hudson, and paused.

Holmes glanced up. "What? Out with it!"

"I went along to Billingsgate but there wasn't any white-spotted char at all. Hadn't been for some time. Not the sort of fish you find at Billingsgate. More likely to get it in the posh shops up at Covent Garden, such as Highfield's."

"I know it," nodded Holmes. "For those with very expensive tastes and the wallets to match." He paused. "But Lestrade said Jacobs had told the police he purchased the fish at Billingsgate."

Watson harrumphed. "But why lie about something like that?"

"Because he has something to hide!" said Holmes.

Mrs Hudson said nothing, and began to clear the plates so she could bring out the pudding. She had laid out the spotted dick when the doorbell sounded. "I'll attend to it," she said.

A moment later Mrs Hudson ushered a ragged little scamp, his face streaked with dirt and his shoes flapping like wet fish, into the dining room. "A boy to see you, Mr Holmes."

"Ah, one of the Irregulars!" exclaimed the detective. "You have a tip-off for us, young man? You and your army of waifs have been keeping your ears to the ground on the hunt for titbits of nefarious deeds and dark doings?"

The boy said nothing until Mrs Hudson pinched him in the shoulder. "Ow! Ah, yes, sir. I brought the thing. Like you said." He held out two sheets of crumpled paper.

"The thing? Like I said?" Holmes frowned.

Another pinch from Mrs Hudson. "Ow! Earlier today, sir. You asked me to fetch you this from the..." He glanced at Mrs Hudson. "Oh yes, the White Star. I mean the White Horse."

"Must have been while you were cogitating, Holmes," said Watson.

Holmes took the papers from the boy. "Passenger manifests? I don't recall... Great Scott, Watson! These are from the journeys Lady Morris took to the Continent, and her return trip. And... dashed if Melvin Jacobs isn't listed as part of her itinerary! He's only Lady Morris's blasted footman!"

Holmes tossed the boy a sixpence and Mrs Hudson hurried the scamp from the house. When she returned, the great detective had already solved the mystery.

"Jacobs stole the jewels while he was in Paris with his employer, and at the docks had them inserted into a fish that he knew must be bound for Covent Garden, for fear all the servants would be searched following the discovery of the crime! Then he went to purchase the exact fish – which he had marked with a cross – to obtain his stolen booty."

"Damned clever footman," observed Watson.

"The criminal mind is a fine example of the adage *necessity is the mother of invention*, Watson. We must away to Lestrade, and have him apprehend the villain immediately."

"You really are quite remarkable, Holmes," said Watson, wiping his mouth with his napkin and depositing it on the remains of his pudding.

"But why," wondered Mrs Hudson, "should Jacobs then hand the gems in himself?"

Holmes and Watson, however, had already gone, leaving her question hanging there above the dirty dishes, dishes that were not about to wash themselves.

It being a Sunday the next day, Mrs Hudson only worked the morning and had the rest of the day to herself. She prepared a hearty breakfast for Mr Holmes and Dr Watson, and gently enquired over the kippers if Inspector Lestrade had successfully apprehended the villain.

"He did indeed," said Holmes. "He has yet to confess to the crime, but the evidence stacked against him is insurmountable, I judge."

"Odd, though," said Watson, inspecting the bottom of his teacup. "Turns out that not only was he not destitute, he is not a Jew. Nor does he live in Aldgate."

Holmes glared at the doctor. "But his wife *is* suffering from typhus, as I deduced."

Mrs Hudson decided not to mention that it was Inspector Lestrade who had offered that information. Besides, she had somewhere to be.

On the passenger manifests Mrs Hudson had seen another name she recognised, that of Eliza Ramsbottom, listed as part of Lady Morris's retinue. Mrs Hudson, when she was younger and used to do for grand houses herself, had worked briefly with Eliza and kept in touch with her sporadically. She presented herself just after lunch at the tradesman's entrance of the tall townhouse in Mayfair which was the seat of the Morris family in town, where Eliza was indeed enjoying a brief repast in advance of her afternoon off.

"Martha Hudson! It's been months! What brings you here?"

In the kitchen they shared a pot of tea and brought each other up to date on their various doings. Mrs Hudson laid her carpet bag at her feet and said, "Paris! How exotic!"

Mrs Ramsbottom agreed, then cast a glance around the empty kitchen. "And somewhat dramatic, too. I don't suppose you'll have heard, but the mistress suffered a burglary while we were in France."

Mrs Hudson put her hand to her chest. "How awful."

"And that's not the worst of it. Yesterday they arrested Jacobs, the footman. Said he'd done the deed, stolen the jewels."

"What a scoundrel!"

Mrs Ramsbottom frowned. "Always seemed a decent type to me. Can't quite believe it. It's so out of character."

Mrs Hudson lowered her voice. "Gambling debts, do you think?"

Mrs Ramsbottom shook her head. "His wife's had a sudden illness, struck down with typhus while we were away. Soon as he came home Lady Morris gave him paid leave to look after her. She's good like that."

Mrs Ramsbottom bit her lip. There was more to this, Mrs Hudson was sure of it. She pressed gently, "Very generous. There aren't many employers who'd do that."

Another furtive glance around the kitchen, then Mrs Ramsbottom said, "That might be part of the problem. She's too generous, sometimes. Between you, me and these four walls, Martha, the finances here are in a bit of a pickle. The bills keep coming in and there doesn't seem to be enough to pay them."

"I thought I heard Lady Morris's son... what's he called?"

"George."

"That's it, George. Isn't he in business?"

Mrs Ramsbottom nodded. "Again, part of the problem. The mistress puts a lot of her own money into the young master's firm. He likes the idea of being a businessman, I think, but he doesn't really have a head for it. I think he lays out more than he brings in, on stock and suchlike. That's really why we were in Paris – he was on a buying trip, and overseeing the despatch of some produce."

"What line is he in?" said Mrs Hudson, taking a sip of her tea.

"Luxury comestibles," said Mrs Ramsbottom. "Very posh food – too rich for the palates of the likes of you and me. He imports it from all over the world, sells it at very upmarket outlets."

"Like Highfield's in Covent Garden?" said Mrs Hudson, peering over the rim of her cup.

"Yes, though I'm surprised you go there, Martha Hudson. Are you going up in the world?"

Mrs Hudson smiled. "I pick up the odd titbit from there, on occasion."

The bell rang and Mrs Ramsbottom sighed. "Strictly speaking I'm off duty but that's her ladyship. I'd better have a look. It's been lovely catching up, Martha."

"I'll see myself out, don't you worry," said Mrs Hudson. She waited a moment until she was sure Mrs Ramsbottom had ascended the stairs, then took up her carpet bag and followed.

From below stairs she emerged into a wide hallway, with a sweeping staircase leading up to the bedrooms. She had a fairly solid idea of what had been going on, now all she needed was some hard evidence. The bedrooms? Perhaps the study first, the door of which lay open to her right. She softly pushed the door and then became aware of a shadow falling over her.

"I've been listening to you, you meddling old bat."

She turned sharply. There was a young man with an ugly disposition, scowling at her. George Morris, she guessed. "It's not polite to eavesdrop," she said stoutly.

He advanced on her, scowling. "It's not polite to shove your nose into what doesn't concern you. And now I'm going to have to make sure you don't shove it any further into my business."

But Mrs Hudson was not about to let him take another step. Before he could close the gap she hefted her carpet bag, swung it wide and fetched him a solid blow to the side of the head with it, knocking him clean out.

The contents of Mrs Hudson's carpet bag would always remain a mystery, but she was prepared to reveal one or two secrets – one, a length of rope, which she had used to tie the unconscious form of George Morris to an upright chair in the study, and two, a long handkerchief with which she had securely gagged him. She had just finished the knots when he came groggily awake and glared at her.

"Now," she said. "Let me see if I've got this right. You took your mother and her retinue to Paris for a short holiday while you conducted business. Did you always intend to steal her jewels, or was it an opportunist act? No matter, that's what you did, and made your way to the docks where companies you did business with were preparing shipments of produce – including a despatch of white-spotted char – for transportation to England. You forced the gems into the mouth of one fish and marked it with a cross so you could find it easily when it had been transferred to its destination in Covent Garden. You intended to sell the jewels to prop up your ailing business, or provide money for gambling, carousing... yes?"

George Morris simply continued to cast her devilish looks. Mrs Hudson tapped her chin. "The only thing I can't work out is, how did Melvin Jacobs come to get the fish? Was he in league with you? If so, why hand them in to the police?"

"Perhaps I can answer that," said another voice, regal and proud. Mrs Hudson turned to see Lady Morris sweep into the room like the figurehead of a grand ship.

Mrs Hudson faltered. "You know? But I thought..."

Lady Morris sighed. "You are a very intelligent and persistent woman, Mrs Hudson. You are the landlady of Mr Holmes, who returned my jewels yesterday, correct?"

Mrs Hudson nodded. "He said you were not particularly pleased to... ah. I think I understand."

Lady Morris smiled sadly. "It was all my idea, I am afraid. I planned to report the jewels stolen and claim on my insurance policies. Then we would sell them on the black market for further gain. Money is... well. Not in abundance, at the moment. I fear I might have to let some of my staff go, but they are all such lovely, hardworking people."

"Mr Jacobs?"

Lady Morris nodded. "He overheard, I think, George dealing with his connections in Paris, organising to visit his supplier at the docks. Jacobs is very loyal and I believe he must have followed George and seen everything, but came to the same conclusion as you, Mrs Hudson – that my son was stealing from me. As soon as we returned to England he went directly to Highfield's, bought the blasted fish himself, and handed the jewels in to the police."

"Insurance fraud, then," said Mrs Hudson.

"I suppose you are going to hand us in to the constabulary," said Lady Morris. "Melvin is too loyal to tell the truth, even with himself in jail. Oh, it is all such a terrible mess. We must be brought to justice. It is all that we deserve."

"But your staff… Eliza… Melvin Jacobs and his sick wife…" said Mrs Hudson. She rubbed her chin. "Mr Morris, do you have people in your companies in France who will swear blind that they saw two local ne'er-do-wells tampering with the fish? That they thought they were trying to steal them?"

George grunted, and Mrs Hudson remembered to remove his gag. He gasped for air and said, "Why yes, of course. I pay them enough. Why?"

Mrs Hudson smiled. "You'll have to pay back the insurance money, of course, but I think we can navigate a way through this mess without too much difficulty."

Mrs Hudson saw Inspector Lestrade out of 221b Baker Street and returned to the parlour to clear away the tea-tray. She said casually, "Good news?"

"Indeed Mrs Hudson, the mystery is solved!" said Watson.

"Turns out Melvin Jacobs was entirely innocent. He just had a hankering for a piece of white-spotted char," said Holmes. "According to Lestrade, two French criminals broke into Lady Morris's hotel and stole her jewels. They were later seen trying to steal fish from a warehouse. They were chased by the staff and must have dropped the gems in one of the crates, which got packed up and sent to England. It was sheer coincidence that Jacobs bought that particular fish."

"I must say, Holmes, you're a dashed genius," said Watson.

Holmes purred like a cat. "It was nothing, Watson. Mere logic and deduction."

"I think this calls for a drink," said Watson. "Doubles?"

Holmes inclined his head. "Entirely appropriate, Watson." He paused. "It was a shame, though, that not all of the gems made it back to England. Either the thieves kept hold of some, or they were lost during transit. A diamond and a ruby, apparently. Still, Lady Morris had them insured, I understand."

Mrs Hudson smiled. If George was particularly careful how he disposed of those jewels, the staff of the Morris household should be kept in wages for some time to come. Not strictly right and proper but… well. It wasn't as though anyone had been hurt, was it?

A week later, with the latest number of *The Strand Magazine* laid out on the butcher's block work-surface, Mrs Hudson carefully cut the pages bearing Dr Watson's lively fictionalised account. The fish had become a goose, the gems a blue carbuncle and the action bore little relation to real life. Still, it was a reminder for her scrapbook.

"Busy, Mrs Hudson?" said Holmes, popping his hawkish head around the kitchen door. "Ah… keeping our adventures for posterity, I see."

She smiled and slid the scrapbook into her carpet bag. "Well, better get on with the dinner, Mr Holmes. The bathroom needs cleaning, the silver must be polished and –"

The bell rang noisily, three times. Inspector Lestrade, for sure.

"I'd better get that, Mr Holmes."

The great detective smiled indulgently. "A woman's work is never done, eh, Mrs Hudson? A woman's work is never done…"

ABOUT THE AUTHOR

David Barnett is the author of the Gideon Smith series of alternate-history/steampunk adventures, coming from Tor Books and beginning with *Gideon Smith and the Mechanical Girl* in August 2013. He is the author of several other novels, including *popCULT!* (Pendragon Press, 2011), and has been a journalist all his working life. Born in Wigan, he is married to Claire and they have two children, Charlie and Alice.

THE FALLEN FINANCIER

BY JAMES LOVEGROVE

"Watson," said Sherlock Holmes as we strolled along the promenade at Eastbourne one sunny afternoon. He was breaking a sociable silence of some ten minutes. "Has it ever struck you how wide a gulf lies between what people seem to be and what they are?"

"I suppose we all project a persona," said I. "We wish others to see us as we would wish to be seen."

"True," said Holmes, "but I meant that however someone appears to the world, the reality of his situation is invariably much different and in most cases a considerable disappointment. Take that young couple for instance. They bill and coo like turtle doves. They are the very picture of love's young dream. Yet I predict that within a fortnight they will no longer be together, indeed will have ceased to be on speaking terms after a highly acrimonious parting."

"Really, Holmes!" I ejaculated. "You are dashed cynical at times. How can you say such a thing?"

"Easily, my dear doctor. Look closer. They are quite clearly from different social strata. The young lady is of good breeding. Her dress, her coiffure, her mannerisms all attest to it. Whereas the lad, though he affects to a high station in life, is of common stock. Note the worn rim of his shirt collar and the button missing on the sleeve of his jacket – sartorial deficiencies which a true gentleman, with a valet at his disposal, would never suffer. Note, too, how his trousers have had to be lengthened at the cuffs and still do not quite fit. He has little money but is making every effort to appear that he does. She, his paramour, has discerned as much but it does not trouble her – for now. She is, as they say, 'slumming it'. She is enjoying his attentions and is happy for him to make love to her. However, when he proposes marriage, as he will do soon, that is when matters will take a turn for the worse."

"How do you know he is going to propose?" I demanded. "Surely that is pure supposition."

"Watson, how often have I told you that you see but you do not observe?" said my friend.

"A maddeningly great number of times," I replied.

"But still you do not take the lesson to heart. Behold the young man's left pocket. See that small bulge? What can that be but a box containing an engagement ring? He is plucking up the nerve to pop the question. Perhaps not today, but certainly by the end of the week, he will have found the courage. That is the point at which his intended will have to reject him, for she is a girl who has been brought up to expect to marry a man with good prospects."

"It could be that she genuinely loves him, Holmes. Have you considered that? Men and women of different classes do fall in love, you know. Or perhaps you don't."

He ignored my little barb. "Then there is that elderly gentlemen perched on a bench over there. What do you make of him?"

I studied the man. He was in his seventies, I estimated, and wore a plethora of campaign medals on his chest. He sat ramrod-straight with his hands clasping the handle of his walking cane, gazing contemplatively seaward, beyond the shallows where bathers cavorted, all the way to the hazy horizon.

"An ex-soldier like myself," I said. "A veteran of the Crimea, though he would have had to have enlisted when he was fairly young. The Boer conflicts too. A military fellow through and through. Never a day's slouching in his life."

"Indeed?" said Holmes wryly. "Yet neither his boots nor those decorations he so proudly sports are polished to a gleam. I would submit that he has never held a rifle or fired a shot in anger. Rather, he haunts the tearooms and hotel bars of this town, cadging drinks and regaling strangers with tales of bogus heroism and derring-do, after which he importunes them for a little cash 'to help an old serviceman through a rough patch'."

"Shame on him if that is so," I said, "and shame on you, Holmes, if it isn't."

My friend smiled thinly. "And this well-to-do family here, coming towards us. How blissful they look. Father, mother, and nanny pushing pram with gurgling newborn within. A very idyll of prosperity and fecundity. What could be sweeter?"

"Now you're going to tell me one of them is an axe murderer or some such."

"Far from it, Watson. In most regards they are as respectable as you or I. Then again, the nanny is wearing a silver charm bracelet that is far more expensive than one with an income such as hers could normally afford. And the father's eye keeps straying to her rather shapely form whenever his wife's attention is elsewhere."

"Are you implying…?"

"I imply nothing. I *infer* that his relationship with the nanny is anything but that of employer and household servant. See how his wife has her arm linked through his? How tightly she clings to him? She senses something is afoot. It is likely she even knows the truth. Wives are not easy to hoodwink, especially when it comes to infidelity. For the sake of her baby, however, and her future, she has elected to turn a blind eye."

Holmes tipped his hat to the family as they passed us. They in return nodded, smiled and offered snatches of formal greeting.

As we walked on I said, "Honestly, Holmes, it is a delightful summer's day and you are like a raincloud, casting an oppressive shadow over everything. Can you only ever see the worst in people? Is there not a part of you that looks for the good in us?"

"Always, Watson, always. Alas, so often in vain. But hullo, what's this?"

A lady was rushing towards us along the promenade, from the direction of the pier. She was in a state of some agitation, her colour up, her stride purposeful. She was only in her thirties but her face was so haggard and drawn as to give the impression of her being considerably older.

"Mr Holmes!" she cried. "It is you, isn't it? I heard you had moved to this part of the country. Pray tell me I'm right. You are *the* Sherlock Holmes, the famous consulting detective?"

"Retired consulting detective, madam," said Holmes. "Those years are behind me. But yes, I am he."

"Oh thank the Lord," said the lady. She threw herself at my friend, clutching his lapels. "Surely you can help me. You must! I am going mad. They tell me he is dead. They insist upon it. They urge me to grieve for him, to be a widow. And yet I know he is still alive. I know it in my heart."

"My dear woman," said Holmes, "pray compose yourself. Your husband is dead, you say?"

"No!" she insisted. "They want me to think that. Everyone is telling me that he took his own life, but not him, not Jacob. He would never do such a thing. A body has not been found, you see. And without a body, where is the proof?"

She was near hysterical. At my insistence, for her shrill imprecations were drawing attention, we repaired to one of the wooden shelters that line Eastbourne's elegant seafront. In truth, the sun was oppressively hot and it was a relief to avail ourselves of shade.

"Now, if you would," said Holmes to the lady, "let us take things in due order. Your name, please."

"But of course," said she. "I am Mrs Thisbe Markinswell. My husband is Jacob Markinswell. Perhaps you know of him?"

"I have heard of a London financier by that name."

"That is he. He works for the bank of Carstairs and Buckingham, on Moorgate."

"A highly successful institution," said Holmes, "with a reputation for prudence and efficiency. Would that all banks followed its example."

"My husband has been a loyal employee for nearly fifteen years," said Mrs Markinswell. "He has risen to senior partner, with responsibility for overseeing investments in the Far East and the Americas. We are, as a consequence, more than comfortably off, as you can imagine." Her pinched face displayed a pride which I'm afraid to say I found rather disagreeable.

"Meaning that he is unlikely to have committed suicide, if indeed he did so, for reasons of penury," said Holmes.

"Exactly. That is one motive the police have advanced, and of course it is utterly absurd. Another is that he has become embroiled in some financial scandal and the shame has proved too great to bear. But that is not the case either. I have checked. His accounts at Carstairs and Buckingham are all in excellent order. At my urging, the bank has had its actuaries go over the books and not a penny has gone astray. Both in his personal and his professional dealings Jacob is impeccably in the black."

"Interesting," said my friend. "How long is it that your husband has been missing, Mrs Markinswell?"

"A week now," came the reply from the distraught woman. "We have a place here in town, you see. Most of the year we live in Kensington, but for the summer we like to come down to the coast."

"I find the South Downs climate congenial myself, and I speak as one who spent the best part of his life in London and whose lungs are probably still grey from constant exposure to an urban atmosphere."

I refrained from mentioning that Holmes' propensity for his beloved shag tobacco was doubtless still leaving its own inward mark on his vitals.

"Jacob always looked forward to coming down," said Mrs Markinswell. "He often spoke about selling our London home and relocating permanently. It wasn't until this year that I began to wonder whether that might be such a good idea."

"Explain."

"Well, we arrived in late May as usual, and my husband began his customary practice of taking the train up to London every weekday. It is a lengthy journey but he prefers to commute like this so that he can enjoy the benefits of being on the coast during his leisure time. However, it wasn't long before I noticed a change in him. He grew withdrawn and irritable."

"As a result of the constant travelling?" I ventured. "Exhaustion?"

"So I thought. It had never bothered him before, though. I asked him repeatedly if something was the matter but received only evasive answers and vague reassurances that all was well. I was reluctant to press him too hard. Jacob is a mild-mannered, biddable man but does not take kindly to being nagged. A decade of marriage has taught me that." Mrs Markinswell gave a brief, stiff smile.

"Might I enquire how suspicions arose that he killed himself?" said Holmes.

"He was last seen in the vicinity of Beachy Head," said Mrs Markinswell. "He was acting erratically, according to eyewitnesses."

"Hmmm. Beachy Head, you say."

A glint had entered Holmes' eye. I knew my friend well enough to recognise the signs. He was intrigued. Something in Mrs Markinswell's account had piqued his curiosity.

"Beachy Head is well known, notorious even, as a place for suicides," he continued. "It has almost become a cliché, the frequency with which people throw themselves off the cliffs there. You believe, however, that your husband is not amongst their number, Mrs Markinswell." This was framed more as a statement than an interrogative.

"I am quite certain of it, Mr Holmes. I imagine you frown on the notion of woman's intuition. I have read enough of your exploits, courtesy of Dr Watson here, to know that you are an arch rationalist. You would no doubt dismiss as superstitious poppycock the idea that the female of the species is sensitive to certain indefinable factors hidden from the male."

"On the contrary," said Holmes. "Often what is called woman's intuition is nothing more than an acute, if subconscious, awareness of the subtle visual and verbal cues given out by others. I have contemplated writing a monograph on the subject but disqualified myself on grounds of gender."

"Suffice to say that were Jacob dead, something in here would have told me." She thumped her chest.

"You suspect foul play, then?" said I.

"Dr Watson, I don't know what to suspect," said Mrs Markinswell. "The police have their line of enquiry, and that is the only one they will pursue."

Holmes gave one of his sharp, contemptuous laughs, like the bark of a dog. Regular readers of mine will know of the low esteem in which he held members of the constabulary. Even those he thought well of, such as Inspector Lestrade, were accorded a grudging admiration at best.

"But you wish to learn the truth?" said Holmes.

Mrs Markinswell nodded adamantly. "It goes without saying. Wherever my husband is, whatever has happened to him, I cannot bear this agony of uncertainty any longer. I have scarcely slept, Mr Holmes. I am going out of my mind with worry. If this were blackmail, I would have been sent a ransom note, would I not? If Jacob really were dead, surely his body would have washed ashore by now. I need some kind of resolution, and I pray you are the man to bring it. Your fee, of course, is not a problem."

Holmes waved this aside. "In my retirement, money is no longer a consideration or a motivation, Mrs Markinswell. I will take on your case *pro bono*. But I should reiterate that I will get at the truth, and you must be prepared for it to be unpalatable."

Mrs Markinswell steeled herself, dabbing her swollen eyes with a lace handkerchief and firming her jaw. "I am ready, come what may."

"Good," said Holmes. "First, Watson and I shall visit the scene of the alleged crime. After that, if we may call on you at home, Mrs Markinswell...?"

She gave us her address, a house in Eastbourne's prosperous Meads area, and we took our leave of her.

During our walk to Beachy Head, Holmes was in a rare garrulous mood, although he talked about everything – the floral displays on the seafront, the geology of Sussex chalk soil, the various species of butterfly we saw – save the disappearance of Jacob Markinswell. Eventually, after an hour, we crested the steep brow of the Head itself. At our feet spread a panorama of glittering aquamarine sea, dotted with yachts and fishing vessels, leisure and commerce commingling. A warm onshore breeze stirred the rough grass and the thickets of gorse and hawthorn. The town of Hastings shimmered whitely across the bay.

It was a beautiful spot, yet I shivered to recall that it was near here that Holmes had watched a schoolteacher, Fitzroy McPherson, die a horrible death from a jellyfish sting, a case he narrated to me and which I have chronicled as "The Adventure of the Lion's Mane"; nor were we far from the stately home wherein had occurred those terrible, almost incredible events which I have yet to set down in writing but may one day do, under the putative title of *Gods of War*.

Holmes echoed the dark turn of my thoughts when he said, "Ironic how, even when presented with a natural prospect as pleasing as this, someone could nonetheless go ahead with terminating his own existence. I am aware that the mind, when in an extreme state of depression, is hardly in a position to appreciate aesthetics. Even so, it seems paradoxical. Such beauty ought to restore one's faith that life is worth living."

"Holmes, are you getting maudlin in your old age?"

"Perhaps, perhaps. As death encroaches, I to tend to cherish all the more the majesty and glory of creation. Now, to work."

He ferreted around for some time, crawling on hands and knees to the cliff edge and peering over, and examining in minute detail various clumps of vegetation. I, for my part, took advantage of the opportunity to rest my weary legs, seating myself upon a small hillock. I may even have briefly nodded off, for I became aware that Holmes had entered into conversation with a stranger of whom I had no recollection arriving on the scene.

His interlocutor was a tweedy sort, out walking an amiable, stocky black Labrador. As I strode over to join them, I heard this fellow say to Holmes, "Why yes, it so happens I did see the gentleman. He was agitated and no mistake. Hurrying back and forth to the clifftop, like he couldn't make up his mind. A horse repeatedly baulking at a fence, that's what he put me in mind of. I was going to go up and accost him, ask him what was the matter. But no sooner had I come to this decision than, damnedest thing, suddenly he wasn't there any more. I took my eyes off him for just a moment – Cicero here had scared up a rabbit and I had to call him back for fear he'd run away and never return – and when I turned to look back, blow me if the chap hadn't gone. Just vanished. Only living beings I could see were a young lady, a farmer mowing that field over there, and two brawny lads hiking."

"Most singular," said Holmes.

"I said as much to myself," agreed the stranger. He spoke with a distinct Sussex burr, a local born and bred. "I even went and checked the cliff, in case he'd finally gone and chucked himself off. I couldn't see anything on the beach below, but the tide was fully in. It's conceivable, I suppose, that he hit the water and was swallowed up by the waves. I raised the alarm right quick, anyway, and soon enough we had a search party going, but no sign of him could be found."

"The others present, they all saw the man too?"

"The young lady certainly did. Pretty little creature. She agreed with me that the fellow had been acting peculiar. She wouldn't swear to it, but she was almost sure he had taken a running jump. Awful business. The poor so-and-so. To be in such depths of despair as to do *that* to yourself."

Holmes seemed inordinately glad to have met this person, whom he thereafter referred to, not without justification, as the Country Squire. "What luck!" he exclaimed as he and I made our way back into town. "It would have taken time and effort to track down eyewitnesses, and one comes along just when needed. Turns out our squire friend exercises his dog regularly, always taking the same route each day along the ridge of the Seven Sisters from Cuckmere Haven. Sometimes the smooth advance of an investigation hinges on such fortuitous encounters. Now to the Markinswell homestead."

The Markinswells owned a fine, large villa on an elm-lined avenue. After a brief exchange of pleasantries with Mrs Markinswell, Holmes and I were given free rein of the house, permitted to look where we wished and speak to any of the domestic staff we chose to.

In the event, Holmes was interested only in two locations: Jacob Markinswell's dressing room and his study. In the dressing room he went through the closets, scrutinising Markinswell's suits. In the study, he pored over the contents of the desk, turning up personal correspondence, some bills, all of which had been paid before due, and a well-balanced chequebook. In other words, nothing of particular interest, until his attention fell on an item half hidden under the ink blotter.

"This, now," he said, holding it up, "may be a clue of some significance."

It was a playbill for a show that was running all season at the Hippodrome Theatre – a variety revue featuring a dozen acts ranging from a ventriloquist to a conjuror to a spirit medium to a small chorale offering a selection of songs from the comic operettas of Gilbert and Sullivan. I scanned the list of performers, but nothing leapt out at me.

Holmes and I went to the drawing room, where he asked Mrs Markinswell if she and her husband were devotees of the theatre.

"Myself, no," she said somewhat frostily. "I don't mind a concert and the opera but I'm not in the habit of exposing myself to lowbrow entertainment."

"But Jacob is?"

"I believe he has attended at the Hippodrome once or twice. On his own, of course. He claims to find it relaxing. He works hard, so I allow him such indulgences, however trivial and mindless."

"Well now, Watson," Holmes said as we departed. "This all becomes somewhat clearer."

"It undoubtedly does, Holmes," I said. "I have seen no evidence so far that contradicts the theory that Jacob Markinswell took his own life. The facts, indeed, seem to point inescapably to that conclusion."

"What about the lack of a suicide note?"

"That, I admit, is problematic, but then suicide can often be a spur-of-the-moment decision, not premeditated – a sudden and catastrophic descent into utter despondency."

"Quite," said Holmes. "But I must show you these threads which I gathered from a hawthorn thicket up on Beachy Head while you were in a state of deep repose. They are worsted wool, and the fibre matches exactly, in colour and weight, the material of Jacob Markinswell's suits, all of which were made by the same tailors, Quiller and Son of Chancery Lane."

"So?" said I. "All that indicates is that Markinswell was up on

Beachy Head and snagged his sleeve on a twig. I would say it bolsters rather than disproves the suicide hypothesis."

"I should have specified that I found the threads *inside* the hawthorn thicket."

"Ah. Is that important?"

"Important? My dear chap, it is crucial."

"How so?"

"In place of an explanation, allow me to treat you to a matinee." He waved the playbill. "What do you say?"

We took our seats in the stalls at the Hippodrome on Seaside Road, just in time to catch the start of the revue. Holmes was being his usual infuriating self, in possession of the key to solving a mystery but loath to share it with anyone – even his old comrade and fellow veteran of many an investigation – until such time as he saw fit. I itched to ask him to reveal all, but knew better than to try. I would be met with a stone wall of silence and a gleeful twinkle in those wise, grey eyes.

I resigned myself to watching the revue, which was, in the manner of these things, good in parts and less good in others. The conjuror was impressive, making objects appear from where they could not possibly be and disappear into places they could not possibly go. The spirit medium, by contrast, was dull, unable to convince that she was in contact with spectral entities from beyond the veil, her pronouncements too nebulous and all too often patently guesswork to sway any but the most gullible. The conjuror made no pretence that what he was doing was fakery. The medium, in her clumsy efforts to persuade the audience that she was genuine, came across as nothing but a fraud. With the former we willingly suspended disbelief, colluding in his illusions. With the latter we could not conquer our scepticism.

The Gilbert and Sullivan singers were polished, if a tad amateur, and a dog act, in which trained poodles were required to jump through hoops and perform other tricks and stunts, descended into inadvertent farce as the animals collectively decided not to heed their master's commands and turned on one another. The curtain was rung down on a scene of canine combat and anarchy, the trainer rushing to and fro in a vain attempt to separate antagonists and reimpose order.

Last on the roster was a girl by the name of Jenny Volteface – a stage pseudonym if ever there was one – who combined quick-change artistry with sketch routines. I have to say she was the star of the show. A slip of a thing, with a delightful rounded face, she ran through a series of impersonations, each more sophisticated and convincing than the last. One moment she was Henry VIII, stamping stoutly across the boards and demanding cake, ale and wives. Next she was Milton's Lucifer, reciting a soliloquy from *Paradise Lost* with a mixture of terrible hubris and wounded pride. She delivered an amusing and somewhat scurrilous skit on Parliament, switching from one side of the House to the other, pretending to be alternately Conservative then Liberal, and showing how narrow a distinction there was between the two parties and their policies. Then followed a retelling of the myth of Persephone, told from the point of view of the reluctant wife of Hades and detailing the niceties and drawbacks of domestic life as the spouse of the ruler of Hell. The whole thing was rounded off by a recitation of Bassanio's soliloquy from *The Merchant Of Venice*, the one beginning "So may the outward shows be least themselves..." and a haunting rendition of the story of Pocahontas, featuring an aria especially composed for the occasion.

Miss Volteface brought the house down. It wasn't just the speed at which she slipped between roles, passing behind a screen in one costume and emerging scant seconds later in another. It was the commitment she put into her acting, the way she could transform herself into any character, evoking the person with her entire body, every gesture and mannerism devoted to becoming someone else. You could believe she was Henry VIII, despite her being of the fairer sex, no less than you could believe she was a fallen archangel, or a puffing popinjay parliamentarian, or a young Venetian man daring all to win the heart and hand of his lady, or a Red Indian chief's daughter pining for love. The audience rose to their feet in approbation, and I don't mind admitting that I joined them.

Before the applause had died down, with Miss Volteface still taking her bows, Holmes grabbed me by the sleeve.

"Now, Watson," he said urgently. "Let us go backstage."

"Backstage? Why?"

Even as I said this, I had an inkling. I was not always as slow on the uptake as Holmes liked to make out.

We left the theatre via the main entrance and slipped round the side to the stage door. A silver half-crown from Holmes' pocket secured our ingress past the stagehand who was posted there as a rather lacklustre sentry. In no time we were knocking on the door of the dressing room marked with Miss Volteface's name.

The person who greeted us was not the actress herself but a gruff and disagreeable man with a coarse thick beard and the manners of a navvy.

"What do you want?" he growled, fixing us both with a suspicious glare.

"To pay our respects to Miss Volteface, naturally," said Holmes in his gayest and most charming voice. "I am an ardent admirer of her work, as is my colleague."

"Wonderful stuff," I enthused, not insincerely. "A remarkable turn."

"Well, you can both –" Here the man invited Holmes and me to leave the premises in an unrepeatably crude fashion.

"Not even an autograph?" said Holmes, unabashed. He brandished the playbill. "Surely the good lady can spare us a moment for that."

A voice came from within, Miss Volteface's, and while I didn't catch her words, the gist was clear.

The man grumbled but let us in.

Miss Volteface was busy removing her makeup in the mirror, still in her Pocahontas outfit. Close up, she was even more beguiling than onstage. She reminded me in many ways of my dear departed Mary – the same broad intelligent forehead, the same flash of wit and hint of mischief in the eyes. I found myself wishing that I were several decades younger, a single man again in the prime of life. These were foolish thoughts, but the sight of an accomplished, attractive young girl makes fools of all men, whatever their maturity or marital status.

"Miss Volteface," said Holmes, "may I be the first to tell you that your skill at imposture is second to none."

"You may tell me that," replied she, winsomely, "but you would hardly be the first."

"Oh, I think in this particular instance I am. It was a remarkable feat that you pulled off up on Beachy Head the other day. You put your talents to the test in a public arena, in the open air, and the results were most plausible."

"Hoy, what's all this?" demanded the bearded man, who appeared to be cross between bodyguard and bulldog. He moved menacingly on Holmes, fists raised.

"You really have no idea?" Holmes answered calmly. "Come now, sir, you of all people should know what I'm referring to. You, after all, are just as much a part of this as Miss Volteface."

I assumed Holmes meant the man had served as some sort of accomplice. Together this pair were responsible for the disappearance and possible demise of Jacob Markinswell. They had contrived to stage an apparent suicide, after having kidnapped the financier and indeed caused his death, either through mishap or sinister design.

It struck me that we were in the presence of dangerous and potentially desperate criminals, and I had had sufficient experience of that to know that violence was likely to ensue. This would not be the first time that events had taken an unexpected, unforeseeable turn for the worse during one of our investigations; and Holmes and I were not the virile young men we used to be, ever ready to meet intimidation head-on. We had aged. We had slowed.

My heart began to race. I found myself wishing I was still in possession of my trusty old service revolver.

Whereupon Miss Volteface said, "It's all right, Jack. We might as well come clean. This is Sherlock Holmes, isn't it? A famous incomer to the area. If he's already figured it out, there's no point trying to string him along any further."

The man called Jack didn't drop his aggressive posture. "What's he doing snooping around anyway?" he barked. "It's none of his business."

"No," said Holmes, "but it is your wife's business, Mr Markinswell, and she has made it mine."

"My…?"

Holmes reached out and gave Jack's beard a firm, insistent tug. It peeled away from his face, revealing the features of a man in early middle age. Greasepaint had been applied to the upper portion of his face, lending it the rough, reddish complexion of someone who worked outdoors and perhaps drank more than was healthy. The bare skin beneath the beard, aside from a few stray flecks of spirit gum, was pale and smooth.

"Mr Jacob Markinswell, I presume," said Holmes. "Not dead. Far from it. Alive and well and on the cusp of embarking on a new life with a new woman."

Markinswell's face fell. The financier slumped into a chair, his hands flopping into his lap.

"The jig's up then," he said in altogether more cultured tones than he had employed beforehand. He sighed. "I thought we'd got away with it, Jenny my dear. Clearly I am not the thespian you are."

"You did fine, my love," said Miss Volteface consolingly. "You were most convincing."

The whole story emerged. There wasn't much to be said. Markinswell had become smitten with Jenny Volteface – real surname Stubbins – after seeing her perform. Relations with his wife had become, if not strained, then unexciting. They had, as a couple, settled into that kind of marital complacency which in some breeds contentment and in others boredom and frustration. An absence of offspring had caused them to drift further from each other. Children can be the mortar which binds a marriage together. Lack of them can be the wedge that fissures it.

"I'm not making excuses for myself," said Markinswell. "But with Jenny I discovered a passion, a love, that had been missing from my life for a good long while, and she, to my great delight, reciprocated. I was ready to give up everything for her. Everything. And I did. I have done. She, for her part, has been willing to take me as I am, unencumbered by wealth and expectation, and help me start again from scratch."

It was Jenny who had come up with the plan of faking Markinswell's death. But how to make a man disappear in broad daylight, before witnesses? Pretend to be him, that was how. Wear his clothes, impersonate him, feint a suicide, then duck into a hawthorn thicket and come out moments later as a woman. Jenny was the "pretty little creature" the Country Squire had mentioned. She had helped promulgate the story that a man matching Markinswell's description had thrown himself over the edge at Beachy Head.

"And now what do we do?" she asked, taking Markinswell's hand. Whatever else I thought of these two, the love between them looked to be the genuine article. The feelings they exhibited were mutual and abiding.

"That," said Holmes, "is not up to me. I shall leave it to you and your own consciences. For what it's worth, my advice is to come clean. This deception is thrilling in its illicitness, I'm sure, but honesty will get you further in the long run. Confess all to your wife, Mr Markinswell. Put the poor woman out of her misery. It will be hard for you but kinder to her."

We left the two of them in the dressing room to debate their future and decide on the best course of action. It was none of our concern now. Holmes was firmly of the opinion that Markinswell would do the right thing.

Out in the mellowing warmth of the late afternoon, we returned to the promenade, where this brief escapade of ours had begun just a few hours earlier.

"A rather tawdry little affair, don't you think?" remarked Holmes. "Hardly worth your writing it up as one of those tales you hawk to Greenhough Smith at *The Strand*."

"I think I should be the judge of that, Holmes," I said. "What it does demonstrate is that for once you're wrong."

My friend arched an eyebrow. "Oh? And how do you arrive at that conclusion?"

"You told me, did you not, that a wide gulf lies between what people seem to be and what they are, and the difference is usually a disappointment."

"I recall saying something to that effect."

"But weren't these two, Markinswell and Jenny, *more* than they seemed to be? Indeed better? Despite the disguises and the trickery and the deceit, behind it there are two people deeply in love."

"Markinswell is rich. That could be her motive for loving him."

"But he has sacrificed all he has for her, and she knows it. It is, in its way, as pure a meeting of souls as can be imagined."

Holmes was sombre for a moment, then surprised me by chuckling. "You, Watson, are a hopeless romantic," he said. "And I wouldn't want you any other way. Now, I don't know about you, but I am famished and parched. The Tiger Inn, hard by my cottage in East Dean, serves an excellent partridge pie and a range of thirst-quenching Sussex ales. We can be there in under an hour if we walk briskly." He made an ushering gesture, squinting against the low sun. "Shall we?"

And side by side, companionably, we did.

ABOUT THE AUTHOR

James Lovegrove was born on Christmas Eve 1965 and is the author of nigh on 40 books. His novels include *The Hope*, *Days*, *Untied Kingdom*, *Provender Gleed*, the *New York Times* bestselling Pantheon series and *Redlaw* and *Redlaw: Red Eye*, the first two volumes in a trilogy. Shortly to come is *The Stuff Of Nightmares*, the first of two Sherlock Holmes novels for Titan Books, and the fifth Pantheon novel, *Age Of Voodoo*, plus a collection of three novellas, *Age Of Godpunk*.

James has sold more than 40 short stories, the majority of them gathered in two collections, *Imagined Slights* and *Diversifications*. He has written a four-volume fantasy saga for teenagers, *The Clouded World* (under the pseudonym Jay Amory), and has produced a dozen short books for readers with reading difficulties.

James has been shortlisted for numerous awards, including the Arthur C. Clarke Award, the John W. Campbell Memorial Award, the Bram Stoker Award, the British Fantasy Society Award and the Manchester Book Award. His short story "Carry The Moon In My Pocket" won the 2011 Seiun Award for Best Translated Short Story.

James's work has been translated into twelve languages. His journalism has appeared in periodicals as diverse as *Literary Review*, *Interzone* and *BBC MindGames*, and he is a regular reviewer of fiction for the *Financial Times* and contributes features and reviews about comic books to the magazine *Comic Heroes*.

He lives with his wife, two sons and cat in Eastbourne.